STORMBIRD

LEON JANE

First published 2020

BARRAMUNDI PUPLISHING

barrapublishing@gmail.com

ISBN-13 978-0-6488208-0-2

Also by Leon Jane:

Shadow Valley (Novella)

For JT + CH - 13.04.1995

PROLOGUE

The repetitive rasping sound of abrasive metal scraping across the axe blade tormented the morning air. Pause gave way only to the axe being turned over to continue the sharpening process. His naturally tan skin glistened in the humid sunlight as beaded sweat smudged filth across his bare torso. Muscles flexed and rolled, bound by his tight skin. His determination exceeded the need to address the ash collecting at the end of a tightly gripped cigarette in the corner of his grimacing mouth.

Children's muffled screams echoed behind sheet iron fencing. He momentarily glanced towards the cage which sat against the fence. He quickened his sharpening action - he was running out of time.

Curious heads peered back from the cage - to the man in the yard. Those of whom were unfamiliar with the process innocently jostled for the best viewing position; his actions were mesmerising. This man, dressed only in short pants, with one foot up on the handle of the pedestaled axe to steady it and both hands holding a metal file, hunched over and working the blade. The seasoned survivors who recounted the fate of previous mates started to cry amongst themselves, huddling together in the back corner of the cage.

A primeval groan marked the end of his tool maintenance as he straightened his spine. A dirty thumb ran perpendicular to the blade to check its sharpness. Further inspection was required and as he brought the blade to his face it caught the sun's rays which reflected about his cluttered yard. A final check involved the blade scraping the back of his arm to shave off a patch of black hair. He grunted in approval after wiping the hair clean from the blade.

Children's screams still permeated nearby.

White knuckles flared through bronze flesh as his hands flexed - angrily gripping the axe handle.

"Shut the fuck up!" He yelled, trying to silence the children. It didn't work.

He needed clarity. Drawing back mucus from a deep nasal grunt, to clear his airways, he discarded the matter in an equally disgusting manner - spitting at a stray cat who was nervously waiting between stacked timber pallets at the chance to lick his bloody axe. Feverishly he wiped stubborn mucus which clung to his lips, with the back of his hand, as he made his way to the cage.

It was time.

Now they were all startled in the cage and scrambled to escape his grasp by selfishly climbing over one another at the back of the small enclosure. Screams replaced cries until a single victim was selected and torn from the group. The victim kicked and screamed in protest until his grip tightened around its neck, starving it of fight. The cage door was angrily slammed shut.

Its legs were bound tightly against its body to prevent it running away - to stop it kicking. Much to its vocal protest he held it firm against a wooden block which lay on the ground. In a quick and purposeful act the axe was brought down swiftly across his body and sliced sharply through its neck, burying the blade firmly into the wooden block, parting head from body.

As he stood, he released his victim. It tried to kick but rolled around on the ground, thrusting in fleeting spasms. Rich blood painted the green grass and flicked up his leg. Muttering profanity he wiped the blood with a rag which was nearby. The stray cat wisely held its distance, but started to drool and bob its head as it peered at the slaughter site with saucer eyes. The man watched on as the life escaped his victim in lessening thrusts. Finally it was dead.

Thud.

Fuck these children.

A black and white soccer ball flew over the fence and landed close to him. It nearly hit him. Without thought he grabbed the ball, smeared it in fresh blood and kicked it as hard as possible back over the fence.

Instantly he could hear their screams which melded into one with the onset of a ringing school bell.

It's only blood. One day those children will learn a valuable lesson.

He picked the rooster up off the ground by its legs and hung it upside down to drain the remaining blood. Later that day he would pluck and dress the bird for dinner.

1 – CRASH

Conflicting is the day,
when we stand before the truth,
of what events will play,
and nibble at our youth.

You've made me this way, so angry, so fucking angry. But you're ignorant to your plight; got me on your side, fed me your bullshit then took advantage of me. Was I your piece of fluff to have fun with, then you fuck me off when shit gets real?

You've left me damaged and scarred. I wish I could erase you like the rash of pimples left across my face from my changing hormones; squeeze you hard and eject you from my existence.

"Yuck! Who writes this shit?" Jack put the book down in disgust. His bus turned the last corner towards his school as he angrily stuffed the book into his school bag. He hated the book.

Standing up Jack pushed forward down the aisle with the other students, ready to disembark. The bus' brakes screeched as the driver fumbled on the brake pedal, causing the children to groan in unison as the bus lurched forward, finally coming to an uncomfortable stop. The bus driver slapped a button on the dashboard and the bus' pneumatically actuated doors sighed as they opened, letting the children pour out. Jack Armstrong impatiently waited for the others in front of him to disperse, then he shuffled off the bus giving the driver a quick, sarcastic smile of recognition. *Thanks for the smooth landing champ.*

It was the start of the school week and another hot school day at Evansdale High; it was building up to the summer storm season. The low morning sun glared out from behind the rows of single level buildings and cast shadows deep across the front of the school grounds. Senior pupils congregated here the most, shielding themselves from the morning sun, hoping to keep their deodorants lasting as long as possible. The seniors met their friends here in the comfort of the building's shadows, to catch up on any juicy bits of gossip about anything which may have happened yesterday and perhaps was too exciting to hold on to until the first class.

Students were everywhere that Jack looked. Although the gathering was large, loud noises were absent – this was left to the screaming juniors at the oval adjacent to the school buildings. Jack didn't care though, he had his Walkman on, earbuds in and was drowning out his sorrows with the song 'Rush' from Big Audio Dynamite. Like the song preached he definitely needed a change of atmosphere. This morning, like every other school morning, was like a morbid funeral gathering rather than the usual teenage hubbub you would have expected. It was too early, their teenage bodies were still waking up, their energy levels slowly gathering momentum.

Jack strode through the front gate and glanced sideways at the usual groups of students - hideous masterminds all plotting together so the whole school could laugh at him as one big, fat, family. At least that's what was going through his mind. As Jack passed the first group of students he kept his head down - not awkwardly but it didn't go unnoticed by others who glared at him.

Sheep.

He suspected he was outcast because outside of school and on free dress days he dressed weirdly to other students who were always trying to impress each other by copying the latest fashions and trends. He didn't conform to the majority. He believed if an 'in' student came to school saying and demonstrating that farting as loud as you could was the 'next best thing' then he wouldn't have been surprised that by the end of the day most of the other students would have torn their shorts or skirts trying to fart as loud as they could. Jack also thought his above average grades put him in a league of students who were seen as nerdy, socially challenged and on the opposite spectrum to anything cool – like being sporty.

The sun reflected from his oily jet-black hair like the shine on a pair of freshly polished boots as he made his way to where his friends usually sat in the morning. *We, the outcasts, are gathered here today...*, Jack thought.

"Morning," he said to his friends who were sitting in a circle. Jack remained standing.

"Hi," Tim and Susan replied simultaneously.

"Morning J-A," Patrick replied. He was the lively one of the group. Although his physical size removed him from all hopes of being athletic, his jovial personality made up for it.

"What have I missed?" Jack asked, his bus was always the last to arrive and he missed anything that may have happened earlier.

"Jonas is here today!" Susan warned, tucking long strands of strawberry blonde hair behind her ear.

"Yeah, you'd better keep a low profile from him in English." Tim added.

"Shit, I forgot we had English straight up," Jack said.

After an acute electrical hum the school bell screamed to life, bringing hell to the quiet morning. Patrick shot a leg out and used this as a lever to lift the rest of his huge body up. Susan helped Tim gather loose pieces of paper that he had been writing on and then she rose, grasping her bag and nursing it at her stomach anxiously - the morning scramble to Form class made her nervous.

Tim's English assignment looked as orderly as the way he dressed - shit everywhere. With his old school shirt untucked, baggy pants and unseasonal, sweaty beanie trying to hold back his scruffy brown hair. He finished stuffing the pieces of paper into his bag; jammed between his lunch and the myriad of other books he carried around. Tim threw his bag down and headed towards the multi-tap drinking trough, which was on the wall opposite to where they had been sitting. Jack followed Tim while both Susan and Patrick watched them along with the other handful of children gathering there.

"I see you've got your shit together for your English essay," Jack joked sarcastically.

"Yeah, the book I was given is dead boring," Tim said.

"Mine's not boring, it's just that the author's demented," Jack said just before he leant over and took a few sips of water. "They wonder why nobody gives a shit in class, when the books we're given to study are written by some washed up writer who's trying to fund their drug habit."

Jack paused and waited while a younger student sucked the last few mouthfuls of water from the water's trajectory then ran off after his jostling mates.

Tim flicked his long hair back to prevent it getting wet and tilted his head to the side to get a drink. Like cows at a water trough Tim and Jack drank at the same time.

"Do you think they have found that stolen money?" Susan asked them when they returned.

"No, some moron probably took it," Tim suggested as they all looked back over at Patrick who was now standing in line getting a drink with some of the other Form students.

"Beats me, but I bet *Haddy* will call another parade today," Jack moaned. Haddy was their nickname for Principal Colin Hadrick. He was holding the whole school under lunchtime detention parades in order to 'squeeze' out the school's staff room thief. These parades would continue until the culprit turned themselves in or someone dobbed them in - either that or the stolen money was returned anonymously. There was even an amnesty period but this had lapsed a while ago.

"This morning's parade and the lunchtime parade has been called off," Tim said. "It's on the notice board this morning, something about Haddy away at a Principles conference."

"Awesome!" Patrick beamed. "Now we don't have to sit on that concrete for *ages*, waiting for *nobody* to own up."

"I heard Jonas had something to do with it," Susan whispered.

Quinton Jonas, or Jonas as everyone referred to him, was the school thug, he beat up little kids for their lunch money and chased girls around the rest of the time - a real gentleman. The whole school hated him and his gang of thug mates. Jonas picked on them the most, and it was Jack who was the main target.

"Told you it was a moron," Tim said.

They walked to the lineup out in front of their Form class and joined Patrick at the very front. The rest of the class assembled behind them after ten minutes had passed.

As they heard their Form teacher's high heel shoes stabbing at the concrete pathway with a clipping noise Jack warned the others, "don't mention Jonas again, we don't want any more trouble than we already get from that asshole!"

"Apart from swearing in public, what trouble would that be?"

"Nothing, sorry Miss," Jack said with his head slung low.

"Well if you can't tell me then you can take the Form roll back to the office and while you're there check out the detention room, because if I hear *you* or anyone else swearing again then you can spend every lunchtime this week there!"

Ms. Smith was quite strict for someone in their early twenties which was a necessary attribute of a Performing Arts teacher – it helped her retain control over the class while they were instructed dance or performance techniques. Deep down Ms. Smith knew her strict nature was from being a single child brought up by both parents who were high ranking military officers. Nancy Smith's strict nature was equally seen in her crisp presentation, which she took great pride in. She wore smart designer clothes - well above the affordability of a teacher's wage, especially a university graduate in her second year of teaching. Her demeanor, along with her selection of clothes, got the other teachers talking about her – and even more so as she kept to herself, leading a reclusive private life. She was quite attractive and her looks also got the attention of the boys in the school, however it was quickly clipped when they realised that she could hold herself quite well and her protective parents were in the military.

"Alright, everyone inside!"

I am tired of crying myself to sleep. I am tired of being reminded of you, but I can't escape your emotional prison. I am told to stand strong, stand my ground and rise from the ashes. But being burnt so badly it's hard to look beyond the reflection of ugly scars.

It's not all doom and gloom. I am getting help, these cuts will heal in time. And like the many smashed mirrors in my presence there will always be many facets of reflection. These objects of vanity will have to be thrown in the garbage; but you know what that's like hey? Throwing pretty things away.

"Look at me when I am talking to you Jack Armstrong!" Ms. Smith shrieked in her usual manner. Jack dog-eared his novel's page to mark his spot and glared up at the teacher giving her his utmost sarcastic attention. "Now as I was saying, Jack, take this student roll call back to the main office."

Reluctantly he rose to his feet causing his chairs' steel legs to scrape against the classroom's linoleum covered floor. Jack moved in and out of the other desks glancing up at the Form teacher, grabbing the roll folder and heading out the door. He didn't bother glancing back at his mates as he was too humiliated being made a spectacle to do this erroneous duty.

Jack made his way to the school's main office, which was a fair walk considering his first class was English and back near his Form room. The school was quiet at this time, with only the scuttle of other kids heading toward the main office to also return their Form room rolls.

In front of him stood the main office, which was the only two-story building in the school. It was a large, red brick building that had an entrance which seemed too small compared to the rest of the building. Because of the restrictive entrance way a couple of other students were leaning on the wall nearby waiting in line to return their folders. From his position, Jack could make out that the other children were younger than he was and when he finally stood in line, he could see that he was correct in his assumptions. He waited behind two younger children, guessing they were three years his junior. One was a horrid little girl with greasy, unwashed hair which was pulled back so tight it appeared to be the only way her face was secured against her skull.

Jack followed them into the room and slid the roll into the pigeonhole marked for his morning class. He turned around and nearly knocked over a couple of other students who rushed in after him.

The school bell rang again, just above his head, reminding him of his English lesson and the long walk back amidst the rush of everyone getting to their classes. Just as he was about to head off in the general direction of his next classroom, he heard a familiar voice beaming down the path. Quickly Jack slipped behind a row of bottlebrush bushes in the gardens that lined the pathway - it was Jonas.

Jack didn't want to encounter this bully so early in the morning - he wasn't ready for the taunts. Jonas was shouting and making weird noises from his mouth, gaining laughs from his goons as they were busy grabbing the odd student and shouting obscenities at them. Jack hid in the bushes until it was safe to continue on. As he made his way back to his first class he thought that it wasn't unusual for Jonas to be sent to the principal's office as they were always in trouble for something or other; that meant Jonas and his goons could walk to the office from any part of the school blindfolded.

"You made it alive," Susan joked as Jack sat next to her in the classroom.

"Yeah, I had a close call with Jonas though."

"Don't worry about him."

"How can you not worry about that ogre? He's relentless."

Susan smiled at Jack, blushing; she turned her head quickly as she thought he gazed at her too long. Still looking at her he turned his head slowly away. Her heart rate quickened so she distracted herself by rifling through her bag for the books associated with the English lesson that they were about to have. Susan thought Jack's beautiful brown eyes were penetrating and could read her inner thoughts. She flicked her long hair out of the way as she rested her school bag on her knees. *Stop it, Jack is a friend,* she thought.

Their English teacher entered the classroom - a little late - still clutching a warm cup of coffee in his favourite ceramic mug which read, 'BITE ME'.

"Now, don't get too settled," Mr. Friar explained, "today we are going to do something different. Today I want you to group up and go outside. Find a quiet spot to discuss your assignment with others in small groups."

"Oh," the class groaned in unison.

"Come on class, you know I've set each of you a different novel to analyse and they are each difficult in their own right. So this will make sure you get help from one another in finishing your report. A fresh set of ideas from another student might be all you need to better your result."

The usual groups formed and started to head outside. Mr. Friar stuck his head out of the doorway and added, "And by the way, so you don't waste this session I want a short summary from each of you about another class member's book to tell me what it is about. And I want that summary before the end of the class."

"Oh," the class groaned again.

"That's all we need, more work," Jack commented as the four friends made their way over to the school boundary where there were some shady trees to sit under.

Tim, Patrick, Susan and Jack formed a group and each spoke about their assigned books. Tim's book was Macbeth by William Shakespeare, Patrick's 1984 by George Orwell, Susan's book was Lord of the Flies by William Golding and Jack's book was called Paperback Writer by John Bird. The other's books were standard senior issue English books, year in, year out, however Jack's book was different. They already knew of Jack's book because he didn't stop complaining about it, but like him, they had no idea what it was about. Both Tim and Patrick quickly decided to pair up and give a short review of each other's books to dodge being stuck trying to review Jack's book.

"Look Susan, please just say that the book is written in the style of 'Stream of Consciousness', and the author has quite an expressive and at times challenging subject matter," Jack explained.

"Are you sure?"

"Yeah, you're not going to get in trouble for being honest, even if your review is short and sweet."

"Okay, my book is a little easier, I'll fill you in."

By the end of the class all the students had written their short reviews on loose paper and made their way back to the classroom - leaving them in Mr. Friar's desk tray. They had only just made it back before the school bell rang out over the school grounds.

"Remember students, your real assignment is due this Friday," Mr. Friar said as his pupils dispersed into the mass of transitioning students.

The remainder of the school day went relatively trouble free for Jack, Susan, Tim and Patrick. They all had their own selected classes to go to like Ancient History, Physics, Speech and Drama or Physical Education; but came together for the core subjects like Maths and the English lesson that commenced the day. The standard school day was broken up into blocks of time, consisting of six classes of forty-five minutes each. The classes were coupled in two and separated by two recess breaks. Jack thought his day was one of the better days he had had for a while.

The group of four friends were all walking towards the school boundary to say their goodbyes when suddenly Jack felt an arm wrap vigorously around his neck from behind. He scoffed as he was caught off guard and dropped his Walkman onto the concrete pathway. Someone had him in a firm headlock grip and he was being dragged backwards.

"Let him go you idiot!" Susan screamed.

"Come on Jonas, let him go, he's never harmed you!" Tim shouted.

Too late, no amount of shouting was going to help their friend. Each of Jonas' goons, Neil Goodall and Stanley McCormack were at the ready with fists raised to ward off any would be rescuers. Susan, Tim and Patrick looked on helplessly and anxiously.

Jonas had picked the right moment to launch his attack. The majority of teachers were in a meeting and the afternoon supervising teacher was being distracted at a safe distance and out of sight by one of Jonas' 'recruited' helpers. *Give any early graders a cigarette and they'll do anything for you*, thought Jonas.

"Fuck. You. Jonas," Jack spat out, he was trying to support his weight off his neck so he could breathe. This left him defenceless and all he could do was kick about.

"Keep trying, you dickhead," Jonas warned, before he let go of his neck spinning Jack out in front of him. His next move was too quick, as Jack was already gasping in air deeply Jonas swung a clenched fist around striking him squarely in the stomach. Jack doubled over in pain and hit the ground face first with a thud. This time all the air escaped him and he started coughing.

"Next time you've got something to say about me, how about you say it to my face, chicken shit," Jonas warned. His goons started laughing and clucking like chickens to mock Jack. As Jonas walked off his mates Neil and Stanley kicked dirt up into his face which got caught in his mouth. Then like sheep they followed their leader.

Susan dropped to the ground and cradled Jack. "I am so, so sorry Jack, I didn't see that coming, there was no way we could help."

Jack sat up with her help and she wiped the dirt from his face and mouth. "It's okay, you couldn't have done anything," he whispered hoarsely. "I've got to learn to keep my mouth shut, you never know who is listening. Someone tipped him off from the Form room line up this morning."

Tim helped Jack get to his feet while Patrick retrieved his Walkman and made sure it still worked. Susan tried to put her arm around Jack to support him as he still looked quite winded, he pushed her away gently but gave her a smile for thanks.

"Here mate, it still works J-A, it didn't have as bad a fall as you though, you be right?"

"Yeah, sure Pat," Jack mumbled. His pride felt more hurt than his body. *I should have seen that coming.*

"Look mate, take it easy, I'll catch you tomorrow," Tim said as he left the group.

"Yeah, see you mate," Patrick added as he also headed off. His mother was waiting in the carpark for him.

"Come on Jack, let's get in line," Susan said as their bus pulled up at the curbside with a screech of its brakes. The younger students in front were pissing Jack off as they squabbled and fought for first place in line, and he was over this day - it was okay up until Jonas' attack. The older students stood back and waited for them to get on first, as they couldn't be bothered to act like a pack of monkeys.

"Jack, are you going to finish that book tonight?"

"Yeah, I am getting close, how about you?"

"Mine's long and boring, it's kind of hard to chew. I am only half way through," Susan admitted.

"But you'll make the Friday deadline?"

"Yeah, looks like I may have to skim over some of the book though, it will send me crazy otherwise." Susan answered as they both stepped onto the bus.

They shuffled down the aisle and found a vacant seat near the back. Jack took the window seat and Susan the aisle. The pneumatic cylinders on the buses' front door sighed with relief and the concertina doors unfolded and closed shut in one motion. Jack opened his backpack, pulled out his book, and said, "Only two more chapters to go, then I am done." He opened to where he left off at lunchtime and read.

I wanted a star, you gave me the Sun. You wanted fun, you gave me a son. It wasn't meant to be, the plug got pulled and it all went away like a vortex into a black hole. My time stood still. You left me standing on the highway, you couldn't even pull me from the traffic, from that oncoming bus.

It hit me hard.

How can you recover when your soul is broken? What therapy would be good enough?

As I look down at my broken fingers, I wish they were magical. I wish they could write away my fears and erase my past. She thinks so - the psychologist.

How can I forget about you, about what you've done to me, when you won't go away? Will I be forever under your control?

The bus bounced over a pothole, Jack looked up from his book and decided to put it away. As the bus approached the next corner all the students standing up moved to try and brace themselves when the driver applied the brakes and their bodies moved forward with the motion.

"This is my stop today, I've got to go and get Mum some groceries, she left me a note this morning, you know her, always cooking!" Susan remarked and with that she stood up.

"I'll phone you tonight if I finish my assignment, maybe we can hang out, listen to music?"

"Yeah sure, see you then," she answered as she gave a small wave with her fingers and headed down the bus aisle ready to disembark along with a hand full of other students.

I've got to try tonight, Susan reminded herself. She was becoming increasingly interested in Jack, she saw her friendship changing, even though her gut feeling was that they should probably remain friends, she knew Jack was beginning to grow on her in a different way. She thought tonight would be a great opportunity to see if he felt the same way. If Jack called she would head over to his house and start making some moves. Susan hadn't thought of what to do yet. She didn't quite know how to go about it. Maybe she could move her body in an awkwardly close position and let him make the first move – a test to see if he too had feelings. "Oh well," she sighed, "tonight, maybe".

The bus continued on, heading out onto the highway, Jack slipped his Walkman out of his bag, put the earbuds in and pressed play with his favourite mixed cassette tape loaded. 'Pretty Fly for a White Guy' from the Offspring commenced as he slouched back on his seat and stared vacantly out the window. He wondered if Susan would go to the end of year formal with him. *Maybe I could ask her tonight?*

Jack had a secret crush on Susan ever since he started to like the opposite sex. How could he not? She lived next door to him for quite some time and she was always there. He thought she was smart and attractive. He found cuteness in the way she sometimes became a little over sensitive about things and he loved the way he could bring her around with a quick quip or a friendly tease. But he worked out early not to push her too far. He remembered one particular day when he felt things changed between them - it was also the first time he realised that he needed to be careful about her feelings. She came over as usual one weekend - a Saturday - just to see what he was up to. He was stuck washing his father's car and asked if she didn't mind helping him to make the job quicker, then they could catch that new movie they were both interested in seeing. He couldn't remember the movie now if he tried - maybe it was Toy Story or Speed or some new release like that. She agreed and before he knew it they were both in the driveway washing the car; he worked a sponge with a bucket full of suds while she rinsed with the garden hose. They were just about finished when the hose slipped from her hands and sprayed across her top and face. Jack looked up about to laugh at her wet predicament, but stopped short when he noticed her wet top clinging to her breasts making it quite easy to see her dark areolas and erect nipples staring back. He froze like a deer in the headlights, only realising he was gazing way too long before it was too late, she had looked down at herself and instantly knew what turned him into an ogling male. A typical guy who now saw her as a piece of meat. She quickly covered herself in embarrassment, dropping the hose and running back home. He didn't see her the rest of that weekend, let alone go and watch a movie with her.

When she finally came around, she never once referred to the incident and he noticed that she wore bras from then on. He didn't mention what had happened, he was too embarrassed to apologise or to bring it up - there was no joke or teasing that would have lightened the mood that wouldn't have been seen as insensitive. What he did learn however, was from that moment on, things had definitely changed between them as she took some time before she came back to visit him at home. She was also distant at school. Jack didn't want that awkward separation to happen again so he tried not to let his growing interest in her show more than that of friendship.

The bus jumped, everyone looked around - it didn't feel like a pothole this time. The bus was approaching the end of its journey on the dual carriageway but was still moving quite quickly. The final stops were in the suburb of Brinsmead, where both Jack and Susan lived. The bus jumped again, Jack felt uncomfortable, something wasn't right. The bus jumped again, students screamed as some were launched out of their seats into the center aisle. Jack held on tightly to the seat rail in front of him as the last jump nearly lifted him as well.

A final jump combined with a small explosion, tearing a hole in the front left stairwell of the bus, caused the children to scream with fear. Jack managed to shield his eyes from a spray of toughened glass, which radiated from the explosion, showering across the students in small cubic fragments.

Jack held on for dear life as blood seeped from tiny cuts across his forearm caused by the glass shower. Looking up he watched the bus driver struggling to control the steering wheel. The driver looked like he was wrestling a bear as he was trying to stop the bus from careering into the heavy oncoming afternoon traffic - but his strength was hopeless. No man, no matter how strong, could control this overweight beast; the steering system was destroyed. The front left radial, void of rubber and at an unnatural angle to the other tyres, hit the bitumen and sprayed sparks up through the floor in all directions like a Roman candle fireworks display. The deafening noise drowned out the children's screams as they all looked wide-eyed about the cabin. Jack was about to see if he could help the driver when he was thrown back into his seat as the bus fishtailed violently. The driver nearly had his foot though the floor trying to work the brake pedal, there was no pushback, no resistance; the hydraulic brake line was cut from the explosion, releasing the pressure from the brakes. Fear washed across the bus driver's face as he realised he had no control of the bus; he too was now a passenger helpless to the young children in his care.

Heading towards the outside edge of the road the bus caught the concrete curb and flicked onto its side like a child was playing with a Matchbox car. The passengers held onto anything they could - but to no avail. All the passengers on the right of the bus were launched into the air, they tumbled down like wet blankets in a dryer, and collided into the passengers who were sitting on the left hand side. One child cracked his head onto a seat support bar while another smashed head first into the top window. The children's screams were lost by metal screeching against bitumen, concrete and dirt - the harrowing noise seemed to carry on forever. The bus hit a timber light pole snapping it like a pretzel but also spinning the bus about its middle. By now other vehicles following in the same direction had locked brakes and were watching the horror unfold before them. As the bus came to rest against the concrete median strip a deathly silence blanketed the devastating scene. Jack, who had ended up wedged into an overhead luggage rack, saw paper and sparks raining down through blurred vision. He tasted a rusty flavoured liquid in his mouth before he slipped into unconsciousness.

2 - RECOVERY

She giggled as he teased the long strands of blonde hair that formed her fringe. He was playing with the way the sun shone through the strands. He liked the different shades of colour he achieved depending on how many strands he let gather in his fingertips and fall away. Brown, blonde, ginger. When he was blinded by the sun from letting all the hairs fall he gathered up more again to shadow his eyes. He loved her laughter, he loved her hair. He continued to play with the strands gently at his fingertips. He wanted this to last forever, nothing else entered his mind.

He felt warm and safe, lying on the thick grass in their neighbourhood park, his head in her lap. She smiled as she ran her hands through his hair.

"Jaaack," she whispered softly, drawing out his name in a low, soothing tone. Feeling sublime and content he just lay there looking up at her, sunlight twinkling in his eyes.

"Jaaack," she breathed again, this time a little louder. "Jaaack," she said again, this time her tone had changed to a slightly more masculine one. He felt pressure on his eyelids and forehead.

"Jack, can you hear me," the male voice said in a deep tone, clearly this wasn't Susan. Jack tried to sit up but he couldn't; he winced as a sharp pain throbbed at the back of his head.

Confusion.

Through blurred vision Jack was now trying to comprehend his surroundings. Was this reality? *Take me back to Susan.*

The light flashed in his eyes again, but this time it wasn't the sun. The doctor moved his pen light back and forth, "Good, good," he said, "he's responsive." He removed his hand from Jack's forehead which he had been resting there in order to keep his eyelids open with his fingers. Upon returning his pen light to his white overcoat top pocket the doctor turned and spoke to others in the room.

Jack came to a sudden realisation that he was in hospital. He had survived the bus crash. How long had he been here? Who was the doctor talking to and what was he saying?

A hot flush washed across Jack's body. It wasn't because he realised the gravity of what he had just gone through, but because of another revelation. Jack just realised his feelings for Susan were more than that of a crush and were stronger than he realised.

A nurse checked the flow from an IV bag that was connected to his hand via a tube. She opened a valve, and the flow increased, causing Jack's pain to dull.

Jack slipped back to sleep hoping for Susan to meet him in his dreams.

And *vivid is the picture,*
that shines like the light of day,
when children's eyes flicker,
as it steals their dreams away.

Snap, snap it shut. Shut it up. Bound by luck, my dreams are stuffed. How can I sleep when a kaleidoscope of nightmares paint vivid, hellish portraits of what I've lost?
I've got to get these plans out of my head and into action. Writing alone can't resolve my issues.

"How poetic," Jack thought. The book he was reading was really going nowhere. He felt like throwing it out of his hospital room window or tearing it in half, like a WWF wrestler would do to a telephone book in front of a chanting stadium. Apart from his lack of strength to destroy the book, the one and only thing that kept him reading it was his impending English assessment based on his analytical review. He put the book on his bedside table alongside a jug of water, drinking glass and the myriad of 'Get Well Soon' cards and stuffed toys.

Jack was too tired to put up a resistance to having the shrine take residence on his bedside table. He'd normally protest and whine to his mother over such trivial embellishments, but this time he actually quite liked them. They were the only colour, the only cheer in his room. Besides, he was lucky enough that his parents were able to afford him a private room. Therefore he was grateful and tolerant to his parents fussing over him. He was also grateful that visiting hours were restricted to two hours in the morning and two hours in the evening.

It was now lunchtime and his stomach had woken him up. Soon the food servers would be doing their rounds with the meal cart. With only the occasional cart rattling past his room and the infrequent whispers of nurses conversing in the hallway Jack's room was pleasantly quiet. Today seemed even more quiet than normal. Perhaps his scheduled discharge today had his keen ears tuned into every noise, listening for anyone coming his way. While he waited he pondered his recovery.

Jack's recovery had gone quite well considering the initial concerns from his head trauma and the potential swelling of his brain. He had only been in hospital just over a week and it was really only due to his concussion; the doctors didn't want to risk the chance of any unforeseen complications. They ran tests to check for permanent damage and monitored the progress of his swelling - which was quite minor. They tested his motor skills, memory recall and behaviour. Head trauma patients quite frequently displayed signs of aggression after an accident but Jack passed all the standard behavioural tests. Although he was visibly bruised, Jack had been spared any broken bones that some of the other unfortunate students had.

Each day over the past week, during morning visitation hours, Jack's mother arrived to bore him with their neighbourhood gossip or anything she had read in the paper about the bus accident. It was during one of these 'information' sessions when she read him the news report about the bus driver, Bill Smart.

She read verbatim each news article which offered information like: '*After examining the bus wreckage traffic accident forensics were surprised that no one had been killed. Even though the bus driver was spared significant injury he was still under police investigation.*' Mrs. Armstrong had received news from a 'credible' source - her hairdresser - with 'inside information' that the police were looking to lay charges for negligent driving.

It was difficult not to like Bill Smart, he was such a kind old gentleman who was so willing to help anyone. The children at Evansdale High however, were cruel to him; they saw weakness in his kindness and called him unfortunate names but the one that stuck was Fat Cat. Like any easy characteristic the children picked out this name because of his large disposition and because Fat Cat was a children's television show - it was kind of unimaginative - so Jack thought.

Most students didn't give Bill the time of day, not even an acknowledgement as they alighted the bus. Jack however gave him a nod or a smile - depending on his mood of course. Jack felt sorry for him and his daughter Sissy, who also attended Evansdale High and was in the same year as Jack and his friends. Sissy was bullied as well. The only reason Sissy didn't hang out with Susan, Jack, Tim and Patrick was because she was quite strange. She was a loner. There was something just not quite right about the girl. Susan would spend some time with her, but came away from the visits and had to debrief her friends on the strange and unusual anecdotes that came out of her mouth. It was sad, but the group of four needed their distance from Sissy even though she was also a social outcast at school. Susan didn't mind being the satellite of their group to orbit them and spending time with Sissy, sometimes she needed a break from the boys as well.

Bill took up bus driving to try and make ends meet as a single parent. It worked out perfectly for him as he was able to transfer Sissy to and from school while earning a living. Although no matter how hard Bill tried to bring up Sissy in a safe and nurturing environment he felt he always fell short because he didn't have an influential female partner for guidance.

A small framed photo, which was affixed to the dashboard of his bus, was the only memory Sissy had of her mother. She died giving birth to her due to delivery complications. When Sissy was old enough to understand she quickly figured out that it was her fault. She grew up thinking she killed her mother, and it didn't help that she couldn't console her father as he retracted emotionally. The burden of harbouring this unreasonable guilt around her whole life shaped what was once a happy little toddler into an introverted recluse with potential self-harm issues.

The school bullying didn't help her situation either. She copped it in both primary and secondary school and no matter how much Bill tried to bring up the issue with the school he saw no improvement. He eventually gave up – his lobbying fell on deaf ears – so he found solace in the fact that he was able to send her off and bring her home safely with no bullying. He thought she could start the day happy and come home with a safe 'landing'.

When Jack's mother read to Jack about how Bill would lose his job and possibly face criminal charges his heart sank. *Surely it wasn't poor Bill's fault. Next time I see him, I'll give him my support - if there is a next time.*

Apart from his mother, and sometimes his reluctant brother, the only other person to visit Jack in recovery at the hospital was Susan. She would meet him in the afternoons after school and assist him with his daily outdoor walking exercises. Jack also took daily walks around the hospital gardens with the assistance of a shift nurse. This was to make sure his swollen limbs and joints were stretched and exercised. Whether with Susan, a nurse or his parents, Jack was never alone - just in case he fell. With the passing of each day Jack was able to walk a little further as his strength increased and his limbs improved. Jack was making a great recovery and was glad that this was his last day - he was over it.

The unmistakable sound of the meal trolley bumping down the hospital corridor broke his train of thought, Jack frowned as he wanted to go back to that moment with Susan, when they were sitting side by side in the hospital gardens, talking about insignificant things. He missed her delicate touch, and the smell of her perfume as she helped him up off the garden bench. Now the rattle of stainless steel cutlery against ceramic plates cut through his daydream like a thousand knives being dropping on the floor.

Oh well, I am starving, and the food isn't too bad, he thought. The trolley stopped outside his room and the door swung inwards. Jack had to rub his eyes because he was expecting a uniformed food server not his English teacher.

"Good afternoon, Jack," Mr. Friar said in a jovial manner. "I hope you don't mind my visit, I took the liberty of asking the young ladies at reception for permission to bring you your food." Without a care for Jack's response he pushed the trolley fully into the room and closed the door behind him.

How did he get past visiting hour restrictions?

"Don't mind me Jack, I had to see for myself that you were all okay and on the mend," Mr. Friar declared. He moved a wheeled food table into position over the bed and placed a covered plate of food upon it, which was on a plastic tray. "Ah, I see you are reading the book I assigned you, so Susan gave you the message that you could, understandably, have an extension on your English assignment?"

"Yes sir, I feel much better, except my head hurts when I read this book," Jack explained as he gave a reluctant side glance to the novel sitting on the bedside table.

"What do you mean?" Mr. Friar asked, looking perplexed.

"Well sir, to be honest, it's nonsense."

"Nonsense?"

"I mean it doesn't make sense, there isn't a plot like a typical novel, nothing about it makes me want to read it and in parts it's actually quite disgusting," explained Jack. He lifted the cover off of his food and watched the steam rise, being careful not to tilt it too much so the condensation underneath didn't dribble all over his food. *Yum, lasagna and chips.*

Mr. Friar ran his short fat fingers through his silver moustache to smooth it out. His frown showed that he was annoyed with Jack's dismissive attitude towards a book that he chose for him. "Jack, the book is different, I know, but I wanted to push you out of your comfort zone," he said as he stood beside the bed. "As I explained when I gave it to you, the writing style is called 'Stream of Consciousness'. That means that the author literally writes everything that flows out of his or her mind."

"Yes I get it, but how does that make for a good read, where is the plot, the climax?"

"I've read it and it's quite compelling, and I am sure when you finish it you'll agree that it's one of the best books that you've ever read," Mr. Friar promised with a smug smile.

"It's so hard to read, that's why my head hurts. Anyway who is John Bird? No one has heard of that author."

"The author is a local, who attends the Evansdale Paperback Writers Group, here at the school," Mr. Friar explained. "Meetings are held monthly - after hours - it's where people new to writing can get help from each other to develop their talents."

"I've never heard of it before."

"It started last year, there are flyers on the notice boards," Mr. Friar said dismissively.

"Great."

"What is it Jack?"

"I was right, it is some half-baked writer," Jack said, choosing not to mention the bit about funding their drug habit. He grabbed a potato chip and dabbed it into the red sauce that oozed from the side of the lasagna. He ate quickly as he was starving.

"Careful what you say Jack, I chair the meetings and I've promised the author you'll write an excellent but honest review."

"Who is in the group?" Jack asked, munching on a potato chip.

"Now, now, Jack, the group has an anonymity code. You know, some authors like the choice of keeping their pen names secret to protect their identities," Mr. Friar explained. "You could join the team but there is a strict screening process."

"Sorry sir, I'll pass." He was starting to become irritated with Mr. Friar's visit. All this information could have been passed on to his parents or Susan. *What's Mr. Friar's real intentions for visiting?*

"Well, I hear you're getting out of hospital today but the principal has given you the rest of the week off. My visit here was also to determine if you are of able mind. So because I see you are thinking clearly, while you are at home over these next few days I expect you to finish the assignment and hand it in first thing on Monday morning," Mr. Friar said, void of his usual jovial tone; he was dead serious.

There's the kicker.

"Good day Jack, and remember, your result from this assignment will heavily weigh on your ability to pass English and consequently finish Year 12 with a passing grade. You don't want to repeat Year 12 do you?" Mr. Friar said. Before Jack could answer he left the hospital room and by either accident or intention he let the door slam abruptly behind him.

Jack threw a potato chip at the back of the closed door and it bounced off, resting somewhere under his bed.

"Mum, stop it, stop annoying me," Jack pleaded, it was late in the afternoon, he was already quite frustrated with how long the hospital discharge process was taking. His day had gone downhill from lunchtime, the unwelcome visit from his English teacher Mr. Friar had pissed him off, and now after a long drawn out process from the hospital he had his mother fussing over his appearance. His mother, along with his brother Clint, had arrived some time ago to pick up Jack and take him home – they were also bored and fidgety. Jack's mother felt the discharge process was taking far too long and was about to lodge a formal complaint at the nurse's station when Jack's doctor walked in for the final check on his patient.

"How are you feeling this afternoon Jack, I bet you can't wait to get home," the doctor said.

"Sure," Jack replied. As soon as the words spilt from his mouth he quickly apologised, "sorry doc, sir, yes I can't wait to get home." He kept his manners in check because out of the corner of his eye he caught his mother's glare. Before the accident he would have received a quick clip to the back of the head to keep him in toe – to remind him to use his manners.

"Okay, let me just check your chart to see if the nurses or shift physician left any details," he said as he grabbed the white clipboard which hung from a frame at the end of his bed. "No, everything looks as it should." The doctor returned the clipboard. "Now Jack, how are you feeling, any mild pain in your head, any discomfort at all?"

"Everything is fine, I feel normal," Jack said, darting a cautionary look at his brother, knowing he would play on the word 'normal' and tease him about being anything but normal. Jack was irritated and wished he could let the doctor know this process was giving him a headache but he didn't want to delay the process any longer and jeopardise his freedom. He wished he was at home, lying on his bed, making mixed tapes with Susan.

"Okay Jack, you've been here long enough, please don't hesitate to contact me if you do feel anything out of the ordinary, nothing is too small or insignificant, after all you have gone through quite a traumatic event."

Jack took a deep breath and sighed. *Thank fuck for that.* He had to mask his enthusiasm as he didn't want to seem rude to the doctor and especially his mother.

The doctor left the room and as Mrs. Armstrong turned her head to the side to pick her handbag off the floor, Clint gave Jack a short but strong punch to the upper arm. *Ouch.*

"Ha, ha, 'I feel normal'," Clint teased as he slurred his speech to imply that Jack was mentally slow.

"Clint, please, let's go, you can grab his bag," Mrs. Armstrong said, missing the physical contact but sensing something had transpired between the two of them.

Clint glared at Jack, not happy with his new duty.

The car ride home felt like an eternity with his mother rabbiting on about trivial indifferences that had been going on in their street. That, and every time Jack looked over at his brother, sitting across from him, Clint punched a fist into the space that separated them on the back seat. It made Jack's blood boil, he wished he could walk home.

Jack's only brother was usually mean to him - brotherly love. One time when they were younger Clint swung a fist out in frustration at him, when Jack was annoying him, which left Jack with a broken little finger. It still doesn't sit at the same angle as his other little finger. Tough love.

Their father would have joined the family today but he worked out of town at a mine site on a rostered system of two weeks away and one week at home - this week he wasn't home. He would have been there to absorb his mother's ranting conversation, but instead the boys had to endure the plucky conversation. All Jack could do was stare out the car window and mumble the occasional, "Yes Mum, no Mum, if you say so Mum."

Jack had his fair share of lying in bed over the last week but now all he wished for was to be alone in his room, earbuds in, listening to music and possibly thinking of Susan. He wanted to be alone in his own surroundings and it couldn't come soon enough. Maybe he could visit Susan tomorrow after she came home from school. He sure needed some sanity in his life at the moment.

3 – FRIDAY AFTERNOON

So take my hand in marriage,
as we're all upon a wheel.
Flip the children's carriage,
drink the pain they feel.

It's staggering to think, with the sunlight in his eyes, he couldn't save them, he is much stronger than me, yet he can't sleep either, because of their cries.

I would have thought that with all my preparation, the bus you threw me under would have cartwheeled from my stoic demeanor.

Life imitates art, one crash at a time.

"What the fuck," Jack said out loud in disgust and bewilderment. *This writer has either written something very coincidental or this is a manuscript for something quite premeditated.*

Jack took a deep breath and looked around his room. He didn't know what to think of the paragraph he had just read, he guessed it was coincidental because he read the publication date and it was 1997 – almost a year before the bus crash. He figured the bus accident had increased his sensitivity to things and the book was dragging on for way too long for his liking – he just wanted to finish it and move on.

His eyes traced the walls of his room and he found comfort in looking at the poster he had on display. An AC/DC poster hung next to a Nirvana, *In Utero*, poster which was flanked by numerous surf brand posters, all of which made for an interesting wall mural but were of little inspirational help. He had to get through this book. *I am three quarters of the way through this thing and today is Friday*, he thought to himself. *Stop procrastinating and just finish the damn thing, at least before the weekend arrives with all its distractions.*

"Come on!" he shouted out aloud and slapped his cheeks. "The bus crash jargon - it's just a coincidence, let's get through this," he said as though he was talking to someone else in the room.

And yet I stand here, staring out his window, wondering what the day will bring. Will another child cross his path?

You would have loved to meet him - He's a good listener. But I bet you would have been scared shitless. After all you are the gutless one who only looks after his brood.

I would have loved to see you shake his hand. He would have broken it, just like he broke the neck of his noisy rooster.

Could this author be old, 'Mad Daris' who lives next door to the school? Jack thought to himself. Daris Kovacevic was an eccentric war veteran who lived adjacent to Evansdale High School. Part of his property boundary shared the school fence line. In many ways Daris was a hoarder as his back yard was filled with rusting paraphernalia that he picked up on the side of the road which people had thrown out for council collection.

That's too obvious, Jack thought. *Someone is using his persona as a character in this book, maybe I can write about that in my report.*

Seriously, now is the time to act, weigh up all my options to realise my greatest dream. Soon it will be over, the way I've always imagined and the way that I've always wanted it.

If only you knew.

If only I could speak to you like the way I spoke to my mirror. It didn't listen and now look at it over there all cracked and leaky.

No, I've got to show you. It is time.

You'll see who the boss is, my friend, the time is near.

Now this sounds like some sort of resolve, maybe this book is getting somewhere, Jack thought. He closed the book but held the remaining portion of pages he had left to read. Holding the book's spine he flipped the remaining pages quickly with his thumb. "Only one hundred pages to go, in this turd of a book," he said to himself.

It was getting late into the afternoon and Susan would be home soon. He decided to have a break and go and visit her for a sanity check. He climbed out the bedroom window of his two story home and traversed the mango tree which had grown beside the house. As much as he loved this 'escape' route he always had trouble negotiating the green ants which called the mango tree home. Getting bitten on the hands, especially between the fingers, was painful and was always expected as he traversed the tree.

Jack pushed past some broken palings in an opening in the timber fence between his and Susan's home. He loved this easy access, which was never repaired, because it was the main passageway for the children as they grew up as neighbours. Now the visits were less about childish play and more related to talking through problems both academically and personally.

"Hi Jack," Mrs. Valentino said.

Susan's mother was dressed in a large brimmed hat and long sleeved blouse to shield herself from the afternoon sun. "How about this heat? The only time I can get into the garden is either in the morning or late afternoon," she explained. The temperature was building this time of year; the grass was scorched brown and the plants wilted. Soon the heat and humidity would be unbearable but relief would be felt by much needed afternoon storms. Local's gave an apt title to how people acted this time of year - 'Mango Madness'; the effects of extreme heat coupled with the same time as mangoes ripening on the trees was used as an excuse to explain why some locals did crazy things.

"Susan's not home yet, how about you go inside and help yourself to some chocolate slice while you wait? I made it this morning." She often showed her generosity in offering her baked treats to Jack and her children.

"Sure, thanks Mrs. V."

"It's in the fridge," Mrs. Valentino called out - Jack had already made a beeline to the kitchen. Peeling back the plastic cling film covering the treat he scooped up a slice with one hand and headed to Susan's bedroom. He had devoured it before he got through her bedroom door.

Susan's bedroom looked similar to Jack's bedroom; posters of pop groups and posters of surfers in various wave riding moments adorned the walls. Her room looked quite gender neutral apart from a fancy white dresser with mirror that her parents had bought for her when she was just a toddler. She had clearly outgrown the girly stage of pinks and frill, but she loved this dresser even though she would have been embarrassed to admit to owning it. Jack kept this secret to himself – he was the only one from school who knew she had it.

While he waited Jack laid back on her bed and looked up towards the ceiling. Her pillow smelt fragrant - her particular brand of shampoo - he breathed her in. Susan's mother trusted Jack in her room alone with her. They knew he had no intention of taking advantage of her; they had been friends for too long and were like brother and sister. Susan's sister, Valerie, on the other hand didn't like how often Jack visited her. She was older and more experienced with the opposite sex and their raging hormones. Also, she had been heartbroken too many times and took it upon herself to protect Susan.

"Make yourself at home why don't you!" the annoyed young woman spat as she barged through the open bedroom doorway. She was taller and thinner than Susan, whom she thought was anorexic. Her auburn hair was tied back in a ponytail, and it gave her face a more pronounced appearance than Susan's. Although she wore plenty of makeup she couldn't mask some of the deeper acne scars. Aside from these minor blemishes she was beautiful and she knew it.

"Sorry Valerie," Jack apologised as he sat bolt upright. He scooted his feet off the bed but remained sitting there looking up at Valerie's imposing stance with a sheepish grin.

"You're damn right you should be sorry, lounging around on my sister's bed like that. I know you've been in an accident but come on, what was it? Slight concussion, no broken bones and you get to have two weeks off school." She was right, it's what other students were gossiping about at school, especially the siblings of the children that came off worse for wear.

"Susan has stuck by you the whole time and what do you show her? That you can drape your dirty feet all over her bed?"

"Look, I said sorry, I was just waiting for her to come home."

"You know what she really wants Jack?"

"What?" *Where is this going?*

"It's what any girl wants this time of year, in their senior year."

"What would that be?" He had no idea.

"The formal, she wants someone to take her to the formal." The end of senior year formal was where Year 12 students got to dress up in formal wear, like ballroom dresses and tuxedos, parade around embarrassingly in front of their parents for gushing candid photos. After the parents left the pre formal drinks the student couples sat, ate food, listened to boring speeches and to watch courageous couples dance. It was similar to the American 'prom' but different in the fact that there wasn't any coronation of the Prom King and Queen. Most of the night was filled with children bitching about who took who and what others were wearing. The other concern on the night was where the after party was going to be and would there be alcohol and weed snuck in.

"But we spoke about it and she said she had no interest in that kind of thing," Jack said.

"And you believed her?"

"Why not?"

"What do you think my best memory from high school is?"

"What? The formal?"

"Yes, it's the one thing I enjoyed, there weren't too many good times for me back then, you know it and I know it. We are all supposed to romanticise about how great our senior high years are, but we all know it's bullshit. What with the 'in' groups, the bullying, the continuous examination and judgement, mix that with a humidicrib of puberty and it's one of the most dreadful times of our lives. But the formal Jack, well I still look at the photos."

If you say so, I wouldn't pin that much on a formal. "Wasn't that a couple of years ago now, when you were in your senior year?" Jack asked, trying not to offend her. He remembered she tried to push for his brother, Clint, to take her but he didn't want to go. Clint made some excuse that he was sick and Valerie ended up taking some guy that she worked part time at the local fish and chip take away shop. From memory, Jack thought she was extremely unhappy because neither Jack nor Clint had seen her around her house much after that. Also, this was the reason why Jack thought Susan showed no interest in going to their formal. Susan didn't want to make her sister jealous. *How could she ever be jealous when she's literally begging me to take Susan?*

"Yes, see what I mean, it's been two years and it's my best memory."

Each to their own.

"Anyway, just think about it. I don't want to see my sister disappointed. Oh and Mum said you can stay for dinner if you want. I just spoke with her as she was chatting to your mum over the fence."

"Cool, what is it?"

"I don't know, anyway, think about what I said," she added as she left the room heading off down the hallway - her room was at the end.

I don't want to go to the stupid formal, and I am sure Susan doesn't want to either, but dinner sounds good - Mrs. V makes some brilliant dinners.

Mrs. Valentino's cooking skills were in fact brilliant. She spent most of her spare time reading recipe books and trying new delicacies. Her Italian background meant she had learnt how to make pasta from scratch which was handed down to her from her Nona. Susan and Valerie also spent a great deal of time learning from their mother in the kitchen. Susan seemed keener to help her mother, more so than Valerie who had lost some of her passion for cooking from working long hours in the local fish and chip take away shop.

But unlike most traditional Italians, Mrs. Valentino hadn't limited herself to cooking food only from her homeland. With each world recipe book that she brought home from the local library she was excited to try many of the different dishes and cuisines. She could be cooking Indian food one night and Mexican the other. Susan loved when she went through a Japanese sushi phase - but she hadn't made that for a while.

Cooking was Mrs. Valentino's addiction; with each new cuisine Mrs. Valentino also went out and bought the bespoke cooking equipment. From Tajines to crepe griddles, you name it Mrs. Valentino had it. But all this came at a cost and on a single mother's income sometimes this was evident in the lack of other activities that they could do as a family; it wasn't unusual for Susan to miss out on high school excursions. This was another reason why Susan didn't want to go to the high school formal, because her mother couldn't afford to buy her a fancy, new dress.

Jack was getting bored so he looked around Susan's bedroom. Her girly dresser intrigued him, he opened the top draw and as he expected it was a mess of 'girly things': hair clips, brushes, hair ties, lip sticks, postcards from her aunt's trip to Europe, coloured pens. A photo of their group of friends caught his eye and he picked it up to take a closer look. *Look at Tim and Patrick*, he thought with a smirk as he saw them taking the piss out of each other in the photo. Susan looked sad, as usual, and Jack quickly put the photo back when he glanced at himself. He hated seeing himself in photos. He closed the draw which stuck halfway and he had to give it a shove to close it. *Too much shit in there.* He opened the second draw hoping to find something exciting, but it was empty. *That's odd, who has an empty draw.* But just as he was starting to close the draw a notepad dropped down into it; the tape that was holding the book to the underside of the draw above gave way. With careful hands he opened the first page of the worn and tattered notebook and read what Susan had handwritten.

<u>For Daddy</u>

My heart burns in times of solace,
I cry myself to sleep,
I loathe this self-pity you bore me,
and my soul that you've made weak.

Happiness is my revenge,
from shadows of your turned back,
proudly I wear this crooked mask,
and the empathy I lack.

So remember your innocent blood,
who clutched their mum with screams,
who relives that day in nightmares,
and wishes for sweeter dreams.

Susan.

That's deep, Jack thought. Susan had told him about her father leaving the family when they were young but he didn't know she felt that way about the situation. *She's clearly holding onto some troubled thoughts about it all. I hope she isn't too scared.* Jack looked up and pondered the times that they had been together, he assumed her unhappiness was because of school life - teasing and bullying. *Maybe it's more than that,* remembering her sullen look in the group photo he just saw. He turned the pages looking for more answers.

<u>Hero</u>

Peering through smudged glass,
beyond the timber divide,
I wish to escape this world,
free from shadows where I hide.

From across the great expanse,
the sun shines brighter there,
one day I wish my hero,
would match my yearning stare.

But he's blinded by the lies,
as I am blinded by the stars,
for heaven is my great escape,
from all these hidden scars.

Susan.

Wow, also very deep. Susan is quite the poet, who would have known. I wonder who this hero is. Jack thought he better put the book back, before Susan came home. He cursed himself for looking through her personal things although what he found both amazed and confronted him.

I love her passion when she has her mind set to do something. I feel like she's the only one in the world who gets me but I don't know how to show my feelings towards her. That feeling I had when I first woke up in the hospital, could it all have been because of the medication? Was it my sub consciousness?

Jack settled back on her bed, he lay there again looking up at the ceiling. He was thinking about what Valerie had said earlier. He had mixed emotions. He contemplated whether he should make a move and show Susan that his feelings towards her had changed. He thought he was lying to himself if he didn't try, even if it meant they could no longer be friends if she rejected him. *Am I being selfish?*

The clock on Susan wall was showing 5 pm; Jack had nodded off to sleep - even though troubled thoughts swam through his head. Being in hospital had changed his metabolism slightly and now he seemed to nod off quite easily. Over time and with regular exercise this should change. He didn't hear her coming through the door so she ran her fingers through his hair.

"Wha..?" Jack woke startled.

"Hello sleepy head," Susan said with a smirk.

"Hi, how long have you been there?"

"Oh, about an hour," she joked.

"Creepy."

"No, you're safe, I just got home. Well I got here a few minutes ago and Mum caught up with me in the kitchen."

"Oh, okay, what are we having?"

"Always thinking with your stomach," she said as she laughed. She blushed as she considered herself being a little too flirty. She turned from Jack to hide her face and put her school bag under her desk.

"Yeah, why not!" Jack said proudly.

"I think it's Osso Bucco with mashed potatoes, your favourite if I remember correctly, you know she loves you," Susan said, referring to her mother.

"Nice, and who wouldn't?"

"Well Jack, you know we all love you," Susan said, blushing again.

"Your sister is a hard case though," he said, frowning.

"She's just had a bit of a hard time after finishing school, trying to find a job and all. Plus she's very protective of me."

"I guess so. Anyhow what is the latest news?"

"Well, today was quite boring, we had a two hour detention this morning. It was so hot in the assembly hall, I wish they would install ceiling fans."

"Still no one owning up?"

"No, I don't know how long this is going to go on for, something or someone has to give. Apart from that, no real trouble, Jonas wasn't there today."

"Well that would have been good for everyone."

Susan sat on her bed next to Jack, she reached down and rummaged through her school bag producing a bunch of papers stapled together - her graded book review assignment. "Look at this!" she said excitedly. It was hard to miss the large, encircled 'A' at the top right hand corner of the cover page.

"Well done!" He was truly excited for her. He gave Susan an impromptu hug which took her off guard. She slowly cupped his back to match his warm embrace. They pulled apart awkwardly.

"Sorry," Jack apologised.

"Don't be."

"I was just happy for you because I know this means you've aced English and it puts your overall grades quite high."

"Yes I know, very exciting." Susan tried to mentally examine the hug and what it truly meant. She turned away from Jack and placed the assignment on her desk.

"Susan?"

"Yes," she was still turned away from him and fussing over some of the loose things on her desk.

"Can I ask you a question?"

"You sort of just did," Susan joked, trying to lighten the seriousness of Jack's tone.

"Well, yes, but I was wondering." *Come on man, spit it out.*

"Dinner time!" Susan's mother shouted from the kitchen which cut through the tension in the air and released the pressure Jack was feeling like a burst balloon.

"Can it wait Jack?" Susan urged, "come on, we'll talk more after dinner." In reality butterflies were doing cartwheels in her stomach. She had to somehow hide her nervousness. She liked Jack, she loved him as a friend, and had thought of the possibility of seeing if it went further than that. Some days, when she was lonely and sad, she even fantasised that Jack would burst into her room, riding a white stallion, and sweep her off her feet. But when that moment came, when that thin line came close to being crossed she wasn't sure if she was ready for it. She wasn't sure if she truly wanted it because everything would change and she might lose him all together.

Valerie was notably missing from the dinner table, Susan didn't care but Jack saw the look of disappointment in Mrs. Valentino's eyes. She blamed herself for Valerie's shortcomings which she believed stemmed from the lack of a father figure in her upbringing. Jack's mother had given Mrs. Valentino plenty of support after he had walked away from the family when the girls were only toddlers. Some attributed her husband leaving the family because of the stress of bringing up two children on a single income, others thought he was weak and didn't deserve two beautiful children. But deep down Mrs. Valentino missed him and his support and the companionship they once shared.

Mrs. Valentino smiled as she watched both Susan and especially Jack eat her homely meal of Osso Bucco. Jack wolfed down the sauce covered potato and sucked the jelly like marrow from the bone. Jack looked up at her sitting at the opposite side of the table and he smirked with a little bit of red sauce dribbling down his chin. She pointed at it and he promptly wiped it with a paper serviette.

"It's your favourite isn't it Jack," Mrs. Valentino asked, already knowing the answer.

"Yes Mrs. V," Jack said, giving a quick smirk to Susan who poked her tongue at him.

"Mum, since it's Friday night can I go to the park after dinner?" She wasn't really asking, she was old enough to make her own decisions, but it was her way of giving her mother some sense of control. If she said no then she would find some way to get out later anyway.

The park, which was located in their suburb, was where some of the local children hung out after school. It was where Susan and Jack met Tim and Patrick on the weekend to catch up and shoot the breeze. When Mrs. Valentino knew Susan was going with someone, her mind was at ease, but when she found out she was at the park by herself she worried herself sick. She figured she needed her space and freedom, and she didn't want her to rebel if she wasn't allowed some flexibility – but she tried to warn her about the dangers of being out at night by herself. Sometimes the warnings fell on deaf ears, and Mrs. Valentino thanked her lucky stars that nothing bad had happened to Susan.

"Sure, why not, Jack will go with you of course?"

"Of course Mum," she said half sarcastically.

"But not too long, I know it's not a school night but we are going to my sister's house tomorrow. I want to leave early, so don't stay out too long, okay?"

"Okay Mum, we won't be too late."

Susan thought her aunty was cool, but she lived two hours away and she didn't really feel like sitting in a car for so long, not this weekend anyway.

"Can't I stay here tomorrow, Jack needs a hand getting his English assignment done?"

"Susan, we spoke about this, your aunty hasn't seen you in a while, besides Jack should have done his English assignment by now, he's had plenty of time off," she said darting a quick glare at him. She was starting to get a little frustrated with Susan's attitude.

"Um, please excuse me," Jack said standing with his head bowed, "I'll just take these dishes into the kitchen."

"Look, now you've embarrassed him," Susan said, raising her voice.

"Okay, sorry, look you'll have Sunday to help him. I just need family time on Saturday, can you just give me that?"

"Sure." Susan's response was frosty.

"Honey, you know I love Jack, but please let the boy learn to take care of himself, it will make him stronger in the long run," she whispered so Jack couldn't hear her from the kitchen.

"Like Dad did to us," Susan stabbed as she stood up abruptly causing her chair to screech across the tile floor.

"That's not what I meant," Mrs. Valentino shouted at her daughter. It was too late, her heart sank as she heard the laundry door slam. Susan muttered something to Jack on her way past the kitchen, and he fumbled putting the dishes into the sink in an effort to follow her. They both escaped into the warm night air while Mrs. Valentino sat staring vacantly at an empty dining table with tears streaming down her cheeks. Although she felt hurt, Mrs. Valentino knew it wasn't Susan's fault for her own acute sensitivity at the moment, as tomorrow marked the anniversary of when she was abandoned by her husband.

4 – PARK

Because it's a beautiful mixture,
and she cries when it is dark,
they bleed for you much quicker,
lying scattered in the park.

"Wait up!' Jack shouted at Susan, she was quite a distance in front and he could just make out the white on her black and white striped leggings, everything else she was wearing was black. She was a fast runner however she hated competing in sports day carnivals at school. The other popular girls would sledge her and bitch about her at the starting line to a race. They tried hard to beat her but they couldn't keep up even with their fancy Nike running shoes that their rich parents bought them. Most of what she hated about it was the lack of praise and celebration for her efforts, so she figured it wasn't worth the effort at all. *Let the nasty bitches please their mummies and daddies.*

"Susan, wait a second!" he called out again, puffing deep breaths in complaint. Jack on the other hand showed no athleticism whatsoever. He didn't mind though, he'd gotten over coming last in running races a long time ago - besides he enjoyed not getting picked for athletic teams.

Finally he could see her slowing down, she had reached the park and dropped onto a park bench under one of the many golden pendas that lined the grassed area. He managed to just work out that she had been crying as she frantically mopped her tears up with the back of a hand. She was trying to hide any sign of 'weakness' before Jack got to her.

She looked up at him as he arrived, shadows from the tree leaves splashed across her face from a nearby incandescent light pole which struggled to illuminate the park.

"You know what makes me most upset, is that she just fucking doesn't get it," Susan spat. She needed to release her anger.

"Woah, what?" Jack asked, catching his breath.

"Mum doesn't realise that I know," she said, crossing her arms in anger.

"Know what?"

"That tomorrow is the anniversary of the day that Dad left us."

"Oh," Jack said, his heart sank, "Susan I didn't know, I am sorry."

"Don't be, I got over it a long time ago."

Not from what I've read.

"And Mum just wants to try and be strong by not explaining to us girls what she's feeling. Every year we have to jump in the fucking car and drive to fucking Aunty Gillian's so they can sit around crying while they tell us to go outside."

"*Swear Bear*, ease up a little!"

"Sorry, it just frustrates the hell out of me," she apologised, "because the last thing I want to do is sit around moping two hundred kilometers away. I'd rather be at home. I just wish she wouldn't bottle up her feelings and then take it out on us. She didn't need to attack you, especially while you were there."

"I don't mind, I could see something was up, and she's right you know, I have taken a long time on that assignment. I just hate it, that's all."

"It doesn't excuse what she said, she's starting to lose her mind if she's attacking you of all people," Susan said, trying to understand her mother, trying to understand the situation.

Jack sat down beside her and they both stared out across the dimly lit park. The park was usually a fun place, but tonight it seemed eerie with the dim light and the somber mood of the pair. The sparse placement of lighting struggled to illuminate the playground equipment which sat foreign in the middle of the grassed area. The odd car drove past which took their gaze and broke the silence between the two friends.

"Come on, let's go sit on the swings," Jack said as he stood, trying to cheer up Susan and change the mood.

"Sure."

"Do you think Tim and Patrick are coming?"

"Maybe, I told them we'd be here tonight," Susan said, still staring vacantly into the night.

The pair sat in adjacent swings, they simultaneously clutched the seat's chain which surprisingly felt cool for such a warm night. Instinctively Jack pushed gently at the ground to swing himself back and forth in small arcs. Susan just sat there, clearly overthinking the evening and her mother, she continued to stare vacantly back in the direction of the park bench and golden penda tree where they had just been sitting. With her head resting against the seat chain closest to Jack her mind wandered to Jack's question that he had for her earlier this evening. She thought her life couldn't get any worse so she decided to get the truth from Jack about his feelings towards her.

"So Jack, do you love me?"

Holy shit, where did that come from? "Um, Susan, of course I love you, you're pretty much my best friend," he stumbled over his words as a hot flush of nervousness washed over his body.

"Not that way Jack, I want to know what you want. Do you want me as a girlfriend?"

Jack hadn't been put on the spot like that ever. Thoughts flooded his mind. *What was she thinking? Is this what happens when her anger builds up? I didn't see that coming. How do I answer her without looking like a dick?*

Susan sensed his hesitation and she sighed. *Why can't I get straight answers from anyone?*

"What's this about Susan?" he asked, trying to bide time.

"Well you were totally going to hit me up this afternoon in my bedroom."

"Um, well, I was going to ask you something and you cut me off for dinner."

"I just want to know Jack, I am sick of all these little wishy washy runarounds in my life. I just want to know what you want, straight up. I want to know if my mother is going to top herself or leave us as well. I want to know if I have any future, and if I do, I want some idea on where I am going," she explained. She was clearly irritated with her life. She just wanted the comfort of certainty. She felt a slight 'electric' feeling around Jack and she wanted to know if he felt the same. She wanted Jack to be her solid ground because she wasn't getting any emotional strength from her sister or mother.

Jack looked away when his eyes met hers and he witnessed the tribulation in her life by the furrow in her brow. Her serious stanch took him off guard. Her cheeks flushed crimson with emotion. *I can't leave her hanging.*

"Susan what I want is...," his answer was cut short by the noises coming from the corner of the park. Jack stood defensively assisted by holding both seat chains. Susan also stood, looking towards the intruders, as their noises became louder.

"Hey guys, sorry we're late," a familiar jovial voice shouted - it was Patrick.

In the nick of time, thought Jack while he shot Susan a quick concerned glance. Her frown broke to a welcoming smile for the two newcomers.

Patrick and Tim moved across the park in stealth like fashion; both dressed in black.

"Hello lovebirds," Patrick jokes.

"Fuck off," Susan retorted.

Pangs of guilt stabbed Jack as he tried to read Susan to see if she truly meant what she just said. He didn't understand her sharp outburst. *Maybe she's doing her best to cover up her own feelings or maybe she doesn't want anything deeper with me?*

"Woah, ease up. Seriously though, what have you two been up to?" Patrick asked, raising an eyebrow in bewilderment in Tim's direction.

"We just got here guys, just shooting the breeze, I didn't know either of you would come. It's good to see you're both still alive without me having to save you at school lately."

"Ha, ha," Tim laughed sarcastically, "we can manage Jonas alright, but you can tell he's been looking for you when his sidekicks pushed us about the other day fishing for information about the bus crash."

"That reminds me, sorry we didn't get up to the hospital, Susan let us know you were okay, so we thought we'd give you space to get better," Patrick explained.

"No problem, it was a bit of a circus up there with my family annoying the shit out of me, I even had Mr. Friar turn up."

"You're kidding?" Susan questioned with a startled look washed across her face. "You didn't tell me that!" Her demeanor had changed, she now looked concerned and her sadness was gone, although a keen eye could tell she had been crying.

"There wasn't much in it, but it was weird. He kept pushing for me to finish and review that book I've got for the assignment. I told him it was shit and he got all stroppy and reminded me it 'hinged' on me graduating," Jack explained as they all looked wide-eyed at each other.

"That's rude and all, I wouldn't have thought he was on your visitor list?" Susan said.

"He wasn't, he was harmless, just annoying, besides I had the nurse button I could have pressed to get them to make him leave."

The group started to move towards their usual sitting spot, a covered eating area which consisted of a timber slatted table with bench seating either side, bolted to a concrete slab. The table was old and worn with visitor's carvings and painted graffiti. Usually there were left over food scraps on the table which had to be flicked off but tonight it was relatively clean. The shelter was a simple square shape consisting of a four post frame with an iron sheeted hip roof. There was no insulation, which made it uncomfortably hot throughout the day, but tonight it was pleasant. It gave protection in the evenings from random bird droppings as rainbow lorikeets, Indian mynas and Torres Strait pigeons flew from tree to tree to secure their nightly roosting spot. Due to its proximity to the coastline the birds favoured this park and they settled on dusk. The noise could be particularly deafening, which is why the group of friends chose to meet here later when the hubbub was over.

"Sounds like Mr. Friar's got a crush on you," Patrick joked as he sat down next to Tim.

"What, he's gay?" Jack questioned.

"That's what my parents think after they met him at the parent-teacher night," Patrick said.

"Well I couldn't tell, and I don't think he pays me any extra attention," Jack defended as he sat down opposite Patrick and next to Susan. They naturally took up those positions at the park table but for tonight Jack was especially happy he didn't have to make direct eye contact with Susan, at least not until there was resolve between them. He didn't know when that would be.

"Yeah, I suppose, he has been harsh to you. But you know what they say, 'treat 'em mean, keep 'em keen'," Patrick laughed.

"Fuck off," Jack said hoping to close the conversation on Mr. Friar.

"Anyway, what are you guys up to tomorrow?" Tim asked.

"Don't ask," Susan muttered.

"I've got to finish that damn essay, it's got to be in on Monday," Jack said.

"*Boring,*" Tim said in a drawn out manner.

"Not as boring as sitting in a car for two hours, hanging around bawling women then driving back for another two hours," Susan spat.

"Ouch!" Patrick said. "Now I know why you look so glum."

She glared at him.

"Feel free to come over to my house with Tim, we are going to dust off the old Amiga 500 and have some Lemmings battles or find some other games," Patrick invited.

"Oh, sounds good," Jack said eagerly.

"Terribly," Susan added sarcastically. "On second thoughts I might enjoy the car ride."

"Aw come on, it's not that bad, you used to love playing Lemmings," Tim said.

"Yes, used to is correct, just like I used to like playing with my Barbie dolls," she said and shot Tim a sarcastic smirk.

"Each to their own, the offer still stands," Patrick said.

"Pass," Susan said as she looked across at the stirring Torres Strait pigeons roosting in a golden penda.

Torres Strait pigeons – also known as the Torresian imperial pigeon or the Australian pied imperial pigeon - are migratory birds, they spend most of the year in the Torres Strait which is between the northern tip of Australia and Papua New Guinea. It's quite a large pigeon, mostly white but in striking contrast it is framed by black feathers - only on the bottom edge of its wing and undercarriage of its body. Like most pigeons it builds a clumsy nest of loose sticks and can be seen in large flocks. This time of year they fly down from the Torres Strait to breed just before the wet season. Quite timid in nature the Torres Strait pigeon is easily spooked, however when they roost in areas frequented by human activity, like a park, they become tolerant. They even muscle their numbers in to displace large flocks of rainbow lorikeets and the evasive Indian myna.

The group spent the next few hours talking, joking and taking the mickey out of each other – what they usually did together. The mood between Susan and Jack mellowed to the point where they were comfortable and relaxed. Susan had time to reflect on how she spoke to Jack and felt a little embarrassed with her outburst. Although she loved the thought of getting some direction in her life she decided to let it go. *Jack had plenty of his own issues to deal with, let alone me adding to his problems,* she thought.

Tim pulled his long hair back and tightened his ponytail, glancing at his watch while doing so. "Shit, is that the time?' he questioned, "I don't mean to wave the old apron strings in front of you all but I promised Mum I wouldn't stay out too late, she needs a hand in the morning."

"Yeah, I better be going too," Patrick said.

"No problem, Mum put a curfew on me too," Susan said solemnly.

"Cheer up, Sues, it won't be long until you're eighteen and you can do what you want," Tim comforted.

"Yeah I know, I should be more grateful, or at least show that I am, but it's hard some days."

"I better get back too, I didn't tell Mum where I'd be, can only assume that she knows. She's usually pretty good letting me do what I want but she's been more annoying since the accident."

"You're lucky, you're mum's the best," Susan stated.

"Good on ya Mum, Tip-Top's the one!" Patrick laughed, making reference to a television commercial for bread.

"On that note, I am out of here, catch you guys later, come on Patrick let's go I'll walk home with you," Tim said.

"See ya," Jack and Susan said simultaneously.

While still seated they both watched their two friends disappear into the darkness of the night. Alone again the relaxed mood also seemed to disappear. Susan lost her smile and looked awkwardly away from Jack. *Come on girl, give Jack some slack, ha, ha funny me.*

"So..." they both said in unison.

"You first," they also said at once, causing the both of them to smile.

"Sorry, I'll go first," Susan said with a sullen look in her eyes. She studied Jack's face and could see the concern in his eyes. She wondered what he was thinking. She swung a leg over the bench seat to straddle it and positioned herself face to him. "Jack, about before, I am sorry for putting you on the spot."

"Don't be Susan, I know how answers in your life would give you peace." He was facing the table, staring out into the darkness. He was mainly referring to her family situation, but he figured

Susan could take it anyway she wanted. He turned his head sideways to catch her eye and gauge her reaction.

"Yeah, it would, but you have your own issues to deal with and I am truly sorry for dumping mine onto you," she apologised.

"What I was going to ask you in your bedroom this afternoon wasn't really about us, well it sort of was, but not, you know, about 'us', if you know what I mean," explained Jack holding up his fingers to perform air quotes, demonstrating the potential irony of using the word 'us'.

"I don't get it, not about *us* but about *us*?"

"Yeah, sorry it will make sense when I ask you."

"Go ahead."

"Well, you know we've spoken about the formal?"

"Yes, and that I don't care about it."

"Are you sure?"

"Positive."

"Not an incy, wincy, teeny, weeny, tiny bit of you wants to get dressed up in a poufy dress and be chaperoned to a dance?"

Susan bit her lower lip. "Now that you put it that way," she laughed and she playfully struck his shoulder.

"Wouldn't you like to see me dressed as a penguin, squawk, squawk," Jack joked trying his best to impersonate what he thought a penguin would look like with wings flapping at its sides.

Susan laughed out loud and in trying to control herself she doubled forward and rested her head against his shoulder. Jack tried to hide his nervous look as he breathed in the smell of her hair.

"You crack me up," she said, controlling her laugh as she sat back upright on the bench seat.

"In all seriousness Susan, if you want to go then I'd be happy to take you." Her laughing stopped and she stared into his eyes. She was trying to gauge his question. She was trying to read him. Now she was even more confused.

Is this out of sympathy for me or does he really like me? I know he would hate going to the formal and I've told him that I don't want to go. What's changed his mind?

Jack turned to face Susan, also lifting one leg over the bench seat. They were now both staring at each other face on. Whether intentionally or by accident he rested a comforting hand on her knee, to reassure Susan that he was serious about asking her to the formal. He quickly pulled it away only realising it may have been there too long as Susan tried to place her hand on his.

"Jack, please, it's okay." She took his hand and placed it back on her knee. "Don't you feel that too?"

His heart was racing, he felt pins and needles darting up his arm radiating from the warmth of her leg. He was totally confused. *I shouldn't be doing this, yet it feels so good.*

"Susan, what are... I mean what's happening?"

She took his hand and slid it further up her leggings towards her upper thigh. His eyes widened as he caught sight of the edge of her tight skirt, which she wore over her leggings.

Holy shit, is this happening? He gulped trying to breathe.

Her heart raced too and in her nervousness her cheeks and neck flushed with a crimson rash. She wanted to move closer and draw him in but she hesitated. *Is tonight the night we cross the line?*

Jack slowly raised his free hand and gently caressed the side of her face. He felt her smooth skin on his fingertips and her silken hair on the back of his hand. He moved it slowly up towards the back of her head and felt her fine chain earrings dangle between his fingers. Jack lent forward inching his face closer to hers all the while never losing eye contact.

Susan battered her eyelids momentarily then closed her eyes as she pursed her lips. Jack too closed his eyes as he leant forward. Her hands reached up and palmed his torso. He felt the buzz from her fingers and his heart seemed to beat uncontrollably in his chest.

Suddenly a loud cracking noise, followed by the shrieks of disturbed flocks of birds shook the quiet night air. Instantly Jack felt a smattering of water flick across his face. They both quickly opened their eyes, broke from their trance and looked out towards the trees that lined the park.

"What was that, was it a gunshot?" Susan shrieked, her voice trembled.

"Maybe," Jack said with concern, "although it sounded more like a firecracker going off, it sounded pretty close."

Susan looked back at Jack. "My God, Jack, what is that on your face?"

He took a hand to his face and traced it down his cheek to where the water hit him. He looked at his fingertips and they were dripping a thick red liquid.

"Is that blood?" she asked nervously.

Jack couldn't believe it, he stood up and looked over towards the tree lined area with a bit more conviction. Susan followed him. There in front of them were dozens, if not hundreds of Torres Strait pigeons, although now they were white, black and red. They were in all states of destruction, in bits and pieces. Susan screamed and Jack wrapped his arms around her to protect her, turning her to shield her from the traumatic scene.

"Come on Susan, let's get the fuck out of here!" He grabbed her hand and led her off running towards their homes.

Their chests heaved up and down as they panted heavily – they were out of breath. They stopped holding hands, as the adrenalin wore off and because it felt slightly awkward – besides their hands were slippery from sweat.

Jack welcomed the safety of the dimly lit cul-de-sac where their homes were. He could hide the anguish on his face - his vulnerability - behind the dappled moonlight. *Where do we go from here? Perhaps I'll wait for her lead?*

They gathered their breath and their thoughts, standing outside their homes.

"Hey, about what just happened," Susan piped up.

"Yeah, how messed up was that?"

"No, not about the birds, about us Jack!"

"Oh, yes that."

"Let's talk about it on Sunday. It's been a hectic afternoon, and I need time to think."

"Oh, okay, sure," Jack said with his head down.

"Hey, I am still here Jack, I just need to think about where we go with this, there is a lot at stake," she reasoned.

He looked up and could see the sternness in her eyes, even in the shadows. Gooseflesh rippled across his body, for a moment it was like he peered into her soul.

"I um, I'm sorry, sure I'll see you on Sunday, but don't stress too much tomorrow, okay," Jack reassured.

"I won't be stressing about that, I can ignore Mum and Aunty Gillian and their carry on. I'll be stressing about us. I don't want to lose you Jack - not as a friend - if we take this to the next level."

"Yes, we've got a lot of history, a lot of good memories," he added.

"Exactly."

"What do we do about the birds anyway?"

"Nothing. There is obviously a messed up person out there, but we can't do anything about it. If we go to the police, they will blame us. It will tie us up and nothing will get done anyway. Let's forget about it and hopefully it doesn't happen again. Agree?"

"Sure, but it was messed up," Jack said, still slightly agitated by the image of dead birds strewn across the park in his mind.

There was an awkward pause, before Jack moved closer to Susan. He lifted a hand to gently touch her upper arm, but she pulled away.

"No Jack, please, give me time."

"I was just..." he said, *going to wish you goodnight.*

"Don't." After an awkward silence she reassuringly added, "I'll see you on Sunday."

"See you then." He disappeared into the darkness towards his house. He thought he cut their farewell off too quickly, but he needed to let her go, to give her the space she needed.

Susan stood there in the dark for a moment. She didn't turn away. A slight pain panged in her head and she winced. She feared the decision for their future lay with her. Jack seemed to be ready, but she wasn't sure anymore. A warm tear rolled down her cheek - it would be the first of many for the weekend.

5 – SATURDAY

Your strength is surely fragile,
and mindset ill at ease,
my resolve is swift and agile,
destroying just to please.

Morning sunlight filtered through a dusty fly screen of an open window. A gentle breeze tickled curtains embellished with a younger child's motif. He lay there awake, watching floating dust particles dancing in and out of the light.

This was his happy time – between sleep and scrutiny.

He could have been listening to music through his earbuds however he chose to lay there vacant of thought. Instead of finding anything useful to do with his free time he counted the number of square foam tiles on his ceiling. Sixty. He never forgot the number but found comfort in checking each morning. This was his freedom but he knew it wouldn't last.

"Jonas, get your lazy ass down here at once!"

And so it begins.

He quickly slipped on his favourite black Guns and Roses shirt, jumped into some board shorts, grabbed his backpack and pushed his way through his bedroom door, careful not to make a noise.

"Coming Mum!"

"About fucking time, what were you doing up there, pulling yourself off?" she barked at him.

"No."

"If I have to clean your stained sheets again, I'll burn them and everything in your room, you understand?"

You've never cleaned my sheets, or my clothes. "Yes, Mum," he said – head bowed.

"Now go down to the shops and get me a packet of Winnie Blues, don't take too long and bring me back the change," she ordered as she pushed cash into his stomach forcing him to take it. "Hurry up, I haven't got all day."

"Sure," he said walking at a brisk pace out the front door. This time he slammed it behind him. Slipping his backpack on Jonas jumped on his bike and headed in the opposite direction to the shops. *Fuck her.*

Across the other side of town in his dankly smelling bedroom, Jack began to stir. His morning was free from family duties and he didn't feel like getting out of bed.

A lawn mower coughed to life somewhere close by and he became restless. His mind sprung to life like a light bulb being switched on and he couldn't stop thinking about his predicament with Susan.

"Ah!" he roared, burying his head under a pillow to drown out the noise and to distract his racing mind. It didn't work so he threw his pillow across the room, it hit his study desk and knocked his desk lamp to the floor. Luckily the carpet softened its fall and it didn't break.

Lying on his side he reluctantly opened one eye, taking a moment to focus. Paperback Writer by John Bird stared back at him from his bedside table. *Fuck this shit*. He dragged himself out of bed, stumbled to the bathroom and decided today was a schoolwork free day. There was always tomorrow to finish the book and the assignment. Nothing like procrastination the day before an assignment is due.

Walking down the carpeted stairs Jack headed to the kitchen like a mindless zombie. His brother was in front of the television in the lounge room watching the top ten music videos on Rage. A note on the kitchen counter with a list of chores to do was a sure sign that his mother had gone shopping at the local markets. His dad was away at a mine site working, but he was due to fly back tomorrow.

Pouring himself a bowl of cereal Jack thought about last night with Susan. He knew crossing the line could mean the end of a brilliant friendship with history if perhaps they broke up in the future. Could they go back to being friends? Jack didn't think so. He thought Susan was too strong willed to go back to being friends - it would be too messy. He only had to look at all the Valentino family members to support his view. Valerie seemed to be damaged fruit that nobody picked from the market. She had gone through a bad relationship at the end of her high school year and she still hadn't gotten over it. Mrs. Valentino buried herself in cooking to escape her reality of losing her husband. Neither Valentino had recovered from the breakup of a relationship.

As much as it pained Jack to see Susan struggle with her emotions relating to her father he was nervous about pushing the envelope too far when it came to starting something with her. He didn't want to 'save' her, he felt she was strong enough to look after herself, but he did think that being with her would be great - for both of them. They could lean on each other for support.

"Hey dickhead!" grumbled Clint, who was hidden by the back of the couch but still watching music videos.

Jack looked across from his breakfast, *do I dignify that?* Jack's brother had many colourful nicknames for Jack, however this one cut him the most, especially since Jack was clearly smarter than Clint. Jack put it down to jealousy and tried to let it roll off him like water off a duck's back - but it was hard sometimes, especially when it was a constant torment.

"What?"

"That list Mum left, it's all yours to do, understand?"

"Or what?" Jack knew he didn't have to ask, he was toying with Clint, but knew he couldn't push it too far.

"Or I'll tell Mum you didn't help and I'll give you a cork on your other leg to match the one you've got," he warned, referring to the bruise on his leg from the bus accident. He knew this was a false threat as his mother would see it and would go berserk.

"Sure."

"I mean it, besides I've got to go to 'work'," said Clint, referring to hanging out with his mates.

Jack didn't answer Clint, he decided to leave the conversation there, it wasn't worth continuing. He finished eating, grabbed his backpack and left his brother who was fixated on a music video by Ween, 'Push th' Little Daisies'. If this was where grunge music was heading, Jack didn't like it.

He needed something to keep his mind off of Susan. Trying to finish reading the novel in his room was the smart answer but not the right answer for him right now. He needed something extra, something more than his quiet room and his obnoxious brother downstairs. Jack headed for Patrick's house on foot, as he didn't live too far away, to join them in their video game tournament.

Jonas' bike jumped the gutter and landed on the patchy lawn with a thud, coming to a stop with a short side skid with the back tyre. He dumped the bike on its side before making his way to the front door to the house of his best mate, Neil Goodall.

Unlike Jonas' house, this house was a home. The gardens were luscious and maintained. The exterior of the single level dwelling was clean and the paint was gleaming. And unlike Jonas, Neil had both parents who lived at home. They were kind and wealthy. They were doctors. They may have been aware that their son was strong willed, but they had little idea on the severity of the terrorising that Neil and his mates did at school. Their lives were too busy and they were never home to act upon the letters that came home advising of Neil's unsociable behaviour - especially about the numerous detentions.

Boys will be boys.

Jonas walked through the open front door to the house - it was forever open. The cavernous high pitched ceiling always caught his eye - it was a refreshing change from the low ceilings he was used to.

The unmistakable organic smell of marijuana smoke drew him to Neil's bedroom, as though he was being dragged from the nostrils by witches' fingers. A hypnotic and repetitive guitar lick – a palm muted e-string, chugging and fat - from Metallica wailed away quietly in the background. Jonas smirked – he was 'home'.

"How the fuck are *we* this evening?" Neil didn't seem phased by his intruder, the drugs had mellowed his reaction time.

"Dude, what's up?" Neil was laid back on his roughly made bed; eyes glazed and bloodshot.

"Give us a chuff," said Jonas reaching across the bed to pluck the half used joint from Neil's fingers. He drew it back deeply and immediately started coughing.

"Time to lay off the smokes eh?" joked Neil, and they both started laughing in fits, making Jonas cough some more. "So man, what have you been up to?"

"Not much hey, just had to get out of the house. The old lady was giving me the shits."

"True? You can't seem to get a break from her."

"Tell me about it!" said Jonas, toking back the last of the joint.

The two of them sat around, laughing at mundane things between long moments of silence in conversation and occasional gentle head banging to a song they liked. The day was getting on and the effects of the drugs were starting to wear off.

"Man I'm hungry, what have you got in the fridge?"

"Yeah, let's check it out."

After raiding the family fridge of leftovers the boys made their way back to Neil's room. "Hey what stick mag's has your old man got stashed away here?" asked Jonas peering into the master bedroom which was directly off the kitchen and first off the hallway. Before Neil could protest Jonas was already deep into the room and was making his way to the bedside table.

"Let's get out of here," Neil pleaded, trying to encourage his friend from his parent's room. Though Neil got away with quite a lot, even this was against his morals.

"Woo-hoo!" Jonas produced a pink sex toy from the top draw. "Your old lady is a legend, smashing this thing!" He waved the dildo about in the air.

"Put that back!" Neil shouted forcefully.

Jonas ignored him, but returned it to the draw anyway, as he eyed a better prize. "Jackpot!" he said joyously and he grabbed a handful of adult magazines. "Let's go," he said, like he was in charge of the looting escapade.

Back in Neil's room the boys flicked through the magazines. They were soft porn publications, mainly topless, if the models were fully naked then their vaginas were always hidden behind a hand or object. The women were in various poses, pouting or with their mouths half opened like they were sipping the air. Neil didn't know they had existed in his parent's room. It troubled him to think that they were needed. He thought they were a loving couple. *Didn't they love each other not to need this crap?*

"Guess what man?" Jonas asked as he turned his magazine on its side to look at the centerfold spread.

"What?"

"We need to figure out how to fuck those geeks up at school." A wry grin spread across Jonas' face as he thought about his devious plan.

"What are you planning?" said Neil flicking through the pages of his magazine, knowing exactly who he was talking about.

"I don't know, something that humiliates the fuck out of all of them together."

"Why all of them?" asked Neil, unsure about Jonas' intentions.

"Don't they give you the shits? They sit there all day, talking geeky, looking geeky, getting good grades, not even trying, going home to their perfect mummies and daddies and looking at us like we're dumb criminals."

"True," said Neil, lingering on a page where the model was on all fours and was painted in tiger stripe body paint.

"Especially that fuckwit Jack," said Jonas as he threw his magazine on the bed, "the way he gave me that smug look, just before I thumped him the other day, they all need a lesson." Jonas stared vacantly across the room, he was clearly pissed off.

"Hey dude, let's get out of here," said Neil trying to make light of his mood.

"Yeah, good idea," agreed Jonas. Standing up he looked across at the smut magazines strewn across the bed and said, "Let's go out and find some real women to look at."

"Cool."

"I know just the right place to look." The glint in Jonas' eye sent a shiver through Neil, and he looked away nervously.

The family car sped along the Kennedy Highway heading south on the Tablelands towards Mareeba. Inside, the passengers were silent as they looked out diagonally opposing windows at the rolling countryside. They didn't focus on the landscape as they were both in serious thought. Their mother drove blissfully along with both hands on the steering wheel.

"Are you right back there Susie?"

"She can't hear you," said Valerie, who was in the front passenger seat beside her mother. She pointed to her own ears to indicate that Susan had earbuds in, listening to her Walkman.

"Oh," said Mrs. Valentino with a frown. "Well we can listen to our own music up here." She turned up the volume on the car radio.

"...and in other news, local police are asking for any witnesses to suspicious activity in Endeavour Park as they try to piece together the events of the explosion which has caused the death of twenty Torres Strait pigeons. RSPCA spokesman Tracey Shaw said it was a cowardly act to target a protected species which are quite timid. Tracey was hoping the culprit would be soon found and charged for such a barbaric act.

Also in local news, Bill Smart, the bus driver for Country Line Transport involved in this month's school bus crash, is expected to have his charges of negligent driving dismissed as Judge

Laura Banks will deliver her ruling today. A spokesman for Country Line Transport had earlier given evidence that a mechanical failure was the cause of the accident.

We'll have fine weather today with a top of 35 degrees."

After a few local ads played and then a jingle, which was to remind you what radio station you were listening to, a song finally began to play. Mrs. Valentino sighed and her body relaxed in the car seat. She didn't like being reminded about the bus crash that Jack was in. She feared it could have been Susan in hospital and it shuddered her to think of what may have happened to her if she hadn't asked her to get groceries from the earlier bus stop. She was glad that Jack pulled through the crash and nobody got seriously hurt. She loved Jack but wished her daughter would spend less time with him and concentrate on her final year, to try and see the year out with good grades. She wanted her daughter to have better opportunities than she did when she left school. Being married early and starting a young family meant that she didn't have any skills necessary for later in life to provide for her family - especially being a single mother.

"It's good that Jack is okay now," stated Valerie, her thoughts were jogged from the radio news.

"Yes," said Mrs. Valentino in a clipped manner, her eyes focused on the road ahead.

"You know they would make a good couple," said Valerie glancing back at Susan to make sure she wasn't listening.

Mrs. Valentino let out another sigh.

"You know he's good for her," stressed Valerie.

"Yes but he's also a distraction."

"Maybe that's just what she needs."

"I don't think so, besides she needs to be careful with that boy."

"Why, he's a good guy," said Valerie sticking up for Jack.

"He may well be, but all 'good guys' want the same thing."

"Jack's too much of a softie to worry about that," said Valerie matter-of-factly.

"Wasn't Eric a softie? Look at where that got you Valerie!"

Valerie's face flushed red as she turned and looked scornfully out her window. She was furious that her mother brought that up again and used it against her in reference to her sister. Her mother sighed once again, still with her eyes on the road.

"That was a mistake and I'd appreciate it if you never brought it up again, especially in the presence of Susie," snapped Valerie.

"Very well, but you can see why I don't want those two spending too much time together, I don't want another emotional trip to the Family Planning Clinic for one of my daughters in her final year of school. Look what it did to you. Susan needs good grades to get out and do well in life."

"Sure, but it wasn't like the news you gave me helped keep me on the rails, Mum!" spat Valerie as she folded her arms, turned her body and faced the window. *Great weekend this is going to be.*

Mrs. Valentino's eyes welled but this time she wasn't letting any tears out. She turned the radio up to catch a song and demonstrate that she had enough of talking. She knew this was going to be a tough weekend and she needed all the emotional strength she could harbor. Her daughters weren't helping the cause.

While Susan sat in the back of the car - earphones blasting - her gaze wasn't taking in the rolling countryside. Her fixed frown indicated she was deep in thought, she wasn't even registering the music that was playing through her earphones. She was contemplating her position with Jack. She wasn't sure about taking their relationship to the next level anymore, her night was sleepless as she tossed and turned thinking about being with him. *He is more like a brother but is that all love should be, with someone you trust and love, rather than with someone that looks good and with someone that is exciting and new to discover. Someone that stirs your interest and challenges your being?*

She glanced up at her sister and then across to her mother. She thought about the rough times these two women had gone through and the rotten luck they had with men. *Maybe it is best to fall for someone you trust? Or is getting burnt by a lover just a woman's natural passage in life? Has it made Mum and Valerie stronger? It doesn't look like it, not on the outside anyway.* Susan adjusted her seating position to improve her comfort, although at the moment she was suffering more psychological anguish than physical discomfort.

Susan shrugged off her vacant gaze and concentrated on the scenery outside to try and establish their location. They had already headed west away from the city, up through the dividing range and were well on their way towards her aunt's country property, in a small town called Dimbulah, on the Tablelands. From some of the recognisable buildings Susan knew they hadn't passed Mareeba yet, which was on the way to Dimbulah.

Maybe a good bawl with Aunty Gillian is what I need. It might be good to get all these emotions off my chest and try to start tomorrow with a new frame of mind. Although, on second thoughts, four women sitting around crying might be a little draining. If Jack is the one for me I might see what Aunty Gillian thinks of the situation, maybe baby steps is what I need right now and maybe I should go to the stupid formal with him after all.

Pulling her earphones out, Susan sat forward in her seat. "Mum, I am hungry, can we stop to get something to eat in Mareeba?" She asked, knowing full well what the answer would be.

Mrs. Valentino tilted her head to the side as she kept her eyes on the road ahead, "can't you wait? It won't be that far Love, besides I've made some sandwiches for lunch which we can share when we get there."

Susan let out a quiet sigh, so her mother couldn't register her feeling perturbed.

Mrs. Valentino was never one to buy take away food – ever – bringing her own food was something she did automatically; a practice that was ingrained from trying to save money as a single mother. Susan craved a juicy burger from a petrol station, the ones in the country always tasted better than the fast food joints in the city. A quick memory slipped into her mind of her mum and dad sharing a burger with her and her sister at a truck stop. They had stopped for fuel while on their way to a remote camping spot. She remembered the family laughing because the ass had fallen out of her burger, all the filling landing on the timber picnic table and she was left holding just the bun. She remembered it was a fun moment, she hadn't gotten into trouble because she was only three and her hands were too small to hold the huge burger. She wondered if her mother remembered the good times like those or chose to dwell on the bad ones to make the anger and resentment she held against her father feel justified. Annoyed with herself for letting this memory slip through the cracks she resumed her frown as she tried to push it deep into her mind by jamming her earphones back in and turning the music up even louder. *Yep, this was going to be a long day.*

"Hey guys," Jack said to his mates who were engrossed in the computer monitor of the Amiga 500. They were playing Dragon's Lair. The dominant orange background scenery from the game illuminated their faces in the dimly lit rumpus room. Toys, CDs, games and clothes littered the floor of the room making it almost impossible for anyone to move around the room freely.

They didn't turn around but acknowledged him with a quiet, "hey."

Jack dropped into an old leather sofa and pushed over a pile of comic books to make himself more comfortable. He looked around the room, showing his disinterest in the current computer game play. To him they were a real time waster - he'd rather watch a movie instead.

Patrick was at the controls, his tongue out in concentration, trying to master the keystrokes necessary for the knight to jump a crevice and dodge the tentacles from a green beast. He missed and the knight fell to his death down a chasm.

"Damn!" shouted Patrick. "That was my last life."

"My turn dude," said Jack thinking that he might as well join in or die from boredom.

"Really? Thought you might have been too tired to play, what with all that smooching of Susan," teased Tim, mocking Jack with kissing pouting lips.

"As if," said Jack defensively.

"Yeah right, when we left you last night you two looked way too cosy," added Patrick.

"Do you want to know what happened when you guys left," said Jack, furrowed lines forming across his face.

"Do tell, I was wondering when things would go off between you two," said Tim excitedly - Jack had his full attention.

"Well they did go off!"

"Whoa dude, high five," said Patrick with his hand raised waiting for Jack to reciprocate.

"It's not what you think, put your hand down. When you guys left we got talking more about...," Jack explained.

"When you say 'talking', do you mean 'talking' or ..." interrupted Tim.

"Let me finish," pleaded Jack. "When you guys left we were talking about stuff and then there was an explosion."

"What? In your pants?" Patrick's humor was always punctual - both friends were rolling around the floor in hysterics.

"Not quite," Jack said with a frown, he was getting over their immaturity. "There was an explosion in the trees. A bomb had been planted and it went off. It was only small but you should have seen the carnage. There were bits of dead birds everywhere."

"Really?" asked Patrick.

Tim and Patrick looking at each other perplexed.

"Yeah it was epic, blood everywhere, I even copped a bit on my face."

"I bet you'd want to cop a load onto Susan's face," joked Patrick.

"Man, fuck up with this shit about me and Susan," Jack was over it, that comment went too far.

"Sorry dude," said Patrick coyly. "I was only joking."

"Yeah but come on, she's our friend too and so what if I were into her, give her some respect."

"Sorry, I won't go there again," apologised Patrick.

Jack was feeling a little off today, maybe he woke up on the wrong side of his bed or maybe his feelings for Susan were growing stronger than he thought and his defensiveness was overly sensitive. Either way Jack didn't feel like being with his mates today.

"You know what, I came over here to hang out with you guys to escape my shit English assignment, but after this I think I'd rather get back to it." Jack picked up his backpack and headed out the door.

"Come on man, lighten up, we were only joking!" shouted Patrick.

"See you later," muttered Jack as he left the house and headed back home. The morning sun was blinding his vision so he had to shield his eyes with a hand held up like a visor.

Gather my tools and my tricks, fill my bag and off I go. Together we'll get to the bottom of this, we'll get the truth out of them all. The day that happens I'll be free. Free as a bird in a storm, huddled on a branch with its mates wondering if after all the wind howling and the driving rain will it still be alive. Will it escape unharmed? I think not, even if it makes it out the other side alive, it will always carry the scars of the ordeal, all the way till death.

My journey is almost complete and when I get to the other side you'll be proud of me, you all will. Don't cry my humble fool for you shall see, when the curtain finally falls and the lights come on, only then will you gasp and stare at each other in bewilderment. Ask as many questions then because I have written the final act and you are the head star.

Sweet dreams, for soon they will be forever.

The End

"Come on!" Jack shouted out loud. It was done. He had finally finished reading the book. As though it was an empty toilet roll he threw the book at the corner of his room, it bounced off the wall, fell and hit the rim of his waste paper bin and landed in the bottom with a thud.

"And he scores!" Jack celebrated like a basketballer who had just won the game with seconds left on the shot clock - arms in the air and shouting to the ceiling. *Good riddance.*

It wasn't over yet - an analytical piece had to be written.
To his credit and surprise Jack stayed in his room until he had finished the assignment. He felt that if he didn't get up and write it then he would spend hours thinking about Susan. How would she feel when he caught up with her tomorrow? He pushed those thoughts to the side and kept writing.

Deciding he better give the book back to Mr. Friar on Monday along with his assignment he fished the book out of his bin. Once again he flicked through the pages, shaking his head in disbelief that something of this nature could be written. *What purpose did it gain?* With that thought he decided to angle his assignment on the fact that the 'Stream of Consciousness' was an outlet for the author to resolve their internal issues. Without focusing too hard on the disturbing and somewhat psychotic nature of what was written Jack concluded that the author had grown throughout the work and had resolved their issues. Jack also reflected on the small poems at the beginning of each chapter and how their message felt softer than the feeling from the bulk of the passages, almost like they were written by two different people. *Maybe the author's bipolar, I wouldn't be surprised.*

Concluding that the work was different and original he thought there was literary merit in what was written and he'd recommend it to anyone who was willing to expand their mind. *Although I really don't think that, it does seem like Mr. Friar knows the author and annihilating the work in my assignment wouldn't go well for my grades.*

Stapling the loose pages of his assignment in triumph of completing it he placed it on his desk and put the novel face down on top of it. Grabbing his Walkman from his backpack he pushed the earbud in and lay back on his bed, he turned his head and looked towards the assignment and novel with a smug smile, like a distant memory evoking joy.

"Oh shit!" exclaimed Jack.

The back pages of the novel were sitting erect like a well-read book, staring back at him were the words which filled him with dread - *Epilogue.*

The car pulled off the highway onto a rural road which soon turned from bitumen to dirt. Clouds of dust billowed from the back of the sedan, settling on the rear windscreen in a thin haze. The girls took out their earbuds as the sound of the car bumping across the corrugation was loud and unsettling. Mrs. Valentino's thoughts of her troubled daughters quickly escaped her mind as she concentrated on negotiating the road conditions.

"It shouldn't be much further," Mrs. Valentino said to the girls as though they hadn't been there before. They all knew how long it would take. Susan knew this was the beginning of the discomfort for the weekend, although the degree of suffering would vary.

Timber fence posts cut from hardwood tree trunks and strung with barbed wire seemed to hold back the rugged bushland. The odd herd of cattle popped into view as the vehicle careened across the dirt track trying to navigate random potholes and ruts.

Susan sighed with relief as she saw the familiar corrugated iron sign ahead which read, "Blackwood Station."

"Okay, who's going to get the first one?" asked Mrs. Valentino as she slowed the car down and stopped in front of the cattle station gate.

"I'll get it," grumbled Susan, agreeing to open and close the cattle gate as they passed the fenced off area. *Anything to get out of here.*

Their mother followed the single lane track which snaked through the property, the cars suspension thudded along, bottoming out on exposed tree roots which stuck out into the track like grasping fingers. Each time the car stopped at a gate Susan reluctantly got out to attend the formality of keeping the cattle contained in each paddock.

The homestead sat at the top of a small rise, positioned for view and for preservation during floods. It was a simple but welcoming home. A wide veranda wrapped around its perimeter and was flanked by lush greenery at the sides. You could tell that the mini oasis was well watered from the rainwater tank as it was in stark contrast to the duller surrounding bushland. The local birdlife congregated here willing to forgo their usual timid nature in order to secure abundant water and life beside their human hosts.

The sedan pulled up out front of the property alongside a work ute and dust dropped off the car like a chicken rising from a dust bath as the women hopped out of the vehicle. Aunty Gillian was already bounding down the front stairs, arms out wide, and wearing a beaming smile. She could sense the tension between her visitors but was overjoyed in seeing them to let that worry her.

"Hello, my beautiful nieces," she said, hugging the girls at the same time. They groaned under her squeezing enthusiasm.

"Hi," said Susan.

"Hello Gill," said Valerie.

"Hi Love," said Mrs. Valentino, giving her sister a long hug.

"It's been too long, come, let's go inside, I've just put a pot of tea on," she said ushering the women inside. "Was it a nice drive?"

"Brilliant," muttered Susan.

The sun hung low in the afternoon sky. For the visitors this was a different sunset than they usually saw on the coast where the mountain range to the west prevented a horizon sunset. As the women stood on the veranda, cups of tea in their hands, they marveled at the orange orb, which painted the clouds and slowly sunk below the tree line.

"Beautiful," said Mrs. Valentino, taking a sip from her soothing tea. It was moments like these that made all her troubles disappear, if only for an instant in time.

"It never gets old," agreed Gillian. She ushered the party to sit down in the worn, but comfortable, wicker furniture that lived on the veranda.

Gillian was still beaming with happiness, she loved this time of year when she saw her family. She loved the fact that it was two older sisters with two younger sisters. She loved this tradition that was set. She also knew that these visits were emotional but she saw the healing benefits of coming together and talking through the pain. In her mind their relationship, their bond was stronger than ever and it was all due to coming together and working through their issues. She felt improvement every year, which was important as she didn't know if these gatherings would be with the four of them in years to come.

"Now, girls, tell me what's been going on in your lives?"

"Not much," replied Susan.

"Not much? This is your final year of high school, wouldn't you be flat out?"

"Yeah, sure. We've got exams coming up," said Susan nonchalantly.

"She's got a boyfriend," spat Valerie with a grin. Both Susan and Mrs. Valentino shot Valerie a daggered look. "Well it's true."

"No it's not," said Susan as she crossed her arms defensively.

"A boyfriend? Do tell," smiled Gillian.

"He's not a boyfriend, now is he Susie," said Mrs. Valentino who stared at Susan until she got a reluctant nod from her. "Valerie is just teasing, he's a classmate who she's been helping get through a rough time."

Both Susan and Valerie wondered why their mother didn't say it was Jack, their neighbour. Gillian knew of Jack, as the Armstrong family had been living beside them since the dawn of time.

"Seriously, why skirt around this one Mum?" asked Valerie as she took an unimpressed slurp from her tea cup.

"I am not skirting around anything, why don't you tell Aunty Gill about your new job offer?" she said, trying to change the subject.

"Like that's big news," Valerie said, dropping the cup roughly on top of the glass topped wicker coffee table.

"Well I am sure Aunty Gill would be pleased to hear about it."

"Ok, Mum. I got asked to manage the fish and chip shop when the owner takes his family on holiday," said Valerie.

"That's great news," said Gillian in an overly excited manner.

"Yeah, it's like a trial, if it all runs well then they will offer me more of a managerial role and there will be training in it as well, I am told," explained Valerie.

"There you go, it is big news, a great offer," said Mrs. Valentino.

"Yeah as big as the cock she had to suck to get it," said Susan under her breath, but Valerie heard and she punched her in the upper arm.

"Ow, why'd you hit me?"

"Valerie!" exclaimed Mrs. Valentino.

"Tell Mum what you said, I dare you."

"Yes, what did you say, I hope it wasn't dirty," said Mrs. Valentino with a concerned look.

"I said, it's as big as the rock she stuck on her finger at the jeweler," lied Susan and Valerie gave her a hard scowl.

"A jeweler, don't tell me you've got a man in your life too?" said Gillian.

"No, Susan and I were window shopping, it was a fairytale dream," she said, continuing the lie as she gave Susan a quick, sharp kick to the ankle. *Well played sister.*

"Tell us what you've been up to Gill," asked Mrs. Valentino hoping a change in subject would calm the girls down and get them off each other's backs for five minutes.

"Oh me, well it's been quite dry up here, we are trying to keep the cattle alive waiting for the big wet. That's where Darrel is now, out making the dams wider."

Darrel was her partner. They met at the country church. Darrel was a weathered man, working hard and drinking harder had aged him beyond his years. He still worked hard but gave up alcohol years ago when he developed a bad case of gout. Doctors couldn't conclude that alcohol was the reason for his gout but from what Darrel's mother told him, it was the reason. Soon after giving up drinking it cleared up and didn't come back. That was the worst two weeks of Darrel's life - being unable to work. He'd rather work than drink so another drop hasn't passed his lips since.

As Gillian went on about how hard it's been since the family last saw each other Susan looked at her face, it was showing signs of age - mostly prematurely -and from living on this harsh land. She wondered why she never had children. She looked beyond the overly annoying nature of her excitement and concluded that she was a wonderful woman and would have made an awesome mother. Maybe she couldn't have children but she dare not ask, maybe another time, perhaps if she caught her alone.

Just as Mrs. Valentino had wished, the conversation quickly turned to discussions about food. Gillian had their dinner cooking all day and the smell coming from the kitchen had them all hungry. Darrel was camping out at the dam, it was ten kilometers from the homestead and he always worked till sun down. He could have made the drive back to the house but knew it was best to give the women room. He didn't want to hang about four sobbing women.

For Susan the meal was hearty and filling, just as good as her mother's cooking. It had been a long day and Susan decided to call it a night. She didn't want to hang around and watch the other women get drunk on wine, then start the downward emotional spiral. She said her good nights, left the others and threw herself on a bed that was made for her. Jamming earbuds into her ears she fell asleep listening to music while the Walkman's batteries went flat.

Soapy water streaked like a roller coaster down the side of her naked body – small milky bubbles collected at the crests and joined the ride when their numbers increased. Steam rose and gently kissed the glass shower screen, like a lover's pant, as she turned her body to rinse the soap off under the cascading water.

She softly hummed along to the music from her waterproof radio, which hung on the neck of the shower rose. As she closed her eyes, tilted her head upwards, she doused her long silver blonde hair under the warm water. The water clapped the tiles, the sound momentarily drowning out her music as she lifted bunches of her hair into the water ensuring it was soaked thoroughly, ready for her shampoo.

Her ears pricked and she tilted her head to the side. Did she hear something? Maybe it was the radio? She lathered her hair with her favourite shampoo, massaging the foam into her scalp.

After rinsing the shampoo she followed her hair treatment with conditioner and decided to shave her legs while she let the conditioner soak and work in her hair. Selecting a razor from the shower caddy she sat down on a raised tiled bench which formed part of the rear wall of the shower hob. She enjoyed the convenience of the raised seat but was annoyed how the small sized tiles left an imprinted pattern in the skin of her bottom – even though it was never long lasting.

She turned side on to the seat and lifted a slender leg into position - on top of the seat. She hesitated for a second, her ears pricked. *I am sure I heard giggling?* Dismissing the noise for an ad from the radio station she continued and soaped her leg to ensure it was lubricated enough for the razor's blade.

The blade slid over her already immaculately smooth leg leaving a track of exposed skin through the soapy lather. She didn't need to shave, yet here she was every night preening herself. Her appearance was important, it was in her upbringing. With meticulous procedure she finished both legs, careful not to nick her skin – which rarely happened.

Closing her eyes once again she dunked her head under the stream of water and rinsed out the hair conditioner. She turned the taps off and gently squeezed the excess water from her hair. Turning off the radio she heard voices close by. *Someone's outside!*

She opened the shower screen door and grabbed her towel, covering her nakedness. From the corner of her eye she saw a shadowy shape – possibly someone's head – drop from outside the bathroom window.

Crash! Something fell over just outside the window.

That must have been my garbage bin. They were standing on it.

She ran over, pressing her head against the window's security screen she could just make out two boys running down the side of her house. The padlocked latch rattled as they jumped over the six foot side gate.

"If I catch you little shits again!" she yelled, but it was too late, they were gone. Probably laughing their asses off.

Her mind raced as she slammed the sliding bathroom window shut. *I've got an idea who they could have been. I'll have to fish them out. Nobody gets the better of Nancy Smith.*

Their Converse All Star sneakers tapped at the concrete sidewalk as both friends dashed through the night. They didn't utter a word as they made their stealthy getaway. They both didn't care if the other got caught, it was a matter of 'all for themselves' as they rounded the corner.

Neil stopped and doubled over panting profusely. Jonas soon realised, stopped and back tracked to his mate – thinking they were safe. Jonas, the fitter of the two laughed, "far out man, that was close."

"Do you think she saw us?"

"Nah, but I copped an eye full of her," laughed Jonas.

Neil laughed along with him but started coughing as he continued sucking in deep breaths.

"Shit man, you'll have to give up the fags," joked Jonas.

"Yeah, right."

"Man, she was prime," smirked Jonas, "you should have seen those titties."

"Yeah, you should have let me."

"I was going to, just couldn't look away," explained Jonas. He was never going to offer Neil a turn. "Come on, let's go."

The soothing scent of lavender permeated throughout the quaint duplex. It radiated from an incense burner which sat upon a display cabinet in her living room. The cabinet proudly displayed group photos of her family in professional portraits, of her parents in military uniform and even her graduation photo in which she looked stunning. This 'shrine' was her world; there was no need for the distraction of a television.

Nancy finished blow-drying her hair and brushing it into place before leaving her bedroom to fix herself some dinner. Her untied hair flowed gently as she walked briskly to the kitchen. Although it was warm she wore a comforting, thick bathrobe. And even though she just had a run in with some peeping toms, she was more than confident to be wearing nothing else but the bath robe she donned.

Careful not to spill food onto its dark purple fabric she tied the waist straps firmly and pushed the robes sleeves back. Tonight's dinner was avocado, salt and pepper on rectangular crackers - her favourite. She poured a glass of water from the tap and added a squeeze of lime from one that was already cut in her fridge. Placing the 'banquet' on a timber serving tray she made her way to the living room. The tray scraped across her glass coffee table as she positioned it centrally. She leaned back and dropped herself into the thick, brown sofa.

Peace at last.

Tilting her head back into the soft headrest of the sofa, with eyes closed, her mind wandered over childhood memories.

"Higher Daddy, higher," squealed Nancy as she leant back in the swing, blonde hair whipping through the air. She felt a firm hand push her in the middle of her back, propelling her through the air. Her frame was small and she felt like she was blasting off into outer space or taking off like her fighter pilot dad.

Nancy smiled at the memory of her giggling with laughter but also of feeling safe in the presence of her father. Another memory crossed her mind, erasing the last like a fresh wave washing over sandy footprints.

"But I did try my best Dad, I promise," she said motioning to a graded paper, which he grasped with an angry fist. It was adorned with a large, red 'A' minus in the corner.

"If this is your best then what the heck are we supposed to do with you?" shouted her dad in an overly aggressive manner. The small hairs on the back of her neck stood as a rash of fear, disguised as a hot flush, raced across her body. Tears welled in her eyes as she looked up to him. She was careful not to let them escape.

Her mother stood there, her arms folded, her eyes narrowed. She didn't speak. She never did. Ever.

Nancy tried hard to hold her tears back, careful not to show her parents any weakness, even after he had thrown the assignment at her and left the house by slamming the back door, jumping on his Harley and skidding away from the property erratically. She felt cold. Ashamed. Alone.

Nancy opened her eyes, looked towards her display cabinet, and wiped a single tear that escaped and rolled down her cheek. She rose and moved purposely towards the cabinet, opening one of the top drawers. Her fingertips cautiously traced across the coiled leather belt, like she was petting a snake. She carefully removed it and returned to the sofa - this time she sat upright on the edge of the sofa. Nancy placed the belt beside her food tray. She rolled her shoulders and let the bathrobe fall away to expose her bare torso. She gathered her long blonde hair, which was draped over her back, and neatly laid it over her left breast.

In a succession of five short snaps she brought the belt across her back in a whipping motion. She didn't flinch as she did it and she was more silent than when her father had done it to her. But like her father she made sure no blood was drawn - no physical scars, no evidence was left. The purple bruise and the stinging sensation left after a few days but the memory of the action - the psychological scars - were always present and ran deep.

Just as quickly as her self-punishment was delivered then the belt was promptly returned to the draw and her hair and bathrobe were returned to their positions.

After her 'dinner' and water she took her tray to the kitchen and returned with her thick laptop. As she waited for the laptop to fire up she sat on the sofa and hummed a lullaby.

When the computer was alive she opened a word processor and started to type. It was mostly poetry and it was mostly to resolve her psychological scars.

Float on whispered wind, on scented skies,
Turn and spin, dance to your own reprise,
Lift, but not too high, take care,
Precariously drift and lead me there,
Your tender journey mirrors mine,
Single feathered seed from dandelion.

The two friends slowly made their way back towards Neil's house. Dogs barked at them and residents yelled obscenities as they kicked an empty aluminium can along the pathway, causing a raucous. They checked if doors were locked on cars parked in the streets, looking for loose change or packets of cigarettes in their centre consoles.

It was getting late and Jonas had a slight feeling of anguish thinking about what he might cop with his mother when he got home. He would rather crash at Neil's house for the night to stay away from her but he knew if he did he might get interrogated about the Sunday plans. He had planned on coming back to Neil's house in the morning to go over his vendetta against Jack, but he knew he could drop in quickly and leave before his mates asked him what he was up to – the whole morning would have been hard to escape their questions.

When they arrived, Neil stood beside Jonas' bike. "I'll see you tomorrow dude."

"What, are you blowing me off already?"

"It's late man," said Neil reluctantly knowing Jonas would pressure him to stay up even later.

"Aw come on. Hey I said sorry back there, there wasn't much time to let you look."

"It's not that, it's past midnight and I'll be wrecked tomorrow. Especially if you want to follow through with your plans."

"Whatever," muttered Jonas, "suppose we need to get Stanley in on it? It'll be sweeter that way."

"Yeah sure." Neil eyed the welcoming comfort of the open door to his house; thinking about his soft bed.

"See ya," said Jonas lifting his bike. Mounting the pedals he propelled forward quickly and after a few meters he jumped the gutter, landing on the bitumen, the bike protesting with a thud.

Before Jonas had left the end of the street Neil was inside, the front door safely closed and he was on the phone. It was very late but he knew Stanley would answer.

6 – SUNRISE ON THE FARM

I'll cup my wounded dove
then tear a jagged line.
A beating heart is what I love,
then whisper, "all is fine."

"Sissy! Sissy!" called out her father. "Where are you?"

No answer.

A pot of food boiled on the stove, it started to thicken so the bubbles spat at the surface like muddy geysers. With a hand shielded by a tea towel, he held the pot and gave it one last vigorous stir with a seasoned wooden spoon before turning the gas hob off.

"Come on, lunch is ready!" Bill Smart rubbed his bald head and looked around for plates to set the table with.

"Coming Dad!" Sissy yelled from down the hall. She just finished cutting the boy's head from a photo before hiding the cuttings and scissors in her desk drawer.

"What's for lunch? It smells great Dad," she said, joining her father in the kitchen.

"One of your favourites, pumpkin soup."

"Yum-o," she replied childishly. Her father didn't mind, she would always be his little girl.

Although pumpkin soup was usually a warming winter dish, Bill's pumpkin patch had delivered a bumper crop towards the end of this year and he was making use of the supply. Where others saw an overweight bus driver, Sissy saw a proud father who loved tending to his vegetable garden. They often ate what he had produced and for that reason they often ate quite healthily.

Sissy sat opposite her father at the small square breakfast table. They ate most meals here; the formal dining table was left in a state of preservation ever since Sissy's mother had passed away.

"Dad, when will you be back to driving me to school?" She looked up at her father as he placed a steaming bowl of food before her.

As he turned to get the breadboard, full of toasted bread fingers for dipping, he shrugged his shoulders. "I am not too sure Love, I'll go to work on Monday for assessment, so depending on what they think it will be Tuesday at the earliest."

"Hope they let you back, since you've been cleared and all," she said with a pained smile. Her father had suffered anxiety attacks from being blamed for the bus crash, and although he wasn't injured in the crash, this was his trauma. His nightmares were a testament to that. She knew that it also woke him up; his night tremors and moaning led to shouting then silence. She cried most nights when it happened because she felt he was the most trustworthy person in the world and he was under constant scrutiny for causing the accident. He always put others first and would never hurt a soul. Nobody was concerned for his welfare. Sissy felt bad for the children on the bus that day. She had been on the same bus but her stop was one of the first and couldn't help feeling that it may have been her in the hospital as well. She was so glad that her father was safe and didn't get hurt. *Who would look after me?*

"Well we can't worry too much about that now can we? My trial was a good result so that will be in my favour, but if they decide my time is up then they might send me to retire early."

"No Dad, that would be awful," said Sissy with concern in her eyes.

"Sis, I've got to face reality, I am getting old and even though I wasn't to blame for the accident I was at the wheel when I wrote off one of their buses. In fact, if I go to the meeting tomorrow with the anticipation of retirement than anything else will be a bonus," explained Bill, always trying to put a positive spin on bad situations; it was one of the methods he used to cope with the death of his wife and being left to bring up a young daughter by himself.

"Let's not think about that Dad, you're the best bus driver they have," she said holding back her springy blonde curls with one hand and dipping toast into the pumpkin soup with the other.

Bill gave a quick smile, even though he was worried about his future, he tried to keep a positive disposition - especially around Sissy. He knew she was his world and without her he would have little to live for. If he kept her happy and safe then that was all that mattered to him. He feared the death of her mother weighed heavily on her and he always worried about her mental welfare.

Suddenly the phone rang breaking the somber mood.

Bill pushed back on his chair and let Sissy continue eating so he could answer the phone.

"Hello, yes it is," he said, giving Sissy a confused look. Nobody called the Smart house on a Sunday unless it was bad news.

"Yes, she's here, I'll just get her for you," said Bill, he put the receiver down on the kitchen bench and looked across at Sissy who gave a puzzled look.

"It's for you Love, says she's a friend, Susan I think she said?"

"Hi Susan?" said Sissy, giving her father a bewildered look. She turned her back to him and faced down the hallway which connected to the kitchen and dining room. She glanced at the dining room table set up for a family of three and a feeling of anguish washed over her body. *I wish Mum was here.*

"Hi Sissy, hope I didn't interrupt you?"

"Nah, I was just having brunch."

"Sorry, I can call back."

"It's okay, what's up?"

"I know I don't usually call you at home, and I'll keep this brief as I am calling from the Tablelands..."

"Oh," said Sissy, cutting her off, and wondering what Susan was doing calling her long distance on an STD call.

"...but I am at a crossroads with Jack." Susan felt relieved to finally say it out loud and tell someone else about her feelings towards Jack. Sissy was the only female friend she could confide in.

"What do you mean?"

"I think I want to take it further with him, more than just a friend."

There was a long pause on the line.

"Sissy? What do you think?"

"What do I think?"

"Yeah, you know us both the best, I don't want to lose Jack's friendship if things go wrong, but he's the best person I trust, and I figure you've got to build a relationship on trust."

"Yeah but do you like him?"

"What do you mean, *do I like him*?"

"You know, *in that way?* I know you like him but that's like having a brother. Do you *like* him, you know?"

"What are you saying Sissy, I don't get it?"

Sissy pressed the mouthpiece to her lips and moved as far away from her father as the coiled phone cord would let her. She whispered, "you know, to swap body fluids."

"Ew, yuck!"

"Well, is he your brother or your lover?" laughed Sissy with a cackle across the line.

"Sissy! Does it have to be that black and white?"

"I suppose it doesn't, but think of it, do you like hanging out with him and don't mind what he gets up to when he isn't with you or do you long for him all the time and want to kiss him all over," she said sending kissing noises and laughter down the phone line.

Susan was annoyed with Sissy but knew that she was different; although she had her quirks Susan trusted her brutal honesty. She still however couldn't handle long periods of her weirdness.

"I don't know Sissy, he has that something that draws me closer. I know what you are saying and on the outside it looks like he could be my brother but I think that I want more."

"Okay, then go with your gut feeling," said Sissy in an annoyed tone, changing her demeanor instantly.

"Look Sis, I trust your opinion, I need a real person to talk to."

"Yeah okay, well my lunch is getting cold."

Susan sensed the change in personality. She may have pushed Sissy's patience too far. She wanted to get off the phone before she got angry.

"Well okay, I am just going to take it slow, nothing official anyway."

"Nothing formal?"

"No nothing too formal."

"Sounds like a good plan, you always have the best ideas. Look I've got to go I'll see you tomorrow Susie."

"Okay see ya," said Susan hanging up the receiver.

Sissy hung up the phone and slowly walked back to the breakfast table, she noticed her father hadn't touched his food and was waiting for her to return. His chivalry sometimes astounded her.

"Everything okay Love?"

"Yeah, she was just having homework trouble."

"Could you help her out?"

"Yeah, she just needed a push in the right direction, I think she'll get the results she'll be after," explained Sissy dunking her toast finger into her soup and taking a bite. She smiled as she felt the warm soup in her mouth; she decided Susan needed more of her help to get top marks in her 'homework'.

Boy Sissy can be a bit testy sometimes. Susan made her way from the kitchen where she just finished her phone call with Sissy. She felt Sissy's aggravation but felt that she genuinely wished her well with her pursuit of Jack. She decided to head outside and rest on the veranda as the others hadn't stirred yet from last night's drinking and crying session. She hoped that they wouldn't hang around the property too long today as she wanted to get back to Jack. She wanted to let him know how she felt and to make grounds on the distance she had placed between the two of them last night after the park explosion.

Sitting on the outside sofa she watched the birds fly in and out of the trees that hugged the veranda. They seemed to be happily playing, like they were chasing each other. Perhaps they were chasing each other away from the prized location of the lush green trees and shrubs, vying for supremacy in the harsh landscape. She wondered how the different birds interacted. Was there a hierarchy based on size or age? What was the tipping point of dominance between a young bird and an older one? Was it when a sign of weakness was shown that the younger bird stepped in and the older, knowledgeable ones stopped giving advice and started taking help for survival sake?

"They are lovely, aren't they?" said Gillian softly, trying not to startle her niece.

"Yes there are quite a few different ones." Susan didn't take her gaze off of them.

"This is my favourite spot, some days I can sit here for hours looking at them, closing my eyes and listening to their songs," she said, leaning against the doorway architrave. "Did you want a cup of tea?"

"Yes thanks Aunty Gill," replied Susan with a polite smile.

Gillian set off to the kitchen and returned moments later with two porcelain cups with steam rising from them. She set them on the coffee table in front of the couch and sat down beside her. They both sat there for a while, staring at the birds before either one took a cup to their mouths.

A large black bird flew in from the surrounding bush trees and landed on the branches of an umbrella tree. It sat there preening itself. Then it broke the morning quietness with its call, like a coowoo, coowoo.

"What's that bird Aunty Gill, the one making all the noise?"

"That's a common koel, he's a male calling for his mate."

"He's got striking red eyes, kind of eerie."

"Yes, he's quite noisy, but I don't mind, it reminds me that the rains are coming."

"Oh, why's that?"

"Well around here we call him a stormbird, he arrives from the Top End to breed just before the wet season, to make sure his young have plenty of tucker."

"So he's not here all year round?"

"No, only this time of year."

"That would give you some peace and quiet in the morning for the rest of the year," laughed Susan.

"Yes it does."

They sat there sipping their tea, still no sign of her sister and mother, watching the Koel dart in and out of the branches chasing other birds away.

"Aunty Gill?" said Susan after long thought.

"Yes Love, what is it?"

"Do you think boys are worth the trouble?" she said turning to face Gillian, her eyes narrowed with concern.

"Oh, maybe that's a question for your mum," Gillian said, trying to play devil's advocate.

"You know what she's like, she's over protective, since Dad left I guess, well since as far as I can remember."

"And you can't see why she wouldn't be, she's been hurt deeply by the man she trusted the most."

"But, I wouldn't get a sensible answer from her anyway, I just want an honest answer without innuendo." Susan took another sip of her tea.

"So you want to know about boys, you think I have all the answers?"

"Well maybe you can help me with just one particular boy," giggled Susan.

"They may well stir your heart but you've got to be careful," said Gillian, cutting Susan's smile to a frown. "I've had my troubles, heck even your sister has had her troubles with them."

"Valerie?"

"Yes, I'll let her tell you about her horror stories with boys, but I can tell you about my experiences." Gillian looked out at the bush land.

"This one is very nice and I've known him for a long time, I am sure he wouldn't hurt me."

"That's what you think. When I was your age I fell for someone I had known for a long time, I thought he was a real gentleman," said Gillian, still looking out at the scenery. "He was a real gentleman until he took advantage of me in a drunken moment."

"Did he intentionally hurt you Aunty Gill?" Susan's sad look showed her concern.

"No, not that way Love, he just should have known better, he was older, wiser and he knew I was vulnerable."

"But I don't think this boy would ever do that, I kind of scare him a little, I think," smirked Susan.

"Just be careful, it can be the most wonderful thing, being swept up in love, but boys, all boys say one thing, treat you like a princess then they all want what pleases them the most," said Gillian bluntly.

"Yes but Jack's not like that."

"Who? Did you say Jack?" Gillian turned her whole body to face Susan. Her narrowed eyes and deep frown lines concerned Susan.

What's the issue with Jack? "Yes".

"Jack your neighbour?"

"Yes, you know him, he's been my best friend for years."

"I know him," spat Gillian, she was clearly distressed. Her hands gripped the top of the sofa and she would have torn out a large chunk of foam if she hadn't taken deep breaths and controlled herself. "Susan," she said slowly, "you aren't going to like what I am about to tell you, but you must listen to me very carefully."

Susan studied her aunty with intent; Gillian was looking deadly serious, she hadn't seen her aunty this way.

"Wha...," muttered Susan before she was cut short.

"You can't see that boy, not any boy, they all want one thing."

"What? But you just said be careful, now..."

"I don't care, I am saying don't see any boys, not while you are finishing your senior year of high school," said Gillian with intent.

"But he only wants what's best for me."

"He only wants what's between your legs!"

"What the fu...," spat Susan.

"It's true, ask your sister about the noble gentleman that wanted what was best for her, but knocked her up in her last year of school!"

"What?" Susan was in shock.

"What's with all the shouting out here?" said Mrs. Valentino sporting a thick pink night robe and holding a steaming cup of coffee.

"Mum, did Valerie have a...did she have a baby?" Susan's look was of disbelief. Tears started to welt in her eyes. "Is that why she went wild after her graduation?"

"Gillian! What have you done?" Mrs. Valentino's mouth dropped.

"I just wanted her to realise what she was getting into with *Jack*," said Gillian, still clearly distressed but determined she had the right to divulge this hidden family secret.

When Valerie came out onto the veranda Susan stood to greet her. With arms out she motioned towards her with deep sorrow. Valerie looked bewildered, her mother looked like she was in a deadlock with her seated sister and Susan looked like someone had just run over a puppy.

"Hey guys, have I missed something?" Valerie said.

"Val, I am so, so sorry, I didn't know," Susan said, tears starting to stream down her cheeks.

"Didn't know what?" She shot her mother a concerned look.

"That you had to go through all that, especially at high school."

"Mum?" Valerie's voice showed a hint of anger.

"I know, seems *Aunty Gillian* has some explaining to do."

"It's too late for that, isn't it a relief to get that weight off your shoulders?" smirked Gillian towards Valerie.

"How about we get all the dirty laundry out?" said Mrs. Valentino, giving her sister a scorned look.

"Let's leave things how they are." Gillian fired a warning look to her sister.

"Then that's how you should have left things Gillian, now look what you've done!" Mrs. Valentino crossed her arms forcefully.

"What gives you the right to tell my sister about my abortion? Don't you think I was going to let her know when the time was right? Now you're sitting there like a smug bitch. Fuck this place and fuck you all!" Valerie took off; she bolted down the stairs and took off along the property access track. She was walking home, she didn't care if she had to hitchhike in her pyjamas.

"Valerie!" shouted Mrs. Valentino. "Come back, let's talk about this!"

"Abortion?" More tears streamed from Susan's eyes as she witnessed her sister stride off into the bush and out of sight.

The car ride home was deathly quiet. Mrs. Valentino only heard the noise of different music coming from each of the girl's earbuds during lulls in the radio station playing in the car. Susan and her mother left straight away, and it took a lot of shouting and convincing to get Valerie into the car so they could make the journey home.

For Susan it all clicked, the annual pilgrimage to Aunty Gillian's property, the late night drinking and crying sessions. Not only were they supporting her mother's emotions about Susan's dad leaving but they were also supporting Aunty Gillian's past and poor Valerie with the loss of her child. They were supporting each other through tragic pasts. *Why didn't they tell me earlier about Valerie? Did they think I was too young to know? Wasn't I good enough to know? And how painful was Aunty Gillian's past? She always looks so happy, what a thick mask she wears.*

When they got home Susan needed space from her family, Jack was going to be the right outlet for her - she missed him badly.

7 – SUNDAY SWIM

Sunday was his day to waste - no chores. His mother was going to pick his father up at the airport and then they would spend the morning together, usually at the local markets or wandering around a shopping centre. It was the last thing his father wanted to do when he got back from the mines, but he agreed as it was spending 'alone' time with her and it was a way to assimilate back into the civilian way of life – mine life was stagnant and generally changed the persona of a worker, due to the isolated conditions, which was predominantly male orientated. His parents would return home later in the day after they had breakfast or lunch at a cafe or had done something else which didn't really interest Jack. His brother took off with his mates on their trail bikes. They were also gone for most of the day.

His parents had asked him a while ago if he ever wanted to join them but he had no interest in being dragged around market stalls in the hot morning sun with market vendors calling out their specials; mix that with annoying tourists and local hippies squeezing past him with their sweaty bodies and it was his idea of a worst nightmare. He especially hated coconut cutting backpackers with their stinking dreadlocks. He was all for freedom of life but he thought the use of a bar of soap wouldn't go astray occasionally.

Jack was alone.

He looked around his room and his vision always came back to that dreaded book with the words 'Epilogue' staring back at him. *Oh well, anything to keep my mind off Susan for one minute.*

Bind our souls together,
before tearing us apart.
Storm through any weather,
beginning before the start.

And you thought I was done, thought I'd had my fun. But like that Deborah Conway song, 'It's Only The Beginning' I too think I've lost my marbles.

Dream at night of soft skin and gentle kisses while I dream of crimson blood dripping from shiny steel blades. You take my essence so I take your life. Like an eye for an eye, let's hope we meet eye to eye and flesh this out.

I'll leave you with a parting thought, a gesture on my part, not that I jest, it's just that I want you to know, why you? Could I fly higher than any bird if you were there soaring with me? Would writing this book make the living fear in me recede like a beheaded snake? Would you think I was a snake if I bit you hard? I am only trying to make you stronger, for I see you as the future, you and her. She needs your guidance, she is a lost soul floating on the surface of sanity. A ripple may drown her but you can save her - unlike me who is as damaged as the reflection in my broken mirror.

Now that you've been shown, go forth and take your kindness with you. Wipe your dirty boots on the doormat of reason. Go, I beg you. Do you want me to show you the way? I've been trying, have you been paying attention?

One last performance, one last release of energy to finish on a crescendo, to help with my therapy anyway. Here goes nothing: Slice my wings lengthways, let the blood flow without repair. If I tattoo your name across my beating heart would it blacken with the pain I bare?

I don't think so.

You left me to tear your infection out, you left me as a bleeding mess. Stuff me in your perfect box and slice the bits off that can't get shoved in - I'll soon conform. I am your germ, your disease, I leave you ill at ease. It's human nature to want to survive but you've strangled my will to live with the umbilical cord of your ignorant existence.

Sigh and breathe, the calming technique that has helped me through the darkness. Thank you for your patience and time, I'll be okay. Smile, I will be fine. Let me close with this final poem and I thank those who helped supply them for my resolve:

And surrender to my love,
where you'll set upon to me,
my crimson dripping glove,
finally sets me free.

"Thank fuck for that!" Jack wished he could burn the book. "Paperback Novel by John Bird, what a stinking pile of hot mess that was!" Jack was seriously thinking of destroying the book and telling Mr. Friar it was accidently thrown out by his mum cleaning his room. At least then he wouldn't be blamed for it.

"Ah!" Jack was tormented by the overlying feeling of hatred for the novel but knowing he had to take it back to school tomorrow with his assignment. *Please I don't want anyone else to go through the pain of having to read this piece of shit.* He put the book down and took some deep breaths. At least he didn't have to change his written analogy of the book. He still concluded that the writer has used this form of writing to express their artistic talent and to use it as a therapeutic method - the words "to help with my therapy anyway' proves it. Jack shuddered still thinking that the writer was somehow trying to communicate directly to the reader. It was almost as if the writer was trying to talk to him. *Fat chance, I don't even know who John Bird is, and even if it's a pseudonym then nothing that I've read connects with me on any fucking level.*

He slipped the book and his assignment into his backpack and kicked it to his cupboard, one last act of retaliation. *At least I don't have to deal with that shit anymore.*

Flopping back onto his bed Jack put his earbuds in and clicked play on his Walkman. A mixed tape Susan had made for him started playing and his mind wandered. He began thinking back to Friday night at the park with Susan. What if the explosion didn't happen? How would things have advanced between them if they managed to kiss? He imagined what her soft lips felt like. Would they be like marshmallows, soft and sweet? His fingers traced his bedsheets like they skated across her leggings in the park. The touch of his fingers through her fine hair - the sweet smell of her hair. He remembered her hand on his chest, pressing on his clothes like a warm iron. His heart began to race thinking about that moment.

His hand brushed across his silk boxer shorts and it bumped into his erection. He hadn't realised it was there, his mind was too lost thinking about Susan. He grabbed his penis and tried to push it back down, "Not now!" He didn't want to think about Susan in that way but his hormones fought him. He blushed in embarrassment but nobody was looking, only the strength of his friendship judged him - his consciousness of their history.

It must have been bad timing but as he stood from his bed, still sporting his trapped, tented erection behind his boxers, his door swung open without warning.

"Aw Mum! Don't you knock?" He grabbed a pillow to cover himself.

It was too late she had already seen her son's crotch. She looked at him in disgust. "Jack! What have I said about doing that in your bedroom?"

"Mum!"

"I mean it, do it in the shower, your room stinks enough as it is!" Jack couldn't help the smell of his teenage pheromones, which were raging and were the cause of his room's dank smell, but his mother typically jumped to conclusions.

"Mum!"

"I just came up here to tell you that your father and I are going out for dinner tonight, you boys can pick a box out of the freezer." She was referring to a frozen microwave dinner.

"Sure, now can you go?"

"Why? So you can finish yourself off?"

"Aw Mum, no way!"

"George, come up here and have a word to your boy," she yelled down the hallway.

"What about?" came the reply.

"About girls and controlling himself!"

"Aw Mum, leave me alone."

"Maybe you should spend less time with Susan, she's affecting your grades," instructed his mother.

"Mum, no, stop." Jack was distressed.

"I mean it. Did you know I had a phone call from Mr. Friar last week making sure that you hand in your English assignment tomorrow?"

"What?" Jack looked mortified.

"Yes we both discussed, that even though you had the accident, there was nothing really stopping you from finishing the assignment," she preached. "He did grant you an extension."

"But Mum, the book was so hard to comprehend."

"Which is why he set you the task in the first place, he said you're a bright student and you need to be pushed out of your comfort zone. I know you had the accident, and yes I know Susan was a good friend to help you through it, but I think that you and her are getting a little *too* close," she said bluntly.

Jack was mortified, he didn't know what to say. *Is that what they truly think? Now my mother and teacher are ganging up on me.*

"And now you are masturbating on a Sunday morning!"

"Whoa did I come in on this at the wrong time?" His father stood beside his mother. "Do you get it? *Did I cum?*" A wry smirk formed across his face.

She frowned at him. *Now I'm dealing with two wankers.*

"Mum, Dad, I didn't do anything. Dad you know what it's like when you wake up in the morning full of pee?"

"Sure, but your mother is right. I've seen you slinking back home late at night. God knows what you get up to."

"But you were young once, she's only a friend."

"I was being sarcastic Jack, I know what you'd be up to. Yes, I was your age once, I know what it's like to chase skirts," said his father.

"But Dad, this is Susan we are talking about, not just some 'skirt'."

"Fair enough, you two have been friends for a long time. I..., we don't want to see either of you getting hurt. We thought you'd stay friends but it seems these longer night 'visits' means you are courting and I don't want you to get serious with her and wreck your grades."

"But she's the best thing that's happened to me." Jack's eyes welted.

"Stop thinking with this," said his father aggressively as he grabbed his own crotch to indicate what he was talking about. He wasn't jovial anymore. "Aren't we the best thing that's happened to you?"

"Dad!" yelled Jack, a lump formed in his throat as a result of his disbelief and anger. A tear rolled down his face. The look in his eyes was like a child getting its first hard smack; it was his disbelief that he had done anything wrong in the first place and the realisation that his parents didn't understand him.

"Come on mother, let's go," said George.

She lingered in the doorway. Jack wondered if she felt empathy towards him.

"Just a little less time with her darling, just until you get through your end of year exams."

Jack reluctantly nodded.

"We are only looking out for you son, you know we love you," she said before she walked off, down the stairs and out of the house.

Jack waited until he heard their car leave before he lay there, burying his head into his pillow and bawling uncontrollably.

"Hey dude! Wait up!" Neil said as he chased after his good friend Stanley. They had just had a visit from their best mate Jonas and they naively had agreed to perform an evil act on Jack early next week at school.

"Just leave me alone, I don't want anything to do with this plan," shouted Stanley.

"Aw come on. Jack and the ogre, Daris, won't that be an epic bit of fun?" Neil flicked his mid length hair to the side and exposed his undercut.

"Have you seen that guy?" he said, stopping and waiting for his friend to catch up.

"Who hasn't? This will be epic!" said Neil with a wry grin.

"Then have you heard the stories? War survivor of a modern ethnic cleansing with post-traumatic stress disorder?"

"Wow, did you swallow a fucking dictionary?" said Neil. He didn't wait for Stanley to reply as he caught up to him. "And yes, we've all heard his stories, that will make it all the more fun."

Stanley wasn't sold on the idea of the prank. He was all up for causing havoc amongst the other students but thought nobody deserves what Jonas had planned. He went along with Jonas' idea but deep down he was concerned.

"What if he kills him, he's built like a boxer?" Stanley lit up a cigarette.

"If he was that much of a threat to the neighbourhood he wouldn't be living beside a school then would he?" Neil put his hand out and Stanley automatically gave him a cigarette and lighter.

Both boys took a drag on their cigarettes as they leaned back on a random house's front fence that they had stopped outside of.

"But I'll be fucked if this comes back on my hands, if anything does go wrong," said Stanley with concern in his eyes. "I also want to graduate this year dude."

"Yeah, I know what you mean, I think that Jonas is going to have to repeat, he hasn't said but I caught a look at his grades last semester and they were shit."

"What about yours, bet your doctor mum and dad don't want their golden boy to fuck up this year?"

"No, they don't." Neil shot his friend a scowl. He took another deep draw of his cigarette and looked out across the neighboring houses. People were going about their Sunday morning rituals, he counted at least five residents mowing their lawns - all looking sweaty and hot. He turned to Stanley, annoyed with suburban rituals. "Like we have a choice anyway?"

"What are you saying? You scared of Jonas?"

"Nah, but he's been getting worse lately. I don't mind stirring up the nerds but he's got it out for that Jack fucker of late."

"True, true. You think he's gone mental?"

"Probably. Anyway we stick with his shit plan for the rest of the year, then we graduate and fuck him off when we go to uni and he has to repeat or he gets a trade or something like that," said Neil.

"What if he's smarter than us?" asked Stanley.

"What do you mean?"

"What if he drags us down to his level so we have to repeat as well? Even worse, what if he gets to have his fun and then frames us for doing it?" Stanley dropped his cigarette stub on the ground and squashed it with the toe of his shoe.

"You think he's that smart?" asked Neil.

"We'll he's got us doing something we don't really give a fuck about, doesn't he?"

"You could be onto something. Like I said to you on the phone last night, let's go along with what he wants but if shit goes south then we stick up for each other. Okay?"

"Yeah, okay." Deep down Stanley was scared of how far Jonas was willing to take his rage on Jack. He feared one act of retribution would see him with a criminal record and ruin any chance of going to university to study to become a lawyer. His father, who was a lawyer, had expectations of Stanley's career choice. Not that Stanley minded becoming a lawyer, he saw the benefits of the high income and the lifestyle it could afford, namely the toys, trips and women.

However, Stanley was different, he had an underlying feeling that he wanted to support the battler in life. He got that drive from attending work experience at a local law firm which provided legal aid. He saw firsthand the underdog's struggle against the corporate world. Attacking Jack was going against all that Stanley believed in.

"Chin up mate, it will be fun, you'll see," said Neil as he slapped his mate on the back.

"It's alright for you, your parents don't give a shit what you do at school," said Stanley.

"You'll be alright, if your old man kicks you out then you can come and live with me," laughed Neil.

"Ha, ha," muttered Stanley.

"Or we can swap parents, your old man's girlfriend is smoking hot!" joked Neil.

"You can have her, she might be hot but she's crazy,"

"What do you mean?"

"She chased Dad around the house with a fucking kitchen knife because she saw one of his clients was hot or something like that."

"True?"

"Yeah and she's loud," Stanley said matter-of-factly.

"Loud in bed?"

"Nah, fucking loud all the time, she doesn't shut up," Stanley explained.

"Still, bet you get a boner when you see her in the morning," Neil joked.

"Shut up. Speaking of mornings, why was Jonas in such a rush to get away this morning anyway?" Stanley said.

"I see what you did there, good change of subject, and I don't know, he had to be somewhere I suppose."

"Yeah?"

"Yeah, he's been going somewhere every Sunday for a while now," Neil said.

"And he keeps this shit a secret? Bet its church or something."

"Fat chance," scoffed Neil.

"See what I mean about being trustworthy," Stanley said.

"Yeah, as long as we have each other's backs, what could go wrong?"

The friends started walking. Stanley had nowhere to be, today was a slow day for him. He normally hated the drawn out Sundays.

"Come on let's go see a bloke I know," said Neil happily.

"What, you out of weed?"

"How'd you guess, and I am sure you need a chuff to steady your nerves old boy," said Neil, laughing until he coughed. He took one last draw on his cigarette and flicked the butt out onto the street, it bounced off of a parked car and landed on the bitumen.

The pictures of bands in dynamic poses and even the still shot of band members exuding their look and attitude is what struck him the most. His rock magazine was full of beautiful pictures and it was a good distraction this morning to keep his mind off his unreasonable parents. It was also a distraction from the bad taste that his English assignment had left in his mouth.

Jack wasn't at all musically talented, he remembered when he was in primary school and the only test for music ability was from a roving music instructor that went from school to school. She sat children down in a crowded class and asked them one by one to repeat the notes on a piano after she had played them. It took all of a couple of minutes. That was it. If the young student could pick up the notes then she recommended them for further music lessons. *What a joke.* Jack knew that to do well in most things in life you needed practice and determination. Not a two minute trial by fire to see if you had talent. Nevertheless Jack knew his parents couldn't afford musical instruments and he probably lacked the concentration to learn. So flicking through the magazine wasn't about the love of music or bands, it was more to do with his love of the graphic arts. Even the ads in the magazine looked sexy - Jack was hungry for more. Would his parents approve of a graphics arts career or one that was more sculptured from his father's route? Sadly Jack knew the answer. But Jack was more upset with the fact that Mr. Friar had held this last English assignment over him and that he needed to do well in it to pass English, which was necessary to give him better options on a career path when he left school, whether in graphic arts or any other direction he was steered.

His ears pricked when he heard the car pull into their driveway as he thought they would be home later in the day. He pushed the magazine to the floor and sat up on the side of the bed. *Susan must be back.* He knew he had to follow the rules and regulations that his parents lectured him about but he also knew that they wouldn't be coming home until later tonight. *She's home early, that means I can get one last catch up with Susan before I've got to slow my visits.*

A car door slammed quite loudly which made Jack jump off the bed and stick his head out of his bedroom window. He just caught sight of Valerie storming off through the front door of their house and also slamming it violently. She slammed it so hard that the door striker bounced off the catch and flew open again hitting the wall of the house. A terracotta pot fell from a stand on their porch and smashed on the tiles sending potting mix everywhere.

Woah.

It looked like Susan and Mrs. Valentino were still in the car talking. He could only imagine what had gone down. *Susan said she hated the visits to her aunt's place, I better give them space, it looks like something intense is going down.*

Jack lay back on his bed, jammed his earphones in and turned up the volume.

Red bottlebrush trees in full flower lined the footpath. Rainbow lorikeets screeched and jumped between the branches along with a few rare scaly breasted lorikeets. They hung out together like drunk mates binging on the nectar, like it was happy hour down at the pub.

The morning was hot and the sun heated the footpath, making a junk mail delivery person wipe his brow with a towel draped around his neck. It was early morning yet he felt like he was half way through an Olympic marathon. Taking a swig from his water bottle he glanced at the rundown property before stuffing the junk mail into the already overloaded letter box. Looking ahead he welcomed the oasis of shady trees that the neighbouring school offered.

Square concrete pavers stained in red oxide, now pink with age and sun damage, formed a pathway to the front door. They were a world away from the cobblestone pavers from where he grew up. But amongst the ramshackle these pavers were the only geometric order to the calamity. And although no visitor would have been welcomed into his home Daris was proud of his neat entranceway. Besides, it met the requirements of the local council no matter how many surrounding neighbours had voiced their displeasure.

The front yard was messy but well-groomed in comparison to the back of the house. The rear of the house had all the hallmarks of a wrecker's yard. Rusted car bodies were stacked and arranged in random order, depending on how the tow truck at the time could unload the vehicle. Pallets were stacked and some of those stacks had toppled onto surrounding car bodies. Weeds and trees had grown between the cars and pallets to form their own mess of a garden. A beaten track between the unmown, long grass led to the far reaches of the yard to where the chicken coop ran adjacent to a Colorbond fence.

In and amongst all the derelict vehicles and timber pallets Daris had taken the time to arrange junk in quite an artistic order. Plastic bottles were in one section, stacks of plastic furniture in another, whipper snippers were piled so high you couldn't see over the stack. Bottles were arranged in crates and bicycles were lined up like an Amsterdam bike rack - except none of these bikes worked. All the tyres were flat and the chains and sprockets were rusted fast a long time ago.

The house was in its own special state of disrepair. Paint peeled off the weatherboard cladding as torn lace curtains puffed in the breeze through windows void of screens. A special kind of odour radiated from the property —one that only the occupant could stand. Most of the neighbours had complained about the stench and the council had been onto Daris about the problem but they found there was little that they could do as he was up to date with his rates. He had shown an officer about his property and found it was quite clean inside. The officer suggested clearing the backyard to remove the potential rodent problem but they were met with stern looks and harsh words. Even so, the locals were forming a litigation case against Daris to have him remove the backyard rubbish in order to mitigate the smell. They were up for a long fight. What they didn't know was they were up against a formidable opponent. Daris had conquered far worse life situations. Daris was here to stay.

The morning heat radiated off derelict car bodies and the iron roof creaked and cracked on the hardwood roof battens as clouds drifted across the sun, changing the roof iron temperature and causing rapid shrinkage. The noise startled the cat that lived with Daris and it flicked its tail in annoyance - a show of defiance. Its belly grew hungry so it sprung off the lounge room pouffe where it had been cleaning itself and headed to the kitchen.

Sunlight flickered and glinted around the small room as it was caught by the small shards of glass being meticulously worked between his fingers and the grozier pliers. He didn't wear gloves nor did he need to as his fingers were hardened with scars. For all the many visible scars that marked his fingers and hands there were many more psychological scars below the surface. He saw solitude and resolve in his craft - in his art. Lead lighting had been his profession but now it only served as a link to his past as there was no need for this skill in Cairns. With the conflict in Bosnia it had been a full time job for him to visit the churches and repair the damaged lead lighting murals.

"Shit!" He was more furious with himself for cutting his finger than the pain it inflicted. He was frustrated with his lapse of concentration and blamed himself for the long hours he had been working on this piece.

A pure white fluffy cat jumped up onto his work table, he didn't seem to care as she licked the blood from his fingers.

"Okay, okay, enough Azra, thank you for trying to help but I better wash this clean." He pushed the cat off the table. She jumped to the floor looking up at him with a disdain expression and then commenced to lick a paw and use it to rub the sides of her face.

From the kitchen sink he looked back at the artwork on the table. It was beautiful, literally a diamond in the rough. The mural depicted a young woman with a headdress on a side profile. Her garment was white and cream, she had her head bowed and hands clasped in front of her. Angels and cherubs flew in individual poses all around the border of the frame. It was quite detailed. The work of a true craftsman. The most striking thing about the work was the blood red tears dripping from the woman's eyes and pooling at the base of the picture. Daris grunted contentedly at the near completed work. His angel - the woman he left behind.

Azra started to meow and she followed Daris to the sink. She bumped her head forcefully into his calves, moving in a figure eight between his legs. Flicking her upright tail all the while.

"Alright, I know you're hungry, just give me a second." He dried his hands on a tea towel. The bleeding had stopped, it was only a shallow cut.

Daris pulled an open can of cat food from the fridge and turned his nose up at the strong fish smell. He knew it would make her shit stink badly but it was the only flavour she ate. His only respite from the smell was to put her kitty litter tray in the laundry and keep the laundry window open to exhaust the fumes. Daris was used to the smell but a fresh deposit was enough to make him gag.

"Here you go." He scraped the can empty into her bowl. She would have buried her head in between the bowl and can if it weren't for the jagged lid of the can darting in her face.

"Always hungry eh?" He tossed the empty can out of his kitchen window in an attempt to get it into a bin that sat on the side of his house. It bounced off the rim and landed inside, upsetting a swarm of flies in the process.

"You know you're lucky you have food, you were born in this lucky country. I wish I could have been born here too." Azra didn't look up as she was too busy scoffing the food down and making unpleasant eating noises.

"But maybe not eh?" Daris sat back down at the kitchen table. "Then I'd be as naive as all the other sheep that walk around here. All the children at the school don't know how lucky they have it."

Daris grunted and continued working on the finishing touches to his mural as Azra finished licking the bowl, moving it about the tiled floor of the kitchen trying to mop up every last skerrick of food.

"She was beautiful," Daris said vacantly, "you would have loved her and I am sure she would have loved you Azra. She loved cats, especially the pretty ones."

His rugged exterior was quite a difference to the tenderness which he showed his pet. Azra was all that he really had in the world.

His other pets were the chickens, but he only saw them as a food source. It was how he grew up in the regional outskirts of Sarajevo. It was the way they lived. They had to kill their food, no supermarkets sold prepared birds to eat and if they did, they wouldn't have had the money to afford it. Cats had to fend for themselves and they grew up to be quite cunning. He looked down at Azra and realised she wouldn't have survived the competition with the stray cats. He looked after her quite well. Even though he tormented her with how lucky she was he would never want her to be subjected to the life he had growing up in war torn Bosnia.

"Had enough to eat?" She just sat there licking her paws and rubbing each side of her mouth. "Don't answer me, your fishy breath would stink."

The cat gave a small muffled meow and kept cleaning. It knew it was being spoken to by the tones in Daris' voice. "That will be your dinner as well as your breakfast then eh, you know I go to the school at lunchtime today. I'll get back too late to feed you, so you'll be alright eh?"

The car hadn't stopped running; turning it off while they were still sitting in it would have been unbearable with the air conditioner doing its best against the mid-morning heat. Susan still looked out the passenger window. She didn't escape her mother's pleading for her to stay and talk about the situation, not like her sister had. The trip home had been silent and arriving home Mrs. Valentino knew she had one last chance to defuse some of the situation before both girls boarded themselves up in their rooms.

"Susan, she was going to tell you one day."

"Why not now, don't you think I am old enough to know? You would have thought I was old enough to know at the time, I am not a baby. What? I would have been fourteen then?"

"I know you think you are strong Love, but it was very hard for your sister. We didn't want to add to your pain," the words spilled out of her mouth, she wished she could have stopped them, but she knew the truth had to come out one day.

"We? So you both made the decision, or did you make it for her? And add my pain? What are you talking about?" shouted Susan, her eyes began to welt and she sniffed to try and hold back the tears. She shifted violently in her seat and forced a long strand of fringe hair behind her ear.

"Susan." Mrs. Valentino struggled to calm her daughter.

"Mum! Answer me. I think I deserve that much!"

"Susan, I know what you've been going through all these years," she held out a hand to try and touch her daughter reassuringly. "I've read your poems."

The answer wasn't what Susan wanted to hear. Her emotions ran from being upset to full rage. Her eyes narrowed and she fumbled getting her seatbelt off. She grabbed her bag, reached for the door, trying to kick it open quickly.

"Susan, please, they are beautiful poems, let me explain!"

"Just no Mum, they are my personal thoughts, how dare you cross the line!" she screamed before she slammed the car door, ran up the pathway to the house and fled for her room. Securing her book of poems was her first priority, getting well away from her family was the second.

Mrs. Valentino sat in the car a few moments longer, she held back tears as she knew this day was coming. She felt more defiant than ever, she had to remain strong to get her girls through this. She felt someone watching her and turning her head slightly, she just caught sight of Jack looking at her from behind the leaves of the mango tree, through his bedroom window.

Lying on his bed he wondered if Susan was okay, she looked pretty angry as she ran into her house.

Car doors slammed again and the Valentino family vehicle skidded out of the driveway and out of their cul-de-sac. Jack didn't bother getting up but he wondered where they were going now. With the amount of door slamming he assumed they had all left, maybe to see a therapist, maybe to do some therapeutic shopping. Sometimes he didn't get them, maybe it was a woman thing. He realised there would have been a plethora of mood swings in a houseful of women. Maybe they could have all their doors taken off so they wouldn't get slammed all the time. *Poor doors.*

Jack thought it would have been hard for his mother living with a houseful of men. She wondered if she ever felt sad not getting a daughter to relate to. He wondered if she felt sad looking after him and his brother, and facing their daily glamour, like washing their dirty socks and skid marked jocks. But Jack knew his mother loved visiting her sister where she got to talk to other women, and especially fussing over her nieces. It was her outlet from all the testosterone that choked her house.

He decided to clean his room up and do his washing, it was the least he could do for her to show his appreciation. Gathering up his pile of school uniforms he carried them down the stairs, prying open the lid of the top load washer with one hand and dumping them in with the other. He threw in an overfilled cup of washing liquid, dropped the washer lid and turned the dial to heavy. Clicking the button in it sprung to life as the water started to fill the bowl. A grin formed across his face knowing he had done some good and it would be a pleasant surprise for his mother.

He didn't see her at first, when he returned to his room, as she was camouflaged on his bed. His blue sheets were the same colour as her skirt and top. In fact he was more taken aback by her tight top and short skirt, it was very un-Susan like.

"Whoa, hey, I didn't see you there. Or should I say who are you and what have you done with Susan?'

"Oh shut up."

"But those clothes? Where did you get them from?" Susan always covered up and always predominantly wore black. She thought the other girls at school who wore tight tops with deep necklines and short skirts were in her word, 'sluts'.

"I found my sister's nightclubbing stash. She'd never want Mum to see her in these so she always changed from her jeans and jacket that she left home in. She told me she changed when she got picked up and went to her mates house for pre clubbing drinks." Susan stared vacantly, deep in thought. "But maybe that was all a lie too?"

"What's with the change, you have always been against this look. We all have. You know, we all don't want to conform like sheep in a paddock."

"I know, but after shit went down this morning I've had enough of being who other people think I should be. I am sick of doing what others think what's best for me. It's time to be me and have fun."

"And you don't think your mum and sister will kill you for wearing it?"

"At this point in my life I don't give a shit what they think. Besides they are gone for now and I am loving this new found freedom."

"But how do you feel? I mean, doesn't wearing that feel awkward?"

"I feel liberated, like layers of crap have literally fallen off. Am I making you uncomfortable?" she said as she sat up. Jack diverted his eyes, careful not to see too much as she lifted her legs in a kicking motion to be able to shuffle to the edge of the bed.

"Sort of, I don't know where to look."

"I can see that! Just relax, it's still the old me in a revived look. Don't you like it?"

"Well yes, it's just a shock to my system."

"I can go if you want. I know when I'm not wanted. I learnt that this weekend."

"No, no, please stay. You look great." Jack said with torment in his eyes. Susan looked happy, smiling there on his bed but he was worried that she was masking deep emotion. Had she gone off the rails and was she going to explode with pent up anger?

"Sounds like a lot happened at your aunt's? Want to talk about it?"

"Not really."

"Are you sure, maybe it's good to let it out?"

"Jack, I want to push that as far away from me as possible."

"Where were they going in such a hurry anyway?" Jack said, trying from a different angle.

"I don't know, they go shopping on a Sunday or some shit like that, they've never asked me along. Suppose they know I hate shopping. Being dragged around clothes shops - such fun," Susan said sarcastically. "But who knows, it might be fun now sorting out a new wardrobe?"

"Right." *Well that backfired.* He looked agitated and annoyed. He didn't want to sit on his bed and he didn't know where to look. Even though Susan had laid on his bed before it wasn't very often or for very long and she certainly didn't show any skin. He was trying to process her, he wanted to help her with her family. She was putting up walls which was also something she hadn't done too often before with Jack.

Susan sensed his discomfort and wanted to change the mood. "Let's do something fun, where are your olds?"

Jack gulped; he hoped she wouldn't notice his nervousness. He was worried that she wanted to do something wild to match her new outfit. He didn't know how to handle the new persona she was exuding. He liked the comfort in the old Susan that he knew. He hoped this was only a rebellious phase that only lasted the rest of the day.

"They won't be back till late tonight, what did you want to do?"

"Cool, let's go for a swim," Susan said with a smile.

Jack sighed with relief.

"Sounds great, Glenoma Park?"

"Just what I was thinking."

"Okay, I'll get you some board shorts and you can wear one of my old shirts."

"No."

"What?"

"I am sure your mum has a bikini that will fit me, they'd be in her dresser drawers somewhere," Susan said and she got up and slipped out of Jack's room before he could comprehend what was happening.

"Hold up! My mum's clothes?"

"Yep, women like to keep hold of things that don't fit them anymore, you should see all my mum's old clothes," Susan said as she pulled the drawer open to Jack's mother's dresser.

This was quite awkward for Jack. He never went into his parents' bedroom. It was like a no go zone out of respect; there really wasn't any reason for him to enter their domain - ever. He felt nervous - his heart pounded in his chest.

"Ah, these look cute and they're my size," she said clutching a pair of black bikinis.

"And your colour too."

"Ha, ha smart ass. Turn around," Susan instructed.

He couldn't believe it, Susan was getting undressed. A fully naked teenage girl in his parent's room, his mother would be livid if she ever found out. His dad wouldn't mind, but for all the wrong reasons. He didn't want to imagine *anyone* naked in his parent's room.

"Susan!"

"I'll be quick, now turn around, no peeking."

He would do anything to defuse this situation so he turned his back to her so she could get it done quickly. He couldn't help it, he accidently caught a glimpse of her naked form in the mirror that hung above his parent's bed, he turned his head to the side quickly but he couldn't unsee the image. His heart raced rapidly in his chest - it was going to explode - he could feel his pants rise in the front and he tried to think of maths problems to divert his attention. He hated knowing that his parents were right, his hormones were betraying his better judgment. But Susan felt so right, she was everything. He wanted to give in to her draw, but he wanted to please his family as well. Conflicting thoughts shot a stab of pain in his head.

He was still facing away with his head down when she cheekily surprised him by giving him a bear hug from behind. He felt her soft breasts on his back as she said, "come on, what are you waiting for? Let's go!"

Standing back she raised her arms, put one foot forward and asked, "So how do I look?" She completed the question by giving herself a quick spin on the spot.

"Nice," was all he could manage from his dry throat. He'd never seen Susan in a bikini before, she always wore board shorts and a shirt when they went swimming. Somehow this triangle bikini and bottoms with thin string sides suited her very well. Her figure was slim and her breasts were petite. He couldn't believe what he was seeing. He felt conflicted seeing her in his mother's bikini, but Susan wore it well. And from memory his mother hadn't worn them in years anyway. She probably wouldn't fit it anymore, not that he'd tell her she had it on. That would be a death sentence.

"Don't get too horny," she laughed. "Your mum has worn this."

"Thanks for that." He smiled seeing the joke. "Not that I would anyway."

"If it makes you happy, I'll wear shorts and a shirt to cover up until we get to the swimming hole."

"Might be a good idea, plus I've got to dink you there anyway and you might get a sore bum on my handlebars."

"Sure, come on let's go." She floated out of the room like a fairy - fresh, light and cheeky.

Jack wondered what he had just gotten himself into. He wondered what happened to the modest Susan who didn't speak to him for days when he accidently caught sight of her femininity.

What the heck, one last splurge before the curfew kicks in.

Jack was right, his baggy clothes did protect her bum as she rode proudly on top of his handlebars. It was a job to keep her legs from hitting the front tyre as her toes gripped the front forks of the bike. Jack needed wheel pegs but he couldn't afford them, besides, he hardly dinked anyone around. This was a long trip for a passenger and he felt sorry for Susan but she seemed to be enjoying herself as she occasionally turned to look at him with a beaming smile.

He was struggling to keep her upright whilst negotiating the undulating bike lane all the while getting whipped in the face by her long hair. In any case this was the fastest way to Glenoma Park for them.

Glenoma Park was a large green grassed area lined with trees and bounded on three sides by the snaking Freshwater Creek. It had plenty of shady areas to swim and was close to their houses. Jack loved it here as it had plenty of flow and some nice spots to jump into the water from the bank. Cane paddocks flanked the western side of the creek, so this stretch of the creek was an oasis for birdlife.

Families came to picnic and play cricket or ball games in the park. The only physical activity Jack and his mates did here was occasionally throw a Frisbee around. With Susan's changed demeanor he thought it might be safer to just have the two of them here today; just as long as he could work out if this was a temporary phase Susan was going through.

They rode through the underpass which got them safely across the highway above. Entering the carpark Jack decided to ride across the ground to the southern side of the park. The grass was lush but bumpy and Susan lifted the weight off her bottom, protecting herself by pushing up on the handlebars.

"Nearly there," Jack promised.

"I don't think my ass can handle anymore pounding."

"Nice way to put it," Jack laughed.

"Shut up. You try and sit up here."

Jack slowed as they reached the tree line and Susan dismounted by jumping forward off the bike.

"That was hard work," Jack's deep breaths was a sign of his unfitness.

"You saying I'm fat?"

"No. It's just hot and the grass is thick. Come on." Jack placed both their towels that he had around his neck on the silty bank. A pair of Torres Strait pigeons who were perched on the inflorescence of an Alexander Palm, which fringed the creek bank, were feeding on the red seeds. They looked wide-eyed at Jack and quickly decided to fly off in a flurry of flapping wings.

Jack got into the water up to his knees and complained about how cold it was. He turned around and saw Susan taking off his clothes that she had borrowed. He couldn't help but stare at her slender figure. She was beautiful. He'd even forgotten that they were his mother's bikinis. She wore them like she owned them.

He glanced downstream and saw a couple of toddlers splashing about on the water's edge. An older woman was keeping a keen eye on them. Possibly a grandparent. They looked like they were having fun and didn't mind the cold - children seemed to have a high tolerance to all things cold.

"Come on, get in, you sook," Susan teased.

"I am, but it's *freezing*."

"That's because it's so hot out here."

"I'll say," Jack said under his breath - he wasn't talking about the temperature.

"What was that?"

"Nothing," he smirked.

"Jack Armstrong, are you flirting with me?"

"What if I was?" He quickly scooped up some water and splashed out at Susan. She squealed when the cold water hit her. With a look of determination she ran, splashed and tackled Jack in the water sending them both crashing down.

They surfaced in fits of laughter.

Susan swished a handful of water at Jack's face with her hand just under the surface of the water. She laughed and splashed downstream to escape his chase. The children who were scooping up silt in coloured buckets looked up at the teenagers. Susan was trapped just before a section of rapids and stooped low in the water. She tried to contain her excitement and hid her huge smile under the waterline. She planned to leap up and spring past him at the right time.

The children's grandmother scowled at the two teenagers for disturbing this quiet part of the creek. She knew cavorting teenagers when she saw them, she could read their body language. She hoped they would rack off downstream. She didn't want her grandchildren to witness any canoodling especially from those with raging hormones.

Look at that child, she's almost naked, no wonder that boy is frolicking around her like some herd bull! Thought the old woman.

Jack was onto Susan's moves, he approached in the crotch deep water with both arms out ready for attack. Susan giggled with his ever closing approach and quickly sprung up and flexed her body to try and escape his outstretched leap. Too late. He grabbed her around the waist and brought her down with a splash in fits of laughter.

He pulled her in towards her as he crouched in the water up to his shoulders. She sat on Jack's legs in the water as they both calmed down. Jack innocently brought his hands down her sides and she wobbled and almost fell off his legs. To steady her he brought a hand up the side of her leg. He was taken aback by the softness of her upper thigh. It felt so good. He kept caressing her there and she let him. Susan's eyes narrowed but she didn't stop him, she felt his touch and wondered if it was his gentle caressing or the cold water that sent a rash of goosebumps across her skin. She wanted more. Water droplets fell from the tips of her wet fringe and tickled his nose - he laughed. Jack moved up to steal a kiss but Susan pushed back and rolled off his legs, splashing in the water.

"We'd better not, not here, there are young kids about," she said looking over towards the children.

Jack wondered if they would ever kiss. They had some close moments - he was ready.

He still thought Susan had a lot to deal with, he still wondered what happened at her aunt's house. But he didn't press. *Give it time.*

The water was cool and refreshing. Their bodies had gotten used to the cold and now they felt relaxed. They both lay in the water in the shallows, heads pointed downstream, letting the water wash through their hair. Letting the water wash away their problems.

After some time, Susan sat up, she let the water pull her hair back into a thick ponytail. She tilted her head to each side to knock the water out of her ears. Jack followed and sat up beside her. He noticed the water catch and glide off her skin, off the small clear hairs that traced her forearms. The black bikini top clung to her breasts and her erect nipples caught his eye, but he looked away quickly before she noticed.

"I wish it was like this every day," he said.

"Yeah it's nice here."

"No, I mean between us. I wish this moment was all that we had, every day. No parents, no school, no bullshit," Jack said as he let handfuls of sand filter through his fingers under the water.

"Yeah, it would be nice," Susan agreed as she placed a hand on his shoulder.

"Do you think there is something here for us?"

"I don't know Jack, I am still thinking about everything. It's such a huge thing to commit to."

"But doesn't moments like this make that decision easy?"

"It makes it even harder for me. It makes me realise what I could lose, not what I have got."

"What does your heart say?" Jack asked.

"If you ask some people, they'll say it's cold."

"But I am asking you."

"I don't know."

Jack turned and looked downstream along the creek bank. The grandmother and children were picking up their buckets and spades and the grandmother was having a hard time coaxing the boy over to get dried. He wanted to keep playing. Much like Jack wanted to keep trying with Susan.

"I hope... I mean I wish there was a way we could take what we have and run with it," Jack said, still looking over at the small children.

"Jack, I need a little more time. I've got some shit to deal with regarding my sister and I don't want to drag you into my problems."

"I'll be here when you're ready."

"I love that, I do, but if we do this, I want to give you my all, not some messed up *thing*. That will ruin any chance of a relationship from the start."

"This is tough Susan."

"If you can wait, the destination will be worth the journey."

"Don't go all metaphorical on me, I just want to be with you."

"I wasn't trying to be, I just don't want to give you my heart if I can't give you my all. Fuck Jack, I don't even know if I am ready? I am scared to give into my feelings."

"Don't be scared Susan, I'll be there to catch your fall."

"Now who's getting all metaphorical," Susan said as she gave him a small swish of water and playfully wet his back.

"Fuck yeah, I've been reading too much of that book. Man, the insights and the poems in that piece of garbage. You'd be glad you didn't read it."

"Hey, that reminds me, did you finish your English assignment?"

"Yeah."

"Great, I thought I'd be with you all day nursing you through the pain of finishing it," Susan laughed.

"That would have been nice, but mostly painful for you. I was over it anyway, I just wanted to get it done," Jack said as he stood up in the water. Water ran down through the thin line of his wispy black chest like a small forest waterfall. His pale skin and inverted chest made a furrow for the water to travel along. She didn't mind that he wasn't in physical form, she thought he was cute. She glanced down at his pants and wondered if he was too excited seeing her in a bikini or was it just some unfortunate folds in the fabric.

"So that chapter of your life is over then, pardon the pun," Susan joked.

"Yeah, it's time I can't get back, I am glad I don't have to deal with it ever again."

He extended his arms to assist Susan up, but she cheekily grabbed the sides of his board shorts and gave them a firm tug. They came down but just stopped short of giving her an eyeful. She was in hysterics, and his frown made it worse, she rolled in the water.

"Okay, you don't get my help then," he said, pulling his togs up but giving her a quick full bum flash first. He sloshed away from her heading back to their towels on the creek bank.

"Oh nice one," she laughed. *Cute bum.* "Jack, please, this time I won't, I promise."

Jack reluctantly came back and pulled her up out of the water with two arms. Susan lost balance and he caught her with their bodies pressing together firmly. She felt his skin on hers, the warmth and closeness sent her small neck hairs on end. She felt his hands lower from the small of her back and cup her bottom.

He lifted her up and they twirled in the water. She loved it and her smile beamed. Taken in by the moment she lent in to kiss him.

"Take it home with you, why don't you!" the grandmother shouted angrily. "There are babies watching you!"

Jack and Susan laughed in hysterics and didn't let go of each other as they watched the old woman shepherd her siblings towards the car park constantly turning back around to scowl at them.

The midday sky was getting darker as a storm approaching from the tablelands hid the sun.

Melaleucas swayed with the gusts of wind like they were beckoning the oncoming storm to come closer. Their yellowing leaves rained down and peppered the parked cars. Anything loose was on the move. Dry fallen leaves from the giant mango tree, which stood tall on the bank above the car park, rattled along the bitumen as they were whisked away. Children in the open grassed area squealed as their beach ball was pushed towards the southern tree line; they wanted to save it from going into the creek. The thick grass swished and rolled in the wind like seagrass in a shallow swell.

The grandmother was now loading her grandchildren into her car and gave one last scowl across to where Jack and Susan were, but they didn't see her as they stepped out of the water up onto the exposed creek bank.

"We'd better go, before we get rained on," Jack said.

"Okay."

Susan quickly toweled herself dry and slipped Jack's loose clothes back on. She pulled at the bikini laces, undoing the knots in both the top and bottom. Pulling them out from under the clothes she shoved them into Jack's stomach so he had to grab them. "Here, take these back."

"You could keep them."

"Your mum would miss them."

"She's long outgrown these, I'm sure she wouldn't know they were gone."

"Jack, you've got a lot to learn about women. Trust me, she would know they were missing."

"Are you sure? They look good on you."

"Gee thanks, but no. Maybe I'll go and get a nice pair for myself. The new Susan needs some new clothes anyway."

Jack shuddered inside, this new personality revolution she was going though hadn't washed away down the creek. *I like the old Susan better than the new one.*

Reluctantly Jack put the wet bikini in his pants pocket and lifted his bike up off its side. "Come on then, jump on."

8 – WRITERS GROUP

The Ford Falcon station wagon pulled up suddenly in the school car park with a squeal of its brakes and it rocked on its spongy suspension. Valerie's eyes had dried but they were red and puffy signaled she had been crying. Mrs. Valentino had done a good job in calming her down, but now it was up to this writers group to help her deal with her emotions. They had been coming here ever since the program started as a recommendation from the child psychologist to help work through her pregnancy and abortion. It had been working but Mrs. Valentino feared this latest conflict with her aunt and sister would be a setback. Being late to the writers group wouldn't help her settle her daughter in quickly either.

Each member of the group was all here for one reason or another. Mrs. Valentino didn't write but came to support Valerie. On the outside, everyone in the group was serious about writing - no one really knew if each other came to resolve any personal issues. They all had a pen name to protect their identity. It was chaired by Mr. Friar and he took great pride in his class.

"Sorry we're late," Mrs. Valentino ushered Valerie to one of the empty seats stationed at a desk which were arranged in a semicircle.

"That's okay, better late than never," Mr. Friar said with a chirp in his voice. He was glad they had made it. Almost a full class. "Now that we are all here, I just want to talk about next Sunday, it will be our final class for the year. We'll have a less structured class and we'll talk more about your future aspirations as a writer. I'll bring in some cake and refreshments, we'll make it fun." His smile beamed around the room, but many of the attendees just gave him a quick smile of recognition. He was always upbeat and jovial.

"Oh, and before I forget, I'll be conducting one last special evening session here this Wednesday at eight o'clock. You don't have to attend but I am sure you all will when you know why." Mr. Friar said with a Cheshire cat grin. "I'll be reading out the book review from one of my pupils for John Bird's novel, Paperback Writer."

Mr. Friar's announcement was met with a round of applause from the writers group. The book review was a long time coming and it would also be the first review for the first novel produced at the writers group. It was highly anticipated by all. Everyone who could, would attend to show their support for John Bird. It was exciting to receive the first review - a milestone for the group.

The class continued on into the afternoon. It mainly consisted of Mr. Friar giving advice to the students as he made his way around to everyone in the class. Sometimes he got each person to read a passage of their work and each student reflected on the writing style, what it meant for them or if they felt it needed adjusting. It was all purely subjective and most of the time the reciter didn't heed any of the advice they were given. As cumbersome as the class was they all enjoyed being with each other. Their common interest in writing actually did wonders for their spirits and drive to continue on with their hobby.

After one lesson held in the middle of the year they had a guest author from Brisbane. She was a wiry woman with a huge personality which commanded the room. Her advice was sound but she was mostly interested in spruiking her own series of crime novels. No one bought a copy and she left feeling quite dejected about the talents of Far North Queenslanders. Valerie thought she was a bit insane. She hoped that all writers didn't end up that way. She was hoping to resolve her emotions through her writing and maybe even earn a living as an author. It was getting increasingly harder to find time to write, especially given her promotion and added training at the fish and chip shop. But one day she hoped to be independent of making someone else rich while she slaved away for them. She hated all the holidays and new shiny things that her boss paraded in front of her.

There was no bell, just a simple thank you from Mr. Friar to mark the end of the lesson.

"Oh and John Bird, as I said, I should expect to see your book's review from my prize student tomorrow. I'll bring it in next week for you to analyse."

9 – SAFE DISTANCE

"Stop, stop, stop. My bum needs a break!"

Jack peddled over towards a large shady tree that covered the bike path. Underneath there was a length of log barricading that would make a good seat to rest on. It had been put there to stop cars, from the adjacent side street, shortcutting across the verge and bike path to enter the main highway. Jack needed to give his legs a rest anyway. He remembered when his brother used to dink him to the park when they were younger. He was brutal though and made sure he hit all the potholes and gutter jumps that he could along the way - no preservation for his bike's tyres or Jack's ass. He wondered why his brother took great pleasure seeing him in pain. Jack on the other hand made sure he took it easy and where he could he let Susan know when the rough sections of bike path were coming up.

"Not far now but man my legs are burning."

"Were you trying to impress me?"

"Not really, I guess I was in the zone, had other things on my mind."

"Thinking about us?"

"That and your sister. I saw the way she stormed out of the car. Is everything all right with her?"

"Not really. I don't know. I thought I had problems but hers seemed far worse."

"Oh?"

They sat there for quite some time, watching the cars speed past on the highway. The storm grew angrier and rumbled in the distance. You could see the rain falling in sheets across the hills as it rolled down the mountain like suds over the edge of a full bathtub. They were safe from the heavy rain but they still caught intermittent drops of rain which was enough to release the sweet smell of petrichor from the hot ground around them. The storm was isolated and heading opposite their direction to the north. The beaches were in for a drenching. The wind and cloud cover to the north had cooled the temperature down but it was still sunny on this side of the storm.

"She had a baby, you know." Susan finally spoke out as she stared vacantly at the light show created by lightning in the clouds.

"What? For real?"

"Well she didn't give birth but it was growing inside her."

"Oh. I am so sorry Susan."

"Don't be, it was news to me this morning."

"When was this? Her pregnancy, that is."

"It was a couple of years ago, when she was in her senior year."

"Oh, I guess that's why she's a bit messed up."

"Yeah but she mustn't know that I told you."

"Of course."

"I trust you Jack and she's guarded that secret from me for so long so she wouldn't trust me again if she found out I told anybody."

"Okay, I get it. There's no need for me to tell anyone anyway."

"Not even your parents."

"No I wouldn't. Why would I when they've smashed me with rules today."

"Rules"

"No more private time with you."

"No way!"

"Yes way, can you imagine how pissed I was?"

"Why? I mean why the rules?"

"They think I was... They think you're a distraction at the moment." Jack said. "*Concentrate on your studies boy!*" Jack did a lame impersonation of his father.

"I see. What made them think I was a distraction?"

Jack didn't see the hole he dug for himself and tried to backpedal out of the conversation. "I don't know, you know how parents are sometimes? If they don't think they have some sort of control of your life then they don't think they are doing a good enough job. Then what would everyone think about them? We can't have anyone gossiping about them can we?"

"Sure," Susan said, knowing Jack dodged her question. A pang of guilt twisted in her stomach. "Mum and Aunt Gillian kind of said the same thing to me about you. They want me to see less of you and concentrate on exams."

"Really?"

"Yes."

"They're all out for us then," Jack said.

Susan was deep in thought and Jack didn't want to interrupt her. He thought he had better get her home because it would be best for her and her sister to talk things over. It would also be good if she were home when they got back so it didn't look like she was uncaring and out having fun. Especially since there was talk about spending less time with Jack. It was best if she didn't appear to be rubbing it in their faces.

These women have so many issues, my home life problems seem insignificant.

They slowed down with one last bump as the bike hit the small concrete lip at the end of Jack's driveway. Once again Susan dismounted unceremoniously by launching herself forward, jumping off and slowing herself down with a short trot. Jack propped the bike up against the low front fence. Susan was eager to get home to process her weekend and wait for her sister and mother to arrive. She knew she was in for some more emotional turmoil and she realised that the swim was exactly what she needed to recharge her batteries.

"Thanks for the swim Jack, it was fun."

"Yeah, all that riding but, I think I need a shower and rest."

"First day back at school tomorrow for you plus exam week starts, it's like we both need a rest today."

"Fun times, are you ready?"

She paused for a moment and Jack thought it was a simple question. He looked at her with a frown. "I am Jack. And I've come to realise that I'm ready to be with you."

"What? Boyfriend and girlfriend?"

"Gee, that sounds pretty official when you say it like that," Susan giggled.

"A couple then?"

"Yes, but not right now."

"Huh?"

"All eyes are on us at the moment, I don't want to get anymore shit from people telling us what to do."

"Since when have we cared about that?"

"I know, but this time we've gotta be serious about things. We'll still see each other at school and stuff, but best you don't come over afterwards."

"Do you think we can steal moments together, without anybody finding out?"

"No. And no public displays of affection either."

"This is going to be hard," Jack reflected.

"I know, do you know how hard it is to have you so close yet you're so far away?"

"Do you think we can make it?"

"I don't know, but we've known each other for so long, we'll make it through anything," Susan encouraged.

There was an awkward pause between the two friends.

"So no cheeky visits?"

"Jack, you're not making this any easier."

"Okay, okay."

"Don't you think we should cool it off a bit anyway? It'll be better that way."

"Yeah but don't you think that sucks?"

"Yeah, but our parents are right - aren't they? It's getting a little intense between us and the timing is a little bad at the moment."

"Wasn't I pretty contained at the creek?" Jack pleaded.

"Yes, but it's only going to get harder not to…It was hard for me too."

She grabbed his shoulders, pushed up on her tippy-toes and kissed him on the cheek.

"What was *that* for?"

"It's a promise kiss."

"A promise kiss?"

"Yeah, a promise that we'll move forward with what we've got once these two and a bit weeks left of school blow over. Think of it as a cute pause on what we've got so we don't ruin things."

"A peck on the cheek, is that all I get?"

"Down boy, this is what I'm talking about Jack. Just a little bit longer and I'll make it worth the wait. Nobody will care what we do then."

Jack gave her a soft wave of his fingers as she skipped away quickly back to her house. *Can't wait.*

10 – HARD LUCK

The bus braked hard and he lurched forward; he gripped the seat handle bar in front with all his strength. It was far too much force for him and his chest crashed into the back of the seat. Ribs bruised and pain flared from the impact zone. He was thrown back into his seat just as violently as the bus stopped dead in its tracks. He felt the tendons in his neck sear in pain as his head was thrown around like a rag doll.

Slumping forward in his seat, his vision was blurred. He couldn't feel Susan; only moments ago their hands were together - fingers entwined. Where was she? He gargled and blood frothed from the corner of his mouth and rolled down his chin. Were his lungs punctured? He wasn't sure if the tightness in his chest and shortness of his breath were any indicators but the insides of the bus started to spin and distort. Stars twinkled in the corners of his eyes and he slumped forward, rolling to the side and across his seat.

He coughed and a thick smattering of blood sprayed across the back of the seat in front. It hung there momentarily then streaked and dripped onto the floor. That's when he saw her. Lying there lifeless. Her pale limbs seemed to be spread in unnatural directions. He tried to scream out her name, but it was muffled and he choked on his own blood. Extending his arm out to reach her seemed impossible as her body had been thrown too far down the aisle way. His weakness was apparent as his arm dropped and he blacked out.

He woke to the sound of running water and children's laughter. A flock of rainbow lorikeets screeched overhead as they flew from a flowering melicope rubra. Boom! The birds were silenced by an explosion in the distance. His eyes came into focus and he was startled by his surroundings. He lay before a clear creek and young children were playing downstream. They had no one looking after them and he had an over extended feeling of trying to protect them. He didn't want to see them fall into the moving water and get swept away and drown. Their steps were clumsy and they fell back on their bottoms close to the water. He yelled out but his voice seemed distant. They couldn't hear him. He was in anguish. He couldn't get up as he was frozen to the bank.

Another flock of lorikeets flew low and down the open canopy of the creek line. This time he saw that they exploded into a million pieces of fireworks.

More laughter turned his attention to the woman in the creek in front of him. She was wearing a black bikini which looked too small for her body. He was sure it was Susan but she was heavier chested, with wider hips and thicker legs. She jumped up and down splashing about in the water and calling him in. His vision was blurred, his head hurt as he tried to focus on her face.

Yet she kept calling his name.

He felt moisture in his pants and he looked down. No this wasn't happening, this can't be a wet dream! He was relieved when he saw the wetness radiate from his pocket from where he saw black strings hanging out.

"Finally Jack, you're awake," his mother said in a disturbed tone as he looked up at her. "Do you know how long I've been standing here calling your name, banging on your desk?"

"What?"

"You heard me, and what's this?" She held up a pair of black bikinis. He looked down at his pocket. It was empty and dry.

My god, what a vivid dream.

He saw the look of disappointment in his mother's eyes. He looked away. There was no escape.

"Um, I can explain," Jack gulped. He was at a loss for words, he had fallen asleep on his bed. It was dark outside, he didn't know what the time was but he guessed it was late.

"I didn't think it was true at first, but when I saw this crumpled on your floor I couldn't believe my eyes!" she said astounded.

"Um," Jack stumbled.

"Jack what are you doing with my bikinis in your room and on your floor?" she shouted.

Jack shrugged. Any answer would have been the wrong answer.

"Also, what are these skimpy girls clothes doing under your bed?" She held up Susan's clothes in her other hand. She had them behind her back all along. It had been a ploy to show her anger in stages.

Jack had nothing but a look of horror on his face.

"I don't know?" *That's it, play dumb.*

"And can you tell me why all your clothes are still in the washing machine? They've gone musty sitting there and it's going to take a lot of washes to get the smell out!"

"Oh no! I forgot, I was just trying to help."

"You forgot, thanks for that, you've given me more work than I needed."

"Sorry Mum."

"Sorry doesn't cut it Jack. I think you need to come downstairs right now and have a chat with your father and I - we've got to sort out what's going on with you. Especially before he goes off to site tomorrow and before you go to school."

"Great," Jack muttered.

She left the room and headed downstairs, he could hear their heated exchanges. No doubt they were discussing how it ended up like this. How the lack of discipline in the family ended up with their son with a pair of his mother's swimming togs and some girl's skimpy clothing under his bed. He could only think that they thought their son was a pervert. A snow dropper maybe? The evidence was glaringly obvious and in their face, especially with the conclusions they had jumped to at lunchtime today.

He decided to face the music. Get it over and done with, quick like taking off a Band-Aid.

"Sit down," said his father in a gruff voice. Jack obliged, his head down. "Your mother and I want to know where you're getting your stuff from."

"Stuff?"

"Yes, do I have to spell it out for you?"

Jack gulped, he was lost. *What stuff?* He could only think of one thing that they were talking about.

"It's from Susan," Jack mumbled.

"Susan?" Slowly repeated his father, looking vaguely at his wife, letting the words sink in.

"I knew that girl was a bad influence. How long has she been giving you drugs?"

"What, no Mum, I thought you were talking about the clothes! There's been no drugs."

"What? These clothes?" she said, still holding on to them. "These haven't come from Susan, I've seen her walking about covered up like a vampire, and she's too prudish to wear these slutty numbers."

Jack couldn't believe what he was hearing. This was the girl that had been Jack's friend for years. Susan was practically like a daughter to them. Why had everything changed? Now they were talking about her with such conviction. What was going on?

"The only reason we can think that you've been stealing these clothes is because you're jacked up on some kind of drug, you're not making any rational decisions boy," his father said.

"Drugs?"

"There's no other explanation," his mother said with her hands on her hips.

"Guys, I haven't taken drugs, not ever."

There was a long silence in the room. A gecko chirped somewhere outside on the patio. A siren was wailing somewhere in the distance. His mother's perfume assaulted the air every time she changed positions for comfort. Jack wanted to go back to his bedroom and dissolve into his bed sheets.

"I tell you what Jack, I am going away for my next two week roster. And I know that coincides with your end of year exams and graduation - I'm sorry. But if your mother tells me of any bullshit stunts like this while I am away then there will be a lot more to deal with when I come back," his father said sternly, complete with flared eyes and engorged veins on his temple.

"Sure."

"Sure? Is that all you can say?" His father was enraged. "How about some respect for your mother and I? We both slave our guts out for you and your brother and look at the thanks we get. This house isn't big enough for the both of us and I know which one of us will be leaving if things around her don't change."

"Sorry Dad, I promise I won't do anything like this again."

"For a start, I don't want you hanging around Susan again, you hear? Not until you've graduated."

"But…"

"No *fucking* buts Jack, get your dick back in your pants, you're parading around here like some jacked up Chihuahua!" said his father. "You know what you're doing? You're trying to extrude your brain though your dick!"

"George!" his mother tried to clip his father's aggressive derogatory abuse.

"Well the sooner he realises what he's doing, the better off he'll be," he reasoned with her. "It's for your own good mate."

Jack's father stormed off downstairs.

Jack was angrier than ever. His fists were clenched and his eyes watered. He wouldn't cry this time, but he also knew when to back down - it was no use arguing. It was time to think smarter about how he progressed with Susan. *Nobody tells me how to feel, especially when it comes to Susan. Fuck them.*

"Come on mate, she'll always be there, you just need to focus on the future. Do you promise to try just for our sake?"

Jack's thoughts boiled over in his mind but he worked out long ago that it was easier not to argue when they thought they knew best. It was easier to be quiet, the yelling usually stopped quicker that way. Pausing for a moment he tried his hardest not to deliver a sarcastic tone in his reply. "Okay. I promise."

11 – MONDAY PARADE

Jack hoped for a better day today; a bad day at home usually meant an inversely proportional good day at school and vice versa - that was his relative theory of happiness. His first day back and he was kind of happy, he was going to unload his English assignment like a weight off his shoulders. He was going to talk to Susan but she wasn't at their bus stop this morning and he wondered if her sister was going to run her in. He didn't mind, after last night's grilling from his parents he needed a breather, he needed some time to think about what they said. Maybe they were right and she was distracting him from finishing his year strongly. But it made his head hurt and his heart tightened when he thought about distancing himself from Susan. He was falling for her in a strong way.

This week was going to be tough. He had a schedule of exams which were going to start tomorrow; he was lucky that his

Monday was free of exams - something he and Susan had reflected on when she brought home his exam timetable last week. During his recovery time he hadn't had a chance to do a great deal of study. Besides, he always crammed the night before and even up to the last minute reading his notebooks just before the teacher opened the exam room and ushered the students in. Procrastination was his best friend and his greatest enemy.

The bus bounced along the road, Jack looked out the window and watched the school kids riding their bikes to school. He pitied them on such a hot morning. They often arrived at school with sweat patches on their backs where their backpacks had been. When the bus pulled up at the school he saw Tim and Patrick hovering around the gate. It looked like an intervention was about to take place, or maybe a celebratory welcome with fanfare and ticker tape.

"Hey Jack, wait up," Tim said as Jack strode past. He wanted to ignore them. Their comments still marred his thoughts, but he wanted to let go of his frustration with his mates - after all they were his mates.

"Hey Jack, we're sorry, can you just hold up a second," Patrick said.

Jack stopped and took his earbuds out. He looked at their confused and frowning expressions. They looked like a pair of dancing monkeys as they tried to formulate an apology.

"Guys, it's been a long weekend, your comments were brutal but can we just forget about it? We're mates and I couldn't imagine if it weren't all four of us."

"Yeah, sure," Tim said with a look of relief washing over his face. "Speaking of all four of us, where's Susan?"

"Don't know, she must have slept in, her sister will probably drop her off."

"Come on then, let's go to the parade, she'll catch up later," Patrick said.

Monday morning was the usual whole school assembly, which was called the parade. Aching asses on hard concrete is what Jack hated the most; long boring messages or presenting of awards that seemed to drag on forever.

"How was your Sunday," Jack asked, trying to spur on a conversation.

"It was okay, we ended up going to see that new movie just out," Tim said.

Patrick elbowed him and gave him a scornful look. "You weren't supposed to say," he muttered.

"What movie?"

"Jurassic Park," Tim answered.

"Oh dudes, I wanted to see that, thanks for asking *me!*"

"Um, you didn't look like you were in the mood to hang around us," Patrick said.

"Was it any good?"

"It was okay," Tim lied. "Patrick was in it."

"What?" Patrick thumped him in the arm.

"You know, Newman from Seinfeld."

"You think I am fat like he is?"

"No, just that you're good on computers..."

"Lucky," Patrick warned.

"...and you've got a hidden nasty streak." he said laughing and running ahead to escape a swinging arm from Patrick.

"Don't worry mate, we'll go again, it was an epic movie," Patrick reasoned with Jack as they strode towards the parade hall.

Tim got caught up ahead by a teacher who he nearly ran into and was made to do a spot pick up of rubbish as punishment. Patrick gave him a sarcastic smirk as they walked past.

"Hey dude, about Susan, sorry about the comment yesterday."

"Don't worry about it."

"Nah, it's okay, it's just that we've been seeing you two guys get really close and I just wanted you to look out for yourself."

"What do you mean?"

"I've seen what happens when you break up with a girl. My brother used to burn girls like they were cheap matches. But one thing I did notice was that they never spoke to him again. There were so many times when we were out shopping when he had to dodge one of his exes - it was never a good thing."

"Sounds tragic," Jack said sarcastically. "But isn't your older brother quite the ladies' man?"

"Yeah, he's had no trouble finding a date, but what I am getting at is when he ends it with them it becomes, let me put this in scientific terms, quite a Supernova. The existence of life is wiped out and there is a deep depressing vacuum of nothing."

"What's your point?"

"I just don't want that nothingness between all of us when you break up with her," Patrick said looking sad.

"What? We aren't going out yet, and if we were, and things went bad I am sure we could work things out so that we'd still talk," Jack said. The truth was he'd been so wrapped up in his own feelings he hadn't considered the dynamics of his group if there was a fallout. This made things much trickier.

"I suppose so," Patrick said, giving him the benefit of the doubt.

"We've been friends for a long time, I am sure we'll be okay."

The bell rang and all the students started to pack the entrance to the hall making their way to their form rows. The seniors held back because they were at the back of the hall. By the time the second bell had sounded all the students from each grade were sitting in an orderly fashion. The principal walked out in front, there was no stage, just a wall stood behind him in the open sided shed. The microphone squealed with feedback as it was turned on and the congregation groaned too enthusiastically in unison.

"Okay, okay, quiet please," Mr. Hadrick ordered the students, his voice booming through the loudspeakers.

Nancy Smith shushed her form group and waved her form roll at them to be obedient. Jack rolled his eyes at her.

"Okay, thank you, firstly good morning students," Mr. Hadrick continued.

"Good morning Mr. Hadrick," responded the students together in a drawn out melody.

"Right, we've got a bit to get through this morning so I'll be brief," he said looking around the hall. "Firstly and most importantly, the stolen money hasn't been returned. The amnesty period is over and the matter has now been handed over to Evansdale Police. You'll be pleased to know that there will be no more parades held for punishment, everyone has got the idea that there are consequences to people's actions. This will be felt no more so than the seniors. As the stolen money was to fund the senior formal, there will be a venue change and there will have to be some fundraising activities, necessary to help bridge the gap.

Ms. Smith will inform the seniors on these activities, so seniors please stay behind after this parade for the additional information."

"Oh man," groaned Patrick. He had no intention to go to the formal and the idea of fundraising sounded horrendous.

As Mr. Hadrick changed his discussion to sun smart awareness Susan slipped in through behind the row of students and sat at the end of their form group. Jack looked up and caught her eye. She gave a quick smile as she sat down. She looked flustered. She was also wearing her usual long skirt and baggy oversized top. Jack figured she had lost an argument at home and was forced to wear what she normally wore. There was no tight top or short skirt today.

As Jack predicted, the parade carried on for an eternity with drawn out notices and awards: exam room notifications, younger grade civic awards, Christmas concert preparation notifications, cyclone awareness, end of year break up notices, band meetings, various extracurricular group end of year break up notices. The various leg change positions hadn't helped Jack from getting a numb rear. Everyone was restless so when the final reading was finished the seniors grumbled with relief. The seniors remained seated as all the other year levels got up and dispersed through the exits.

"Right, now I know some of you have exams to get to but this is important to let you know about the formal," Nancy Smith said as she gathered the group together. "This may not be pertinent to you all, since some of you have chosen not to attend the formal, but I am only going to say this once so you can all listen in."

"We are down two thousand dollars all thanks to the theft from the staff room. What that means is that we can't have the venue at the Cairns International Hotel."

There were several groans which radiated around the group. The group of about 120 seniors all gave looks of concern.

"Therefore we have to hold the formal here in this hall."

"Oh no," a girl said in the group.

"That's shit," said another.

"Here?" said another.

"Okay, okay, quiet please!" Nancy Smith said to control the group. "I know that this is undesirable but we were not able to come up with the funds to pay for the venue, we also lost five hundred dollars in a booking fee, because we had to cancel, so we are out of pocket two and a half thousand dollars."

"To be able to have food, DJ and decorations for the night we have to raise funds. So the only quick and profitable solution is to have a car wash."

More groans radiated around the hall.

"It will be compulsory for all those attending the formal and it will be this Saturday morning at the Evansdale Shopping Centre car park."

Further groans started to infuriate Ms. Smith.

"There will be no acceptations to the rule, you will all be helping at the car wash. And be warned, we will not be offering adult services so boys and especially to the girls, make sure you dress accordingly otherwise there'll be strict repercussions."

Everyone glanced at each other comprehending how their existing weekend plans were now ruined. Jack wasn't going to the formal, Susan had shown no interest, so he was safe, and it was probably for the best at the moment with his parents on heightened alert with him. The seniors dispersed in a more orderly fashion than the junior school, because most of them had exams to attend for which they were now running late for.

"Jack, wait up," Susan called.

"What happened this morning?"

"You don't want to know."

"Did it involve a wardrobe malfunction?" Jack laughed.

"More like a wardrobe mafia, my sister saw me leaving in her old high school skirt and she flipped out."

"Oh," Jack said.

"It's probably okay though, it was a little breezy under there," she laughed. "I had to change and she dropped me off."

"So it's okay between you two?"

"This morning seemed like a setback between us, you know – with stealing her clothes, but she seems more civil with me. At least we are talking."

"Cool."

"Yeah, one day she'll tell me all about it I guess."

They said bye to each other and headed off in their different directions to their first class. Susan had a biology exam, Tim and Patrick had chemistry exams and Jack had a final Ancient History lesson before his exam tomorrow. They all had English before recess and Jack was looking forward to getting rid of his assignment and the book that had taken so much of his freedom. He was glad reading it was over, now he had to concentrate on his exams to prove to his parents that he was more than just a boy led by his genitals.

By the time English came around Jack was quite bored - equally so because Mr. Friar was running late. But then he saw his unmistakable bounced walk, as he flitted past the classroom windows, and made his way to the front door. He was beaming with excitement.

"Oh hello Mr. Armstrong," was the first thing he said as he addressed the class. "So good to see you. How's the body holding up?"

Was he genuinely interested in Jack's welfare or was it all to do with getting his writing group buddies novel reviewed? "Fine sir, it's like the accident never happened."

"Good, good. And your report?"

Jack didn't hesitate, he rose from his chair, grabbing the assignment and novel from his bag and made his way to the front of the classroom placing them on the teacher's desk.

"Ah, thank you. I can't wait to grade it."

A huge relief washed across his body. Jack was at a stage where he couldn't care less what mark he was given for the assignment, his reward was that it was gone. Never to return again.

His daydreaming hadn't bode well for him on his way back to his desk, Jonas stuck a leg out and tripped him, causing him to lurch forward and crash into other student's desks, much to their annoyed glares. Jack turned to see Jonas smirking.

"Be careful Jack, you've had one too many crashes of late. I'll grade this shortly and get you the results by the end of the week," he said with a smile in his voice. "Okay everyone, since we are starting exam week, let's go over some of the literary pieces we have read throughout the year and reflect on the trials and tribulations, their idealisms and we'll sit a spot exam to keep you on your toes."

The class groaned but got on with the task. The end was in sight for the year. Only a few more hurdles to jump.

It was like a chanting noise and it was coming from behind the toilets which were adjacent to the drama building. If Jack pricked his ears he could almost make out the works. It sounded like hissing in a way, maybe some of the girls were practicing for the end of year concert - though it sounded quite morbid. Curiosity got the better of him so he decided to take a look.

The chanting got louder as he approached and it took him a few moments to register what he was seeing. A circle of girls all fluffed up and full of scorn like brooding hens seemed to be pushing someone about as though they were a human pinball, bouncing from one to the other.

Dust floated above dirty white ankle socks and grubby shoes as the pack danced around their victim.

"Sissy, Sissy, Sissy," the girls chanted.

"What the?" Jack said. *Seriously does this shit still happen?*

No one saw or heard him approach, they were too transfixed on their goal. Total humiliation.

"Hey, leave her alone!"

"Piss off Armstrong," Meredith said as she broke ranks and faced Jack with her arms crossed.

"I mean it! Leave her alone!"

"Girls, Sissy's lover is here to rescue her, the dork in shining Alfoil!" Meredith said, resulting in a round of laughs.

Jack broke through the circle of girls and was confronted with Sissy who by now had tears streaming down her face which caught dirt and matted her curls. She looked down in embarrassment which was a bad move because she didn't see the one last shove she was given, sending her crashing to the ground.

"You want to take her place Jack-off?" Meredith threatened.

"Fuck off. All of you, just fuck off!"

"Aw, look girls, maybe he does have a backbone," Meredith said to more laughs. "But he's still just a weakling, maybe more of a sissy than Sissy."

Jack would never punch a girl but his anger was rising, his face full of scorn.

"Come on girls, we wouldn't want 'Jack-off' to go all psycho on us," Meredith said. "Even though he's gutless, just ask Jonas."

The parting comment was a reference to the building tension between Jack and Jonas, the beating he coped before the bus accident. Jack thought it was all over. Two weeks off school to recover wasn't enough. There was always going to be tension between them but it seemed Jonas had been spreading rumors while he'd been recovering, to keep fueling the fire.

Jack turned to help Sissy. Her schoolbag had torn and books were spread across the dirt. Most of them had been trodden on. Jack felt sorry for her. He helped her up by the arms and assisted her to sit on a fence log barrier – the style of which bordered most of the walkways around the school; they were used to prevent students from short cutting across the grass lawns and to keep children on the concrete pathways.

Sissy was too embarrassed for words and she mouthed 'thank you' to him while she dusted off her long skirt and wiped the tears from her face - only muddying it further from the dust mixture. She knew she shouldn't have gotten herself into that situation but she was trying to save time by shortcutting through the buildings where she stumbled upon the group of girls; it was a case of wrong place, wrong time. This was their hangout - they were drama girls.

"Are you okay?" Jack asked, the vigour of his concern was still fueled by the adrenalin pumping in his body.

Sissy looked away in shame, her pride had been bruised but she was okay. She could normally defend herself but the girls took her down like a pack of cunning hyenas – she thought they laughed like hyenas anyway.

"I'll be fine," she whispered.

Turning away Jack took to picking up her possessions and tried to gather them into her torn bag. He had it all together when one piece of paper dropped out of a book. It flipped on its edge before falling into the dust.

Crouching he carefully gathered it up and realised it was a flyer for the school formal. Sissy pounced, snatching it out of his hands like a hunting cat taking its prey.

"Sorry," Jack said, not realising its importance to her.

"Don't be, it's okay," Sissy said, annoyed that it slipped from its hiding place.

"It's for the formal right?"

"Yeah."

"Are you going?"

"No!" Sissy's sharp glare cut like a knife.

"Oh, okay."

After an awkward silence. "Are you?" Sissy asked cautiously.

"Not me either," Jack said with a smile.

"Jack, did you want to go with me?"

"To the formal?"

The question took Jack by surprise. *Susan doesn't want to go but if I went with Sissy what would she think? If I go with Sissy would it be out of sympathy especially after this? But the look in her eyes! It's like I'm denying a puppy some food if I don't answer her.*

"Um," Jack hesitated. *Come on man just say no!* He watched her pull a strand of curls from her eyes as she looked up at him blinking. She touched her hair and smiled, looking away shyly – all the flirting rules in the book, but she knew what she was doing.

"Um, I suppose." *Fuck!*

"You don't have to, I just thought it might be nice."

Being in a bus crash is nice, getting birds blown up in your face is nice but going to the formal! "Yeah, nah it'll be good," Jack lied.

"Awesome!" Sissy said, her mood had piped up. "How about coming over and meeting Dad, he'd want to see who is taking me to the formal, out of respect and all."

Woah, this is moving along way too quickly. "Um, okay but how about Wednesday afternoon?" He needed time to smooth things over with his mother and especially break the news to Susan.

"Cool, you can stay for dinner then." Sissy seemed to skip away cheerfully like nothing had ever happened.

12 – MEET THE PARENT

Wednesday afternoon came around too fast for Jack's liking. Even sitting exams during the day hadn't drawn out the impending appointment - meeting Sissy's dad. He would be happy to say hello and shake his hand but now Sissy had made a big deal out of it and they had to have a sit down dinner. It was only a formal, they weren't getting married.

Pausing at her front door Jack's nerves got the better of him and he let his heart race in his chest. Although he saw Mr. Smart every time he got on the bus, this was his home, this was his daughter. Did Mr. Smart think he was trying to take his daughter away from him? Jack knew how he felt about Sissy, this was only for her sake, but did her father think he was trying to take his daughter's innocence away from her? He shuddered at the thought. Sissy was okay looking but she exhibited a personality that Jack couldn't stand. She was too airy. He definitely would never consider her as girlfriend material. There was someone special out there for her but it wasn't Jack.

The mat at the front door said 'Welcome' and it was true, everything looked welcoming. The house, although old and small, was well maintained and in pretty good condition – it looked like it had full time maintenance staff looking after it: freshly painted, windows clean, pathway from the front gate pressure washed, plants meticulously trimmed, gardens mulched. Jack assumed that driving a bus in the morning and afternoon was all that Mr. Smart did, and that the rest of his time was devoted to his little palace.

He was tired of looking around and hanging out on the front porch like a nervously grinning garden gnome or an anxious child door knocking at a stranger's house for fundraising. *Let's get this over with.*

His knock was met with a warm welcome, Jack received a firm handshake, beaming smile and he was almost pulled off his feet as he was ushered inside quickly. Jack had assumed wrongly. *Maybe Mr. Smart wants me to take his daughter off his hands?* It was a cool change, an air conditioner was running and Jack instantly was drawn through to the back of the house to where the smell of something delicious was cooking. Sissy was nowhere to be seen. Jack was still nervous, he was hoping Sissy would protect him from this awkwardness.

"So Jack, you want to take my beautiful daughter to the formal?" Mr. Smart's voice was deep and commanding - no mucking around, straight to the point.

"Um, yes sir."

Mr. Smart frowned. Jack's response had been a test. He wanted a strong boy to date his daughter. The weak response had proven otherwise.

"Your parents, they must be proud of their son showing responsibility and respect, to take my daughter?"

"Yes sir, they are proud." Jack didn't know what Mr. Smart was really on about. *Mum was way too happy for me to go with your daughter, guess she loves the distance it will put between me and Susan.*

"I hope you've got good intentions."

Ah, so that's the responsibility angle, he thinks I want to deflower his daughter? "Oh, yes sir, I wouldn't dare hurt Sissy, she's a good friend."

Mr. Smart felt some comfort but wondered why he'd never heard of Jack being a friend until this week. If he was such a 'good' friend then this wouldn't be true – he had his doubts about Jack but he seemed like a nice boy on the outset and from seeing him on the bus.

"What do your parents do?"

"Dad works at the mines, fly in, fly out, and Mum's a cleaner at one of the hotels in town." Jack's answer was clear, these questions he could handle.

"Very good. Armstrong, I've heard that name before." Mr. Smart looked Jack over with a curious eye.

"Probably because my brother caught the bus a couple of years ago before he graduated."

"Ah, yes, what was his name? Don't tell me, Clint, that's it. He was a good boy, what's he up to now?"

He's a stay at home loser. "Um, he's still looking for work, he had a gap year and he'd had trouble with a few jobs. He wanted an apprenticeship, so he's still waiting on a few responses."

"He's leaving it a bit late, two years out, he should be door knocking business, pestering them."

"Yeah, Mum and Dad are always on to him about it, but he seems more interested in riding his motorbike with his mates."

"Ah well, we're only young once."

Jack wasn't enjoying the third degree questioning and looked around nervously hoping Sissy would save him at any minute.

"You hungry?" Mr. Smart said as he stirred the large pot bubbling away on the stove top.

As long as you aren't serving Sissy chopped up in that pot? "Um, yes, can't wait."

There was a long pause and Jack looked around the kitchen to divert the awkward silence. It was odd that only pictures of Sissy hung on the walls.

"About the crash Jack," Mr. Smart said, still hovering over the stove top.

Jack was wondering when it might be brought up. "Please sir, it's quite okay."

"No, no I must apologise. I count my lucky stars every day that no one was killed. For the life of me I don't understand what went wrong. The guys down at the depot reported it to be a mechanical fault, but they don't buy into it."

"They blame you?"

"No, I've worked there for twenty five years, they trust me like no one else. They are certain someone else tampered with the steering system, but the investigators couldn't find anything out of the ordinary." He paused to taste the sauce on the wooden spoon. "It's got us all stumped. How have you pulled up, are you okay?"

"I am okay."

"Not physically, mentally. I have nightmares you know?" Mr. Smart offered.

"I haven't told anyone, but I have them too, but I'll be okay."

"I am so sorry Jack, if there is anything I can do to help?"

"No sir, I'll be okay sir,"

"Please, my father was sir, please call me Bill."

"Okay sir, um Bill."

They both smiled, now Mr. Smart looked at the doorway which led off the kitchen, Sissy was taking her sweet time.

"What do you do for fun Jack?"

"I hope he's not giving you the third degree," Sissy said as she entered the room with an explosion of enthusiasm, wild red hair flailing about which made her boy's clothes look very plain. Jack was surprised by what she was wearing, he'd never seen a girl intentionally dress like a boy before unless it was for school sports day. Even Susan who liked baggy clothes at school wore skirts and strappy singlets at home.

Maybe Mr. Smart always wanted a boy? Jack thought. "Um, no, hey Sissy!" Jack's relief of her arrival was a little too obvious.

The trio moved into the dining room, Jack was still weary of Mr. Smart, but he guessed he was a typical protective father. Jack hadn't experienced this, his parents were protective but more so for potential dangers in their natural environment: flooded creeks, snakes, crocodiles, riding their bikes, wearing sunscreen, crossing the road. Jack also hadn't seen it with Susan's mother as she was more concerned with how she was going mentally after her father had left them – if there were concerns over boys with Susan, Jack hadn't seen Mrs. Valentino's warnings.

Sissy was also hard to read. Her wild look matched her wild personality, it was hard to keep a conversation going with her, and maybe that was the artist in her. Jack did like her paintings and wondered what other talents she might be good at.

"Please sit down," Bill said. "I know it's an early dinner, but we've got to go out this evening, Sissy has her writers group to go to."

"Writers group?"

"Yes, I'm sure Sissy will tell you all about it while I go plate up dinner."

"So you have some more hidden talents?" Jack asked as Bill left the room.

"Um, I suppose so, I don't think I am too good though."

"You sure? If your paintings are anything to go by then I am sure you're brilliant. You know, left brain and all."

"Gee thanks, you think my brain is sexy?"

Here we go again, left field. "Um probably, but I'd have to see," Jack joked.

"Maybe you could scoop it out after dinner, for dessert!"

"Aw, yuck Sissy!"

She laughed and gave a little snort thinking how clever she was. "I'll read you some of my work after dinner, does that sound better?"

"Cool."

There was an awkward silence as they both heard Mr. Smart scraping the pot on the stove and clinking lids as he was getting dinner ready.

"Hey, who else is in the writers group? Mr. Friar mentioned it to me once, but made out it was some secret society." Jack said.

"Oh it is, I could tell you but I'd have to kill you," Sissy said bluntly.

Jack smiled as though she were joking but his gaze was met with a deep frown. *Serious shit then.*

Jack tried a different angle. "So do you know John Bird?"

"No. Should I?"

He could tell she was lying by the way she looked away from him when she answered.

"What about poetry with the line, 'flip the children's carriage, drink the pain they feel'?"

"Interesting, sounds quite dark, I like it. But no, I am not into poetry, and I've never heard that line before. Why all these questions Jack?" Sissy's eyes narrowed.

"It's something that has been bugging me for a while. But hey, I'll get over it." Jack said, not quite sure if Sissy knew what he was talking about and not really caring if she didn't. Sissy would have known who Jack Bird was, she was in the secret writers group. They were sworn to strict secrecy and Jack was getting nowhere with her, maybe it was something he could bring up with her again some other time. Surely she'd give him some ideas on who was who in the group. He had a terrible gut feeling that someone in the group, namely John Bird, was behind the recent spate of accidents that had included him. Jack wondered what it would take for Sissy to break the secrecy.

He could tell he had agitated Sissy and now there was more awkward silence as she made shapes in the tablecloth by gathering folds with her butter knife. Luckily Mr. Smart bound through the door, holding plates of steaming food, just in time to save Jack.

"Hope you're hungry, I've made a lot!" Bill smiled. Jack wondered where Sissy got her personality from, or how it got so twisted, because Mr. Smart was charming.

The rest of the dinner went well. Sissy acted quite normal around her dad, although at times she was a little childish in the way she looked for his attention. Jack realised she must have had a hard upbringing with no siblings and no motherly guidance. Mr. Smart had done quite well considering he was on his own. They spoke more about the bus accident, about Mr. Smart's employment, future even on how Sissy was trying to get into university and do an arts degree. Jack hadn't thought that far ahead, he was still looking at options. He hoped he had more initiative than his brother though.

Jack helped Mr. Smart clean up the table while Sissy mysteriously went back to her room. *What the hell is she doing in there?*

"That's okay Jack, you go, Sissy will be waiting for you."

"Are you sure sir, um Bill?"

"Yes go ahead."

Jack placed the tea towel he was using on a hook, wiped his hands on his pants and headed for the hallway.

"Oh and Jack."

"Yes Bill?"

"Make sure you keep her bedroom door open."

Jack flushed red with embarrassment. *Surely he wasn't thinking I was going to try anything with his daughter?* "Yes sir," Jack said, slinking around the corner.

The room was at the end of the hallway, next to the bathroom. It was a small house so Jack could tell that Bill's room was closest to the lounge room. The third room looked like it was for storage as it was dark and Jack could make out stacks of boxes, varying in shape and size.

Sissy was quietly sitting at her desk when Jack entered her room, her fingers twirling a lock of curly red hair as though she was deep in thought. She seemed to be writing something on a piece of paper. Jack didn't disturb her as his eyes wandered around the room. Unlike his room, hers wasn't adorned with band posters, rather there were quite a few paintings and Jack assumed they were her own work. The subject matter varied yet the style was all from the same person, all jarringly abstract yet somehow beautiful in their delivery. There were so many paintings hanging on the walls that the room smelt like one of the art rooms at school; a mix of wet acrylic paint or the smell of pastel chalk hung in the air. It was quite different to the smell of floral perfume in Susan's room. Jack didn't mind it though, it was his kind of smell, all industrial, like progress and work had been done there.

Sissy stirred a little on her chair. "You can come in you know, close the door, sit on my bed."

"Um, actually your dad just told me not to."

"What, not to get on my bed?"

"No, to close your door."

Still not facing him Sissy stretched her neck to the side like she was trying to release built up tension. "Well get on my bed then."

Jack sat on the edge of her bed and looked as uncomfortable as a dog being taught a new trick, and not knowing if they were being disobedient to their master while hoping they were doing the right thing.

"Good," she said as she heard her old innerspring mattress ping under his weight. "Now, I've just finished one of my latest chapters, and I'll read to you a paragraph. Let me know what you think?"

"Okay."

Sissy turned in her chair and holding the paper out in front of her she read out loud the paragraph.

"Her skin burned to his silken touch. He didn't realise how he made her feel, how her heart knocked like the pounding of a herd of brumbies hooves across a furrowed mountain track. Her spirit raced like the horses in the crisp alpine air, he had that effect on her, yet he didn't know it. He was trapped like a fly in the web of a widow making spider. She could lay it out for him, bare her soul but she wanted him to want her the same way - she wanted him to conquer her. If he wasn't ready then she would have to wait. Wait for the spider to suck his entrails out and leave him a shell of a being. Then she would be there to catch his fall from the web. To cradle him and to bring him back to life. He'd realise that she had been here all along, his feelings for her would blossom like a night bloom, whose flower's nectar is only for the moth, not the bee. In the end he would be drunk on her nectar and they would be one."

Sissy paused. She rubbed an eye like she was stubbing the flow of tears. Jack didn't pick up on that or the probable message in her writing.

"So what do you think?" She said impatiently.

"Um, it's beautiful Sissy, it sounds like a romance novel. What's it about?"

"Oh thanks, it's pretty rough at the moment but yes it's a bit of a high school romance with a love triangle. The main guy's a dick though and doesn't know when he's got a good thing, he's stuck in a loveless relationship, but it all changes after a few tragic events."

"Oh, a bit of a thriller as well?"

"Yeah, you could say that. I was heading that way with it but not sure if I should turn it into a murder mystery instead."

"Oh well, I am sure you've got the talent to make it into a great novel, no matter which way you go with it," Jack said.

"Thank you, you're too kind." She smiled at him and tossed the paper back onto her desk. She jumped onto the bed and almost launched him off the other side. She laughed and Jack also saw the humour in it.

"Hey, with the formal, my dress is red so you'll have to wear a red flower on your lapel."

"Okay, wow, you've got your dress already?"

"Yeah, you have to, this time of year, all the school formals are on and there isn't much to offer in Cairns. I had to order mine from Brisbane."

"That sounds expensive?"

"Yeah it was."

"Sissy, I hope it wasn't too much?"

"It's okay, I found a way to fund it," she said matter-of-factly.

"Cool, anyway I'd better go and let you get ready for your writers group. Your work sounds great and I can't wait to read it when it's finished."

"I don't know if I'll ever be finished."

"What do you mean?"

"Jack, it's tough, do you know what it takes to get a story together? There is heaps of research, you've got to make sure your work is homogeneous, that the story will be interesting, that the characters are realistic and likeable. It's a tough job, but I find it rewarding, especially when someone like you says that they like what they've read."

"Or what they've been read to." Jack smiled.

"Yes. So with my story it's coming along, but I might need to do some more research or method acting if you will."

"Oh, okay," Jack said, not quite understanding what Sissy was on about.

"Before you go, there is something I want to show you."

"What is it?"

Sissy looked deep into his eyes, he gulped as she blinked longingly at him. She slowly unbuttoned his shirt from the top down. His heart raced, he wanted to stop her but he was frozen. Her eyes penetrated into his soul. He couldn't turn away. She slid a hand between his open shirt like a snake negotiating an opening between hanging curtains and she gently traced her fingers across his chest. She played with the wispy hair that grew down the centre of his torso before settling her warm, firm hand high on the left side of his chest.

"I can feel your heartbeat," she breathed softly.

Jack gulped again. A bead of sweat rolled down from the side of his forehead. His eyes momentarily breaking from her gaze and darting to her open bedroom door.

"Relax, Dad won't see us, he'll be engrossed in the news," she said rolling her eyes - like the news was a waste of time for her.

"Sissy, please!"

"Don't you like this?"

"Yes, but..."

Before he could think she took hold of his right hand and brought it up under her loose t-shirt. His palm brushed her erect nipple before she pressed his hand high above her breast - she held it there firmly.

"Can you feel my heartbeat?" she asked with a smile in her eyes.

He was surprised about how well he could feel her heart. "Yes, but Sissy..." Jack stumbled. He was confused. Was he betraying Susan? She said they needed a 'pause', but he was sure this wasn't what she'd meant. "I really shouldn't."

"She's not here Jack," she said, knowing his hang-up for Susan. "It's just you and me. All that's holding us back are these thin slips of clothes." she whispered. She could hear the TV in the lounge room and her father let out a gentle cough. The thought of getting caught excited her.

"It's not that Sissy. I don't really have those feelings..." He stopped himself short of making her feel bad. He really wasn't into her. She was a friend and he was trying to figure out how she could have gotten the wrong intentions about him.

"But Jack, I know how you truly feel." She lowered his hand to fully cup her breast, moving her free hand she touched the front of his pants - he flinched. "See, I can feel you're loving this."

Jack pulled his hand from her shirt quickly and stood up, backing away from her bed. He felt like he was cheating on Susan. He couldn't believe his body betrayed his feelings for Susan.

Suddenly Sissy lurched forward and threw her arms around him, like a bear hug, she jumped up and kissed Jack with an open mouth. Her tongue darted into his mouth and before he knew what was happening she bit his bottom lip hard.

"Nice." She released him, standing back with a grin.

Jack back-pedaled closer to the open door and stood away from Sissy.

"What? Did you just bite me?" Jack said in bewilderment, touching his lip, looking for traces of blood. The pain was sharp.

"It was hot, wasn't it?"

"Hot?" Jack thought it was quite the opposite.

She gave him a box of tissues from her dresser as a peace offering. Dabbing his lip he inspected the blood blotched tissue paper with a furrowed look. "What the fuck Sissy, what were you thinking?"

"Sorry, I got carried away."

"Carried away? Who bites people?"

"Vampires," she chuckled.

"Look Sissy, thanks for this evening. Your dad is great..."

"...but I am a bitch," she said, finishing his sentence.

"I wouldn't put it that way. You just need to calm down. I don't know how I would have given you the impression that I wanted anything more than friendship between us." Jack said as he stemmed the blood flow and discarded the tissue into her wastepaper basket.

"But Jack, you're the only one who stands up for me. You look out for me and I love that. I was just showing you my appreciation."

"That's a pretty funny way of doing it, especially the bitey part."

"But you didn't mind touching my tit," she said looking quite dejected.

"Sissy! Please" Jack raised his voice, he was feeling quite annoyed and didn't care if Mr. Smart heard him. "You made me touch...can we just leave us as friends."

After a long silence she looked up at him with puppy dog eyes. "Sure, whatever you want."

Jack wanted to go home, his lip was starting to throb. "Look, I'll see you tomorrow."

"Are we still on for dance lessons?"

Jack hesitated. He was trapped into the formal now and wanted out. What did he sign up for? She gave him a puppy dog look and his heart grew heavy. "Sure, but no more biting."

She waited for him to walk down the hallway, she heard him wish her father a goodnight before she closed her bedroom door. She turned to her cupboard and opened the doors revealing her shrine.

A mirror bordered with a thick padded frame in the shape of a heart hung in the back of the closet. The mirror's frame was covered in mostly red dyed feathers; the occasional pure white ones accented the frame. Either side of the mirror a naked Ken doll swung from little string nooses. Their lips were smeared with a heavy handed application of lipstick and graffiti covered their little bodies in the form of slogans like, 'love sucks' and 'I h8 boys'.

It was like a bower bird's nest in the way that all the trinkets which covered the top of the drawers in the cupboard were all of one colour group – red. Although a bower nest was made by the male to attract a female, Sissy had made this shrine as a kind of offering to the object of her affection. She hoped one day he would see it, the level of her detail as an indication of her devotion, the strength of her love.

She normally would have lit some red candles but she thought it wasn't a good idea this evening. She took the bloody tissue out of the wastepaper basket and placed it in a small crystal bowl at the centre of the shrine. Sissy smiled at the thought that this was now her most prized treasure. It sat well amongst the copies of the only cut out photo of Jack's portrait from the high school yearbook.

13 – MIDWEEK MEETING

Cane toads sat around the post of the street light like they were old mates talking about old times. They could have been misconstrued for little worshipers praying at a timber post shrine. But in reality they were just waiting for a bug to drop to the ground so they could nab it for dinner. One by one cars pulled up in front of the school, turning their headlights off, and getting washed from the orange glow of the street lights above. Walking past the introduced amphibious pests the members of the writers group entered the confines of the wire mesh fence, down the covered concrete path and towards the back of the school where the newly constructed tiered lecture room sat beside the auditorium.

Mr. Friar busied himself with multiple copies of Paperback Writer by John Bird. He had ordered a stack of them and made sure there was a copy on each desk of the lecture room. The room had been built for theatrical performances and also to have senior students get used to the lecture rooms at university.

When all the members had taken a seat, Mr. Friar addressed the group like he would an English class.

"Welcome everyone, I am glad you could all make it, everyone is here," he said with a spark of happiness in his voice. "You can see I have given you each a copy of the book. I've read it and I know some of you have had passages read to you by John Bird, but I want each of you to take a copy home and have a good read. Like me, I am sure you will all agree that it is a stroke of genius. The prose is multilayered, full of analogy, laced with irony and most importantly captures complete emotional resolve, not only for the reader but for the author, John Bird."

Mr. Friar gave a clap, which echoed about the lecture room. He anticipated he would be copied but nobody took the lead so he continued on with his speech.

"So ladies and gentlemen, we come to the analogy of our first published novel's review. I know, it's not a professional review, but it is from one of my most gifted senior students. So, as I am sure you are as excited as me, let me read the review and then we can analyse it and see what it means for John Bird, and potentially what it might mean for you all as writers. We can all take some valuable insight to this review as I am sure you'll all be seeking reviews for your own works when they are completed."

Mr. Friar read Jack's review, pausing on poignant points and mulling over critical aspects. It was as though Mr. Friar had written the novel himself and was taking all the criticism personally. Throughout his whole life he didn't take criticism well, from when he was a teenager at school to when he came out to his parents as a gay man. His mother and father weren't shy in showing their disappointment. They didn't forcefully punish him yet their lack of empathy and interest in his life from then on was enough to snowball his feelings - he became very guarded.

Mr. Friar went on to university to study English, his major was William Shakespeare; although many argue about Shakespeare's sexuality, there is no denying his flamboyant celebration of both sexes through his work. Mr. Friar studied all of Shakespeare's masterpieces, including Julius Caesar and Macbeth; these plays portrayed a time when homosexuality was also misunderstood and punished. However he saw Shakespeare as a bastion of acceptance and built fortitude through the proclamation of innuendo, both apparent and hidden, in his works.

Mr. Friar became a teacher to hopefully mould young minds from becoming contempt and small minded when it came to sexuality and acceptance; via the use of expanding student's readership through diverse authors, of many backgrounds and persuasions.

While members flicked through the small book in front of them, Mr. Friar continued to read the review. "The author finds themselves lost in their personal torment, like a drug hazed stupor we trudge through the sticky mess of uncertainty only discovering resolve towards the end. It was hard to digest this novel as we were often meandering through meaningless garble in the format of 'Stream of Consciousness'.

"Although I found this book difficult to read I found similarity between their life struggles and my own, often at times I found coincidental events and it was like the author's voice was reaching out to me.

"The work was dotted with poetry that was rhythmic and dark, perhaps a little too different to the written work, and I questioned its necessity, however it did add to the chaotic imagery painted inside. The poetry was the very structure required to backbone the work.

"I would find it hard to recommend that anyone didn't read it. Words are hard to best describe this work however I found this work to be: soulful, humble, imaginative and terrific."

There was a laugh from one of the rows, Mr. Friar looked up with scorn.

"So class, I gave this review a High Achievement, not that the student necessarily needed to write a positive review," Mr. Friar concluded.

There was further laughter from the second row.

"Who is that? Alex Dimov, what do you find so funny?"

"Well Mr. Friar, a man of words like yourself didn't see the reviewer's hidden message? I hope you haven't registered that high achievement yet," said Alex Dimov.

"Yes I have, and no, what do you mean *hidden message*?"

"Well, and I am sorry John Bird," Alex Dimov said in the direction of the author. "The student said 'I found this work to be soulful, humble, imaginative, terrific. The first letters of those words Mr. Friar, S...H...I...T. It's quite ironic given the positive adjectives but I am afraid that they found this work to be shit."

The penny dropped. Mr. Friar flushed red with rage. He couldn't believe he had been duped by Jack Armstrong.

John Bird stood up, grabbed their belongings and stormed out of the lecture room. They were followed closely by other authors who wished to give support.

"Ah John Bird, I'll look into this, and everyone please don't forget this Sunday we'll have a break up party here, no analogy, nothing too hard, just friends with a common interest who need to celebrate our achievements..." Mr. Friars' voice trailed, he sat on a desk and looked down at his copy of Paperback writer in disbelief. *Not the outcome I wanted but it is only a review.*

Out in the carpark the cane toads had grown in number but not changed in stance. Moths and cane beetles buzzed around in kamikaze fashion. Some of the toads hopped onto the road, scared at the flood of humans pouring out from the school gates.

"Look, don't worry about the review, I found your book brilliant," one said.

"It's only a review, someone's opinion," said another.

"Let's get home," said an older woman, she feared the repercussions would be a backward progress in their psychology.

"Next time I see him, I am going to wring Jack's scrawny neck," John Bird said in anger.

14 – DON'T TALK TO ME

Susan was very distant with Jack when she saw him in the morning. They both walked to the bus stop but there was an unnatural silence between them. Jack tried to start up a conversation but she ignored him by putting her earbuds in and her head down. Every time he tried to get her attention she looked the other way. The bus ride to school wasn't any better.

By the time they reached school Jack had had enough, he wanted to know what was up. He skipped after Susan as she pushed her way quickly through the marauding pupils.

"Hey Susan, wait up." Jack grabbed her swinging arm and spun her around.

"Don't touch me, and don't talk to me!"

"What?" Jack racked his mind thinking what on earth had made Susan so angry with him. "But you didn't want to go to the formal with me?"

"How can you be so naive? If that's what you think this is about, then don't talk to me again, ever!"

"Come on, what is it?"

"I mean it Jack, don't talk to me, especially with that!" she said pointing to his face.

"Please Susan, what is it?" Jack touched his swollen lip gingerly.

"What do you think I am? Stupid?"

"What?"

"Your swollen lip, it's from her love bite!"

"No, you've got it all wrong!"

"Tell me you both didn't kiss then." Susan stopped walking away from him and stared him in the eyes looking for an honest answer.

"Well, um..." Jack stumbled.

"See! I was right," Susan said and stormed away from him.

"But it's not the whole story Susan, please listen to me!"

"You know what Jack, just no, go and be with her, Sissy will be waiting for you."

"I was only trying to help her out, to go to the formal with her because she had nobody and she was down and out."

"You know what your problem is Jack?"

"No, what?" Jack asked, knowing that it was a loaded question but trying to figure out the source of Susan's rage.

"You're so busy trying to please everyone else that you end up hurting the ones that love you the most."

"Please Susan!"

"Just go, be with her, I am happy for you both." She finally broke away from Jack as he stood there in disbelief. She was glad that her back was to him because he wouldn't see the tears streaming down her face.

Damn Sissy! She must have told Susan, but how? Did she call her and warn her? Nobody is that psycho. Sissy must have planned this all along and made sure there was evidence to see that it may have actually happened. Why can't Susan see it for what it truly is?

Jack stormed off to the locker room. It was a small masonry brick building attached to the senior toilets. Jack hated needing a locker but the weight of his textbooks gave him back pains if he didn't use one.

He didn't see it at first, the strange smell struck him like a punch to the nose. He couldn't tell why the flies had been hovering outside his locker door but now it was apparent.

Foreign to his locker contents – a brown paper bag sat neatly in the middle of the only upper shelf of his locker. It looked like a Chinese dumpling money bag with the way it was bunched in the middle and tied with brown string - Except this was no money bag. Wet blood stained the base of the bag, coupled with a rank smell, ensured there was no tasty treat in this money bag.

Dark blood, thick and drying like a cooling lava flow had seeped through the paper bag, snaked its way across his loose assortment of books and papers and had dripped down the inside face of his locker door. It pooled in the pressed up lip that formed the edge of the door. Whether intentional or not, this one bag had left a trail of destruction.

Who the fuck has left this here? How did they get into my locker?

Jack contemplated whether he should move it or call for a teacher – he wanted to report it, it was clearly planted. Intrigue gave way to proper due course and he carefully lifted the bag, trying to peel the congealed base from the textbook that it was sitting on. His efforts were in vain and the bag tore across the line between wet and dry, exposing the ghoulish contents.

Jack gagged and dry reached. He wanted to slam his locker shut, to shun his eyes from the horrid sight, but he thought best about spreading anymore blood through his locker from the blood that sat in the door frame. Other students looked at him like he was having a fit, they frowned, quickly closing their lockers and leaving him and the smell that they thought he caused – like he had left his lunch in there for days.

Who is going to clean up this mess? This hot, stinking, fucking mess!

Disgust grew to rage. Jack had had enough. It was all stacking up and this latest offering was justification for being somebody's target. He peered back into his locker and shook his head in disbelief. Someone had opened his locker between yesterday afternoon and this morning, managed to walk past hundreds of students, and possibly some teachers, and plant a bag full of raw animal hearts.

Jack couldn't tell what animal the hearts came from but he was sure they weren't human -they were too small, and there were too many. They could have been pig hearts, rat hearts or even chicken hearts, for all he knew they might have even been cane toad hearts.

So many decisions were flashing through his mind but he thought the smartest thing was to quickly pick up the book that the heats were stuck to and throw it in one of the industrial bins at the back of the tuck-shop. If he reported this to any teacher he could potentially cause a bombardment of further crimes from the perpetrator. If he was going to find out who did it he would have to figure it out for himself. From the theatrical placement of the bag and its contents he had a good idea of who it might have been. Only a fellow student could have known which one was his locker and could have gotten past everyone without being seen as not belonging in the area.

Jack thought ever since he picked up that novel and read it, his life has been littered with events and potential vendetta against him. He didn't know who to trust, but he knew he had to stop it, before it escalated too far and took his life.

He knew now that he could only trust his two mates, Patrick and Tim, they were the last ones left talking to him. Sissy was too weird and Susan hated him at the moment - she would take a bit to come around.

Who was after him, what had he done to them? Was it a student or teacher? Obviously it was someone he knew or someone who had come across his path. Was it Jonas? Was it Mr. Friar? Did Mr. Friar work out his hidden message in his book review and seek revenge? Jack grew frantic and nervous, he didn't know which way to look - everyone it seemed could be a suspect. He wanted so badly to confide in Susan, but she was way too angry to approach – he had to resolve the issue of Sissy.

Was it Sissy, she seemed to be a bit unstable? Was she jealous of Susan? Was Susan jealous of Sissy - not likely she had proved that with this morning's argument, but maybe she deeply resents Sissy and wants to take it out on me for my bad decisions?

When he found her his nerves were on edge and he wasn't thinking properly. Susan had rejected him for virtually cheating on her - it was the furthest thing from the truth and he wanted answers from Sissy. She was sitting in the shade against the commerce class wall. Rows of computers sat idle at their workstations. Jack shuddered at the memory of being in that room for Year 8 typing classes and wondered where typing was ever going to get you in life.

He had to clip his rage, he would never intentionally hurt a female and he flushed red with embarrassment at the thought of it – but his rage was pure. She sat there knowing he was standing over her, sensing he wasn't happy she ignored him while she plucked the petals from a weed's flower. This made him livid but he stood his ground. While confliction flicked through his mind like the pages in a Refidex he thought that the whole ordeal was probably his fault for getting himself into the situation in the first place – alone with her in her room. But she took him by surprise and lashed out like a viper, sinking her teeth into his lip. He wanted to throw the whole formal back at her, tell her to stick it, yet here she sat like butter wouldn't melt in her mouth.

He couldn't wait any longer, he was over the games she was playing. "Why did you tell Susan we kissed? Now she won't talk to me. Is that what you wanted?"

"I didn't tell her Jack, she must have figured it out for herself, the way you've been playing coy with me."

"Coy? What are you thinking? And how could she figure anything out, she hated me first thing this morning, you must have called her last night when I left."

"Not me Jack, but thanks for thinking that I am a conniving bitch, gee that doesn't hurt," she said sarcastically.

There was an awkward silence between them, he didn't believe a word she was saying and only thought she was playing him to make him feel bad. He wanted true answers and yet he still felt like he was being played like a puppet.

"I know you're cranky," she finally said, "but your rage strengthens my understanding of the strong feelings that you have for me, you just didn't want Susan to know about them yet."

"What the? Sissy, I don't know why you would think that I *want* you, I haven't done anything or said anything to show it!"

"Well I know there was something there in my room between us, I could feel it."

"Like fuck there was!"

"Getting ahead of yourself there lover boy, we only touched bare skin I know, but I guess we could go there if you want."

"Sissy! Sorry I used the wrong words but you make me so mad. You've stuffed things up between Susan and I, she is who I want, not you!"

This comment seemed to sting Sissy like a sharp slap to the face. She flicked the flower head to the grass and grabbed her school bag that was propped against the wall beside her. She cuddled it in front of her like an expectant mother, then she unzipped the main compartment.

"Oh no you don't," Jack said angrily. "I don't need any more bloody surprises like the one you left in my locker this morning."

"What?" She looked up at him, squinting from the glare of the sun eclipsing his shoulder.

"You know what, and I get the symbolism, bleeding hearts for love or some shit like that!"

"What, there were actual hearts in your locker?"

"Don't play innocent with me?" Jack looked to the side in thought. *She looks too surprised to have done it, then who could it be?*

"Not me Jack, seems like I have competition," she smirked.

"Great!"

"So I guess you want out for the formal, I guess my dad could try and get a refund on the dress, but it will break his heart to see his little girl not dressed up," Sissy said with a sad look.

"What makes me want to go with you now? Guilt surely won't change my mind. Why don't you take someone else?" Jack said, the thought of not going or having anything to do with Sissy was beginning to sound great.

"Jack, there is nobody else."

"Sure there is."

"Nobody who gets it, who gets me. We are alike Jack, people here laugh at us because we are different, because we aren't sporty or cool. You get that and that's why you stuck up for me and that's why I want to go with you and not some random guy."

Jack felt his heart sink. She was right, if her final year was going to be memorable he wanted it to be good for her, he knew she had a hard life at school and he knew what it felt like.

"Sissy, don't pull anything like you've just done again otherwise you can go to the formal by yourself."

"I promise," Sissy said softly, with a huge smile. *I love it when you talk cross to me.*

Susan made sure she was the last on the bus in the afternoon and sat well away from Jack at the front of the bus. She managed to fire a serious glare at him before she sat down in a heap like a sack of potatoes being dropped in a shopping trolley - the air protested noisily as it escaped a hole in the bottom of the vinyl covered foam padded seat. It was the exclamation mark to her frustration.

Jack couldn't stop looking at Susan, at the back of her head. A knot of anguish twisted in his throat. Little did he know, but his week was about to go from bad to worse.

15 – OVER THE FENCE

The following day they had him targeted before he even realised what was happening. They worked swiftly and as a team. Pack hunters. His slight build was easily lifted in one quick motion, almost too easily. Before anyone could see they had picked his body up from his wrists and ankles, and swung him like a dead body, up and over the fence. As he crashed and banged on the other side of the fence, like garbage at the tip, they slinked off pissing themselves laughing.

On the other side of the fence, Jack's head hit a block of timber on the way down and he was out cold before he could comprehend what had just happened.

"Hey Susan," Jonas said as he joined the line for morning form class. "Since I just took care of some dirty laundry, did you want to come with me to the formal? I am sure you'd scrub up just fine too."

Neil and Stanley snigged. They knew the innuendo behind Jonas' statement and they also knew what her response would be, the hatred had run deep for Jonas for many years. Stanley had come around to the plan of throwing Jack over the fence, sometimes it was easier to go with the flow then to fight against what he knew was wrong.

"I'd bet you'd scrub up alright as well," she said. "Especially washing off that ogre smell that permeates from your body. Why don't you go back to the swamp where you came from? You swamp Neanderthal."

His mates sniggered again but were quickly stopped by an instant jab to their ribs with a purposeful punch from Jonas.

"You stupid bitch," he whispered under his breath. "Hey it's Friday, you want to come out with us tonight and party?" he said, trying a different tack.

She didn't answer Jonas, she turned her head as she saw him sideways glance at Ms. Smith who was walking towards the lineup of students.

"Okay everyone, quiet now, let's get this over with quickly today, I've got things to organise for tomorrow's car wash," Ms. Smith said hurriedly. She extended her arm to indicate they were to head inside the form room.

Patrick and Tim looked at each other from the front of the line. They just heard the commentary between Susan and Jonas and they wondered why he was asking her to the formal. They knew

Susan was angry at Jonas but they didn't think he'd have the gall to ask her to the formal. Perhaps it was just another taunt.

Patrick was worried, he hadn't seen Jack this morning and he knew he was upset about yesterday. The bloody mess he had seen in Jack's locker still made him shudder.

After the second bell, they were all seated in the form room and Patrick sat beside Susan.

"Hey, have you seen Jack this morning?" Patrick asked.

"No, and I don't care where he is."

"Awe come on, what's he done that's so bad?"

"He's existed." She turned to the side to prevent further discussion and to stare vacantly out the window.

It wasn't the throbbing pain from the cut to his ear that woke him, it was more the wet sandpaper that was repetitively rubbing his cheek. He groggily opened his eyes and it took some time to adjust to what was before him.

Two glossy orange marbles with brown, spider leg lines radiating from black dots peered at him. They seemed to be floating in a cloud of white wool, parted by a little pink nose. His brain registered and he pulled back from the cat who was licking a cut on his face.

"Oh man! Get away from me!" Jack shouted.

"Careful boy, don't scare my Azra!" said a stern voice, with a thick accent from the corner of the room. Nevertheless the cat bolted out of the room.

Jack turned his head quickly and saw him, leaning against the kitchen counter, drying a white ceramic plate. Jack's heart raced, this was the man every student feared, he was an urban legend –

Mad Daris. Jack's face went white, he sat up on the derelict couch where he had been placed and pushed back into the armrest as far away from Daris as possible.

"Relax boy, if I wanted to harm you, I would have done it by now," Daris said unfazed by Jack's reaction. "But I am warning you boy, you'd better have a good explanation as to why you were in my yard. Were you trying to steal my chickens?"

"Uh, n-n-no," Jack stuttered. His throat was dry with nervousness. His eyes were locked on Daris and he dared not scan the room.

"Then what eh?" Daris said with hands raised, tea towel in one, ceramic plate in the other.

"I - I was thrown over mister, by other kids."

"Bullies eh?" Daris asked with intrigue.

"I - I guess so mister," Jack said as he quickly wiped sweat off his top lip with his uniform shirt sleeve.

"Ah, weaklings, you know nothing about self-defence, you let yourself be beaten up, why are you happy to be the victim?"

Jack didn't answer, but it was more of a statement than a question Daris wanted answered. Jack nerves were overwhelming him as the sweat began to bead down the centre of his back. He wondered if he would make it out alive. Daris' form was quite foreboding, his exposed upper arms from his worn t-shirt were rippled with muscles. His back was lean and also thick with muscle – like the man had worked hard his whole life.

"Please mister, I am sorry I ended up in your yard, can I please go?" Jack pleaded.

Daris grunted and spit a thick wad of mucus into the kitchen sink, he wiped his face with the tea towel and looked over at Jack with a frown, "Not until I teach you a valuable lesson."

"Jack Armstrong, Jack Armstrong," Ms. Smith repeated. She looked over towards where he usually sat in the room, looked down and wrote 'A', for absent, alongside his name for the day. She continued to read out the remaining student's names, only lifting her head if there was no response.

Tim looked at Patrick and shrugged. Both boys had no idea where Jack was, they hadn't expected him to be away – this was exam week and they knew he had exams today. They both surmised that he was probably late, having stayed up studying. Looking around at Susan, Patrick caught her writing something on a scrap of paper. He wondered if it could have been a letter to Jack.

The final bell rang before classes and exams and the students were excused from the form room and were on their way.

"Hey Susan, wait up," Patrick protested as he tried to catch up with her. "Do I look like I can beat you in a running race?"

"I am not in the mood for any of your lame ass jokes."

"It's no joke Susan, I just wanted to see what was up with you and Jack?"

"Why don't you ask him? I am sure he'd be happy to brag about it."

"About what?"

"Sucking face with Sissy, that's what."

"No way!"

"Yes way, and it was after a nice family dinner with her and her dad."

"You're shitting me?"

"Patrick, do I look like I have time for this?"

"Sorry, I can see why you're upset."

"I am not upset, he can have her, besides I've already moved on," she said dismissively.

"Yeah? With who?"

"You'll have to wait and see, I need a man who can take charge of his feelings and knows what to do about them," Susan said. She walked off to her first exam leaving Patrick to become engulfed in a sea of traversing students. He couldn't believe that Jack and Susan would no longer become an item - he was certain they were supposed to end up as high school sweethearts.

"Please mister, let me go and I won't tell anyone," Jack pleaded.

"After we're done here you won't want to tell anyone, little boy."

Jack's heart raced, he looked around the room. There was a door leading out of the kitchen which he could see was out towards the backyard. If he ran that way, maybe he could jump the back fence over some stacks of pallets or crates and he'd be safe back in the school grounds. The only problem was that Daris was in between him and that option. The other way was just behind him, it looked like a hallway led off the kitchen and towards the front of the property. The only problem with this direction was that it was dark and Jack wouldn't be quick enough to work out which way to go, also Jack assumed that the front door would be locked so it was most likely a dead end.

Maybe Jack could overpower Daris, but that looked impossible given the opposing form he would have to combat. A third and less appealing option was to jump out of the kitchen window which faced the side of the property. The only problem here was that the window was a casement window and it didn't open up fully – so smashing it and jumping through it was the only possibility. Jack didn't have enough time to find something large enough to throw through it and then he'd have the problem of getting past the jagged edges of broken glass. Jack thought that the only way out of this situation was to use his brain and try to negotiate with Daris.

"Um, mister, I see you are good with glasswork, have you been working on that one for a long time?" Jack said as he pointed towards the leadlight mural on the kitchen table.

"Eh? That? Yeah, it's been awhile I guess," Daris said as he glanced over at the table – his mind seemed to drift away as he stared vacantly.

Good it seems to be distracting him.

"She looks pretty, is she someone close to you?" Jack asked looking at the woman in the mural with blood dripping from her eyes. He gulped at the thought of how she came to be in that predicament. *Was it like my situation? Had she also seen too much?*

"*Was* boy, she *was* close to me!" Daris was losing his temper; he was struggling to keep himself in check.

Jack gulped and sweat dripped from his brow. *That backfired, quick think fast.*

"I can tell she was the love of your life, I am so sorry for your loss."

"Yes boy, she was, she will always be the love of my life, such a waste of a beautiful life."

"Please mister, I'd love to hear more about her?"

"What are *you* to me? Just a stupid boy, from a stupid school, in a stupid country. You want to know about my wife? How did she die? You would shit in your pants," Daris' sadness was evident in his voice. He took a step towards Jack which made Jack reel backwards into the couch. Any further back and Jack would be sitting on top of the backrest.

"Arrgh!" Daris screamed, he grabbed his right hand and balled it into a fist. Jack pushed into the corner of the couch, he was trapped, the best exit - the backyard – was blocked and he was leading himself into danger by edging towards the dark exit.

Daris looked up and Jack and frowned, "sit boy, sit. I am not going to hurt you."

"But you said you wanted to teach me a lesson?"

"I do, but I am not going to hurt you." Jack stared wide-eyed at his balled fist. "My arthritis is playing up – big storm coming."

"What do you mean?"

"In Bosnia, they gave me a name, *olujna ptica*. It means stormbird, we have birds over there, they visit before the storms come. My friends say my calls were like stormbird, before the rain comes. But it's just my arthritis," Daris said in broken English.

Jack stared at him massaging the joints in his fingers as his face grimaced in pain.

"But you were going to teach me a lesson, you looked quite angry before your hand gave you pain."

"Yes, I want to teach you how to stick up for yourself when you are being pestered by bullies."

He didn't show it but Jack sighed with relief and his heart rate dropped. He still felt awkward and scared but somehow he thanked his lucky stars for being alive.

16 – HUNT IN PACTS

It was lunchtime when Jack had finally left Daris' control. He had thanked him for teaching him about how to deal with bullies but deep down he knew it would be easier said than done to implement some of the tactics. At times during the lecture Jack's mind had wondered, especially when Daris went off track and started to talk about the harsh life he had in war torn Bosnia. He also didn't find out about his wife and Jack thought it wise not to broach the subject again. It was intriguing however, the mural depiction of her with bleeding eyes, it left him more troubled thinking about that than the whole ordeal of being in Daris' house in the first place.

Jack headed to the school office to explain his absence, he would have to come up with a lie, like he was sick in the toilets and couldn't get up to ask for help. He knew he had missed exams but hoped he could sit them next week during the last week of school.

Jack swore that he wouldn't tell any teachers that he was at Daris' house as Daris was afraid he would be deported for having a student alone with him. Although he was part way through the process, Daris was finding it difficult to provide all the necessary documentation to gain Australian citizenship. He had pleaded with his case worker that most of what they asked for had been destroyed, he was lucky to have his passport. Daris' case had further slowed as his citizenship was caught up in his proof of refugee status. The paperwork and legal red tape added to the scars of his horrid past. At times he wished he could escape into the Australian outback, possibly the reason he chose Cairns as it was regional Australia. But he knew that he was much better living here with citizenship politics than with political and religious genocide.

Jack kicked at a broken pencil that lay on the walkway as he waited outside the school's main office. He looked around as students came out of their classes for lunch. He wanted to head off and skip the rest of the day: the blood in his locker, Susan ignoring him, being thrown over the fence into Daris' control, and Sissy creating drama all stacked up against him. But he knew he had exams in the afternoon and they were important. He wanted a better life through getting into university so he had to suffer the short term pain of high school. He sighed as he stepped up into the office and waited for the receptionist to acknowledge his presence.

Mrs. Healy, the school nurse, had doted over Jack until the point of annoyance. He didn't know what was worse, being held hostage by Daris or by Mrs. Healy. Jack knew it was all part of protocol: recording temperature, asking about vomit times and amounts, what he ate last, was he on any medication, how he was feeling. Jack had to navigate his way through the interview with a series of lies and half-truths. He had felt like vomiting when he saw the chicken hearts, when he had the cat licking his face, and when he smelt the bad odour of cat facies in the front room of Daris house as he was let out the front – but he didn't. He felt terrible but it was more emotional than physical as he looked out the sick room window wondering if Susan would ever talk to him again.

The nurse asked if he was up to finishing the rest of the day as she could call his mother and he'd be given a leave of absence. She left him in the room while she checked with the principal if it was okay to finish exams that he had next week. Mrs. Healy came back into the room beaming as usual with the good news. But Jack didn't take her offer, he'd rather stay as a show of defiance to Jonas. Besides he still might get to speak to Susan in the afternoon and that would be worth anything Jonas could dish out to him.

Jack ate his lunch on his way to where his mates sat. He was pleased to see their familiar faces but his heart tightened when he noticed Susan's absence.

"Hey guys," Jack said.

"Hey man, where have you been?" Patrick asked. "What's gone down?"

"Jonas and his goons tossed me into Mad Daris' yard first up this morning."

"What the!" Tim said in shock.

Patrick looked gobsmacked. "And you're still alive?"

"Yeah, just." Jack sat down on the concrete next to his mates.

"What happened over there? How'd you get out? Did he do anything nasty?" Patrick rattled off questions like Tony Barber on Sale of the Century's Fast Money segment.

"Nothing happened over there, I got out down the side."

"Bullshit! If you got out then why has it taken until lunchtime to get here?" Tim said.

"I don't know," Jack said, not thinking of a quick comeback in time.

"He did get you, did he touch you, like *touch, touch* you?" Patrick said with concern on his face.

"Fuck off, like I said, I didn't see him, I got out, I've just been in the sick bay, I got a whiff of all that chicken shit over there and I felt ill, plus I had to get the scratch on the side of my face checked out didn't I?"

"How'd that happen?" Tim asked with concern.

"I landed on some wood or something, it knocked me out."

"Geez, sorry man, sorry for the questions," Patrick said.

"Don't worry about it."

"You've had some bad luck this year mate. The bus crash, seeing birds blown up in the park, having to read that shit novel for your English assignment, punched by Jonas, bloody hearts in your locker and now getting thrown over Daris' fence, and to top it all off, Susan has the shits with you." Patrick surmised.

"Thanks for the update Sherlock, like I didn't know my life was already shit enough," Jack said, shooting Patrick a frown.

"Sorry dude."

There was quiet amongst the boys as Tim and Patrick absorbed the story Jack had told. Jack was deep in thought, he was clearly disturbed as he pulled randomly at the straps of his school bag.

Feeling dejected, Jack sprung to his feet, and he drop kicked his school bag against the classroom wall that he had been sitting against.

"Guys, I need your help, I need you to come with me."

"What? Why?" Patrick asked as he looked at Tim with concern, he was worried about Jack's state of mind.

"There's no time to explain just yet, quick, I need to get to the English classroom before lunch ends."

They were a good five hundred meters away from their destination. Three buildings with large grassed areas between each separated them from the English classroom. Patrick grunted as he lifted his large body up – he didn't like having his lunch hastily shortened but figured he needed to help his mate. They walked briskly although Jack wanted to run. He didn't want to draw unnecessary attention to the trio as they approached their target classroom.

"Okay, I need one of you out here to stand guard, while one of you helps me search in the cupboards."

"I'll come in, but what are we looking for?" Tim said.

"That stupid book, Paperback Writer. I think it's the key to all the shit that has been going down."

"How?" Patrick didn't quite follow what Jack was saying.

"I'll show you when we find it, it's got to be here somewhere." Jack opened the unlocked door, looking briefly sideways for any onlookers before he entered the room.

Across the far side of the classroom stood three closed cupboards. They housed textbooks, class group reading fiction, practice exams, activity papers and writing material. The classroom was only locked at night because none of the material stored in the cupboards was worth stealing. Jack figured the novel he was after had to be here, Mr. Friar was surely going to use it in future classes as study material.

The boys opened the cupboards as Patrick waited nervously outside. His back was to the door and Jack noticed his head turn from side to side like a carnival amusement where you put the ping pong balls into the clown's mouth and hoped not to get the shitty plastic prize. Jack hoped that Patrick would calm down otherwise his suspicious demeanor might blow their cover.

Angry with himself for not realising the direct link to his woes and the words in his assigned novel, Jack tormented over the reality of what it meant. Who was John Bird and what did they have against him that made them go to the lengths of writing a novel, getting access to a writers group that was chaired by his English teacher and being able to have enough influence within that group to get Jack to specifically read the book, all the while the clues to future acts of violence were hidden in the words.

"You remember what the cover looks like Tim?" Jack asked as he rifled through books.

"Yeah, it's that skinny book with the picture of a phoenix on the cover?"

"That's the one," Jack said as he focused on going from shelf to shelf. "Guess they truly rose from the ashes when they wrote that."

Jack finished going through the first cupboard at the same time as Tim had finished checking his. They both closed the doors and moved onto the last cupboard. It sat in between the two other cupboards. Jack casually pulled on the handle and his fingers slipped off the door knob – it was locked.

"Since when are these locked?" Jack was in disbelief.

The school bell rang outside the room. Patrick cracked the door open just enough to poke his head through, "Found it yet, the next class will be here any minute, let's go!"

"No, not until I open this cupboard." Jack was determined.

"Come on man, we'll try again later. How are we going to get into it anyway?"

"I don't know, it's only a wooden cupboard, maybe we could pry the lock open?" Jack looked around the room. It seemed hopeless there were only desks, chairs and wall posters in the room. It was quite sparse of break-and-enter tools.

"Come on Jack, let's go, I am sure there will be another window of opportunity to get into the cupboard later." Tim looked quite stressed as he noticed other students start to congregate outside. The nerves had got to Patrick but he looked like he was walking over to the students to distract them.

Jack looked around the room one last time, and that's when it stood out. "'Window of opportunity', I like that, thanks for the heads up Tim."

"What?"

Without explanation, Jack raced over to the side of the classroom. The room side wall was made up of a row of sliding glass windows in aluminium frames that went from halfway up the wall to line up with the top of the door frame. Above these windows were a row of louvered windows – too high to open and close without a ladder – except for the aluminium pole with hook attached that was hanging from one of the louver window closing arms.

"Brilliant!" Tim saw Jack pull the pole down and head back to the cupboard. "Come on we better be quick."

The pole was long and awkward but Jack was determined to open the cupboard and expose its secrets. Tim manned the end of the poll while Jack forced the hooked end into the small gap between the timber door and catch. The pole length actually worked in their favour as there was enough of a moment arm to pry the door open by busting the timber around the lock. The door was damaged but Jack didn't care – there had been too many hostile events against him and he was determined to find evidence and answers.

While Tim returned the pole Jack frantically scanned the open cupboard. Children outside were getting noisier and Patrick had long gone. Jack heard the classroom door latch click and figured Tim had fled as well.

Jack was running out of time, the book wasn't there. Out of anger he pushed a stack of textbooks over and rested his head on a shelf, pillowed by his forearm. A book that he recently hoped he'd never see again, that made his life a misery while he chewed his way thought reading it was now the key to his happiness and he longed to get it back. But it was over and he was going to get caught by the next class teacher; he didn't care – he had far worse happen to him of late.

He looked up in dismay, vacantly staring towards the back of the fruitless cupboard. He had to squint to focus, but there it was, it had been hidden behind the textbooks that he had knocked over. He quickly grabbed the book and shoved it down his pants as he heard the classroom door open and close behind him in a violent manner.

"You'd better have a good explanation as to what you are doing in here?" shrieked the all too familiar voice of Ms. Smith.

The end of lunch bell had rung out long ago. There was a gentle breeze rolling across the sports ground, tickling the grass and tossing empty chip packets like they were an urban tumbleweed. The thick planting of trees at the western edge of the school grounds made a cool spot to hang out and escape the midday sun. This is where Susan had come to find solitude.

She had nowhere to go and no one to be with. Her exams were finished for the day and she was free to study anywhere in the school grounds. She wanted to go home but had to wait for the bus. Other students walked off like sheep heading towards Evansdale Shopping Centre to loiter. She didn't want anything to do with that, her small friend group were disbanded and she felt happy in her misery, picking at the grass and poking twigs in the dirt.

She was angry with herself for trusting Jack. *How dare he come to school sporting a love bite like it was a trophy!* She told him they would be together, she guessed he couldn't wait and needed any female affection.

She was angry with Sissy for moving into her territory and taking Jack away. They were friends, she was the only female friend she had and she broke that trust. All those hours talking about how she liked Jack and she wanted to get closer to him but didn't want to lose their strong friendship and Sissy took advantage of her situation. Sissy moved in, she swooped down like an owl onto a mouse. She didn't think she'd ever care to talk to or confide in Sissy ever again.

She was still smouldering over not being told of her sister's pregnancy and although her mother and sister were now all on talking terms she knew keeping that secret from her had put a strain on their relationship. At the moment, Susan was finding it hard to trust anyone. Sitting here contemplating her future was her strongest resolve.

The wind blew in stiff gusts causing the branches to sway and the leaves of the trees to rustle loudly - the sound was deafening. It looked like dark clouds were gathering at the tops of the close mountain range. Large leaves fell off a beach almond like sheets of motley coloured paper. It was supposed to be a happy time of year but with the onset of another afternoon storm and the smattering of leaves like outcast debris Susan thought her afternoon couldn't get any worse.

She pulled out her notebook, holding the edges down from the wind like she was protecting her essence from escaping, pulling a long strand of blown hair behind an ear and she began to write to resolve her emotions.

> Where is my hero now?
> Watch me rebuild these walls,
> to shadow my existence,
> and murder your hapless calls.
>
> Why trust you again?
> What was once all there,

is now wiped like your bloody lip,
which with others that you share.

Who are you now?
I don't believe your mistake,
others may devour your kindness,
but to me you are all fake.

When will you give up?
Just leave me as broken,
you've bruised my blackened heart,
with the lies that you've spoken.

What is there for us?
Just a frail tender thread,
and what we once had,
may as well be dead.

"Hey there, what are you writing?" a familiar voice spoke above the rustle of trees.

"Nothing for you, go away Jonas!"

Jonas was alone and he ignored her request as he sat down opposite her and leaned up against the trunk of a large gum tree. Susan frowned and closed her poetry book putting her prized possession back in her bag.

He squirmed a little and groaned in complaint, standing up quickly as he realised he just sat down on an ants nest. He looked down at her with a grimace, trying to flick the ants off his pants, as he caught her giggling at his demise.

"Not funny." Jonas moved away from the tree trunk, but he still maintained the distance between the two of them.

"Couldn't have happened to a nicer guy," she said with a sarcastic smile.

"Hey, I can be nice."

"Yeah, I haven't seen that side to you yet, why do you bash my friends and give us shit all the time?"

It's a good hobby, gets me through the day. "I don't know, I guess I can be an asshole sometimes," Jonas shrugged his shoulders.

"How about *all* the time."

"Ouch. Look I am sorry," he lied. "I guess I am going through some tough shit at home and I stupidly take it out on people that I see as weak."

Susan was taken aback by his apparent honesty. It was hard to tell if he was lying as his delivery was quite raw. She suspected he may have had trouble at home so there was an element of truth about it. "Yeah, but it's still no excuse, in fact it's quite cowardly to pick on people you think are weaker."

Jonas flushed with anger, but he controlled his temper. "Yeah, I guess I have been."

There was an awkward silence between the two students. Jonas could sense there was more to Susan's cold mood than his presence.

"Hey what's up? You can talk to me if you want a different outlook on things." Jonas offered.

"Thanks, but no thanks."

"So something is bothering you?" Jonas pressed again.

"You are, just go away."

"Aw come on, I am trying to be friendly here. I even have ant bites on my ball sack!"

Susan laughed, she'd never heard someone say that before. She didn't find it terribly funny but with her pent up emotions and his awkward behaviour she couldn't stop laughing.

"Hey, it's not that funny!"

"Sorry," she said coyly. "It's just that I am also going through some shit at the moment."

"Yeah? Well we all seem to have our problems," he said. "Yours wouldn't happen to be called Jack?"

Susan looked at Jonas squarely. She normally wouldn't have spoken to Jonas let alone have confided in him but she was fragile and she let her guard down.

"He's not a problem anymore."

"Wow, I didn't think you two would fight." He looked out across the school oval. "I thought you two would be prom king and queen."

"You've been watching too many American movies, we don't have prom king and queen here, besides he's going to the formal with Sissy. I am not going."

Jonas saw the opening he needed, he circled his prey and discovered her weakness.

"Look, if you want to go, for whatever reason, whether to make him jealous or if you just want to go – I'll take you." Jonas said, he looked at her gauging for a reaction.

Susan thought about the offer and what it truly meant. She knew Jack had hurt her but if she went to the formal with Jonas that would be like a dagger to the heart for Jack. She didn't think he deserved it.

"Thanks, but I'll pass."

"Aw come on, you'd love it. It might be a way to get there and have a special moment with Jack, a dance or something – it will be a surprise for him."

"Some surprise."

"Look, you can blow me off once we get there if you want. Come on, Jack won't know you are going, if he has feelings for you, then once you are there, then who knows what will happen?" Jonas said with his hands up in the air.

Susan went quiet. She wondered why Jonas was so determined to go to the formal especially with her and especially when he had options more suited to him like Meredith. She knew he must be up to something but came around to the idea of surprising Jack – in a good way. She would use it as one last attempt to see if he would stand by her even if it meant Jonas would be the means.

"Well if you want to go with me then we better go to the carwash tomorrow," she said. *If he's serious about it, he'll turn up.*

"Cool, I'll see you there." Jonas stood up.

She watched him flick dirt and leaves off his pants and put his heavy backpack over his shoulder like it was a rag doll. She wondered what he had in there, he never seemed to study so she doubted it was books.

"Hey if you want to blow off some steam, the guys and I are having a small party at Neil's house on Saturday, you're more than welcome to come and listen to some tunes and just hang out." He walked backwards away from her with a smile.

"Sure, why not." *All or nothing.*

"Hey guys, thanks for the backup," Jack said sarcastically. "Now I've got an afternoon detention with Ms. Smith."

"Wow, lucky guy, did you get the book?" Patrick said with no apology.

"Yeah, just in time."

"Great, now show us what you mean about the hidden messages," Tim said with intrigue.

"Hang on, let me get to the sections." Jack pulled the book from his bag and flicked it open.

His face showed lines of determination as he started scanning from the beginning. He smiled when he found the first reference and held the book up towards his mates like he was practicing for a speech recital.

"So, tell me what this reminds you of. *'Flip the children's carriage, drink the pain they feel.'*"

Both friends looked at each other, then turned and shrugged at Jack.

"Aw come on! What if I said flip the children's *bus?*"

"The bus crash? You think that means the bus crash?" Tim said.

"Yes of course. Then how about this, *'they bleed for you much quicker, lying scattered in the park'.*"

"The blown up birds in the park?" Tim said.

"Exactly! And what about these lines, *'I'll cup my wounded dove, then tear a jagged line. A beating heart is what I love'*."

"So you're linking that to the chicken hearts in your locker?" Patrick piped in.

"Yes, you don't agree?"

"It's a bit of a stretch, but I suppose," Patrick said. "What else is there?"

"Well the last two poems talk about stormy weather and a crimson dripping glove, which I guess refers to blood."

"So what do you think, this writer can conjure up a storm?" Patrick asked as he took the book out of Jack's hands and began scanning the pages.

"No, that would be impossible, maybe they are planning to attack me when things get bad metaphorically speaking or maybe they might attack me during a storm? I don't know, all I know is that all these events are too coincidental and they seem to be directed towards me."

"So what do you want to do?" Tim asked.

"Let's find out who John Bird is before they act on their final threat, maybe 'crimson dripping glove' is about stabbing me?" Jack said with a concerned look.

"How do we find out who he or she is?" Patrick said.

"Well I know the writers group meetup on a Sunday at lunchtime, here at the school. Let's have a stake-out and see who all the members are, that way we can try and figure it out."

"Hang on, before we go off halfcocked look at this in the epilogue, they say thank you for the help with the poems," Patrick said as he pointed out the line to Jack and Tim.

"Well let's go anyway, the culprit may not have written the novel, perhaps they just wrote the poems, so they may not be John Bird. But we've gotta try; it might be harder to work out but it's my only chance to protect myself and maybe put an end to all this."

"Yeah and it would be interesting to find out why you are such a target in the first place," Tim said.

"Yes, very interesting," Jack said as he took the book back and shoved it into his school bag.

The noise of children escaping to freedom from the end of the school day was loud and sporadic. They seemed to cut, dart and weave every which direction and quite annoyingly for Jack as he pushed past the throng heading in the opposite direction. His afternoon detention was going to be worse than a lunchtime one - at least his mother would have never found out about a lunchtime detention, but now because he would miss his bus he would have to be picked up after hours. Jack felt stupid for getting caught, his day had been shit and this was the cherry on top. With his head down, feeling sorry for himself, he pushed on toward the performing arts building for which Ms. Smith was head of.

The white performing arts building stood tall against the covered parade hall. It was the only two story building in the school. Jack often thought it was built in the wrong position as it was hidden, not taking advantage of fully showing its artistic facades. It would have been better placed more central to the school but its position was subject to a school growing too quickly which overshadowed proper planning – at the time the school was built for functionality.

Afternoon detentions were housed in the room decided by the teacher on duty as the main office was closed at four o'clock each day. As Ms. Smith was on duty Jack knew he had to make the journey towards the back of the school to her detention room, which was the main auditorium of the performing arts building. At this time of day it was quiet at the back of the school as all the students rushed to the front boundary in fluid motion to make their way home.

Jack passed rooms which contained practicing dancers who moved gracefully across the timber floorboards in front of a mirror wall. The students were oblivious to what was happening outside the room and were concentrating on keeping in time to the soft music playing from a portable stereo which sat on the floor. Jack assumed it was some type of contemporary dance. He didn't get it. He didn't get how they could be marked on such a style of dance and what that would lead to in life. He didn't think they were bad at what they were doing, just that he thought there was no real use for it in life. It might be entertainment but to Jack it was more of a hobby. Each to their own, he thought.

On finally arriving at the performing arts centre office Jack knocked on the glass door to let his presence be known. He could see Ms. Smith sitting behind her desk in the corner of the front room. She looked up at him and glared, showing her authority by ignoring him and making him wait. Her office was separated only by partition to the other three desks in the room. Jack thought it might be awkward for Ms. Smith to be in close proximity to the other teachers and wondered why there was no solid divide to the room but he figured it was the way the room was designed or perhaps the department also grew far too quickly for the original design and the desks were jammed in just to fit. *Maybe that's why Ms. Smith was always so cranky,* Jack thought. Ms. Smith finally looked up at him again and pointed to the door to indicate for him to enter the office.

Her tone was aggressive and her speech clipped. Jack submissively bowed his head out of respect, he was also embarrassed to have detention - this was his first time in all his twelve years of schooling. Jack carefully listened to her instructions and obediently conformed. He politely excused himself and headed down the passageway between the close buildings and entered the main auditorium. He was to allow himself into the building, sit close to the main door and write a short essay on how his behaviour could impact others. If he finished earlier than the two hour detention then he had to write lines, 'I shall not disobey school rules' until she came and dismissed him. She wanted to see at least five hundred lines. If he were to skip detention then the punishment would be doubled.

The main auditorium was a cavernous room. The seats were arranged like a reclined stadium and reached far into the back of the room. When he looked up the ceiling was high and he could see all the hanging lighting in black above his head. The stage sat proudly at the centre of the room and was at least two metres off the surrounding floor. There was a sunken section in front of the stage where a band could be set up. The polished timber stage floor was flanked by red velvet curtains which were thick and heavy in appearance. The lighting in the room was soft and dull, which gave the room and even further cavernous feel. Although there was nothing in the room, it still had a grand feeling to it. Jack couldn't work out if it was the acoustics or the lighting but the room felt grandiose.

The first hour dragged. The silence of the room played tricks on his mind, the acoustics were designed to absorb sound and the room had a blanketed quality to it. So every creak or ping made him look up. The loudest noise which alarmed him every time was the occasional ping of the iron roofing as it contracted from the cooling effect of the afternoon sun being shielded by a cloud. He was quite bored and the essay he had to write was meaningless. He imagined this is what solitary confinement would be like except his isolation was amplified by the size of the room. In his writing he couldn't explain how the cupboard lock was busted so he lied and said that was how he found it in his defence. He wrote that he regretted entering the classroom when he shouldn't have been there and he will in future show greater respect for others property and rules. Jack figured if he wrote his five hundred lines quick enough he could spend the rest of his incarceration with his head on the desk. He knew it would be 'the calm before the storm', before he had to face Ms. Smith and then his cranky mother. He knew she'd be more upset over having to drive to the school and also the embarrassment that he caused her by having to talk to Ms. Smith about her disobedient son, and the implications that had on making the family look bad.

It was about five minutes before his detention time was to be over when he heard the click of the main door being opened. It was enough warning for Jack to sit up straight and gather his papers. Ms. Smith strode in with a presence as she made her way to Jack. With her silver blonde hair tied in a bun, her skin tone lipstick, her white vest and suit pants she almost looked angelic. Jack could see why the other guys in his classroom sniggered and spoke about what they wanted to do to her if they had a chance. Jack wondered about her background and why she was so strict. Usually the pretty girls at school were easy going even if they were bitchy.

Her designer pants made a swishing sound as she approached and Jack's eyes followed her movement across the auditorium floor to where he was sitting. She stood erect with arms folded, legs slightly parted when she stopped - her posture showed dominance.

"Show me what you've done!"

Jack handed her the loose papers he had written his essay and lines down on, he fumbled as he gathered the papers, trying his best to present them in an orderly fashion. She frowned at his inept composure.

"So you think you've learnt a lesson here, Jack?" She asked wide-eyed with lips pursed in anger.

"Yes Miss."

"Good, I don't want to see you here ever again."

"No Miss."

Jack was about to get up out of his chair when she slammed the papers down on his desk causing him to double back in his chair. He looked up at her in confusion. Her face had changed from commanding to angry like the flick of a switch.

She gripped both sides of his desk and lent in uncomfortably close to Jack's face. "You don't get it do you?" She snapped.

"Get what? Um Miss?" He was quite confused, he gulped in nervousness.

"Discipline. You don't understand the term do you?"

"Miss?"

Pushing back off the desk she stood up and paced a short distance away from him before turning on the spot and standing over him.

"All of you little shits don't know what real discipline is; you come to school thinking that you're all here for a good time, that you can play, muck around and it's okay. You are all led by your hormones - girls wearing slutty clothes pining over boys; boys walking around like life size erections sniffing the air as though there were bitches on heat.

"There is no discipline in any one of you - if there was then you wouldn't be here writing lines for breaching a direct rule that you cannot enter a classroom unless you've been asked to. Then you've lied to me about busting into the cupboard causing damage to school property. If there wasn't the carwash tomorrow and if it wasn't the last week of school for you seniors next week then I'd haul your ass up to Mr. Hadrick's office and you'd be paying out of your own money to repair the damage."

"Yes, Miss," Jack eyed the door, hoping he could leave soon.

"Is that all you have to say?"

Jack wanted to bite his tongue and say nothing else but he had had enough. "Well you see Miss, I beg to differ, I am not like one of those guys you described, like I am on heat or something like that and I do have discipline." Jack looked directly in the eyes.

"Your actions prove otherwise. Tell me, what was your reason for breaking into the cupboard? What did you steal? Did you know

I could have called the police? Did you also steal the formal money from the staff room?"

Ah, that's why she's come down on me like a tonne of bricks, she thinks I've stolen her formal money. "Oh no Miss, that wasn't me. I didn't steal the money."

"You haven't convinced *me* Jack, what were you doing in that cupboard?"

"I was looking for a book, a novel Mr. Friar had made me read for an English assignment. I wanted to get the book because I was afraid I had missed something in the text that was important for the assignment."

"It's the last week next week and you think I'd believe that story. Assignment writing would be over, would it not? It's all exams now."

"Yes, but I was given an extension because of my accident." He hoped she would believe his story. It was a lie but he was clever to shadow the truth.

"Your story would almost have worked up until the part where you didn't go directly to Mr. Friar and ask him to open the cupboard for you, or ask where the novel might be," she said with raised eyebrows.

"I was frantic Miss, this assignment is important for me to pass English and to graduate this year, I couldn't find Mr. Friar, he was in a staff meeting or something like that and I was afraid I wouldn't get a chance to catch him with my busy exam schedule."

She paused to think about his answer. "Very well, but you could have gone to the main office, they would have had a key. Your story is very loose Jack, it makes me think you are hiding something. It all comes back to discipline. If you had proper self-discipline then you wouldn't have been in that situation in the first place, you would have finished your assignment properly and thoroughly enough not to be in that predicament in the first place."

"Yes Miss." Jack looked past her serious face to the analogue clock on the wall. It was five thirty and his mother would have been furious waiting in the car outside knowing that he should have been out at least half an hour earlier.

"One last thing."

"Miss?"

"Make sure you're not late tomorrow, I need as many hands as I can get, we need to raise enough money to cover the theft."

"Yes Miss."

Sweetest Thing by U2 played out on the car radio, she tapped the steering wheel to the cheerful tune knowing all too well that it wasn't 'blue skies up ahead' like the song preached. For her it was big, black storm clouds that were going to unleash on Jack's ass. Getting detention was not what an Armstrong did.

The gentle breeze through her open car windows wasn't enough to cool her down, to dry the sweat from her brow or to stifle her rage. She didn't know exactly what trouble Jack had gotten himself into - Ms. Smith had left that detail for Jack to explain to her - but she was sure as hell going to give him a serving for tarnishing their family name. Jack's mother was ready to prevent him going to the formal with Sissy, but she knew it would be healthy if he spent time with a girl other than Susan. If Jack's father hadn't been away for another week then there would have been severe consequences, perhaps no social events or even after school breakup parties. There would have been a family discussion about sending him somewhere to work, via one of their family contacts, so he could work out his holiday period. But Jack's mother was on her own with this one and she would have to let it slide, she didn't need the extra stress in her life - not that she wouldn't give Jack a piece of her mind.

Twisting her loose wedding ring around her aged finger with the thumb of the same hand she impatiently looked out the car window towards the front entrance. She steamed furiously in the humidity of the car, too cranky to step out and wait under a shady tree, too mean to run the car for air-conditioning.

Jack scuffed his shoes along the covered concrete pathway. A willy-wag tail danced in front of him and chatted like it was protecting its nearby nest. He didn't give a shit about its bomb diving - he knew they never made contact no matter how protective they wanted to be - how much worse could his day get anyway.

"Mr. Armstrong, a word if I may," said Mr. Friar from behind him. Jack groaned, he was about to find out how bad things could get.

Fuck me, Ms. Smith has already told him about the book and now he'll want it back with a reason why I took it. More detention is on its way.

"Jack Armstrong, I know you can hear me, please, I need to ask you an important question."

Jack stopped and turned on the spot. "Yes sir."

"Can you please explain to me what shit means?" Mr. Friar said with his arms crossed. He looked like he was in no mood for humour.

"Sir?"

"Yes, what does shit mean to you?"

"Shit sir? Excrement?"

"Yes, in your book review. The first letter of each word you used to describe Paperback Writer forms an acronym for the word shit. So are you making fun of the book, saying that it's shit?"

That didn't take long to work out, so he knows nothing of me taking the book. "I don't know what you are saying sir, I think you are looking too hard into something for a meaning. It must just be a coincidence. The book was very good," Jack lied.

"I am not sure I believe you, but since on the outset it appears you've written a favourable review as you did find the book enjoyable then I'll give you the benefit of the doubt. Please be more careful in your future work Mr. Armstrong," Mr. Friar said in a cautionary tone.

"Yes Mr. Friar, I'll be more careful in the future."

"Good, you'll be pleased to know that I gave you a High Achievement for your assignment. That means if you pass all your other exams you should have a positive outcome for the university selection criteria."

"Wow, thank you sir."

"Yes, your analogy was well structured, even though I was slightly dubious about your final comments."

"Yes sir, I am sorry for that, I'll be more careful in the future," Jack said with a smile. He skipped away, towards the car park.

"Have a good weekend Jack."

"Yes, thank you sir, you too," Jack said, knowing all too well the weekend was off to a bad start with the impending confrontation with his angry mother waiting in the car park. The irony of it all was it was all about to turn to shit.

17 – CAR WASH CAPERS

A morning rain shower had cooled the air. Olive-backed sunbirds flitted around and bathed on water droplets that had gathered on the leaves of gardenia bushes – these had been trimmed into neat hedges that lined Evansdale Shopping Centre car park. Apart from a few carpentaria palms there was little shade and the morning sun had already begun to show its strength. Ms. Smith had anticipated the weather and had borrowed two temporary marquees from shopping centre management which were erected at the back of the car park. This position took advantage of the large highway roundabout outside the car park which was the junction of the Northern Beaches Highway and the Tableland Range Highway. This would make great exposure for their setup and signage and hopefully punters would see the carwash in progress and drive into the shopping centre car park.

Students hadn't arrived yet however Ms. Smith was there adding the final touches to the signboards. '$5 Small Car, $10

Large Car' was written in large letters. Ms. Smith had done the maths and realised that there had to be quite a few cars washed today in order to make the formal anything other than substandard. So Ms. Smith had to improvise and she had also set up a table under one of the marquees with an assortment of snacks and cold drinks that customers could purchase while they waited. A stack of chairs from the school were dropped off earlier by Mr. Hadrick, who conveniently couldn't hang around this morning; he didn't want to get caught up in teenage chaos that he believed the morning would turn out to be. Ms. Smith hoped students would soon arrive to help her unstack the chairs and arrange them under the second marquee - also for waiting customers.

Ms. Smith was wearing smart casual wear. There was no surf brand shirt for her but her clothes looked like they were what rich kids wore to their weekend tennis matches at their private retreats. Her clothes never looked worn, they didn't look like she would ever get a sweat up in them.

This morning's weather hadn't perturbed Ms. Smith, the patchy sky would give relief when a rain cloud covered the sun and the occasional drizzle would also help cool things down. And the rain wasn't heavy enough to stop people getting their cars washed. If anything it may help due to the road grime getting sprayed up onto the back of people's cars.

A slow stream of cars were entering the car park. The Shopping Centre was due to open in an hour so Ms. Smith knew that this must have been the start of students being dropped off by their parents. And arrive they did, in a mishmash of colour; it was different seeing the students out of uniform in their casual clothes. They all did pretty well to obey Ms. Smith's strict dress code – she only had to address a couple of students who tried to wear a top or pair of shorts that were too revealing. Ms. Smith had also anticipated this and brought some baggy shorts and shirts that were ill fitting, but they did their job.

One student brought a portable CD player which at first annoyed Ms. Smith but then she warmed to the idea as it made the students work well together and the customers didn't seem to mind. 'Boom Boom Boom Boom!!' by Venga Boys played out on the stereo and the customers enjoyed some of the drama class students putting on an impromptu flash dance.

When Jack arrived with Sissy they were dropped off by Jack's mother before she was to go shopping; Chandlers was having a closing down sale in the city so she wanted to go bargain hunting, she had her eye on a new blow dryer.

Jack was amazed at the performance his mother gave in the car ride to the car wash. She was in a polar opposite mood to when she carried on to him the evening before. It made Jack sick how nice and welcoming she was to Sissy; to keep up the masquerade of a happy family. Jack's mother was annoyed that he was spending time away from his studies to go to the formal but she was happy that he was taking someone other than Susan, she felt this was healthy for him not to be so engrossed in Susan, besides Sissy seemed like a lovely girl. She was so polite and full of manners. It was something she hadn't told Jack's father about, it was something he wouldn't understand; the importance of going to the high school formal and the life long memories that it produced.

Car wash customers began to line up in the car park. Whether by word of mouth about the cause or from the students who were waving signboards at the oncoming traffic, the car wash was becoming quite popular. Ms. Smith was beginning to feel relieved that they would meet their target funding. The smell of grilled sausages and onions wafted around the car park as one of the student's parents donated the food and their time to cook them. They were determined that their child's formal experience wasn't going to be diminished by the money theft.

Sissy and Jack worked together washing, careful not to get their clothes too wet. Jack worked a sponge while Sissy washed off the suds, taking care of one car at a time. She loved watching his care to detail as he the washed a car body in a circular motion with undiminished effort; she stood there transfixed – daydreaming that the car was her and that he was taking tender effort to wash her body. He looked back at her and had to snap her out of her dream to remind her he was done and she could work the hose. He wondered what went through her mind – she was definitely no Susan.

Jonas was there too; worry played with Jack's mind at what he might do this morning, and he also wondered who he was taking to the formal. Jack dared not make eye contact with him and he made sure he and Sissy worked as far away from him as possible. Jonas was hanging around Neil and Stanley who seemed to be partnered up already. Jonas looked like a loner at the moment and Jack wondered if his partner was turning up at all.

The morning was getting away from Ms. Smith, she was too busy keeping an eye on the till and liaising with customers to address the growing trend of boys taking their shirts off to show their muscles and girls trying to raise the lower half of their shirts by tying knots in them to expose their midriffs. She had to let it slide as they were all working hard and the money was streaming in. Ms. Smith had to pull up a small water fight that got out of hand as the hose had sprayed some of the customers sitting under the marquee. Those students had to have time out.

It was just past lunch when he noticed her turn up. Jack hadn't seen how she arrived but her presence was definitely known. Coincidently, 'Dub Be Good To Me' by Beats International started to blare out from the portable CD player. Her cheeky denim shorts were cut so high they would have made Daisy Duke blush. She sported a white fishnet crop top over a fluorescent orange, Lycra bikini that said, 'look at me' like a beacon in a storm - and it worked; active hoses were let go of and flailed like cut snakes, heavy sponges dropped in buckets of suds, heads turned and jaws dropped. She minced past Jack like a strutting catwalk model and didn't even acknowledge his existence. What little bum cheeks she had bounced and jiggled in the sun as she made her way across the carpark. Ms. Smith flushed red with rage.

Susan's anger had turned to revenge and she was laying it on thick. Jack was afraid of how far Susan was going to take this, his heart weighed heavy in his chest and he felt queasy with mixed emotions. But it seemed there was nothing he could do but watch this trainwreck pan out. If and when she fell, he'd be there to pick up the pieces, hopefully she wouldn't be too damaged along the way and he could put her back together. She got what she wanted, his attention, but now what was she going to do with it?

She made a beeline to the one person who would twist his angst like a jealous knife to his heart – Jonas. With a bright pink and blue Stussy singlet and brooding chest, he changed his surprised expression to a cheeky grin. Like a fly to shit, she'd landed on her prize.

Jonas quickly took his singlet off and offered it to Susan, she dismissed it with a wave of her hand. Her heart skipped a beat as her eyes drew to Jonas' chest. His pectoral muscles were raised like two large bronze, smooth mounds – her thoughts betrayed her as she imagined sinking her teeth into them. She flushed pink as her eyes lower to his rippled torso – imagining she could play checkers with his six-pack abs. *Yum*, she thought – she was only human.

Traipsing her extended fingers across his chest he stood there glaring at Jack as she circled her target. Jack wanted to run, but he had a commitment to Sissy, to the formal. *What is Susan doing here? Surely she wouldn't be going to the formal with Jonas, not after all we have been through this year.*

Nancy Smith had seen enough to know what was going on. She also was all too aware of the clothes, or lack thereof, that Susan was wearing. It was bad enough for the fellow students to be exposed to this caper let alone strangers rocking up in their cars. God knows how many men would ogle at this young piece of meat. She grabbed a towel and stormed straight over to the hot zone - she needed to defuse the situation.

"What do you think you're doing?" Ms. Smith shouted, her voice raised to compete with the music. "Turn that stereo off at once!"

The music was stopped and the car wash went quiet as all eyes were fixed on Ms. Smith.

"Susan, what are you trying to prove, wearing that get up?"

She rolled through the possible answers in her mind but she ended up succumbing to the enormity of the moment. "Nothing Miss."

"It doesn't look like it, in fact it looks like you are trying your hardest to humiliate yourself."

Susan saw rage, she was sick of her mother, sick of her sister and now sick of her teacher jumping down her throat thinking what was good for her and telling her who she should be. And if Jack didn't want her how she was then he'd have to get used to the new Susan. She had had enough. "Um, I don't think so, to me it looks like you're making a fool out of yourself, screeching like a bitch!"

The students laughed as Ms. Smith went red with rage. She grabbed the towel and launched herself forward in an attempt to cover Susan's body. As she did so she was met with Jonas' arm in a blocking maneuver which was too high and glanced off her shoulder clipping her chin. It sent her backwards as she was taken off guard.

Jonas laughed at the sight of her silver blonde hair messed and wild like a mop being flicked out of a wash bucket. Susan smirked but deep inside she was worried that Ms. Smith was hurt. But she stood her ground.

Rubbing her jaw she looked Susan in the eye. "You might want to think twice about who you hang around," she said to Susan.

"What Miss? You ran into my arm, it was an accident," Jonas said with a smirk.

"Just like watching me shower at home was an accident?" Ms. Smith scowled.

"What? No, I wouldn't do that," Jonas said, trying to defend himself but he didn't look convincing as he looked away from her.

"What?" Susan whispered. *She must be lying.*

Ms. Smith again tried to wrap the towel around Susan who stood there frozen in the moment. Jonas lifted his arm to fend off Ms. Smith and this time she grabbed his hand and twisted it back on itself. Jonas winced in pain and dropped to his knees on the hard bitumen. The watching crowd gasped like they were all trying to draw breath at once. Ms. Smith twisted his arm behind his back, pushing him over onto his chest and drove him into the warm bitumen. She pressed his hand into his back with her knee and had him pinned down. Her father's military training had bode well in her upbringing.

"What the hell, Miss? What have I done?" Jonas protested.

"I suggest you and your girlfriend take your circus away from here."

"What? We've done nothing!" Jonas shouted.

"Miss, he's not my boyfriend."

"I don't care, you've come here to cause a scene, you have no respect for authority. There are reasons why I didn't want anyone dressing like that, but you are so caught up in your own self-worth you don't care why. I want both of you out of here now!"

"But Miss, I was only having some fun," Susan said. "I hope we aren't going to get in trouble over this?"

"Just go, you've crossed a line, you're going to be no use to us here. I should have you both on detention next week and get your parents up to the principal's office to explain your behaviour, but since we are supposed to be having a fun day, and fundraising, I'll overlook this altercation and put it down as a learning curve for all of us. I suggest you leave now before I change my mind."

Ms. Smith backed off Jonas and threw the towel at Susan who promptly caught it and wrapped it around herself.

"Come on, let's go, this blows anyway," Jonas said to Susan as he brushed his knees and flicked small bitumen stones off his chest that had become imbedded in his soft skin.

18 – CLOSE ENCOUNTERS

The tail lights of the purple Holden Torana GTR-XU1 glowed red and lit up the surrounding trees as it came to a slow stop in the doctor's driveway. Jonas cut the engine, and the V8 coughed and sputtered with overdrive – like it didn't want to be told it had to go to bed. Jonas had tried to impress Susan by revving the engine and speeding along the highway to Neil's family home, and the car's engine wanted to keep having fun, to keep partying – but now it was the passengers turn to party.

Jonas was jealous of Neil's life and of all the 'toys' and freedom that his parents gifted him, but he didn't mind taking his rare sports car out for a spin whenever he got the chance. Neil's only restriction was that he brought it back in one piece and that he didn't screw any girls on the back seat – he didn't want his baby smelling like a whore house and he didn't want to replace the covers on the back seat.

Susan shifted her position in the brown vinyl clad bucket seat and looked at Jonas. He smiled back at her, his hands to himself, he quickly jumped out of the car before Susan could speak. He popped her door open for her and it creaked with its aged metal hinges. *Quite the gentleman,* Susan thought.

"Thanks for sticking up for me today, nobody has put themselves on the line like that for me before," Susan said sincerely.

"Not a problem, I could see she was being too harsh on you," Jonas said, motioning for her to head towards the entrance to the house, "ladies first."

The stale stench of marijuana hung in the air. It was a foreign smell to Susan and she turned her nose up at it. He led her past Stanley and Neil who were sitting on a couch taking turns with a bong. Neil held it up to Jonas offering him a toke but he dismissed it with a wave of his hand.

Music videos were playing on a projected image on the wall. The sound system was turned down low but enough to hear the dulcet tones of the heavy metal band working rhythmically to their wild head swinging and body lurching. Neil's parents were once again away, at a doctor's conference somewhere in the world, entrusting Neil to look after himself. The Saturday party was a common occurrence.

"Come on, I'll show you Neil's room, he's got a better collection of CDs in there," Jonas said as he grabbed a bottle of wine off his stoned mates - he took a swig and showed Susan the way. She nervously followed, she felt so out of place but she felt like she mattered.

Behind the closed door of Neil's room all Susan could hear outside was the drum beat to the music. She still smelt the stench of cigarette smoke and marijuana mixed together.

"Take a seat," Jonas offered, motioning towards the unmade bed.

Susan sat obediently at the end of Neil's bed while Jonas flicked through the long row of CDs which were stacked in a low bookcase.

"He's got a lot of music," Susan said coyly.

"Yeah, anything you prefer?"

Susan didn't know what to offer, her taste in alternative music might have offended Jonas and she wanted to impress him.

"How about AC/DC?"

"Yeah, not bad, bit old school, but this might be better," Jonas said as he picked a CD case out of the rack, popped it open and inserted the disc into the portable player sitting on top of the bookshelf. He skipped a few tracks and after a moment she could hear a jangly guitar and drum solo which led into the soft ballad of Daniel Johns. The song soon broke out into a rhythmic guitar riff and thrashing drum beat as Silverchair's 'Pure Massacre' screamed to life.

"Nice," she lied.

He turned it down a little so they could talk.

"You're different lately, I didn't really notice how pretty you were before today," Jonas said.

"Thanks," Susan blushed. "Time for a change I guess."

Jonas took another swig from the wine bottle. "So you're not hanging with those dorks anymore?"

"No," Susan said looking around the room nervously.

"Cool," Jonas said, he noticed her fidgeting and offered her a drink from the wine bottle. "Hey relax, are you sure you want to party with us?"

"Yeah, why not?" The alcohol burnt the back of her throat as the warm wine took her off guard, but she kept it down, trying not to cough.

"Well, we like to party hard, you think you can keep up?"

"I am up for it," Susan said. "You're not the only tough one here."

"Woah, relax, I didn't think you weren't," Jonas said with a wry smile across his face. "So does anyone know you're here?"

"No, I didn't think I needed a babysitter."

"You're feisty, we'll have some fun tonight."

"What do you mean? I am having fun."

"This isn't fun yet, trust me, I'll teach you how to have *good* fun," Jonas said as he brought a hand up and brushed her hair from her face. He traced his fingers over her lips and she flinched turning slightly.

"Relax honey, you've got some beautiful lips."

She regarded the complement as repugnant as his smelly wine breath slothed across her face, offending her senses. A knot twisted in her gut and she glanced at the closed door; she cursed her decision to come into the room.

"No thanks, can we go outside?" Susan said as she pushed the offered wine bottle from her face.

"We are just starting Love." Jonas ran a firm hand up her inner thigh; Susan squirmed.

"Please, don't."

"Come on babe, I'd love to taste your nice lipstick? Did you steal the makeup from your mum?"

"Ha ha, no I didn't smart ass."

"Well the colour's a bit slutty."

"Fuck up with your comments," Susan frowned, she didn't like Jonas' dark humor.

"Suppose the colour would look good around the base of my dick."

"Hey that's no way to talk to a girl!" She turned away from him and backed towards the side of the bed.

"Are *you* a girl? Let me check." Before she knew what was happening he ripped open her top and exposed her chest. Her black bra shielded his ogling eyes.

"Nice, a little flatter than I am used to," he said with a cruel grin, holding the torn top open. "Still there's one last check just to make sure *you're* a girl."

Her heart knocked hard in her chest.

She smacked his searching hand away and held her top tightly closed. Her wide eyes darted towards the closed door, she was trapped, she was frozen with fear.

But before she could get up he had struck her hard in the stomach with a closed fist at full force. It knocked the air out of her and she doubled over in pain. He took advantage of her hunched position and flipped her over on the bed as she gasped for breath. He quickly pulled her from behind, towards the edge of the bed, with her hips up high. He pulled her arms out from under her which forced her head into the bed. She let out a muffled scream.

She thought she was safe wearing jeans to a party with a boy she should have had better judgment with but it was no barrier for his strength; in one swift tug he had her jeans and pants off down to her thighs.

"No!" she screamed through tears and spit.

He slapped the side of her bare ass and it sent a stinging pain across her skin. "Bingo, we have a winner," he laughed, "a little hairy but it'll still do the job."

She tried to move but he was one step ahead and he grabbed her around the back of the neck, his grubby fingers gripping the side of her throat with brute force. "Now, now, where do you think you are going? You wanted to party with the boys, I am just going to show you a good time," he whispered into her ear. "You play well and the boys outside will treat you fine. They might even want a turn."

He released his grip and she coughed for air, she couldn't find the strength to touch her throat where his fingers once were; they had branded an impression into her neck.

She could hear his belt buckle jingle and his pants unzip just over the dull beat of the music outside combined with the stereo playing in the room. Tears streamed from her eyes as she wondered if she would get out of this alive. She didn't want her first time to be this way.

"I've got to teach you a valuable lesson...," he laughed.

Susan's mind screamed inside; it was her way of dealing with the situation, with his stupid statement, with his stupid actions. She felt his heavy hands grip the sides of her buttocks and linger there. The sound of a smashing bottle was heard outside and she felt one of his hands come off her as he turned his body to look towards the opening door.

"Hey, not yet, wait your turn," he said angrily to the shadow entering the room.

Before Jonas could react a swift foot kicked out and stuck him squarely, hitting his bare testicles from behind sending him to the floor in an instant. He writhed in pain. The assailant picked up a baseball bat from a dresser and swung it clearly around and struck him on the lower arm. The cracking sound indicated a bone was broken. He screamed in agony. The second swing of the bat meeting the back of his head and sending him into unconsciousness.

"Please, leave me," murmured Susan, hoping her turn wasn't next.

"Come on, let's get you the *fuck* out of here," said her sister as she helped her pull up her jeans. She grabbed one of Susan's arms and hoisted her off the bed.

"Valerie?"

"Yes, come on hurry, we've gotta get out of here. I've sorted out this one but the others think he's getting lucky with sisters. It won't take them long before they realise their buddy is out of action."

Susan looked at her sister. Her turned face was full of determination but she could tell that she had disappointed her big sister. Tears streamed down her face as she realised that it was her own fault for getting herself in this position and that she also put her sister in danger as well. She didn't know how she would ever repay her for saving her from this monster. She knew she owed her life to her sibling.

Although she should fear the punishment her sister or mother might deal her once they were home, her main fear now was the repercussions that Jonas may deliver to her, or her family and friends.

"Val..." Susan whispered.

"Save it."

"But I just want to thank you."

"Don't. I don't want your thanks, there are others that need your thanks more than me."

"Mum?"

"It wouldn't hurt if you treated her better."

"I love her but she knows how to hurt me."

"Don't you think that's being a little selfish?"

"Yeah, but it's how I feel."

There was silence in the car. The sound of the tyres murmuring along the bitumen road felt rhythmic and soothing. Valerie concentrated on the road ahead as she sped towards home.

"Did he do anything?" Valerie asked, breaking the silence.

"No." Susan clutched her stomach feeling the pain in her abdomen. She knew what her sister was asking.

"Are you sure? Because if he did anything to you..."

"It was close Val, he was so close to hurting me." Tears streamed down her face. She pulled her legs up into a crouching position in the car.

"I am not going to lecture you, no 'I told you so' rants, I just want you to know I love you so much and this is the reason why it kills me when you don't listen to me."

"I know, but he was so nice to me today."

"Don't give it a *fucking* excuse. They are all the same, they all want one thing."

"I am sorry, there is no right answer to why I got myself into that position. I was being selfish. I was being ignorant."

"And these clothes Susan? You are asking for trouble. They aren't you," Valerie said glancing over at her sister.

"I know, I was escaping being me and it burnt me."

"Are you going to be okay?"

"Yes."

"You sure?"

"Yes."

"What about school, isn't he from your school?"

"Yes, but I don't know what he'll do to me, to any of us," Susan said looking nervously out the window. "I want to report him."

"You've made a mess of this Susie, it doesn't excuse what he's done or what he was going to do but the system will be against you. There is no use reporting it, it'll go nowhere. At least he'll get nowhere with the cops if he wants to report me for breaking his arm. It'll make him out as guilty."

"But what if he tries this on another girl? What if this is his thing and he does it all the time?"

"I said no!" Valerie shouted.

"So what do I do, there's one week left of school and I've got exams," Susan recoiled. "I can't *not* go to school."

"I don't know sis, you've got to be careful. Do you think he'll let it go?"

"His grudge against Jack at school has escalated. He doesn't let things go."

"Then why get caught up with him in the first place?" Valerie's face glowed red with determination and anger.

"I don't know."

"Don't give me that shit. Give me your fucking honest answer, why?"

There was a long pause before Susan finally spoke, "I am sick of people telling me who I should be, how I should act."

"Who's telling you what?"

"You. Mum. Wear this, don't talk to this boy. Be home at this time."

"Tonight is the *fucking* reason why we are protective of you. We love you, we don't want you to make the same mistakes we made. We are trying to help you."

"If you hadn't suffocated me so much with your rules and regulation then maybe I wouldn't have gone off like this. If I had made a few mistakes on my own I would have learnt earlier and it wouldn't have gotten to this."

"You think you are that good? You think that you stub your toe and you'll learn not to get run over by a truck?"

"You're taking things to the extreme."

"It's like I have to, so you understand me," Valerie said.

"Then why didn't you tell me about your baby? Why wasn't I allowed to know? That made me so angry. Like I was untrustworthy, like I was a child and couldn't handle anything."

"With decisions like you've made tonight it's little wonder why we didn't tell you," Valerie spat.

There was another long pause in the car. Both women were furious.

"How'd you know where I was anyway?" Susan finally said.

"Like I said, I am not the one you should thank." Valerie stared cursedly at Susan.

"Jack?"

"Yes, he saw you walk off down the close and when he realised who picked you up he came over and warned me that you could be in trouble."

"I've wrecked it between him and I haven't I?" Susan rubbed the tears from her eyes.

"I am pretty sure he still cares for you Susan."

"Yeah, but it's going to take some mending."

"I don't know, you'd have to talk to him. That's the bit that hurts us all Susan, we've all wanted to talk to you, to work things out but you've put up these walls and won't let us in."

"Has anyone thought how hurt I've felt? Jack has gone off with Sissy, you've been holding this pregnancy secret for years. Mum doesn't want me to have anything to do with boys. You've all pushed me away and then you get angry when you get the distance you want."

"I don't know about Jack or Mum but I've been as honest as I can with you, Mum said when the time was right she wants to let you know." Valerie said. "When Mum told me...When I found out about Mum and Dad I took it to heart like you have now. I went off the rails and didn't want to listen to anyone. I was seeing a boy while I was at school and well, we did it and I ended up pregnant; it made matters worse."

"When Mum told you what? Valerie, what about Mum and Dad?"

"Look it's not about what Mum told me, it's about you getting yourself into dangerous situations. We thought Jack might get you... I mean I didn't expect you to end up with the high school bully, not after what you and your friends have all been through."

"Valerie, this is what I am talking about, all these secrets, don't you think I should know? Especially if there are more secrets about Mum and Dad that I don't know about! You know anything about Dad has made me so fragile."

"Exactly, which is why Mum has decided to tell you after you graduate. She didn't want what happened to me to happen to you."

"It *didn't* and it *wouldn't* have," Susan said angrily.

"Not from what I saw, I'd say it was very close to happening, if not worse. I chose to have sex, I didn't chose to get pregnant that was my mistake. Your choice to have sex was being taken away from you - who knows what messed up shit you'd be dealing with if I hadn't come along."

"Yes, but this secret you have..."

"Susan! Haven't you learnt anything tonight, let it go, Mum will tell you, it's not up to me."

Susan turned in her seat and looked at the reflections of the street lights rolling across the bonnet of the car. She was furious but conceded she was the luckiest girl alive tonight.

"Sorry sis, and thank you."

Susan's head pounded with thought. A short moment in time of pure evil can ruin a lifetime of purity forever.

19 – SUNDAY SCHOOL SKIRMISH

The boy's pact had been an easy assignment to follow; meet at the back of the school just before midday, negotiate an easy access to the auditorium, establish a secure line of sight to the main entrance, note who entered the writers group, then disperse and reconvene later that night to debrief over the possible culprit. It would take an hour or two maximum.

Jack, Tim and Patrick had entered the school grounds through the back fence. They skirted the buildings ensuring they kept a low profile. The difficulty they posed was getting close enough to see who entered the auditorium without getting caught. They needed a plan to maintain a good distance and to get the evidence they needed – a list of who was in the writers group.

As per usual Patrick had overdone his commitment. He had seen one too many stake-out movie scenes and had brought a plethora of snacks in his backpack. He was prepared to stay for a week but Jack insisted it would probably only take an hour out of their Sunday. Jack didn't know if Patrick was more committed to the stake-out or to an 'eat out'.

The best vantage point would have been from Ms. Smith's office or from inside the auditorium. Both options were way too risky. Jack didn't want to get caught breaking into a school building again, this time his luck would have run out and the police would have been called.

There had to be another option but the boys were running out of time.

"What if we hide down the walkway a few buildings down, we'll see them come from the car park," Tim suggested.

"That would be okay, but what if one of them did what we just did and they come in from a different way? This school has too many entry points along the boundaries," Jack said.

"Yeah but surely they'd all come by car and through the front gate?" Patrick said as he munched away on a space food stick - clearly ready for anything required of the mission.

"We can't screw this up, it's their last meeting of the year, and we may never get another chance to see who is in the writers group. There has to be another option," Jack said.

"Look, I don't know, maybe we could split up and each of us man a different entry point," Tim said.

"Not a bad idea, but we could still miss someone and that might be the person we need to see," Jack said.

"How about we get into Ms. Smith's office?" Tim offered

"And how do we do that?"

"I can pop a lock, I learnt that long ago when my sisters locked me out of the house. Hunger can lead you to drastic measures." Patrick said as he opened a Tiny Teddy biscuit packet.

"It sure looks like it can," said Jack. "You have the tools to do this?"

"Sure do, I learnt from Scouts to 'Be Prepared'," Patrick said.

"Come on, I don't like it but it's a matter of life or death," Jack said.

The boys ran to the passageway between the two buildings. Jack was right, the vantage point from the office was perfect. There was a direct line of sight from the glass door across the way to the main entrance of the auditorium.

Both Jack and Tim turned to face the exposed passageway while Patrick worked his magic on the lock. They didn't know how he was going to open the door, but he promised it would be easy.

"Hey guys, this isn't going to be easy," Patrick said on inspection of the door. They groaned at being misled - what were they thinking? "Well it's not like the doors at home, I can see the striker clearly engaged in the housing there, that's what I shove my knife into to pop the lock. Here it's not visible, the whole frame is protected by an aluminium shroud."

"Striker? Housing? Shroud? Are you Patrick Fucking MacGyver? Jack teased out of frustration.

Patrick shot Jack a frown, he was trying to keep his friends focused on the problem.

"Well, what is 'Plan B'," Tim asked. "And we'd better think fast, I just heard a car pull up."

Jack shrugged, he looked around like a frantic dog trying to find an escape route, but in reality he was trying to find a protected vantage point. In frustration he grabbed the office door handle and jiggled it, to his surprise it moved freely, it wasn't locked! The boys looked at each other, amazed at the find.

"It's open, do you know what that means?"

"That Ms. Smith is here somewhere?" Tim said.

"Exactly, all we can hope is she forgot to lock the door when she left? Or perhaps she's still here somewhere on the school grounds, maybe she's gone out to get some lunch?" Jack said.

"We can't hang around and wait, we'll get sprung," Tim said nervously.

"It's our only shot guys, maybe it's worth the punishment if we get caught," Jack said.

"Yeah but aren't you on thin ice? You've already had a run in with Ms. Smith, you said she thought about calling the cops on you, I don't think we would be so lucky this time," Patrick said looking around wide-eyed.

"Come on, if she comes back we'll just have to hide in the back of the office and wait it out, our plan of meeting up at home would have to wait until we sort it out. That's the worst case scenario anyway," Jack said.

"No, the worst case scenario is that we all get caught, then what?" Patrick said.

"We are in this together, we've got no other choice and we've run out of time." Jack pointed towards the group of people walking up the pathway towards the auditorium. "Quick, inside."

Entering the office on the weekend was the wrong thing to do, but it added a sense of excitement to their planned stake-out. Tim was secretly enjoying the thrill of it, Jack just wanted answers and was numb to the potential risk, whereas Patrick was trembling with fear - he was no good in these situations.

They decided it was best for Patrick to head to the back of the office and wait, he was too nervous to be of any help. Tim sat up on a low cupboard which was positioned under a row of windows and he hid behind curtains. He could press his head against the glass and peer through an opening in the curtains to look down the passageway to see if Ms. Smith was coming. If she was returning from either lunch or the toilet she had to approach from the same way. Jack squatted low at the office door and peered across the passageway to the auditorium's main entrance. He was partially hidden by a low cut, open garden between the two buildings. He could be seen from the other direction but it would have been difficult unless you knew what you were looking for.

Mr. Friar was the first to arrive, distinctly recognisable in his trademark tweed jacket - Jack never understood why he continued the look well into summer. When the others arrived Jack shouted the names out so even Patrick could hear at the back of the office.

"Look who we have here, it's Sissy, we knew that already. Ah, look it's Mad Daris, wow he scrubs up alright when he's got more clothes on," Jack said in reference to Daris never wearing a shirt as he went about his property. "There's Mrs. Valentino, ah and Valerie, so that's where they were going that other Sunday."

"Anyone else?" Tim asked, his head still pinned to the window looking out the curtain gap.

"Let's wait and see," Jack said. "Surely there are more than that."

"We can't get caught here, we've got to call it soon, let's give it five more minutes," Tim said.

"Yeah okay, Ms. Smith might be part of the group?"

"We can only hope, so we don't get caught red handed in here," Tim said. "Oh, hang on, she's coming! She's way too close, we're going to have to hide with Patrick down the back."

The boys moved from their positions and scrambled down to the back of the office. They hid behind a partition and all struggled to squeeze themselves under a desk, but with adrenaline pumping through their bodies they managed to fit.

They heard the office door click open and Ms. Smith enter. They could hear the rustle of what they imagined was her lunch wrapper, followed by her chair wheeling backwards behind her desk and the huff of her leather seat cushion as she sat down quickly. Their ears were oversensitive, picking up on any sound and trying to process it and recognise it.

Jack looked at his watch and mouthed, "great," as he knew they could be in for a long wait.

Time seemed to drag on for what felt like an eternity, but the boys dared not move. It was quite boring up until Ms. Smith's desk phone rang.

"Ms. Smith. Oh hello Mr. Hadrick. Yes sir, still at it, grading papers. No sir, I won't be too much longer. Yes, oh yes, well thank you, I've considered your offer and I'd be pleased to accept the vice principal's position next year. Yes, yes I do love being head of Speech and Drama but I am up for the change and for the challenge.

"Yes sir? Oh yes, well I've got my suspicions about one student in particular but I want to make precisely sure that I am correct before I make the accusation. We can then call the police on the matter. Yes sir, two thousand dollars is too much to ignore.

"Okay, sir, yes you have a good day too," said Ms. Smith ending the phone call.

The phone was hung up and Jack, Tim and Patrick all looked at each other. It seemed Ms. Smith was on the war path, Jack was her target and a promotion was up for grabs. Jack guessed she was offered the position on the results of her investigation; cracking the case on the money theft would secure her role as the vice principal. Jack knew she was onto a false lead, but wondered if he might be set up to take the fall.

Jack slowly moved position to let the blood flow back into his cramped legs before he heard Ms. Smith pick up the phone receiver and dial a number.

"Hello, yes sir it's me. How have you been? Good. I have some really good news, yes, yes but hear me out."

There was a long moment of silence in the office, Jack could only think that the person on the end of the line was deep in a one way conversation.

"But please, can I just say position is only a stepping stone to the top job. Yes, yes sir, I know, *'strive for excellence at no cost, reap the rewards others have lost'*, yes I haven't forgotten our motto. No sir, okay, thank you, but..."

There was a long silence and Jack could just make out the beeping sound of a dead phone line. Ms. Smith finally replaced the receiver, she stood up quickly forcing her wheeled office chair to crash into the bookshelf behind her desk. She picked up her handbag, her car keys rattled as she grabbed them from her desk, and she headed for the office door.

The boys were hot and cramped, they could sense freedom was only moments away. Patrick, who was going purple from trying to hold the pressure, accidently let out a short squeaky fart. The boys looked at each other wide-eyed and mortified.

Ms. Smith paused at the door, turning her head in the direction of where the boys were hiding. Their hearts pulsated in their chests, sweat beading down their faces. If anyone moved their world would be shattered and they would be spending time at the police station this afternoon answering questions. Their graduation would surely be under contention - Jack couldn't face repeating Year 12 especially with Ms. Smith vying for the principal's position.

As Ms. Smith took a step towards the back end of the office a book fell off her bookshelf and crashed to the ground. She would have normally returned to fix the mess, her obsessive compulsive disorder usually wouldn't allow for things to be left out of place, however she had more important issues to deal with and that meant visiting her special cabinet at home. She dismissed the squeaking sound as two more books yielded on her bookshelf before they fell so she clicked the door lock over and closed the door behind her with a forceful heave.

The boys waited for a further minute before they moved just in case Ms. Smith returned. Patrick couldn't hold out any longer and his body released the remaining gas in his bowel with what seemed like a twelve second fart. Jack and Tim wailed as they tried to escape to freedom and the wrath of Patrick's ass - the smell was overwhelming - while he sat there and laughed his heart out.

The smell of freshly heated sausage rolls hung low in the auditorium, it drew the gatherers across the entrance way to the small table set up haphazardly in the middle of the vast hall. A small membership fee afforded the writers group rewards like the cheap supermarket bakery offerings that were presented before them.

Milling around the table the members of the group exchanged pleasantries. The writer known as Mick Axeman wasn't shy and grabbed a paper plate to load it with cake, biscuits, party pies and sausage rolls - much to the disgust of the others. Some were willing to pick one or two treats from the assortment while others turned their noses up at the food. Mick Axeman didn't mind, more for him.

"Okay people, I am glad you could all make it, except um, someone's missing," Mr. Friar said as he stood on tippy toes trying to see if someone was being blocked by his vision by another. "Ah, yes, Sam Shield isn't here, does anyone know if he's coming?"

"I don't think so," John Bird said.

"Oh, really?' Mr. Friar said in disappointment.

"Yeah, I think he's giving his arm a break. He's been working hard at being himself lately," John Bird said.

"Well that's unfortunate, I had some really important news to tell you all."

The group stopped and listened, they were intrigued by what Mr. Friar might have to announce. Was it a book deal or an excursion next year to visit a publishing house?

"What is it Mr. Friar, you have all our ears," Felicity Grey said, munching on a lamington from a packet.

"Well someone can tell Sam Shield," Mr. Friar said. "Everyone, the exciting news that I have is that Paperback Writer has been accepted for a reproduction deal by Crazyhome Publishing and they want to meet John Bird for a deal on future works!"

Alex Dimov played with her wiry red hair, she looked pissed. *Why does that bitch get so much attention?* She decided to excuse herself to the toilet with the pretense of leaving the group, to make her way back home. She had much to think about.

John Bird was taken aback. *How could they like my work? I thought it was worthless. I thought I was worthless.*

"That was intense!" Tim said with a nervous smile. "Ms. Smith is one tough nut."

Yeah, I've got to wait for my heart to stop smashing around in my chest. Imagine if we were caught in here?" Jack said.

"We'd be fucked," Patrick said as he pulled himself up from under the office desk. "But my ass would have saved us, she would have been knocked out from the gas, giving us a quick getaway."

"It's a wonder we're not all dead," Jack said, frowning in disgust.

Patrick laughed and quickly went quiet as he realised the stupidity of what he said.

"So out of all the people you saw go into the writers group, who do you think could be John Bird?" Tim asked.

"I don't know, I didn't expect to see Valerie and her mum there. It could be any of them, even Mr. Friar." Jack said.

"What if they aren't even here today?" Patrick said.

"It's possible there are people missing today, but I reckon John Bird is here, Mr. Friar is too proud of them, it's the last meeting and it sounds like John Bird is his best product."

"So, we're no better off finding out who wrote the novel, and who is trying to hurt you?" Tim said.

"No, and I don't know how we could narrow it down," Jack said.

"Let's talk through what we do know," Tim said. "First there's Mr. Friar, he's been quite weird and possessive over that book and he's been possessive over making sure you and only you review it."

"True, and then there is Daris, who you would have thought was crazy enough, but he actually seemed quite willing to help me."

"Help you? I thought you said you didn't see him, when you were dumped into his yard?" Tim said with a frown.

"Um, yeah, it was the other morning, when I was walking past his house, he um, he yelled out to me to watch out when I didn't see a car coming as I was crossing the road," Jack lied.

"Whatever," Patrick said dismissively, "What about Sissy then? Isn't she crazy?"

"Yeah, I guess she is, she's all over the place sometimes and I could see a split personality there but she is quite keen on making sure I go to the formal with her."

"Doesn't that say something, could she be infatuated with you enough to hurt you?" Tim asked. "Like a stalker?"

"Perhaps, we can't rule her out," Jack said. "And I don't know where Valerie and Mrs. V stand in all this, I've known them for years. Valerie has been pretty protective of Susan and Mrs. V is always helpful, she spoils me with her cooking."

"What about Susan?" Patrick asked.

"What about her?" Jack said defensively.

"Don't get me wrong, I wouldn't have thought about her if her mother and sister weren't here, couldn't she be caught up in it somehow?"

Jack thought long and hard. "I suppose she got off the bus at the right time to miss the crash, she was also at the park with me when the birds were blown up."

"Yeah and now she's ignoring you and off with Jonas," Tim said, Jack shot him a harsh glare. "Sorry mate, she's treating you badly."

There was a long pause. Jack's mind turned over like he was coming around to the idea.

"I suppose you could be onto something, she even writes poetry, which makes the bulk of the threats," Jack said. "It still doesn't help me, I mean it could be Jonas for all we know."

"I don't think so, I couldn't imagine him writing his own name let alone a novel," Patrick said.

"After this week, I don't know what is possible," Jack said looking deflated. "I suppose all we have is a list of people that I've got to keep an eye out for."

"We're here too Jack, we'll keep an eye out for you too," Tim said.

"Thanks guys."

Jack darted his head around the office nervously. "We'd better go, before we get caught by someone else."

"Yeah, true," Patrick said. "Hey you want to find out who got Ms. Smith so flustered."

Before the boys could protest he picked up the receiver on Ms. Smith's desk, hit redial and then the loudspeaker button.

Everyone froze as the harsh voice grated down the line. *"How dare you call me back, you have nothing further to say to me on the matter, it disgusts me to think that after all these years, of all the training we've put you though, that you haven't learnt the most valuable lesson, 'anything less than perfection is not acceptable', we just want the best for you, your mother and I."*

The phone was slammed down on the receiver at the other end sending a cracking noise across the speaker of Ms. Smith's phone, followed by the pulsing dead line tone.

The boys looked at each other, wide eyed, mouths open in utter disbelief.

The wind blew hard and his bedroom sliding window rattled in its frame. The afternoon rain was horizontal and it blasted the side of the house and iron roof in heavy pulses. The roof insulation wasn't enough to muffle the roar. The sounds of frogs, which seemed like they were in their thousands, were singing in symphony to the downpour. The orchestra of the storm, which was quite loud, was surprisingly calming. Although it was only a band of storms lashing the coast the weather had turned bad and it was getting worse as the monsoon trough strengthened.

Jack wasn't preoccupied with the weather; the way in which it turned people's dull lives exciting, the way it gave people something to talk about and wonder what Mother Nature might dish out for them. His family usually ran about the place making sure things were secure; all of which seemed too late and pointless – at least to Jack anyway.

Jack found more resolve lying in bed wondering where he went wrong with Susan; why she went off with so much hate and why, of all people, she went off with Jonas. Susan thought he'd kissed Sissy but she wouldn't listen to his explanation. He knew Sissy had probably stirred Susan up that morning. He wanted to let Sissy know that he was only going to the formal with her out of sympathy, but he felt he shouldn't otherwise it might tip her fragile mind over the edge. Jack had got himself into this predicament, he hadn't foreseen the dramas that he had caused and now he was madly thinking about how he could correct the situation - with all his smarts, Jack had never been a good chess player.

In his heart he knew Susan had nothing to do with the premeditated acts in the novel but his mind was clouded with her actions over the last few days. He shook the negative thoughts away.

It had been very quiet over at the Valentino house. Their car was parked in the driveway, which meant they were home in this weather, but he couldn't see any lights on. That didn't mean too much, but he usually caught sight of Susan's bedroom light on. That was always one of the indicators that she was up for a visit. After the carwash theatrics he thought it might be best to approach her tomorrow at school. He was certain he would cross paths with her as they had some of the same exams.

Deciding he wasn't going to penetrate the fortress of walls that Susan had built up since their big argument Jack wracked his brains on how he could get in contact with her.

He sat up looking across to his desk and in a lightbulb moment an idea sprung to mind. *I'll show her how I feel the way she likes to express herself – poetry!* Jack thought if he could get a letter to her, maybe tomorrow, then surely she'd read it and see how he felt. It was a long shot, perhaps his only chance.

Roses are red,
you dress in black,
please forgive me,
I want you back.

"No, too childish," he said to himself as he crossed it out furiously.

My heart is heavy,
it weighs in my chest,
of all the girls I know,
I like you the best.

"No, too dumb, fuck this poetry shit, I'll write her a letter instead," Jack said as he tore the page out of the notepad, scrunched it up and threw it away like a bad memory.

Jack spent the rest of the evening and into the night writing, and rewriting a letter. He only stopped for dinner with his brother and mother, his father was still away at the mine site. When he had finally finished his waste paper basket was piled high with balls of discarded draft letters. He looked at and smirked which quickly turned to a frown as he realised, given the chance, his mother would unfold each and every page to read what he'd written. *She can't make a fool out of me twice.* Jack pushed the pile of paper down into the bin and pulled the plastic bag liner around it, tying the top ends into a firm knot. Then he shoved the bag into his school bag ready to drop it into an industrial bin at the back of the school tuck-shop tomorrow.

Flopping into his bed he hoped the lateness and constant rain on the roof would drown out his thoughts and he'd be able to get to sleep quickly. It was no use, his mind kept racing with thoughts of Susan and what she could have gotten up to with Jonas.

Jambing earbuds in, he listened to his Walkman - a mixed tape that Susan had made up for him earlier this year. It was working to sooth his mind until 'Glycerine' from Bush came on and it struck a chord with him.

He turned onto his side, looked towards his window and whispered, "goodnight Susan," as a tear rolled down his check and soaked into his pillow.

"I'll kill that fucking bastard!" Jonas screamed as he held the weight off his left arm to reduce the excruciating pain emanating from the break in the bone. He winced in pain as he felt the two separated bones spar against each other in his arm as he over corrected its natural straightness.

Stanley's father didn't hesitate to rush Jonas to the Cairns Base Hospital emergency department when he saw Jonas in so much pain nursing his arm. Jonas' mother was incapacitated at home, passed out on the floor from an all-night bender - she wouldn't have been much help anyway with their dilapidated car sitting in their driveway with a flat battery.

"Hold on mate, it shouldn't be much longer," Stanley's father said to comfort him. It had just ticked over an hour since they checked in at the front desk - it was typically the minimum wait time at the emergency department.

The over-the-counter pain killers were starting to wear off and they weren't as strong as Jonas needed. After his attack he took a few large hits from the bong Neil and Stanley were using. This helped subdue the pain until the morning. Jonas didn't think it was that bad, until he tried to move.

His mates were too stoned to remember who entered the bedroom to inflict the wound. It could have been anyone, they heard the screams but thought Jonas was in fits of pleasure and they didn't want to interrupt him - they never did. They hated his womanising ways and were too fearful of letting him know.

Jonas was full of rage, and the attitude from the overworked nurse on reception didn't help ease his mood.

He was determined that Jack had come to rescue Susan. He thought Jack attacked him in a moment of weakness and Jonas wanted to settle the score. Right now his mind was filled with too much pain to think straight but he knew he had to pick the right moment. This time he wasn't going to play fair. This time Jack was going to feel his retribution, his angst, the fire from the devil's belly - Jonas was going to unleash all the pent up torment from his troubled upbringing.

20 – WHERE IS SUSAN?

'*...with a top of thirty two degrees today and a UV index of extreme make sure you turn before you burn after 15 minutes.*

'*Stay listening to 4RRR-FM, Regional Reef Radio, for future updates on that tropical low forming in the Coral Sea.*

'*Coming up we'll have Mayor Tom Pyne in to discuss your concerns with our region's disaster relief funding and he'll give you some handy tips to keep your property cyclone safe.*

'*Now this band out of Seattle toured Australia early last year on the back of their world tour, 4RRR-FM, giving you all the hits and memories, this is Soundgarden with 'The Day I Tried To Live'...'*

The radio alarm caused her to stir like a butterfly's first movements within its chrysalis. It had turned on at five past seven, it was set this way to miss the news and capture a song, sometimes there was talking overlap which she hated.

Her Monday morning routine was going to change today, but she forgot to turn off her alarm so she shot an arm out from under her Doona and clicked the radio off with her head still buried somewhere under the mess of bedding. Any other day she would have loved to listen to that song, but today - especially after the trauma of Saturday night - she didn't want to be reminded that she was alive.

She was thankful that Valerie came around to the idea and was going to take her to see the school nurse, Mrs. Healy, on her day off to report Jonas. Susan knew Valerie meant well about not reporting the attack, but she couldn't stop thinking about what Jonas was going to do and if he would try it on some other poor girl. Susan was thankful that Valerie agreed to not let her mother know what happened; she was more embarrassed that she got herself into the situation and didn't want to stress her out about it. Susan could see the irony in keeping something from someone to not hurt their feelings and she guessed it was karma that had dealt her a lesson. She wanted to stop the trend of emotional trauma so the sisters agreed that this one time they would close the lid on what happened. But Valerie had adamantly insisted that anything else in the future had to be openly discussed to keep their family strong.

Susan hid her pain behind the guise of an illness as she knew she had one week left of school and there was no way she could miss exams. With Valerie's support, Susan was expecting that Mrs. Healy would give her leniency, perhaps permission to take exams at another time.

Monday morning was Mrs. Valentino's weekly shop and she negotiated that the girls should go to the school to sort out Susan's expected absence while she shopped. She would have changed those plans in an instant if she knew the truth to the nurse visit – she would have sat beside her daughter and held her hand through the reporting process.

After a lengthy shower Susan immerged slightly invigorated on the outside but an emotional torrent on the inside. Her stomach still hurt from the punch and a purple bruise, the size of a fist, was beginning to bloom. She winced in pain as she touched its perimeter. She was glad it was there, she hoped it would be enough evidence to prove her side of the story. Doubt crept in her mind at the prospect of Jonas having the chance to defend himself over the matter. Her head was in the wrong place and she had second thoughts over the appointment.

The heat in the car didn't help the mood between the two sisters. The car's air conditioner was playing up and needed looking at by an air conditioner mechanic - something Mrs. Valentino didn't have money in the budget for at this time of the year; Christmas was fast approaching and she loved the extra cooking and baking for the season, and she loved showering her daughters with gifts. She was quite generous at Christmas, Susan wondered why, as the rest of the year they lived quite frugally. She thought her mother was either guilty of their troubled family upbringing in a single parent family, or her own upbringing was stifled and she was living through her own children's happiness. Susan thought it was quite fake and it added to the friction with her mother.

By the time Susan and Valerie were sitting in the small waiting room of the school administration office they were both quite grumpy and Susan thought she could smell her sweaty armpits. Even the school bus had better air-conditioning than their family car.

"Please come this way," Mrs. Healy said as she welcomed them with a larger than life smile.

Her white uniform was a little over the top, even the upside down fob watch pinned to her top was especially excessive especially since they were in a school not a hospital. Susan thought a feeble attempt to latch onto the job position as she's somehow missed out on getting a nursing position at a proper clinic. As silly as Susan thought it looked, everyone knew it commanded Mrs. Healy respect, especially with the junior students. Each child with a sniffle to a cut saw her and appreciated her medical wisdom and care. She was well liked by all in the school.

Susan didn't trust her though, maybe because of the white clothes. *Everyone needs some black to wear.*

"Now what can I do for you Susan?" Mrs. Healy asked as everyone took a seat in the small school sick bay.

"Um," Susan began. "I don't know."

"Well if you don't know then I can't help you."

Bitch. "It's hard Mrs. Healy," Susan said with her eyes to the ground.

"Come on sis, I am here for you, if you don't tell then he'll do it..."

"I know, I know," Susan interrupted. She looked up at Mrs. Healy who was all wide eyed with concern. *Maybe she does care.* "I um, I got into a situation." Susan nervously played with her ponytail, picking it up and dropping it, flicking it off her shoulder.

"Yes, go on Love."

"I shouldn't have been there."

"Susan, please, that doesn't matter," Valerie said.

Tears began to welt in her eyes as she retraced the moment in her mind, over and over again. "He was going to hurt me," she cried.

"Where is Susan today?" Tim asked as Jack sat down beside him.

"I don't know, I guess she's still pissed with me, maybe she's *that* angry she doesn't want to see me at all, I hope she isn't blowing off her exams over it," Jack said as he looked over at a vocal group of Year 8 students playing handball in their lunch hour on the concrete pathway.

"Did you try and see her yesterday?" Patrick asked.

"No, I thought I'd give her space, I might try this afternoon."

"Any idea about who is out to get you Jack?" Tim asked.

"Nah, I've got no idea," Jack said, he was over the whole problem but needed to keep his wits about him. "Are either of you going to the formal, maybe I need extra eyes about."

"No, you're on your own with that one Jack," Patrick said with his arms out.

"Yeah, sorry Jack, since it's the end of school my parents are taking us to Brisbane on holiday," Tim said.

"Lucky you," Jack said. "So I am on my own."

"Yes, have fun, good luck with that," Tim said with a laugh.

"Yes well I have to get through tomorrow night's dance class yet," Jack complained.

"Yeah I don't get that, why learn the waltz, I mean it's grand and all but are people really going to dance?" Patrick said. "Remember the 'Heel and Toe Polka' in grade 7? That was hell."

"I'll say," Tim said. "Sucks to be you Jack."

"Gee thanks, I guess Ms. Smith wants to see something formal about the formal. We're all going to be dressed up - why not make it even more awkward than it is."

"You'll love it," Patrick teased.

"Hey, *you* aren't going on holiday, why don't *you* take Meredith, I hear she's got nobody to go with since Jonas picked Susan." Jack was angry that his support options were diminishing.

"Whoa Jack, I was only teasing, I am sure Susan wouldn't stoop so low. And look at me, when was the last time any girl looked at me, except to get out of my way so they wouldn't get crushed."

"Sorry man, I guess we're all feeling sorry for ourselves at the moment," Jack said. "I just wish I had a wingman to back me up, the formal is going to be bad enough, I'll be looking at the earliest moment to bail on Sissy."

"You sure miss Susan, don't you?" Tim asked.

"Yeah."

"She's really giving you a hard time over Sissy," Tim said.

"Tell me about it."

"Well, I guess she's not treating you good anymore!" Patrick broke into the song, 'You Don't Treat Me No Good' by Sonia Dada, and Tim joined in.

Jack would have normally got up and walked away but he was over it all. He didn't even have the energy to lash out a friendly arm punch at his mates. He just sat there and listened to them sing a cappella style and hoped the end of lunch bell would come quickly to drown out their carry on.

"Okay Love, so you're saying this boy that you went to a party with came onto you and punched you and tried to take advantage of you?" Mrs. Healy asked. She finished jotting notes down and looked up at Susan over the top of her horn rimmed glasses. She studied Susan, looking for the truth in her reply.

"Yes."

"And tell me Susan, were there drugs at this party?"

Susan anxiously played with the frayed tear in her black denim jeans, she looked over at her sister and shot her a look, waiting for a sign of encouragement. All Valerie could do was narrow her eyes and wait for Susan's response, she too wanted to know the answer. How did her sister get involved in such a predicament that was so out of character - what happened to the smart sister she once knew.

"Well, yes there were drugs there, but I didn't take any and I didn't see the boy take any either."

Mrs. Healy sighed as she closed her note book, sat upright in her chair and straightened her dress as though she were dusting her favourite biscuit crumbs off her lap. "Ms. Valentino, do you realise how difficult it would be to peruse this allegation, it would be your word against his. Now that you've indicated drugs were involved it would be dismissed in any police action or court decision."

"All he would have to say is that you were both under the influence and there was a misunderstanding. Are you sure you want to take this matter any further because as far as I can see there isn't a strong case here?" Mrs. Healy folded her arms, her seat backrest creaked as she reclined into it.

"What are you saying? He tried to hurt me, he had his pants down and he was going to put that thing in..."

"Please Ms. Valentino, from what you said, no rape has taken place. Yes he punched you in the stomach, I can just make out some bruising, but even with that he can plead innocence and say you got that from falling over."

"But what about all the talks, all the pamphlets and discussions on seeking help if an assault takes place?" Susan said in disbelief, tears streamed down her eyes as she realised her argument was futile.

"Yes Ms. Valentino, the government promotes the awareness program for students who are victims of sexual abuse and or violence, it has been running quite well."

"So there is nothing you can do for my poor sister." Valerie clenched her fists in anger.

"No, the paper work would tie me up for weeks, and all for an event that quite frankly looks like a lovers tiff. I suggest you take your poor sister home and teach her how to present herself around boys so she isn't so alluring and suggestive," Mrs. Healy said frankly. "There are other cases which would be of more importance than this one, and I don't think it would be fair for others to miss out on getting help because of that, don't you think?"

Mrs. Healy took out a piece of paper and wrote down a small note, after she signed it she handed it to Susan who grabbed it with a trembling hand. "I'll authorise the rest of the week off for you and I'll organise for the exams that you miss to be specially sat in the following weeks. Go home and rest, use the time to reflect on how much worse your situation could have been."

She didn't wait for any further comment from the sisters and she stood up and left out the back door. The sound of the end of lunch bell screamed to life outside. The two girls were left in utter shock at the result of the meeting.

"If she had of kept going on I would have got up and clock her, I was ready to slap the bitch," Valerie said. "Sorry sis, I was in total shock to what she was saying, I can't believe it, what sort of nurse or fucking liaison officer is she?"

Susan buried her head in her hands and wept uncontrollably, she realised that Jonas had gotten away with the assault and that there was potential for it to happen again, not only to her but to some other girl. There was also the thought of Jonas' retribution. Did Jonas see who hit him with the baseball bat? And if he did or didn't, would he still blame Susan for his injury and still come after her? She also thought about how her life didn't matter, and she was only a case to dismiss, would she even want to live if Jonas hadn't been interrupted by her sister? She felt her sister's warm hand rubbing on her back and she sucked up the tears, she pulled her head up and looked at her through puffy eyes.

"Thanks sis, you tried, the best thing you've done for me is save my life, but I am terrified of what may be coming."

"Don't worry about that, I've set things in motion, that areshole won't come near you ever again let alone look at you sideways once what I've planned comes into play," Valerie said with a wry grin.

21 – STORM BREWING

It was like walking from a barren landscape into the Garden of Eden once he passed through the opening in the fence. On the Armstrong side there was a lawn, mowed on most weekends but not to the standards of some of the neighbours. On the Valentino side it was like Jack entered the world of Narnia through the magical wardrobe, it was hard for him to describe but it was a beautiful stark contrast to his bedroom window outlook.

The lush buffalo grass was thick and padding underfoot, it wrapped around the stone border garden beds forming a sea of green pathways. The backyard wasn't a typical layout as the area to play cricket had long been replaced with freeform garden beds, all layered with tropical plants.

The hard work had been established years ago by Susan's father, Tony. After he left Mrs. Valentino kept up the maintenance, it was one of the things she didn't mind doing, and although it reminded her of her estranged husband she also found it was a healthy pastime along with her cooking.

Bromeliads of various shapes, as though they were flicked with paint of opposing colour, were grouped in like colours which added a striking effect. These shorter plants made up the foreground against the taller shrubs like caladiums, vincas, pentas, golden candles and towards the back were the taller gingers and heliconias. The shrubs and gingers flowered at different times and provided Mrs. Valentino with fresh cut flowers at the dining table most of the year round.

Old trunked cycads dotted the gardens, canopied by a saraca tree to the back with its orange flower lined trunk. A dilapidated tree house sat awkwardly in the fork of a poinciana tree, a wooden seat swing hung from one of its large branches. These were the only remaining structures in the garden that Tony had built for his girls, the only remaining evidence that he once cared.

She was there, long loose clothes on to escape the sting of the afternoon sun, digging away at the garden bed, loosening the roots of stubborn weeds - freeing her landscape of foreign irritants.

"Hi Mrs. V, is Susan home?" Jack asked coyly.

"Yes, but she's not up for any visitors," she said with her back to him, still busying herself with the gardening.

"I just wanted to see her Mrs. V."

"I am afraid she doesn't want to see anyone, that includes you Jack," she said reaching for a taller weed behind a cordyline.

"What's up Mrs. V? Is she okay?" *Surely this still can't be over Sissy, something must be wrong.*

"She went to see Mrs. Healy today, she's got a stomach bug and she doesn't feel in the mood to see anyone, she told me that much. You won't see her for a while, not until after school has finished anyway."

"Oh, that sounds terrible, please let her know that I came around and that I hope she gets better soon."

"Sure Jack, I'll let her know." She turned around and sat on one of the garden border rocks. "You know she's lucky to have you in her life, you have turned out to be a fine young man."

"Thank you." The complement caused Jack to blush and break eye contact by looking around the garden. "Gee, you keep a lovely garden Mrs. V."

"Yes, but sometimes it can be hard work."

"But it is lovely, I wish I could be good at something."

"You're only young Jack, you've got the rest of your life ahead of you." Mrs. Valentino looked across the yard. "Now if you don't mind I want to get the rest of this weeding done, I hear a big storm is on its way and I probably won't be able to get out here for a while if we get a tonne of rain."

"No problem. Oh, and if you don't mind can you please give Susan this letter, I've been meaning to let her know what she means to me for some time now."

"Sure." Mrs. Valentino removed a dirty gardening glove to receive the folded paper.

Jack turned and passed back through the fence opening as quickly and silently as he first appeared. Mrs. Valentino waited until she heard him enter his house through the lower level – the bang of the screen door indicating that he was inside. She carefully opened the letter and read it with a deep frown. She pursed her lips in displeasure, carefully folding the letter back up.

She sat there in thought, her maternal instincts got the better of her, but she resisted the urge to dig a hole in the garden and bury the letter under the mulch. Instead she folded the letter in half again to make it smaller, and she reached up, tucking it into a crack between the floorboards and wall of the dilapidated cubby house.

"You might be a fine young man Jack, but my Susan isn't ready for *your* immature love," she muttered to herself as she made her way back inside.

The phone ringing on the wall broke the awkward silence between all three family members sitting at the dining table. Jack's mother looked up at it like it was a welcome relief. She bounded to the phone and answered it with a big smile on her face.

"Hello," she said with an authoritative but pleasant tone. "Yes, who's speaking? Oh hello Sissy, yes I'll just get him for you."

Jack's body slumped with disappointment, he didn't want to speak to Sissy, he had hoped it was Susan. *What was she calling about?* Mrs. Armstrong returned to the table to finish her dinner and passed the receiver to Jack as he pushed back on his chair leaving a half finished dinner on his plate.

"Hello?" Jack said with a puzzled look.

"Hi," came the familiar chirpy voice from the other end. "Did I interrupt your dinner?"

"Sort of, but it's okay, what's up?"

"Just checking to see if you're still okay for dancing lessons tomorrow?"

"Sissy, I'll see you at school, I could have told you then."

"No you couldn't have because Dad wants to know if you could pick me up and take me there tomorrow, he's got to work late, they have safety training or something like that to get through. So if I waited till tomorrow then I wouldn't know if I had a lift."

"Oh, okay, sorry I'll ask," Jack said, he held the receiver to the side and partially blocked the mouthpiece to direct his question away from Sissy. "Mum, is it okay if we swing by Sissy's house tomorrow and give her a lift to the dance classes?"

"She's over in Redlynch right?"

"Yeah, up Michelangelo Drive, near the shop."

"That's not too far out of the way, not a problem."

Jack turned back to his conversation with Sissy, his brother giving him a sarcastic expression with his tongue out. His mother didn't see it as she was beaming with delight at the possibility of Jack seeing a girl who wasn't Susan.

"Mum says it's okay."

"Cool, thanks."

"I'll see you tomorrow," Jack said, he was hoping to get off the phone quickly.

"Wait a sec, I did interrupt your dinner didn't I?"

"Sissy, it's okay."

"So mummy and brother are sitting there eating dinner looking up at you with awkward grins?"

"Yes."

"Oh I am sorry Jack, I didn't mean to."

"It's okay."

"Is it hot there Jack? It's starting to get oh so hot here," she said, changing her voice to a sultry tone.

"What? What do you mean, we've got the air conditioner on?" Jack's frustration showed on his face as he turned to glance at his family. His mother still sporting a beaming smile and his brother still scowled at him.

"It's getting a bit hot here Jack."

"Sissy, please."

"I thought you said it was okay to call you during dinner."

"I am sure you didn't mean to, it's okay." Jack was now pissed off and it was hard not to show the anger in his voice.

"So if it's okay to call you now then you wouldn't mind if I were to slowly take my free hand and gently explore my hot body. My fingers are running slowly, up and down. Oh Jack, you're making me feel so hot," she breathed softly down the phone.

Jack flushed red, he turned his body fully away from the dinner table. He was embarrassed and furious.

"That's okay Sissy. Yep, see you tomorrow, bye." Jack hung up the receiver abruptly. He could only imagine Sissy pissing herself with laughter at the other end of the line. Her father was obviously not home. He took a moment to compose himself before returning to the table.

"She seems like a lovely girl," Jack's mother said, taking a sip of coffee while trying to control her smile.

"Yes, she is, she's special." Jack took a fork full of food, eating it angrily.

The first Jack heard about the storm was from the ABC news weather report. Jenny Woodward was talking about the potential development of a tropical low from the Solomon Islands. Over the next few days it would be monitored to see if it had the potential to develop into a cyclone. This time of year was cyclone season, so it was quite normal for weather reporters to get excited about any low that formed in the Coral Sea.

If it formed it would be called Tropical Cyclone Rona, the weather reporter declared. Jack listened with interest but wasn't alarmed, it was a common occurrence of living in the northern tropics to be dealt a cyclone watch or two during the wet season.

Jack kissed his mother on the forehead, wished her goodnight and headed upstairs to his bedroom. He was tired and wanted to listen to music before he endured another day of school tomorrow, and the pain of having dance classes with Sissy in the evening. *Such a waste of time.*

He felt a heavy blow to his upper arm, the pain wasn't instant but the force pushed him to the side and losing balance he knocked his head against the bathroom wall. Steading himself against the towel rail he turned to see who interrupted his teeth brushing process.

"Hey dickhead!" Clint said aggressively.

"What the? What was that for?"

"Just for you being an idiot."

"What?"

"Yeah, if you hadn't been so stupid lately then Mum and Dad wouldn't have worried about what I've been up to, but since you're such a dickhead now they are on my case as well."

"What do you mean?"

"Just stop fucking up, I don't want to look for a job, now they are on my arse about it."

Clint gave him a shove to the back of the head and Jack turned to swipe at him but he missed as he left the room. *Arsehole, it's got nothing to do with me that you're such a loser.*

He likened his brother to a tropical storm, full of rage and tempest, meandering aimlessly through life and deferring the real problems in his life by causing uproar and fury. Jack thought Clint had real problems and didn't know why he took out his frustration on him so much, he was his brother but it felt like he could have been a stranger. He thought siblings were supposed to love one another and look after each other, but the way Clint treated him, Jack felt like he couldn't have been any more of a hindrance in Clint's clouded life.

Jack sometimes thought that just because you were family didn't give you an excuse to treat each other with such disdain. It hurt how he observed his family treating strangers like royalty, like their lives mattered more, like the portrayal of happiness was stronger than actually making the effort to ensure there was happiness within. Jack saw all this like an influential, young minded child glued to mindless Saturday morning cartoons.

He finished brushing his teeth and out of frustration he threw his brother's toothbrush across the floor, he restrained himself from throwing it into the toilet, he couldn't care less about the implications - how much more strained could their relationship possibly get?

22 – DANCE CLASS

A mishmash of casually dressed students loitered about the entrance to the auditorium. The door was locked and Ms. Smith was unusually late for the one and only seven o'clock formal dance lesson. She wanted the formal to have a special moment that the students would remember forever. She didn't want the night to get lost in rubbish modern music. She knew the students wouldn't thank her now, they wouldn't thank her in the future but in years to come when they were reminiscing about their senior years they would remember this dancing and that would be thanks enough.

Jack and Sissy sat in silence in the back of the car, Jack's mother frequently staring back at them through the rear vision mirror. Jack was sweating with nerves, he was expecting Sissy to slide a hand across and grab his crotch, but she behaved and it didn't happen. The dance lesson was supposed to end after three hours and Jack's mother would return at ten o'clock. Sissy politely declined the offer to be returned home as her father was picking her up after his training.

Jack's mother spared him the embarrassment of a kiss, but gave the pair a group hug and endearing words of encouragement to enjoy their dance lessons before she left. *Thanks Mum, more fuel for Sissy*, Jack thought.

Making their way to the auditorium Jack's stomach started to knot with butterflies. He was unsure if he'd see Susan and Jonas at the rehearsal, he wouldn't be surprised if they turned up and made a scene. His head hurt at the thought of Jonas touching her, leering in his direction to show his dominance over her - another conquest.

Shaking the thought he turned to Sissy and smiled. Her light fabric dress waved in the breeze, she pulled a stubborn spiral strand of fringe and tucked it behind her ear. She looked back at him and smiled. She grabbed his hand and thanked him for coming to the dance rehearsal with him and let him know it meant a great deal to her. Jack told her it was no big deal.

In reality Jack wished he was home in bed listening to music. He tried to hide a yawn by looking away from Sissy and checking out who else had turned up. Thursday night at school was a tall ask, especially to learn dance moves for a formal that he didn't really want to go to.

A hurried sound of high heels could be heard clipping up the covered walkway. The unmistakable silver blonde head of hair of Ms. Smith swished from side to side as she pushed her way to the front of the pack.

"Sorry I am late everyone, I just got held up at home. Please, let's get inside and get the rehearsal underway."

Slow melodic music filled the cavernous auditorium from a small portable stereo which sat against the side of the stage. All the lights were on so the students could pay attention to the instructions and dance moves. Ms. Smith was a brilliant teacher which was reflected by how quickly they picked up the moves to the four step waltz. In her mind there was not enough time to teach her pupils anything more elaborate than the waltz so she decided to have a bit of fun and finish with the ludicrous moves to the Chicken Dance which had most of the students in hysterics.

Sissy and Jack, caught up in the moment, fell into each other's arms as they tried to stop laughing. It may have been the lateness of the night or the fact that the end of the year was imminent as the stress of exams was almost over but they lingered a little too long as they pulled away from their embrace.

"Sorry Sissy, I didn't mean to..."

"It's um...fine Jack, please don't worry. See how much fun we can be together?"

Pulling his arms away they strayed down the length of her arms and their fingers met gingerly. As though it was natural their fingers entwined and locked together. They stood there, stunned in the moment, staring into each other's eyes.

"It has been a good evening."

"Yeah, I'd love to have more like these...with you," Sissy replied.

Jack blushed and looked down, Sissy was nervously playing with the hem of her short dress - lifting it gently and dropping it, exposing her upper thigh with each movement. Jack looked away as his heart quickened.

Just as quickly as their fingers found each other, Jack pulled away suddenly. "Sorry Sissy, um I should...we should get going."

"Yeah, looks like Ms. Smith is packing up." Sissy looked over at her pulling the stereo lead out of the socket.

"Come on, I'll walk you to the front gates."

Along the way, Jack's mind wandered, he was caught up in the moment of having a great time with Sissy. *Look at her, she's beaming with excitement, does she genuinely like me that much, to be so happy around me? With Susan it's different, she's my world but sometimes the friction between us burns and I get so frustrated that she can't see we'd be awesome together.*

And yet here is Sissy – warm, caring and so willing to please? Is it too easy? Should love be easy or should it be a challenge? Have I got it all wrong?

Jack was woken from his daydream by the large bus pulling up in front of them. Sissy gave Jack a peck on the cheek and climbed aboard the bus.

"Need a lift? I can drop you off mate," Mr. Smart said cheerfully from the driver's seat.

"Nah thanks, Mum is coming to get me, she won't be long."

"Okay. Oh, please thank her for picking up Sissy this afternoon," he said before the pneumatic doors sighed and closed. Jack gave a wave and Sissy blew him a kiss from mid-way up the bus. Jack thought it was quite the transport and wondered how it was growing up being taken everywhere in a bus. It was probably quite restrictive in where they could actually go.

Looking down at his cheap Pulsar watch he checked the time, it was a quarter past ten - his mother was late. A stiff breeze blew and a heavy cloud drifted across the moon like it was being tucked in for the night.

He didn't hear her footsteps approach, but as she announced herself he turned startled. "Jack, a word if I may," Ms. Smith said in her sharp tone. Before he could turn around and reply she had him in a strong headlock and was dragging him back towards the school into the dark shadows of the buildings.

His nostrils flared as he tried to breath, her grip was suffocating. She had sufficient elevation to her elbow, tilting his head back putting further pressure on his esophagus. It was quite like the headlock Jonas had placed on him a few weeks ago but Ms. Smith's stronghold felt more tactical - well-practiced. And unlike Jonas' hold, Ms. Smith had allowed Jack's feet to touch the ground as he scrambled backwards.

She whispered in his ear but he couldn't understand what she was saying. Shock had turned into fear. He knew she hated him, she blamed him for the theft of the formal money, she directed all her anger for her hatred of teenage unruliness towards him.

Why me? Doesn't she realise she'll get in trouble over this? Dismissed from teaching - there goes her promotion. Or is she planning on killing me and hiding any evidence? Sissy would be the last one to have seen me alive, there would be no account for the time she left and when my mother would turn up. I can't believe it, of all the culprits we overlooked Ms. Smith.

Fuck she's got a strong grip!

Heavy metal music pulsed and squealed, singers screamed in demonic chorus. Smoke thick with sweat hung in the air like a grey blanket. This was the den of the devil.

A black arm cast lay in front of him like a blank canvas. It was heavy and itchy. It was a constant reminder of his resolve. He had nothing else in his life that mattered. He didn't even care what his mother was up to, she was insignificant at the moment. He felt relaxed knowing that he now had purpose - to make Jack pay one last time.

Taking one of the cigarettes out of a packet he stole from his mother, he lit it, drew deep and relaxed as the nicotine washed over his body, slowly unwinding the withdrawal like a rubber band untwisting.

He picked up the white correction fluid pen, shook it vigorously and began to draw artwork on his cast, some demonic symbols and finally crosshairs with the initials JA squarely in the centre.

"After your detention with me I decided to check you out, so I had a meeting with Mr. Friar about your academics," Ms. Smith said.

"You what!" Jack shouted angrily, rubbing his neck as though to remove the sensation of Ms. Smith's arm imprint.

"Yes, it appears you have been letting him down."

"What? I don't understand, what has all this got to do with you!"

"Jack, Jack, your anger is unnecessary," she said with a smile. "Please hear me out."

"Hear you out? After you just dragged me back here to kill me, you've half choked me anyway, what are you going to do, finish me off in the dark so my mum can't see?"

"Jack, settle down," Ms. Smith said angrily. "What are you accusing me of?"

She grabbed his throat with her right hand, took hold of one of his hands with her left, pinning it behind his back. He struggled to release her grip on his throat with his free hand. With an unusually strong force she slammed him hard against a glass sliding door. His head cracked against the glass in a jolting motion.

"Ah, what the fuck!" Jack screamed as she released him.

"Mind your language," she hissed. "That's the trouble with the youth these days, no manners and no respect."

She pushed forward and used her body to buffer hard against him, she gripped his throat again causing him to cough in protest. Releasing the pressure slightly so he could breathe she leant even further forward, her face close enough to his that he could smell the sweet odour of her foundation makeup. Her red lipstick glistened in the dim orange glow of a nearby bunker style wall light.

"Please, what have I done to you?"

Ignoring his discomfort, her eyes glazed over as though she was transporting her mind to another time.

"All I ask is for excellence, Nancy."

"What the? Who's Nancy?"

"Silence, your mother and I have read your report card, we saw you tried to rub something out, so we contacted your teacher, and guess what she said?" Ms. Smith ranted like she was having a one-sided conversation.

Jack was in shock, who was this woman in front of him? She was crazy, was she having a childhood relapse? Jack figured he should go along with whatever she wanted and try to pick the right time to run for his life. Every time he struggled he could feel her grip tighten.

"Yes, we saw the smudge next to the A and she told us you got an A minus in English, that she had to drop you a level because, although you were excellent in your assessments, you spent a great deal of time distracted by daydreaming," she continued. "Do you want to explain that? No, I didn't think so. My daughter doesn't daydream, it's a sign of weakness. In the battlefield the enemy will exploit any weakness, then where will you be? Dead!"

A light shower of rain, which speckled the car windscreen, caused orange halos around the streetlights as she made her way to Evansdale High School. The radio was on low as the music at this time of night had switched over from mainstream artists to alternative - indie performers. She enjoyed music but drew the line at drug fuel musicians who smashed guitars and radiated feedback down the speakers.

She was irritated to leave the comfort of her home at this hour and longed for the school term to be finally over. These extracurricular activities were a distraction from her everyday life, however they were mentally draining. Although during the early years of motherhood she longed to have a daughter, a little doll to play dress ups with, she now couldn't imagine the friction and impossibility of adolescence. She pitied Frances Valentino and the drama that her two daughters had caused her. She couldn't imagine living with all the pheromones raging, although she felt that her two boys acted like girls at times.

As she turned into the school car park she couldn't help but notice the absence of other cars and students being picked up. Her heart raced at the sight of the empty car park.

"Shit!" She glanced at the car's clock. "I'm an hour late!"

Too scared to notice the car arriving down the street, Jack still couldn't take his eyes off Ms. Smith, she was in some sort of trance, and her stranglehold was still strong.

"Ms. Smith, can you hear me?" he pleaded. "Please let me go, if it's my grades you're worried about, can't we talk about that later?'

Like the flick of a switch, her eyes rolled and she looked sideways at the beam of the car's headlights which crept up the grass bank towards the school buildings.

"What? What are you talking about Jack?" Looking at her hand around his throat, she looked confused and dropped her hold. She pushed back off him and he crumbled at the drop in pressure.

"Jack, I am so sorry, please let me help you up." She extended her hand out. "Look, I didn't mean it, I just wanted to offer you some career advice."

Jack looked up at her confused, he gave her the benefit of the doubt and took her hand as she helped him up. He was still disturbed by her actions and scowled at her.

"Mum's here, I better go."

"Before you go, I wanted to offer you an invitation to a career evening at the defence force base. Like I said, I discussed your grades with Mr. Friar and we agreed that you have a brilliant future ahead of you, but you just need discipline, the defence force is an excellent conduit for that." Her smile did little to comfort Jack.

And end up as twisted as you! "Sure, why not Ms. Smith," Jack lied, hoping that in doing so she wouldn't turn back into the crazy person she just was.

The beep of a car horn caused them both to look in its direction.

"I'd better go, Ms. Smith, Mum is waiting."

"Please Jack, you've pretty much finished your school year, you can call me Nancy."

23 – TAKE AWAY DINNER

"Yes, yes, I know, Gill listen to me, at the moment they hate each other, so with a little coaxing they will be back to being civil with each other," Mrs. Valentino said as she held the receiver and stood at her kitchen bench staring vacantly at a saucepan of simmering water, waiting for it to reach boiling point.

"Gillian please, we've stood together for this long, our family will hold well for many years to come," Frances Valentino said. "No, you need not come down, everything will be okay, I'll make sure of it, besides a cyclone is coming and you're safest up there. Who knows, after this weekend we'll probably be all up there cooking dinner in your kitchen, utilising your power."

Mrs. Valentino dropped a cup of sugar into the water and gently stirred it with a wooden spoon. She didn't need to brush the sugar crystals from the edge of the boiling syrup line as she had learnt that she could pick the saucepan up and slowly swish the liquid to catch the edge of the pan. She watched eagerly to make sure her caramelised sugar wasn't taken too far and became too bitter.

"You should see her dress Gill, we went shopping earlier this week to cheer her up. No, no she's been sick, but she seems to be getting better," Mrs. Valentino continued as she took the hot saucepan off the stovetop.

"I couldn't convince her, she said she didn't want to go, but we ended up finding this gorgeous dress and I bought it to cheer her up, what girl doesn't like to dress up like a princess even if she doesn't want to go to the ball, well in this case, the formal."

They finished their conversation by talking about the impending cyclone and how they grew up living through previous cyclones. Gillian remembered their whole family huddled in the lower level of their family home while the wind howled like a demonic beast as branches and loose items crashed about outside. Mrs. Valentino laughed at the memory of them gazing outside at the power of the storm, however they all got the shock of their lives when overhead power lines arced together just outside their home, they all shit themselves at the massive display of blue and green sparks of light.

She continued cooking, stirring the egg based custard, she was making this recipe a little different, a special treat for the end of school year, so she decided to chop up pistachios and add them as a crunchy element to the dessert. Cooking this early in the morning would give each crème caramel plenty of time to set.

It was a morning of mixed emotions, the last day of school for the seniors. Female seniors were crying amongst each other, giving hugs like it was the last time they would see each other alive. Male seniors were walking around like they were lost, like they wanted to cause trouble but didn't think it was worth it. It was going to be a long, slow day, a necessity to strike off the school calendar.

You could easily pick out the seniors, they were out of uniform in their casual clothes. A special parade was organised to send them off. There was a report on the impending cyclone, and it was determined that its landfall would be days away so the formal was still going ahead, however if conditions deteriorated quickly then plans would change. They would be kept informed.

It was the last farewell, they would once again be dispersed into the world as juniors in an adult world. A feeling they hadn't experienced since grade 8 when they entered high school. They would have to learn the ropes at either new workplaces or at university. They would be reborn into the world, of nimble existence, full of bravado, ready to be moulded and shaped by society.

And here they sat, cordoned like lambs and just as innocent under the watchful eye of the shepherd - Mr. Hadrick. The farewell parade was long and boring and it made the seniors wish for the day to be over. *Surely life events aren't this drawn out in the real world*, Jack thought.

The rest of the day was a non-event, Susan didn't miss out on anything except the farewell parade and the multiple classroom breakups while reflecting on the years gone by while eating from plates of finger food.

Jack did his best to dodge Jonas, only catching a glimpse of him walking between two buildings. He noticed the cast on his arm, covered in white graffiti and just dismissed it for a bike riding accident. He hadn't seen him all week and wondered if the broken arm was the reason, maybe he was busy riding motor bikes as his brother had done to waste his senior years.

Their school day finished early as there was no point staying around till 3:30, so early buses were organised for students and parents collected the rest. Some of the students, who were lucky enough to have their licences, borrowed their parent's cars and were seen driving erratically past the school with toilet paper streaming from the windows. These incidents were kept to only a few as Mr. Hadrick had warned that any such acts could see the perpetrators graduation certificates and results being kept in the office until action was taken. It was something nobody wanted this time of their school life as it held them up from accessing university or a job and held them accountable to the school that they so desperately wanted to break away from.

Jack caught the bus and gave Mr. Smart a smile as he boarded. He was sad Susan wasn't there to join him on their last bus ride. Looking out the window he thought back over all the good times with his friends. He closed his eyes and thought about Susan. He could smell her perfume; the scent of her shampoo in her hair. He felt a warm hand gently run across the top of his leg. *Susan, you've come to join me.*

"Hey you," she said with a smile. "Looking forward to tomorrow night?"

Jack sat bolt upright in his seat and pushed over towards the window, causing Sissy to pull her hand away and frown.

"Come on Jack, you know you'll love it."

"Yeah sure." *Now she's copied Susan's perfume and shampoo? That's kind of freaky - but I'll give it to her for trying.*

A neon tube flashed intermittently inside the acrylic shop sign which hung under the footpath awning. It had been like that for months at the Fish-N-Chip takeaway shop. The owners were either too busy or too mean to fix it. A stray dog, likely a neighbouring yard escapee, paced back and forth wide eyed and panting under the awning to escape the driving rain. It frantically searched the skies wondering where the light and sound came from, hoping the noise would end. The passing storm had delivered its tempest and was dying off with a few distant flashes and grumbles.

Jack trudged barefoot through the groundwater, along the pathway, annoyed that his mother sent him out in the wet to get dinner. His umbrella kept him dry but the heavy rain and squally gust had wet the bottom of his long pants. Although he was annoyed he figured it was better than staying back at the house. He brother and mother were giving him the shits as they were all cooped up in the house and had nowhere to escape each other's bickering. He was glad his father was still a week away from coming home otherwise the house would have had more drama than an episode of Neighbours.

Under the awning he folded his umbrella and lent it up against the shop front. The cheesy shop logo, which was a potato chip catching a fish out on the reef, stared back at him. It too was looking like it needed maintenance with its faded colours and peeling paint. *This guy makes a mint and he can't give the place an update?*

Jack waited as a customer bashed their way out the single, self-closing screen door. His hands were full of wrapped fried food and the guy was using his back to push the door open. Jack sprung forward to help hold the door open.

"Thanks mate," he said before rushing off to his car which was drowning in the flooded gutter.

When he entered the shop he saw Valerie's unmistakable auburn hair bouncing around as she managed the deep fryer station. She looked like she was working alone. There was one other customer, not the usual amount for a Friday night, the weather must have been a deterrent. Still, there was nothing like warm fish and chips on a cold, wet night.

She caught his eye, gave a nod to let him know she wouldn't be long as she prepared the order for the waiting customer. It was a barefoot, young mother with a snotty nosed toddler who had lined up all the tourism pamphlets across the floor like he was playing Thomas the Tank Engine and Friends. The mother didn't mind, it kept him from nagging her as she looked about the shop nervously. Jack wondered if she had a partner and if he were waiting at home hungry – perhaps that's why she almost looked as anxious as the dog running circles out under the awning. She picked at scabs on her arm and turned away when she noticed Jack staring at her.

Jack thought he would be relieved when the mother and child left but somehow he didn't anticipate the awkwardness between

Valerie and himself, now in the empty shop. He held some comfort in the loud rain on the roof, it was a slight distraction.

He could see his family's order, wrapped up in white butcher's paper with Armstrong written in black Nikko pen across it, sitting in the food warmer beside all the other precooked food. She was about to talk to him when the phone rang and she held out a finger to indicate she wouldn't be long.

Looking around the shop Jack wondered why she stuck it out working in a place like this. He knew that she'd been getting management training but to what end? He hoped for her that she'd leave this place and get into a solid job. Maybe it was a stepping stone for her but all Jack could see was slave labour in progress. While she made her boss rich he was always off somewhere on endless holidays, while she was stuck here working the fryer, day after day. Jack wondered how real the management training was and were there any caveats that benefited the owner more than Valerie. Jack wanted to ask her but didn't know the right way to approach the subject, ultimately it was her decision anyway. She seemed like a headstrong girl who didn't take crap from anyone. She could handle herself.

While he waited he amused himself by looking at the old tabletop arcade game. The graphics were pixelated and the game was ancient but it still got the punters dropping their twenty cent pieces into it like they were feeding an addiction. Jack sat on one of the bobbin shaped plastic chairs and rested his elbows on the smudge glass of the game machine. It smelt like a mixture of bubble gum and burnt plastic, maybe there was even teenage sweat – he couldn't pinpoint it – but it was a unique smell that reminded him of a games hall. Jack's parents couldn't afford a home computer, so he always went to Patrick's house to take turns on his Amiga 500. That's probably why he didn't get caught up in the whole computer game scene.

Jack heard Valerie return the phone receiver to the holster on the wall.

"Hey Jack, how's things?" she beamed, happy to see a familiar face on such a dreary night. "What's on your mind, you look deep in thought?"

"Nothing, I'm good, it's been a long year." *Except that I've got a psychopath called John Bird who wants me dead.*

"But you look so sad, Jacky-boy," she said with a reassuring smile.

"I don't know Valerie, life was going great up until Sissy bit me. It's like the kiss of death, now Susan doesn't want to talk to me, she won't even let me see her," Jack said, disenfranchised with himself.

"I know she hated that Sissy kissed you."

"But it was hardly a kiss."

"It wasn't so much the kiss Jack, it was that you put yourself in that situation, for it to be able to happen. She thought you were smarter than that."

Jack had no answer. He looked into the warmer at the fried food options and didn't like what he saw.

"Cheer up, she still likes you."

"Yeah?"

"Of course, she's just had a rough week, she needs time away from the world."

"What's happened?"

Valerie busied herself behind the counter, she didn't want to be the one to let him know about Jonas. She thought it best to change the subject.

"Are you still going to the formal?" she asked.

"I don't know, I really wanted to go with Susan, but she showed no interest. Now I am stuck with Sissy. I've done too much to upset Susan. I think I'll bail out on Sissy," Jack said as he ran a finger along the well-worn stainless steel countertop creating a smudge line.

And we're back on this topic, well that didn't work. "I don't think it's you Jack, she'd be more upset knowing you weren't going because of her." Valerie looked down at his vacant behaviour.

"Really? It sure is hard to read you guys?"

"What? Us Valentino's?"

"No, you women."

Valerie laughed off the comment and busied herself by fussing over the contents of the bain-marie. She placed his order on top of the counter in a plastic bag and then added a small plastic container of salad to the order.

Jack frowned, "What's that?"

"It's salad Jack, you should look after yourself, it's no charge."

"Gee thanks"

"No problem, oh by the way Mum said to drop in to our house before you go home, she's made a batch of crème caramel, your favourite dessert. See we look after you, you've got the main, the salad and now dessert sorted."

"Thanks again, I am sure it will all be nice."

A gust of wind blew hard and the roof trusses of the take away shop creaked in protest of the wind load on the roof. "Are you sure the formal is still on, it's getting messy out there with that cyclone on the way?"

"Yeah, Ms. Smith wouldn't cancel it even if the world was blowing up, besides we've been told it's 48 hours away and that's still plenty of time to have the formal tomorrow night and be home safe for the next day. If they were worried they would have cancelled it I guess."

"Ms. Smith is still there? She sure rubbed me up the wrong way when I was there."

"Oh really?" Jack said with an inquisitive tune in his voice.

"Yeah, what's it to you?"

"Oh nothing, she hasn't changed, she rubs me up the wrong way too."

Valerie laughed, "Well look after yourself Jack, and have a great time tomorrow night."

"Thanks Val." Jack grabbed his family's order and headed outside.

Back out in the rain Jack's mind was still confused as ever. *I wish I could have asked her about the writers group and who John Bird was, but she seemed so helpful and I didn't want to upset her, I suppose she'd flip if she found out I knew she was in a writers group.*

Jack held the warm food close to his chest and pulled his umbrella low to shield himself against the wet squally gusts as he made his way home in the storm.

24 – FORMAL

Sunlight filtered through a gap in the curtain and woke Jack with a startle. There was a break in the rain and the sun had managed to find a way through the clouds. He felt groggy, like the food coma from last night hadn't passed like it should have. Lifting his head from his pillow he peered through glazed eyes - that's when he saw it.

Blood.

It was dry but it was quite a large, round stain radiating from where his head had left a furrow in the pillow. Touching his face he searched for the source and his fingers stopped at his nose to examine the sticky fluid.

Nose bleeds, since when do I get those?

Sitting upright in bed he shifted his body forward to stand but crumbled under his weight and fell with a thud onto the shag pile carpeted floor. He didn't anticipate the imbalance in his body and he flushed hot and cold. His face went clammy and knew what was coming but couldn't lift himself quick enough as his body convulsed as he vomited across the carpet, leaving a thick white mess.

Shit, that's going to stain.

Feeling better after the purge he wiped his face on his shirt sleeve and picked up his room waste paper bin, some tissue paper and started to attend to the stinking muck. He nearly dry reached at the smell. He noticed green lumps throughout the vomit and curiosity got the better of him as he picked a piece up for closer inspection.

"What the fuck?" Jack said out loud. "Ratsak!"

Twisting it between his fingers, the little compressed pellet of rodent poison was unmistakably identifiable. Looking back down at the carpet there had to be quite a few pellets that he had thrown up.

"That bitch just tried to poison me!" Jack said with anger. *And she said I should look after myself and eat the fucking salad, well I guess John Bird just revealed herself!*

It was going to be a hard day to get through and an even harder night. Mrs. Valentino had complained vividly for her to get out of the house and stop moping around but Susan wanted the warmth and comfort of her surroundings. She didn't want her mother's advice and she was sick of her sister preaching to her. She wanted a warm hug, she missed her father.

In the last week she had missed him dearly and longed for the fun times they had playing in the backyard. She loved it when he chased her around the gardens like he was a tiger in the jungle. She squealed with delight as he pounced and nearly caught her. She knew he could have caught her at any time and she loved that those games seemed to go on forever. But now it seemed like a distant memory.

She wanted to escape to the backyard, to sit in the cubby house and make mud cakes and tea for her daddy, but she knew that would never happen again. Feeling dejected she waited for a break in the weather so she could sit outside on the tree swing and reminisce about her father pushing her, or how he worked in the garden while she played sea monsters and princesses in the cubby house.

She was glad she was back to her usual fashion sense as the leggings she wore provided warmth in the cool summer breeze that came with the rain. The humidity was at bay as the oncoming cyclone made the summer seem more like an early autumn. She donned a thin cardigan and traipsed out into the waterlogged yard and sat gently on the wooden swing seat made by her father.

It was cool and a stiff gust blew, she pulled her cardigan tight, wrapping her arms around herself as she slowly rocked on the swing. She wanted to draw deep on her memory and think of all the good times she had with her father, but it was difficult as she only knew him for a short time. Her memories were also patchy and usually associated with a strong emotion, like when she was hurt or when she was happy -more often than not it was when she was hurt. Like when she fell from the cubby house, landing in the garden below, the fall onto the soft mulch cradling her fall but it still knocked the wind out of her. Or when she tripped running back to the house and landed hard on the concrete pavers taking off bark. Her father was not always there in her memories to comfort her - it was mostly her mother.

But here standing before her was a legacy to his influence, evidence to his existence, proof that he cared - the cubby house. She remembered the feeling of joy when it was revealed to her behind draped bed sheets on her second birthday. However, the cubby house was a reminder of sadness, as later that year it would be the last time she would ever see him again.

Looking away from the structure she couldn't help but see the Armstrong house. The house was white with green trim. It had been a sanctuary over the years. Jack didn't know it but Susan felt great comfort in the distraction of their friendship. It's why she had been so cautious to pursue a deeper relationship with Jack. This last week she tested the boundaries and pushed as hard as she could. She knew she had damaged their friendship and the bond that had been created over all their years together. She hoped one day Jack could see why she had done it.

It was these two men who she wished were in her life again. However her father was lost in time and she knew she had pushed Jack too far away. She wiped a tear from her face and looked up to the sky. The clouds were thick and dark, she sensed it was about to rain heavily again. She didn't care to get wet so she stood up and turned toward the safety of her home.

A strong gust blew and she steadied herself against its force. Leaves blew across the yard and red flower petals rained down from the poinciana tree as the branches whipped about. She felt a wet leaf stick and flap against her ankle, bending down to remove it, she was surprised to see it wasn't a leaf but some folded paper.

She decided to sit back down on the swing so she could steady herself while she inspected the paper. She carefully unfolded it so as not to tear it at the wet and fragile folds.

Susan,

I look across at your bedroom window, the light isn't on but I know you're home. I wish I could join you, to hold you and to let you know how I feel.

I look across and see rain splashing down your window-pane like the angels are crying. Too corny? Yes, look at me writing a love letter. I am not writing what I think you want to hear, it's what I feel.

I tried poetry, you should have read it, you would have laughed, they were shit.

But I look out my window like a sad puppy waiting for its owner to come home, the lump in my throat is a reminder of the tears I am courageously trying to hold back. I might be a wimp, but I am your wimp.

We've grown together, so close, like there was more than just a friendship, like we are more than just situational brother and sister. I know you're scared just like me when you realised how terrifying that is, to want to be with someone so bad, but you know all the pain you've ever felt will destroy you if things turn ugly. But I want to take that chance, because I can't imagine life without you in it.

I wish I could be with you, to comfort you and to ask for your forgiveness for letting someone get between us. I was stupid and naive to think you wouldn't have minded. I now know what it feels like, it tears at my heart thinking of you with anyone else

I am still going to the formal with her, it's only a formality nothing more. I'd love you to join me, I'll ditch her in an instant just to have at least one dance with you.

I know you still don't want to see me, you are so strong willed, it's what I love about you as well, so I am going to leave this letter with your mum, I hope that is okay, she's been good to me over the years and I love how she'd made you into a beautiful person.

I miss you,

Love,

Jack.

Tears flowed, she bawled uncontrollably while she read. Susan carefully folded the letter in her trembling hands and protectively tucked it into a closed fist inside her cardigan pocket. She looked up into the stream of cool rain as it started to pour down. It washed over her face, matching the strength of her warm tears, but not fixing her pain.

Jack agreed with the old adage, 'time flies when you are having fun', but he thought it was ridiculous how quickly time flew this Saturday, he wasn't having fun - all he wanted to do was resist the onset of the formal. It didn't help how his mother fussed over his presentation, making sure his tuxedo was pulled and plucked into shape. She wanted him to fix his hair with his father's gel and put on some of her light foundation to mask his freckles and pimples but he resisted. She ranted and raved about how smart he would look but he was glad he stuck to his guns - he didn't want to look like a clown.

Clint had seen the tension brewing in the lounge room and he quietly slipped out the back door. Jack could hear him kick start his trail bike and take off down the road. *Lucky bastard.*

"Now, don't let me forget your lapel rose in the fridge," Jack's mother instructed. "And make sure you don't crease that suit, don't sit on the couch, you'll have to sit at the dining room table while you wait. I won't be long."

"Yes Mum," Jack said reluctantly.

She headed upstairs to get ready. Not only was getting dressed up in these clothes embarrassing enough, but having to have your mother attend welcoming drinks was going to be unbearable.

Now time seemed to slow down, he wanted this night over and done with.

The blood had long since turned a rusty brown colour, but the tissue had been opened up to reveal a butterfly shape, similar to that of the Rorschach test - the inkblots used by some psychologists. Sissy thought it was pretty and as such it still remained pride of place in the middle of her shrine. It was the most valuable piece in her collection. She was well on to her way of securing her ultimate prize - Jack.

Tonight she knew she would get an even bigger piece of the prize.

Red satin and tulle spilled out from the waist in overlapping segments. The waist to the bust was quite tight and highlighted her slender figure and accentuated the size of her breasts. The short sleeve caps and the plunging neckline added to the wow factor. She was glad to have spent the obscene amount of money for the dress; she wanted to show it to all the other girls at the formal, especially Meredith and her bitchy buddies.

All of her physical assets were well hidden throughout the school year as she wore an unflattering school uniform consisting of baggy t-shirts and long flowing skirts. She didn't own short skirts to show off her legs and she didn't tuck her t-shirt in tightly - like the popular girls did to highlight their torsos.

She had taken most of the day to straighten her tightly coiled hair, which was stubborn but well worth the effort in her eyes. Looking back at her reflection in the mirror her smile beamed as she admired the stark contrast in her look. She had to talk to herself to make sure it was her standing behind the mirror – for now, with her hair straightened and dyed she uncannily looked exactly like Susan.

Spinning left and right she twirled in front of the mirror, laughing and giggling. She loved the dress and the new look. She gathered her hair up wondering how she looked if she wore it up, or dropping it to see it down once again. She decided a simple princess style would suit her best. She knew it would showcase her innocence. Something she hoped Jack's heart would race over, something she hoped Jack would conquer.

Cherry red lipstick was her choice to match the dress, she kissed her lips together to ensure an even coating and then she applied a quick foundation and light blush. Her transformation was remarkable.

"Are you almost ready Love?" her father asked outside her closed door.

"Almost Dad," she replied smiling.

"Okay, you don't want to be late, we've got to pick Jack and his mother up yet, remember?"

"I can't wait!"

After she fixed her hair, she gave her shrine one last look over, kissed her fingers and placed them on a photo of Jack. She fumbled around in her dresser draw looking for the things she needed to take in her small, matching tote bag. Finally she opened a small decorative box on her dresser and gently pulled the necklace out.

"This is for you Mum, I wish you were here," she said as she slipped her late mother's necklace with locket charm over her head, quickly adjusting it so it hung neatly between her breasts - ensuring it caught the eye.

"Where do you think you're going?" she slurred through drunken lips and eyeing him with snake eyes. "And why the fuck are you dressed like a cop? I hate cops!"

"It's a tuxedo, I am not a cop, and I am going to the school formal!" Jonas yelled.

"Like fuck you are!"

"Why not?"

"Cause you're not going to get some little slut knocked up, that's why," his mother hissed.

"What the...like that's going to happen," he said coyly, trying not to get distracted by the horse racing on the television.

"You're just like you're good for nothing father, you'll chase pussy no matter who you're with...," she stopped to cough her lungs up and spit on the carpeted floor. "You know how many bitches he's fucked?"

"Mum, please!" Jonas pleaded with her to stop her rant. He knew how badly it would end if she didn't stop. He wasn't ready to dodge anything she could pick up to throw at him, in another one of their living room showdowns.

"All right, all right, go then, have fun," she said, changing to a sarcastic tune. "Who are you taking anyway?"

Jonas didn't know if he should answer her, but he was tired of her abuse so he yielded. "Meredith Mum, and before you slag her off she's not a slut."

"Oh yes, she's nice that one," she said with a wry smile. "Pity though."

"Pity what?"

"Well, you think I am stupid, you think I sit here and drink and don't know what my boy gets up to?"

"Yeah, well what, what are you carrying on about?" he said with furrowed eyes.

"You said she wasn't a slut, but I saw you sneak that little whore in here a while back," she said as she crushed her empty beer can in anger. "Wouldn't her mummy and daddy like to know that a dead shit like you has been fucking her in his shit hole bedroom?"

She threw the beer can at her son and he quickly dodged it. The can hit the plasterboard wall behind him, scoring it with its sharp edge and spraying remnant beer up the wall.

Jonas saw red. He had brought Meredith home, but it was only to lend her a Metallica CD and sell her some weed. His home was the last place on earth he'd bring a girl home to impress or fool around with.

He liked Meredith and although she'd given him a blow job for a bag of weed one time at Stanley's house, there was nothing else between the two of them. He didn't even know if she liked him.

His rage was at boiling point. His mother's derogatory comments towards Meredith were a direct attack on his judgement. He felt like Meredith was more worthy than his mother and he couldn't take her comments any longer.

He grabbed his bag and headed for the door, he wanted to get out of there before he did something he regretted.

"Oh, did I strike a nerve, does the truth hurt?" she jibed as he walked past.

Without thought he grabbed his mother around the shoulders from behind, he picked up her deteriorated body from out of the couch, unaffected by the strain beneath his cast, and threw her towards the television. She screamed and wailed but was too impaired to stop her fall, and as she crashed down her head struck the television screen, creating a large divot and spider web shaped crack.

She was out cold.

The house lights and television flicked momentarily before the house went into total darkness. The nearby street light cast a dim glow throughout the living room.

There was deathly silence.

"No Mum, family hurts."

He quickly headed back into the kitchen, grabbed a carving knife that had been tossed into the sink, before escaping out into the wet night.

The polite beep of a horn outside stopped his mother's fussing over the white snow on his shoulders. She asked him to stop his nervous head scratching because the loose dandruff it caused was going to make him a laughing stock. Jack's cheeky reply about it being the least of his worries didn't go down well. She was proud of her son, no matter what others thought of him. She wished his father could be here to see him in his smart suit.

They were both gobsmacked when they stepped out the front door and saw the gleaming white stretch limousine parked on an obscure angle in their driveway. Jack sheepishly looked across at Susan's house to see if she wasn't peeking through her window – he sighed with relief at the blackened windows. And much to his surprise he was grateful that the limousine had blackened windows as well. He didn't want to get caught being inside the thing, especially with Sissy.

"I hope you don't mind the surprise, I borrowed her from work," Mr. Smart said as he stepped out of the driver's seat.

"Oh my, she's beautiful, thank you very much Mr. Smart," Mrs. Armstrong said with a smile.

"Yes, impressive," Jack added.

"Not as beautiful as my lovely daughter," Mr. Smart said as he walked around the front of the car and opened the rear passenger door, all the way down the back, for his new passengers. "Come on, before the next burst of rain."

If you say so, Jack thought. Jack stood back waiting for his mother to pull her long black dress underneath herself and slide onto the leather seat sideways. He followed and as he sat down, he was taken aback again – this time in a shocked way.

Sitting smugly in the middle of the rear-facing passenger seat was Sissy, but Jack had to look twice to make sure it wasn't Susan.

"Wow," Jack said. *First her perfume now her hair, it's like she's trying to replace Susan.*

"Thank you, you look handsome yourself," Sissy said with a smile. "And you look lovely too Mrs. Armstrong."

"Thank you, that's such a pretty dress, it's gorgeous." Mrs. Armstrong said as she made herself comfortable.

Bill Smart sat back down in the driver's seat, he turned and spoke though the lowered privacy partition. "Okay ladies and Jack, all set, let's go."

Turning the radio on for some music to lighten the mood he caught the end of the local radio station weather update.

'Tropical Cyclone Rona has just been upgraded to a category 2 storm, it's currently located 500 kilometres due north east of Cairns, traveling in a south west direction at approximately 8 kilometres per hour. A cyclone watch is current for coastal communities between Lockhart River and Innisfail, a cyclone warning is current for communities between Cooktown and Cairns. Residents are urged to make appropriate plans and to keep listening to your local radio station for further advice. The next advice is due from the Bureau of Meteorology from 11pm tonight.

For all your weather news, favourite songs of all time, stay listening to 4RRR-FM Regional Reef Radio...'

The MTV version of 'All Apologies' from Nirvana came on the radio, with her fingers, Sissy tapped the leather seat to the melodic beat of the drum, and looked over at Jack and gave him a wink.

Heavy rain caused the students to exit from their various modes of transport in an ungainly fashion. Long dresses were held high so girls could run and jump over puddles to get under the covered walkways as quickly as possible. Concerned young men, mainly sporting black tuxedos with variations in lapel flower or bow tie colour, tried eagerly to impress their fair maidens by supporting them - ensuring they didn't trip and fall in the mud.

It seemed like the weather created a waste of effort to arrive in a classic or ultra-modern vehicle; opportunity was missed to take the perfect photo of couples up against their cars. Parents were heard muttering that having the formal at the high school was going to mar their children's memories. They complained that the porte-cochère at The Cairns International Hotel would have been perfect under these conditions. They hated that the formal funding had been stolen and they kept this resentment dear to themselves. Ultimately they blamed the school for their lack of security.

Bill pulled the white limousine in behind a silver XY GT Ford Falcon and waited for its occupants to alight from the vehicle and for the car to move on. It sat there and revved a couple of times much to the delight of students gathered under cover. One rowdy boy wound his arms around in a circular motion to persuade the driver to do a big burnout. The Falcon revved once more and the driver dropped the clutch while his foot was on the brake pedal. The tyres screamed to life and the vehicle stepped out sideways sending a shower of gravel and thick smoke from beneath its wheel arches.

Bill frowned and beeped his horn.

The Falcon driver stepped off the accelerator and coasted forward giving a small wave out the window. The students under cover laughed and carried on like it was the highlight of their school year.

"Quite the entrance," Jack said with eyebrows raised and a wry grin.

"Yeah, if it wasn't raining so much I would have gotten out to give him a piece of my mind," Bill said with a frown.

Bill drove forward and much to Mrs. Armstrong's protest he jumped out into the rain to open the rear barn doors to let his passengers out.

"No need to run ladies, there are umbrellas under the seat compartments."

"How civilised," Mrs. Armstrong beamed.

"Come on Jack," Sissy said as she grabbed his hand and pulled him from the limousine. He didn't mind her forcefulness but his heart skipped when she entwined their fingers and held his arm close to her side.

Obscurity was the word that crossed Jack's mind as he saw students in their fancy clothes gathered in small clusters around their parents, who looked like they pulled their clothes from the far reaches of their wardrobes. It was quite a contrast, coupled with the sight of the older family members holding champagne or beer glasses while their younger offspring stood doughy eyed in wonderment and of innocence - like alcohol had never passed their lips. For Jack it was quite fake and quite forced. But knowing this didn't abate his nerves in any respect.

Jack's eyes wandered around the parade hall, focusing on each group of people, as they stood at the back of the hall. The students and their parents were arranged in groups exactly like the student groups at their school. All the surfer kids were in the same area, the athletic kids in another, the stoners were in their own area. Then there were the academics, who were poorly represented, as Jack figured that he and Sissy were pretty much the only ones in that category.

You could feel the tension in the hall, the students were eagerly eyeing off which dining table they would sit at to ensure their group of friends all sat together and that the various groups didn't blend. That would have been social sacrilege.

Jack looked beyond the decorated dining tables, with their white table cloths, and small shielded candles which circled tropical floral centerpieces. Chairs were wrapped in white cloth but Jack could tell they were the uncomfortable classroom chairs with the plastic molded backs and black metal, triangular legs.

Beyond the cluster of tables was a lectern and a ten metre cleared space with a disco ball cheerfully turning overhead at a low speed. The light wasn't shining on it yet and the dance area was flanked with coarsely hung fairy lights. On the back wall were the words, painted on butcher's paper, 'Seniors 98'. Under the lettering was a collage of photos of seniors taken throughout the year. Jack figured it was the handiwork of the senior art students.

"Who are you looking for Jack?" Sissy whispered under her breath as she saw her father walk through the main entrance. "She's not coming, I heard she had a massive barney with Jonas."

"What?" Jack said, gaining her full attention.

"Yeah, Meredith was happy to let me know when she tripped me over at the shops this morning," Sissy explained. "Meredith said she is going with him now, along with some other choice descriptive words for Susan."

Mrs. Armstrong spun her head and glared at Sissy momentarily at the mention of Susan, she moved herself to properly get to know Mr. Smith as he had been hard to talk to while he drove them in.

Turning his head to contemplate what Sissy had said, Jack spied Ms. Smith over in the corner of the hall trying to operate the audio system with a tech student. They must have resolved the problem as the music started up, blaring at first and then it was turned down to a respectable level. Jack recognised the tune to be 'This Is Your Night' by Amber.

Once the PA system was running, Ms. Smith commenced the evening. She began with a short address and a few toasts, thanking the parents for the hard effort they had in making sure the school year went well and their compassion was not unnoticed for the tough year they've had. The address was finished with a round of applause.

Jack noticed Meredith standing with her friends and was glad he didn't see Jonas.

After a short while Ms. Smith indicated it was time to farewell the parents before the night proceeded. "Jack, Sissy seems like a lovely girl and Mr. Smith is charming. Have a lovely time tonight, if this weather gets too much then come home early," Mrs. Armstrong said. "Oh and here's $50 to get a taxi home, I won't wait up."

Jack felt his mother push the money into his hand, but if felt foreign, he looked down in bewilderment and it took a moment to register what else she'd given him with the money.

"Mum!" Jack said with a strained voice.

"I want you to be safe Jack, I don't want my boys to get into trouble."

"But Mum, a condom?" Jack said under his breath, looking around, flushed red with embarrassment.

"It's not like I am giving you permission," she said with a clipped tone. "Remember when you were in Scouts, 'Be Prepared'."

Jack winced at the connotation. His mind now drew correlation between having sex and standing around the scout's parade giving the three finger salute while condoms were raining from the sky. He shook his head to rid his mind of the thought.

"Anyway Love, I just want you to stay safe, I'll see you tomorrow, I won't kiss you in front of your friends, but good night, I love you."

Jack gave her a quick smile and shoved the $50 note and condom into his pocket. He watched her and Mr. Smith, along with other parents, head off out the main door and into the night.

Thank goodness, that's half my worry gone.

The squealing feedback from the PA system indicated that Ms. Smith had turned the microphone back on and was about to order everyone to their seats. It seemed to work as everyone started to secure their seats at the dining table without her prompting.

"Okay everyone," Ms. Smith said across the speakers. "Now that I have your attention I'd like to formally welcome everyone to the 1998 Evansdale Senior's formal."

The applause was loud and enthusiastic - it drowned out the rain on the iron roof above.

"Now please be seated and we will commence the dinner and speeches."

"Great, we've got to sit through more speeches?" Jack complained.

"It won't take long," Sissy said, grabbing Jack's hand. "Come on, let's find a good seat, somewhere away from the bitchy groups."

Music started up again, this time it was louder and someone flicked a switch and the mirror ball was lit up. It was too early for dancing but it started the party mood for the night.

As they settled at their table Jack kept a cautious eye on who might join them. There were ten chairs to a table and Jack wondered how he was going to ignore the others at the table through all the dinner courses and speeches. He figured he would have to hide in engrossing conversation with Sissy and he wondered what would have been worse - his table intruders or Sissy.

"So, Sissy," he began. "I know who John Bird is, do you care to explain why she's got it so against me? Did she explain that in your *little* writers group?"

"What? You know who she...ah...it is? I don't believe you."

"Okay, it's Valerie Valentino, I know, I saw your last writers group for the year and I saw who was in it."

She raised her eyebrows and rolled her eyes. "Yeah, she's in it, but not everyone was there. Bet you can't guess who else is in it. I'll give you a clue, he's not here yet."

"No way!"

"Yes way, and Jonas was at every class but the last one!"

"But he can't be John Bird," Jack said in shock. "Valerie tried to poison me with Ratsak!"

"Oh, how exciting," Sissy smiled as she clapped her hands together in a childish manner. "But I don't think she's capable of that, no matter how tough she likes to think she is."

"Well you're wrong, I chucked my guts up with all the evidence this morning."

"And yet you're still alive."

"I know, you don't believe me?"

"Jack, what I believe in is *us*," Sissy said with a smile.

A gust of wind blew hard and flapped the tarps that had been tied up to cover the gap between the concrete floor and corrugated iron wall that ran up the length of each side of the building. These were added for the formal for privacy and protection against the weather. Normally the sides of the parade hall were open for ventilation in warm weather and to allow students easy ingress. Now the parade hall had one entrance at the front and a small side opening towards the back of the dance hall for access to the toilet block. From here Ms. Smith could also make her way to her office where she kept the valuables, like awards and prizes for the night.

Jack thought the wind blew hard again and smashed the main doors open but he was shocked to see what had caused them to swing violently open.

Jonas.

It took Jack only seconds to realise that Jonas was very angry. The furrowed look, the purpose in his swagger. He was dressed in a tuxedo and was drenched, like he just walked through a shower. Dripping wet Jack knew that Jonas wasn't angry because he got caught out in the rain, this look was far more determined.

Jack tried to keep an eye on Jonas but he lost him in the crowd - Sissy hadn't helped as she momentarily distracted him by asking him inane questions. That was Jack's first mistake for the night.

He felt the rough graze to the back of his head like someone had taken a rock from outside and used it to nudge him with. But Jack wished it was that simple. Turning around he saw the culprit - Jonas had forcefully bumped Jack with his arm cast.

"You and me outside now, fuck-head!" Jonas commanded before he walked off towards the main doors.

"You can't go Jack, he'll kill you," Sissy pleaded, her voice full of worry.

"It's okay Sissy, I knew this moment was coming."

"But you can't, he'll seriously kill you," she protested.

"Probably, but it's been leading to this moment all year. He's had it out for me and we need to settle our differences. I can't run scared of him or anyone like him in the future," Jack said with worry in his eyes. "Like my father says, 'you've got to stand up for yourself otherwise you'll be a pussy all your life.'"

"Yes, but tonight is no time to play heroics, I want you in one piece, I've got plans for the two of us."

"Plans?"

"Yeah, I can't have you broken for them."

"Don't worry," Jack said as he stood from the table. "Daris has taught me how to look after myself."'

"Daris?" Sissy said with a confused look in her eyes.

She couldn't stop him and she just sat there in disbelief as she watched Jack follow Jonas out of the parade hall and into the heavy rain of the night.

Outside the rain was getting worse. The chorus of frogs and the mating call of male cane toads was testament to the only living beings enjoying the deluge.

Jonas gripped the metal handrail that barricaded the walkway from the deep open drain that ran alongside the pathway. Looking out into the black night he was furious. His mother had raised his anger level, and tonight was the perfect storm for his emotions to boil over. In his mind Jack wasn't going to survive the night without payback, without retribution for his broken arm and for his pathetic existence. Glancing across his shoulder he saw a familiar form heading his way.

"I heard you like raping girls!" shouted his visitor angrily over the heavy rain.

Jonas turned to face the aggressor. "No, I've never done that, what's it your business, and what are you doing here?"

"I am here to warn you," Daris said with steely eyes, "because I know what you did."

Daris moved closer to Jonas causing him to back up against the handrail in discomfort.

"Hey back off!"

"Like overpowering the weak do you?"

"What would you know?"

"I live next to the school, the walls talk, I know everything," Daris mused.

"So, what's it to you?"

"Why do you think I live beside the school," Daris said holding his arms behind his back and looking around. "I am here to protect all the children."

"Good-o, fuck off then because you didn't protect me when someone smashed my arm, go and be someone else's superman!"

"I am not here to protect you, you smart arse," Daris said angrily. "I am here to make sure you don't rape anyone else, ever again."

"Why? She didn't need rescuing, she was into it anyway."

"So you did it!" Daris said with wide eyes, and muscles flexed in his taught arms.

"No, man, look at my arm, someone smashed me before anything happened."

"So you were going to?"

There was as silence between the two of them as they squared each other off. Jonas was the largest, muscle bound senior of Evansdale High, but he was no match for the strength of Daris.

"Fucking answer me!" Daris said angrily. He pulled his arms around to his front and exposed what he had been hiding.

"Whoa man, what the fuck? An axe!" Jonas was now visibly shaken by the imposing sight of Daris. "I um, I thought being rough was what girls liked, you know, take the lead, being the stronger one."

"You small minded shit," Daris said. "Let me teach you a lesson about raping girls," he said as spit dribbled down his face. Daris dropped the axe to the ground and reached out to grab Jonas' arm.

"What the fuck," Jonas frantically protested, dodging his grasp.

The second time Daris didn't miss and he swung Jonas around taking hold of both his arms from behind.

"Let me go you fuck-head, what do you think you're doing?"

Jonas flexed and twisted and slipped from Daris' hold. He spun around and thrashed violently towards Daris. With quick and stealth-like movements Daris threw two purposeful punches at Jonas. The first connected with his kidneys and knocked the wind out of him, as he hunched forward to cradle the impact Daris swung his right fist around and it connected with his cheek. The blow was too strong and Jonas was out cold before he hit the ground.

"I am going to do to *you* what *you* wanted to do to that girl," Daris said as he picked up Jonas' limp body and hoisted him up over his shoulders like a rag doll.

With his axe in his free hand and Jonas on his shoulder he headed off towards his house in the driving rain.

Rain streamed down outside like water from a shower head – it was heavy and torrential. The water flow also continued inside the square shower hob. She sat on the tiled floor looking up at the water, letting the warm flow wash over her face and penetrate her eyes. She wanted to wash away dreams, her desires and her pain. Cradling her legs in the seated position she rocked back and forth to let the water stream flush over her hair, to warm her scalp and to numb her thoughts.

She'd been sitting there for an hour and the warm water started to get colder. She had emptied the hot water system, but she still sat there, closing her eyes, thinking how her cold heart would soon be in equilibrium with the cold water.

She would have sat there longer but she was beginning to hate how her body trembled uncontrollably as she shivered. She stood and turned the water off. Not bothering to dry herself she walked naked and wet to her room. Flopping onto her bed, she cried into her pillow thinking how much she hated herself.

Her mind wandered to the letter she found. She knew the letter was written recently and wondered how it ended up in her backyard. *Maybe Jack knows me better than I think, but I hardly go out to the backyard anymore let alone the cubby house.* It only proved more frustrating for her as her apparent loss of control of her life was growing. *He said he would give it to Mum, maybe he chickened out and put it in the cubby, thinking I'd eventually find it?*

She was scared of Jonas but she had moved beyond what had happened. All she could think about now was how she lost Jack, she had pushed him right into the arms of Sissy. Tonight was supposed to be their night and she hated herself for the lost opportunity of being there for him, of being the girl in his arms.

She had dried the letter out in the oven, on low temperature, and she had read it over several times. It made her cry each time. She needed an emotional rest so she had folded the letter and tucked it under her pillow.

Lying in her bed she looked up at her ceiling aimlessly. Her eyes were puffy and red from crying. She knew she had ruined things between herself and Jack. Turning her head she stared at the dress hanging from her open wardrobe. It was supposed to be for Jack, but she had intended to wear it for Jonas. Tears flowed thinking of how that would have hurt Jack. She was so wrapped up in her own self-pity that while trying to make others around her feel her pain it had all come back to hurt her. She wondered if Jack would ever forgive her. She wondered if she should get out of bed, put the dress on and run to the formal.

She was scared of Jonas but she was terrified of Jack and the thought of letting down her walls to allow their emotions to meld. She didn't want to let her misery ruin Jack, to change his course in life. To make his life worse.

Thunder cracked closely outside as the heavy weight of guilt wrapped over her body like a thick blanket - stifling her will to move. She wished her pain would suffocate her and take her last breaths. The thought of Jack dancing with Sissy, dressed to perfection, arm in arm and smiling cheerfully held her back. She knew Jack would be better off with Sissy. Sissy didn't seem to have the hang ups that she knew she had.

She needed to escape her bedroom and she needed to pee, so she pulled herself off her bed and made her way down the hallway of her empty house. Her sister was at work and her mother had left earlier to watch a movie - she wasn't interested in movies, nothing seemed to interest her anymore. The house was dark, only lit from the occasional flash of lightning. Sitting on the toilet in the main bathroom she thought about how her life had gotten so bad, but she realised that there were others out there far worse off. She still thought her existence had been worthless.

Passing her open bedroom door, she paused while she had one final glance at the dress hanging in the open wardrobe. Tears rolled down her cheeks yet she found the strength and resolve to push forward. Her mind was made up as she headed for the kitchen.

The top draw rolled open and the utensils clinked as the runners hit the backstop. Lightning flashed outside and shone through the kitchen window, its blue light reflecting off the shiny stainless steel utensils. Shadowing her hand over the knives she made her selection for the largest one she could find.

"This is for you Jack," she whimpered through streaming tears.

Jack walked out through the main doors of the hall. He felt his face dampen from the spray of rain in the wind. His heart raced as he looked around expecting to see Jonas thumping his fist into his palm, ready to pummel him. But he was shocked to see a familiar face.

"What are you doing here?" Jack said.

"What?" Clint replied like he wasn't out of place.

"Come on man, this is my formal, what the hell are you here for?"

"I just wanted to say..." he said pausing to gather his thoughts, he looked out across the school ground, the rain was quite heavy and water was pooling and making mini lakes everywhere, "...this is hard for me, I am sorry for everything."

"What?"

"I treated you like you were different, I know that you are, but I am sorry."

"Where is this coming from, like right now, in the pouring rain, on this night?"

"I know, it just reminded me of when I was going through what you are now, and that I should have done everything to be with the girl I liked, but I let that slip through my fingers, and now she's lost for good."

"What makes you think you can't turn things around with this girl?" Jack said, wondering which girl he was talking about.

"I can't, my ship has long set sail," he said. "But don't give up, you've still got time to be with Susan."

Jack stood there puzzled, he didn't have time to ask any more questions as he saw his brother retreat off into the shadows of the wet night. He stood there and wondered how weird his night had been and wondered how much longer he needed to be here. He was ready to bail. Before he headed back inside he just made out the familiar sound of his brother's motorbike being started up through the noise of the downpour, then he heard him accelerating off into the distance.

The motorbike drove right up onto the footpath under the shop awning and out of the rain. Clint was glad he had his motorbike, it gave him great access to areas over cars which were parking quite a distance back from the flooded gutters. It wasn't a great ride on a wet night but he was desperate to right some of his wrongs tonight.

"Hi," Clint said as he eyed Valerie behind the Fish-N-Chip shop counter.

"Hey, how's things?" she replied, surprised to see him.

"Wet, looks like you've got a quiet night."

"What's with the visit? You are not cooking for yourself tonight since your brother and mother are at the formal?"

Clint gave out a strained chuckle. "Yeah, something like that."

Valerie shrugged her shoulders as she watched him turn away from her and he walked over to the drinks fridge. Ever since high school she didn't understand his demeanor. It wasn't a brooding type, just a lot of arrogance. She guessed he picked up that trait from his father - he too exuded an aura of dominance. They were in the same grade but they didn't share the same relationship as Jack and Susan. There wasn't that closeness or bond.

"You know we could have been a couple," Clint finally said as he placed a drink on the counter.

"What makes you say that?" Valerie said with raised eyebrows. "You hardly spoke to me in high school."

"Yeah, but I was going to ask you to our formal, before you went off somewhere. Where did you go actually?"

"I had my reasons, and you were never in with a chance," she said smiling back.

"Your loss then."

"Whatever," she said annoyed. "Did you want to order anything?"

She wanted him out of the shop as quickly as possible. It wasn't enjoyable serving customers that she didn't like. She watched his eyes as he scanned the overhead menu display. She found him attractive but his personality was ugly. She didn't mind the bad boy type, and she suspected he was trying to work her over by treating her mean, but she wasn't sold. She had lived beside him for far too long. She needed a stable boyfriend and in her eyes he wasn't boyfriend material - he didn't even have a job or future career prospects.

"Can I get a hamburger, please?"

"Sure." Valerie went back to her fridge to pull out a premade burger patty and slapped it on the grill. It sizzled in protest to the heat. She wished she could give him a grilling like the meat to work out how he ticked.

"I um, I am sorry for being such a dick."

It took her off guard - she narrowed her eyes at him and questioned the integrity of his sincerity. "What? What's the reason for your change of heart? You've always been a prick."

"I don't know, you don't have to believe me," he continued. "But I am sorry for not being there, for all that you've been though."

"What do you mean?" *He couldn't know about me, what I've gone through.*

"I know all about you, and your sister."

"You what?" she yelled. "How could you possibly know?"

"I've heard your mother and mine, talking in the garden, just outside my bedroom window. They probably thought I couldn't hear, but I could."

"If you know what I think you do then you can't tell Susan!" she breathed frantically.

"Don't worry, your secret is safe with me." Clint rolled his eyes. He pointed to the burger patty as he noticed it was cooking on one side for far too long - he didn't want the burnt bitter taste. "But I should have given you some support, especially when you went off the rails."

"That's none of your business!" *That imbecile knows way too much!*

"True, but I could have been a friend and I could have supported you."

He watched as she flipped the meat and turned the grill off, anticipating the rest of the cook from the residual heat in the hot plate. She didn't feel like finishing her shift after this order and wanted to close up and go home. She slapped the burger together in the most haphazard fashion - not her greatest food presentation but she was happy with the result.

"At the time I wasn't in a state of mind that I needed help, I would have told you to fuck off, which I am pretty much going to do now," she said as she wrapped the burger and tossed it onto the counter.

He raised his hands in peace. "Whoa, hold up, I didn't mean to offend you, I was only trying to keep the peace and let you know I could help you in the future."

"I'll be okay, and no charge for that," she spat. "Can we call it quits on this conversation, I want to close up and go home."

"Sure, I am sorry. I've also let Jack know tonight that I am sorry for being a shit brother. I mean, I guess I looked at the differences in your family, about not knowing where you belong and I saw the special treatment Jack got from Mum and Dad - so I lashed out at him. I punished him for no reason."

"Good for you, you better have not told him about Susan and I," she warned. "And what's with all this feel good shit all of a sudden, what's your agenda?"

"Relax, he knows nothing yet, unless Susan has told him."

"She doesn't know either, that's why you can't say anything!"

"What?" Clint looked bewildered. "I am so sorry, your secret is safe with me, but don't you think she should know?"

"Not yet, and it's not up to you."

"My lips are sealed," Clint said as he took his drink off the counter.

"You didn't answer me before. What's with the big change of heart, why tonight? Can't you see you've always been such an arrogant prick to me?"

The comment was like a slap across the face for Clint, he paused, considering his answer. "It's been stewing with me for a while, and tonight's formal has brought up the past, I could have been more compassionate. God knows how hard it was for you getting pregnant with that guy you were going to take, what was his name? I didn't end up seeing him, wasn't he from a different school?"

Valerie was tired of Clint, she was tired of other people's judgment of her. She knew she was a stronger person than the high school senior she was two years ago. The writers group had helped her immensely to deal with her emotions in a creative way, her mother had supported her with that process - that's all the help she needed. She didn't need Clint's lame ass help that was a century too late. She didn't care anymore about his or anyone's feelings so she responded the only way she knew how to. The words spat out like a madman mowing down a captor with an uzi - much to her satisfaction.

"It wasn't a guy from school, or any other fucking school," a tear slipped from her eye as she continued, "not that it is yours or anyone else's fucking business but if you have to know, it was my boss, the owner of this fucking shop!"

25 – DARIS' REVENGE

The knife's cold blade dug into her skin as she pushed it with careful pressure against her wrist. Small red blood deposits welled up from the cut line it created, like a fine bracelet with small glistening rubies. Susan was flirting with danger, coaxing herself to continue, daring herself to push harder.

As a distraction she gazed across the room at the dress. She thought it was ironic that the dress resembled the flow of blood from a wound. Its burgundy colour flowed out from a tight bodice. The red lacework was intricately detailed. The front was modest but the back was open to the top of the buttock in a revealing spade cut. When she tried it on in the shop her long hair had covered the opening from her mother, but she knew it was there and had intended to wear her hair up in a bun. It was like her, sweet and innocent from the front but there was a dark side concealed from behind.

Susan was beyond tears - her determination in her resolve. The only evidence of her emotion was her puffy red eyes and the lump in her throat. She knew she could hide that behind makeup, but she wanted the truth to be set free, to free herself of her paralysis.

Taking the knife she stabbed it hard and deep into her desktop. It pierced her poetry book that was open on a page - the poem for her father.

She was ready to take the final steps in her tortured life.

The dress slipped over her naked body, it felt warm and still smelt of incense, impregnated into the fabric, from the boutique store where she and her mother had bought it. She smoothed the dress over her body, pushed her arms though the long lace sleeves. Slipped her middle finger through the end clasps of each arm sleeve.

A thunderclap cracked through the night sky close by. The house rattled.

Taking the cool steel blade from her desktop she positioned the blade up to her wrist.

"This is for you Jack, we'll be together soon," she whispered.

In a final motion, she pushed the blade sideways across her wrist, she felt the resistance and pushed harder in a cutting motion, from the heel of the blade to the tip.

It was quite unceremonious and she felt instantly relieved - finally some purpose, a new direction in her life.

She let the blade drop to the floor along with the dress label that she had just cut off from its hemp cord.

"I'll see you soon Jack, my love, I am coming."

Walking back into the parade hall, Jack felt odd. He didn't expect to have seen his brother, he didn't expect a deep and meaningful apology and he had no idea where Jonas had gone. It was a weird series of events. If it wasn't raining Jack would have checked the sky to see if it was a full moon. That could be the only logical explanation for the craziness.

Sissy was ecstatic to see him and to see his face didn't sport any damage.

"What happened, I didn't want you to go outside, and it looks like you've been spared his anger?" she shouted over the dance music.

"I honestly don't know what just happened, but I'm glad Jonas wasn't there when I went out," Jack said. "Let's hope we don't see him again tonight, in fact I hope I never see him ever again."

"True, come on, Ms. Smith wants us to get into couples for the formal dances."

Great, more pain.

Just then the music stopped and Ms. Smith commanded the PA system with a harsh squeal of feedback over the speakers. She ordered the couples into formation on the dance floor and gave the nod to the hired DJ to play an instrumental waltz. Like robots the seniors performed their square step waltz in unison and as expected without any flare - like one would expect from only one evening of lessons. But Ms. Smith saw the romance in it, perhaps it was how everyone was dressed, or how the light from the mirror ball danced across the twirling couples or perhaps it was Ms. Smith's affinity to tradition, but Jack had to admit it was the happiest that he'd ever seen her. In a way it was a little freaky, like she was in a trance and her mind was transported a million miles away. He wanted it to stop but he could see Sissy was also enjoying herself.

At the end of the first song, all the couples stopped and clapped, giving themselves reward for their efforts. Sissy was caught up in the moment and she hugged Jack from behind. Wrapping her arms sounds him in a warm embrace. Jack didn't mind her affection, he went to grab her hands but she slipped them down his sides and slid them into the pockets of his pants. Jack thought she wanted to get closer to him and he closed his eyes and let the moment wash over him. That's when he jolted, stiff and uncomfortable, when he realised she'd found the small square packet in his pocket.

"Oh Jack, so you *are* on the same page as me," she beamed as she held the packet out in front of her like a small trophy. "Yes, yes, yes, Jack! I love that you have come around, this will be great."

"Sissy, it's not what you think," Jack pleaded. But it was too late, Sissy had already pushed her way past other students on her way to the toilet via the back exit. Her resolve was strengthened. The permission for her next phase still clutched strongly in her clenched fist.

He paused and wanted to run, to leave the formal and go home - maybe try and see if Susan was still up. But he knew he had to clear himself with Sissy and he reluctantly slipped through the gaps in the crowded students on the dance floor and passed out the back exit - to catch up with Sissy.

An analogue clock ticked in another room, it was out of sync with the drip from the tap in the kitchen. These noises were the only consistent sound and were barely audible over the incessant rain. Gusting squalls showered the roof and external walls like a madman was blasting the house with a firehose. There was no end in sight as Cyclone Rona continued on its path, spinning towards the coast.

A small desk lamp lit the kitchen table allowing Daris to marvel over his finished lead lighting mural. He traced his fingers over the female form at the centre of the work. His fingers lingering over the red blood that was portrayed with individual flecks of glass.

He heard the groans in his left ear and chose to ignore them.

Remembering the boy who called himself Jack who not too long ago sat in the very same spot that was now holding his new captive. He knew this new child was very troubled and too needed help, but in a different way. He wondered if it was this child who threw Jack over his fence.

There had to be a reason for a child, so young, to be full of angst. Daris knew what it was like to grow up in turmoil, he had seen the results of living with burden - but he wondered how this child's upbringing could ever compare to his own, especially since he was brought up in a war torn country and here he was in the 'lucky' country; with never a war on its own soil. *How dare this child complain about the inconveniences of life - this child would never know about freedom and what it cost to achieve that dream.*

There was slight movement out of the corner of his eye, and Daris still chose to marvel over his artwork.

Suddenly Jonas' body jolted as he finally peeled the hazy layers of slumber caused by his concussion. "What the fuck! Let me go you sick fuck!" Jonas screamed in vain, he winced in pain at his own outburst as a tight squeezing headache blanketed his skull. Rain bucketed down on the iron roof, masking his cries for help. He struggled against the tight ropes keeping him captive on the wooden chair. He tried to stand and kick but his legs were also bound. He tried to squirm and wriggle himself loose but it was of no use.

He thought against screaming again as he couldn't hear any noise from the formal so he quickly realised that there was no chance of them hearing him.

"You should have kept to writing your stories, Jonas, or should I call you by your pen name, Sam Shield?" Daris said. "I know you joined that writers group to work through your demons."

"Like that's any of your business."

"Meh," Daris said, still concentrating on his work.

"Fuck you!" Jonas spat in his direction.

"You know you've got some issues boy, and I want you to tell me them tonight."

"Like that's going to happen."

"Well if you think it's okay to rape girls, then yes it is going to happen."

"You think I did it, somebody told you, who was it?" Jonas glared at Daris.

"You don't listen, nobody told me, I know everything."

His white cat entered the room. It was woken by their argument.

"Azra, keep quiet." Daris pushed the cat off his legs as it tried to rub itself on him in repetitive head bumps. "You'll eat soon, there'll be plenty for both of us."

"Man, you're not going to eat me?"

"Quiet boy! If I wanted to eat you, you'd already be bubbling in my soup pot," Daris said, still looking at his artwork. He moved containers with offcuts and chips of small coloured glass off to the side. "The trouble with you kids these days is it's all me, me, me."

Jonas' cheeks flushed red with anger. If looks could kill then Daris would be choking from the pressure Jonas could only imagine about unleashing on him. His eyes were bloodshot and bulging; he couldn't care less about any stupid story Daris had to offer.

"You see this!" Daris screamed holding up the small shards of glass and scrunching them in his hands. The blood instantly poured out like a red thick honey. He let it drip onto Jonas' tuxedo and stain his blazer. "This is the blood from my wife's eyes!"

Jonas pushed back in the chair, trying to distance himself from the dripping blood. Daris now had his full attention.

"My wife, she was beautiful, now she's gone," Daris said. "We were running from the government, from the soldiers, we got separated in a stampede for freedom.

"It was many days later but I heard she got caught by the troops," Daris paused and sat back down to trace his bloody fingers over his artwork.

Daris had stuck a nerve as Jonas started to whimper, and Daris looked up at him with steely eyes.

"You know what they call it? Ethnic cleansing!" Daris spat. "I heard she was pregnant to the soldiers, many of them violated her."

Daris eyes started to welt, he grabbed a tea towel and cleaned his bloody hands.

In a calm soothing voice Daris continued with his story. "To me she was still innocent as the day we were married. Azra and Daris in the chapel, bound by God and love. But they kept attacking her, raping her, even after the baby died during birth, even after she was too weak from the loss of blood."

Daris cried as he threw the tea towel into the kitchen sink. "I cry every night, every time I close my eyes the nightmare is relieved."

"I am sorry sir," Jonas said - the welt in his eyes proof to his sincerity.

"You? Sorry? Meh," Daris said falling back into his chair. "When you bully these other children, when you treat girls with disrespect, I wonder what excuse you could possibly have to justify your actions?"

There was a long pause in the kitchen.

"Well boy, answer me!" Daris screamed. "Do you want me to fucking get the answers out of you?"

"Please sir, no, let me go, I won't do it again, please!"

"I don't think you mean it," Daris said as he grabbed the axe which was propped up against the wall.

"Please sir, you don't understand!" Jonas shrieked. "I was never going to *do* it. *She* paid me to do it! To scare Susan!"

26 – FINAL DANCE

Mrs. Valentino dropped the car keys on the kitchen counter. She walked through the house turning lights on, she was frustrated that the house had been left in darkness.

"Susan? Susan are you home honey?" her mother called out.

"I don't think she's here," Valerie said as she changed out of her work clothes.

"She's gone alright, the dress is gone too," Mrs. Valentino said. "And she's left this knife on her bedroom floor, how many times have I said to her to clean up after herself?"

Valerie joined her mother in Susan's room. "Oh my God, look there's blood on the knife," she looked around frantically for other clues to her whereabouts. "We've got to find her, before she's done anything terrible!"

"Where do you think she's gone?"

"I think she's taken off to the formal."

"Why? She wasn't interested in it, I said she should go to the formal, we bought the pretty dress to cheer her up and she just didn't care to go," Mrs. Valentino said dismissively.

"Yes, but you don't understand."

"What don't I understand, Valerie what are you saying?"

Valerie pulled the curtains apart to look out into the night. She was worried that her sister was emotional, alone and out in the bad weather.

"We didn't tell you, because we didn't want to worry you, but she was nearly raped, she's going to the formal where that boy will be, I don't think she'll be in the right frame of mind."

"What! When did this happen?" Mrs. Valentino said angrily. "Haven't we learnt about not telling each other things?"

"I know, you would have thought I'd have known better, but it was tough, looking into your sister's eyes and knowing she's been through a lot, and all the things that she doesn't know."

"You know I will tell her about *that*, she hasn't finished her exams yet, now that she has to finish them in the holidays, I'll sit her down when I know she'll be ready."

"But she's still messed up over Dad leaving, and she's lost her best friend Jack, and she doesn't know what's right, she rebelled and it backfired with this boy."

"So you think she's going after Jack? To be with him even though she could run into this other boy?"

"Yes."

"Quick then, let's go get her, before it's too late."

He was amazed at her strength, her arms flexed and slipped over it with ease. Her head bobbed and darted over it, her now straight hair whipped and flicked with her determination. He hadn't seen that side to her and he was both impressed and shocked. He saw her wedge the short steel star picket that she pulled from the nearby garden bed, in between the door handle and door frame and she pulled back with all her might. It was like she was determined to break into the auditorium, and she did.

She turned and smiled at Jack before she slipped through the doorway. She was oblivious to Jack trying to stop her - she was deafened by the constant downpour, she couldn't hear his protesting shouts.

"Jack, we should be together," she said in the quiet room - rows of seats elevating to the back of the room, being their only witness.

"What?" Jack looked around nervously.

"I want us to be together tonight." She grabbed his hands together tenderly. "Don't you think this is a beautiful place to finally be true to each other?"

"This is school Sissy," Jack said. "Look, I've got to clear things..."

"Jack, please." She placed a slender finger on his lips. "It's time to stop talking, it's time we did what is natural, we owe it to each other."

She slipped her purse onto a nearby seat and turned her back to Jack. Gathering her long hair off her back she turned and whispered to him, "Please Jack, can you help me with the zip."

"Sissy, you don't understand!"

"Come on Jack, we're here, all alone," she said turning back towards him. "I've felt you before Jack, I know you want me."

"You've got me all wrong Sissy!"

"I've seen the way you've looked at me tonight Jack, your eyes don't lie," she said as she flicked open her purse in search of something. "Don't you want a piece of me Jack? I know I want a piece of you."

Not the condom again.

Jack didn't want to wait for her to pull his condom from her purse, so he grabbed Sissy's arm in an attempt to stop her. She spun around quickly and pulled him in closer with her free arm. Losing balance they both fell to the floor, and Jack cushioned her fall as she fell on top of him.

Sissy squealed with delight, the sound reverberated around the cavernous room, her white teeth shining in the dim light through her bright red lipstick as she sported a joyous smile. *Now he's finally turned into my man.*

The taxi driver warned Susan that the weather was getting worse and that she should stay home, but she was determined to find Jack and nobody was going to change her mind. Looking out the back passenger window of the white Commodore she smiled when she saw the glow of light coming from the back of the school. She paid the driver and ran off towards her goal.

Bursting into the parade hall, the music finally overpowered the noise of the rain. She scanned the room and disappointment weighed in her heart as she couldn't see Jack or Sissy amongst the jostling and bobbing students.

"Your boyfriend is in the auditorium with his new lover," Meredith laughed. "She's probably going down on him right now."

"Piss off, I don't see your Hulk here anywhere, don't you have him on a short leash?"

"At least he's faithful to me," Meredith spat.

"Yeah? Why don't you ask him what he tried to do to me?" Susan said. "He likes any port in a storm."

"Whatever, why don't you run along little bitch," Meredith said with a grin. "Oh and when you find your friends, however tangled up they are, give me a *blow* by *blow* description of their positions, you might learn some lessons, I hear Sissy is good with her wrists."

Susan felt the burn in her ears as her blood rushed in rage. She gathered her long dress and ran away from the group of cackling girls. She was determined not to cry but couldn't help a tear escape. Susan took to the back of the hall and escaped out the back exit, into the night.

At first she couldn't hear anything over the noise of the rain, but once the large auditorium door closed behind her and silence filled her ears she began to hear their muffled sounds within the soundproof cavernous room. Susan's mind went into overdrive and she couldn't help but think of the worst possible scenario. Jack and Sissy's naked bodies entwined in thrusts of pleasure, backs arched as they drive their bodies, pushing themselves further into each other, joining as one. Sealing themselves together in a rush of orgasmic release - forever as one.

Susan's eyes welt out of frustration, out of anger and out of loss. She wanted to see it for her own eyes, the betrayal of a lifelong friend, and betrayal of her trust. Her life couldn't get any worse, she wanted to stand over their bodies and let them know she wasn't ignorant to their secret. She wanted Jack to stare at her in the eyes and see her love leave her body like he killed her from the inside out.

As she made her way over to the far side of the room their muffled noises grew louder. Susan was sickened by the moans, whimpers and screams. She bide her time and wondered if she should wait for them to finish or to catch them out in their final thrusts. She thought it would be best to interrupt them as they were reaching the end - it would prove greater impact that way. This would be her only control of the situation.

The exit sign overhead provided the only illumination at the side of the room. It was all Susan needed as her eyes adjusted to the dimly lit corner. At first she couldn't believe it but she knew it was something she should have realised. Sissy was still in her flowing, red dress and was straddled on top of Jack, she had him pinned to the floor. Their bodies were writhing around and he had her by the wrists.

Wrist action indeed!

Susan knew Sissy had been quite aggressive in pursuing Jack, her position of dominance showed her true nature. Susan didn't miss her hair change and her blood boiled. *How dare she try to replace me!*

Storming over to them, her heart pulsated. They both turned their heads towards her, Sissy and Jack's eyes widened like they were caught. Susan stood her ground with her arms folded, waiting for their pathetic excuses.

It was then that her eyes furrowed as she tried to process what she was actually witnessing. She saw the reflection from the metallic object in Sissy's other hand, and that's when she heard Jack whimper.

"Susan, please help me, she's trying to kill me!"

As their car pulled up in front of the school, Valerie turned to her mother, "I think you'd better tell her tonight Mum, I think you owe her that much."

"I told you I would, when she's ready! Don't tell me what to do!" Mrs. Valentino spat.

"If you don't tell her then I will!"

"If you do, it's the last thing you'll do as a Valentino!"

Tears welled in her eyes, but Valerie didn't care anymore, she knew that she owed her sister big time. She knew she might lose her over it but she couldn't carry the guilt anymore.

"Come on, your sister's safety is the first of our worries. Let's not turn the night into a bigger drama than it has already become." Mrs. Valentino stepped out into the rain clutching her handbag.

Valerie punched the glovebox of the car, and winced at the pain. She wished she hadn't let her family baggage become such a huge problem. It was something she would have to live with forever.

The office felt warm and cosy compared to the environment caused by the torrential rain and wind outside. Ms. Smith sat in her leather office chair and sipped on a much needed coffee. She let the aroma of the Arabica coffee beans drift and waft around her - she loved fresh coffee and had made sure a proper espresso machine was one of her first purchases in the office.

She sat back in the chair, causing the leather to grumble with her movement - it was a moment of peace she savored before she had to go back to ensure the students were behaving and that they were having a good time.

Written on a 'With Compliments' card, addressed from the deputy principal, was a short poem that she had been working on for some time. Tonight, the mark of the end of the school year, the sign of changes to come, she finally grew the courage to carefully slide the card inside the envelope.

solace trembles on echoed knell,
withered roses offering sickly smell,
while conjuring beauty in thickened dreams,
eclipse blackened hearts, cut bloody streams,
death drips along frosted thorn,
silent screams awaken your stillborn.

Her short pink tongue licked the envelope seal, it would be the last time she touched her father's fingers. She would send the letter off, like a white carrier pigeon in flight. She imagined a flock of white pigeons flapping wildly as they took flight from her hands. Sending off her message, bidding her family farewell.

She was stronger now, not the scared little girl who sat on the dining room floor bawling while her parents argued over her achievements.

She looked across the passageway from her office. She had to look twice and squint but it was glaringly obvious the auditorium door had been broken into, the bar device was left fallen on the pavement. She quickly dialed the police - more than ever she was determined to catch the culprit.

There was a bang on the Valentino's car roof so hard it left a large dent that instantly began to pool with water. A bloody hand slapped on the glass as Daris, filled with rage, searched through the windows. He roared with anger, looked towards the light being projected from the back of the school and trudged through the mud on his way to administer justice.

"I just want a piece of you!" Sissy screamed as she tried to break her arm free from Jack's grip. Her eyes were emotionless and her breath was panicked.

"Get off of me, you're a psycho!" Jack could feel her thighs squeezing the breath out of him as she pushed forward with all her strength. "Susan, please get help!"

Susan was about to pull Sissy off Jack from behind - adrenalin outweighed her rational thought processes.

Suddenly the lights to the auditorium came on and Susan froze. In Sissy's hand, clutched like a dagger around the shank, was a large pair of metal, dressmaker's scissors. Susan looked around frantically but couldn't see anyone. She didn't know if Sissy would break free and swipe at her or lash out at Jack. She didn't know who to turn to for help.

"Sissy, get off him, he doesn't love you!" Susan shouted in desperation.

"Yes. He. Does!" Sissy grunted. "And I love him. More than you could ever know!"

"Susan's right, I don't love you," Jack shouted, not caring anymore about Sissy's feelings.

Sissy gave an angry frown and then her expression changed instantly to a big smile. "I don't believe you Jack!" she laughed. "I felt the way you've looked at me, the way you were all hard in my hand in my bedroom, the way you're all hard for me now - I can feel you Jack, you want me."

"What..." Jack said looking quickly at Susan to gauge her emotion. "Not true!"

Sissy pushed forward with an unexpected force causing Jack to slip and lose grip of her arm that held the weapon. She stabbed the blades of the scissors violently towards Jack's head.

"No!" Susan screamed, holding her hands up in despair.

Jack spun his head to the side and felt the tip of the scissors scrape down the side of his head, behind his ear. Jack screamed in pain as blood started to flow freely, matting his hair and staining the carpet.

He heard the scissors drop to the floor and thought it was time to act. Jack let go of Sissy's other arm to try and push her off, but she managed to dodge his attempt.

Jack felt the sharp stinging pain across his face as she slapped him without warning. "That's for trying to stop me and for luring that bitch to my formal," she said. "Now hold still, I need a better piece of you."

Maneuvering her hands with deft she grabbed the scissors again and without resistance she took a large cut from Jack's hair.

Susan felt a sudden push from the side and was bowled over - she didn't know what hit her. In a blur of white Sissy was knocked off Jack and pushed backwards onto the carpeted floor with a thud.

"Ms. Smith!" Jack shouted as he righted himself. "Be careful, she tried to cut me!"

Sissy screamed as Ms. Smith overpowered her and flipped her over, pushing her head sideways into the floor while pinning her hands behind her back. She sent the scissors careering across the floor in a rattling clatter. "You've got a lot of explaining to do young lady."

Susan raced to the side of Jack. She applied pressure to the back of his head to stem the flow of blood. It wasn't a deep cut and the blood was starting to congeal. She gave him a reassuring hug from behind, she knew he wouldn't remember it as he was in shock, but she needed to show she missed him.

"I love him Miss, I just wanted to keep him, piece by piece," Sissy babbled as tears started to flow, she looked across at Jack being supported by Susan.

Everyone's heads turned as the sound of heavy boots tramping across the floor in a running motion and the harsh sound of two way radio talk offended the air as two police officers entered the auditorium.

"Is this the offender?" one of the young constables said.

"Yes sir," said Ms. Smith as she struggled with her squirming captive. "I had to apprehend her, she was attacking this student."

"We'll take it from here," said the other senior police officer. He made his way over to where Ms. Smith had Sissy pinned to the floor, took out his handcuffs and snapped them over Sissy's wrists.

Sissy had calmed down, she knew there was nothing more she could do.

"We'll take her down to the station for questioning, can you please contact her parents and let them know where she will be?" said the older police officer as he assisted Sissy up off the floor.

"Miss," Jack piped up.

Both Ms. Smith and Susan looked at Jack with concern. "What is it Jack?"

"You should ask Sissy where she got the money for her dress," he said looking at Sissy with conviction.

"You bastard, I did it for you," Sissy screamed. "Two thousand dollars was money well spent, I know you wanted me, I saw the way you looked at me in this beautiful dress!"

"Oh my," Ms. Smith said with her mouth open in shock.

"It's okay madam, we'll get this young lady's statement on the stolen money as well, she's got a lot of explaining to do," said the older police officer.

Ms. Smith thanked the officers and made her way back to her office to make an important phone call to Sissy's father. She was glad she had someone to blame for the school break-in and theft, but she was concerned that she had to inform the students' father that their daughter was about to navigate some trouble times. She had seen it before, when her parents had received a call about her petty crimes during her final year of high school. Like her, she knew Sissy was acting out because of something in her life and she knew Sissy would be on a long road to recovery.

"Constable Watson, will you please start taking statements from everyone here while I take this young lady to the safety of our patrol car," said Sargent McCloud.

"Yes sir," said Constable Watson. "Ah Sarg? Should we call QAS?" The rookie cop always made sure it was acceptable to call in the Queensland Ambulance Service, especially on a busy storm night where there were many calls for help.

"Son are you okay?" Sargent McCloud said, directing his question to Jack.

"It's just a scratch, I'll be okay."

"Very well, no need for the ambulance then," Sargent McCloud said to his junior officer. "480 to Cairns."

"Cairns to 480 copy," came the voice across the two way radio from the Cairns Police Office command centre.

"We have the offender in custody, just finishing up here, show us returning to base," Sargent McCloud said.

"Copy 480, everything fine there?" asked the operator.

"All okay here, signs of a 104 and 105, we'll be transporting one for questioning," said the Sergeant.

"Copy 480, show you returning to base, 11:15."

Before Sargent McCloud turned to head for the door a barrage of people burst through into the auditorium.

"Susan!" Mrs. Valentino shouted. "Are you hurt? Are you okay?"

"Mum? What are you doing here, I am fine."

"I heard you could have been in trouble, Valerie told me all about your attack last weekend."

Susan shot Valerie a scornful look. Valerie defiantly stood beside her mother and looked around at the scene of chaos.

"I am okay," Susan said. "And I'll be okay from now on, I am stronger. Jack on the other hand was attacked by Sissy!"

Susan was attacked? Jack thought. Jack's thoughts went into overdrive – he wondered if his headache was from the scissor wound or the myriad of thoughts running through his head. He looked around at everyone, he was surprised to see Mrs. Valentino and Valerie as well. Even though Sissy had just attacked him he was still wary of Valerie and her alias John Bird.

"Sissy, did you do all this?" Jack asked.

"Do what?" she said with a smile, she was happy he was finally speaking to her without contempt in his voice.

"The bus crash, the blown up birds in the park, the bloody hearts in my locker, the food poisoning, you're part of the writers group, are you not?"

"You're blaming me for all that?" Sissy shouted.

"Yes!"

"How so?"

Jack and Susan looked at each other. Susan knew what Jack was saying, it all came flooding in as she realised that Sissy was responsible for Jack's attacks.

"You're in the writers group, you stole my poems and rewrote them, and they're *too* coincidental to describe the events that have happened," Susan said.

"You're supposed to be my friend!" Sissy screamed.

"And you're supposed to be mine."

"What do you mean? Up until just now you *were* my friend, but not anymore," Sissy said.

"How can you be my friend when all you want is Jack? That's it isn't it? All these things you've done, they are some sick twisted show of affection for Jack. You've only gotten close to me so you can get close to Jack. Isn't that the truth?" Susan said.

"Wow, I am glad you've taken notice. Why do you want him when you can't treat him right? You've been a tease to him, you've been harsh to him and for what? Last week you even threw him away like a useless piece of shit. So I want him for myself, I will treat him right, I'll make him happy!"

"So it's true, you planned all these attacks and you even taunted him in a book that he had to read," Susan said.

"What book?"

"That English assignment, the one Mr. Friar set him to write a report for, you know, Paperback Writer."

"By John Bird?"

"Yes."

"That wasn't me," Sissy said.

"What about the poems?"

"I can't write poetry."

"Then who wrote that book?"

"Ask your sister!" Sissy spat.

"What?" Susan was shocked, her own sister had written the instrumental piece that was like a manual on how Jack was going to be harmed.

"Come on Love, all these things can be recorded at the Police Station," said Sargent McCloud before he led Sissy out of the auditorium. "Constable Watson, make sure you take down what's being said, I've got a feeling there is more here that just break-and-enter, theft and common assault."

Through the open door to the auditorium, Jack could see the wind pushing the rain about. The shrubs in the garden were swaying backwards and forwards like they were head banging to thrash music. Jack was just as confused as Susan. *If Sissy didn't do all that stuff, then it has to be Valerie.*

"Valerie, is that true?" Susan asked. "Are you John Bird?"

There was a long pause, the only sound was the howl of the wind outside. Valerie turned her head and looked at the opening like it was her only escape. Before she could answer she mouthed, "sorry," to her sister and fled out the door into the night.

"Miss! Miss! Come back, I have questions!" Constable Watson shouted in vain. He was a rooky at his job and didn't want to call for backup otherwise he would look like he was incompetent. He knew she wouldn't get away from the authorities as he had her mother and sister here anyway. He decided it was best to get everyone's statements and then they would pick Valerie up in the patrol car later that night or in the early hours of tomorrow.

"Mum, she's run away from the guilt, so *she* is John Bird?"

There was an awkward pause before she answered. "Yes, she's John Bird."

"But why? Why does she want to kill Jack? I don't believe it. We've talked about Jack, she loves him. She thinks that he's the best thing for me."

"Yes she does," Mrs. Valentino said quietly.

"But the poems Mum? It's written well before the incidents happened. It's like they were premeditated and they were acted upon. She *was* trying to kill Jack."

"Don't blame your sister, she's gone through a lot."

"There is no one else to blame, she stole my poems, changed them up and planned all these vicious attacks. We've got to send the police to our house. She's got to be locked up."

"No. No she doesn't. Nobody is sending police anywhere."

"I can send a unit out to your house madam, what is your address," said Constable Watson.

"No you won't," said Mrs. Valentino.

"Madam, please your address," pushed the constable.

"It's 14 Fr..."

"Susan shut up this instant!" Mrs. Valentino demanded.

"Please madam, you are obstructing police, let me know your address or I'll take *you* to the station for further questioning."

"Mum, what the hell, just tell him!"

"I won't."

"Okay madam, you'll have to come with me," Constable Watson said in annoyance, he knew his shift was about to get extended, especially on this night with deteriorating weather. "I'll take down the rest of your names so I can get statements from you all."

"Mum please, there are lives in danger here. I could have been caught up in one of those explosions."

"I won't put any of you in danger, not your sister or you."

Constable Watson grabbed Mrs. Valentino by the arm.

"Let me go, let me talk," Mrs. Valentino said angrily.

"What is it?" Susan said.

"You think you're so smart. You want to know the truth about you and your sister?"

"What truth?"

"I told your sister the truth about you two in her final year of school and look where it got her. Knocked up with no grades to amount to, she ended up as a pathetic fish and chip server."

"I think I deserve the truth," Susan demanded, tears started to pool in her eyelids.

"Is that right?" she said. "Well the truth you shall have Love. Just remember I did everything because I love you. I love you both."

"And I love you Mum, but please before the officer takes you away."

"The truth is Love, that you and your sister were adopted."

"What?"

"Yes, that's right. Your father and I couldn't get pregnant. We tried so many different things. Doctors, natural treatments, health farms. It was ultimately me who couldn't bore a child. I was sterile. So when the adoption path was offered we decided to register and we fell in love with you baby girls from the moment we saw you."

"Why didn't you tell me earlier?" Susan's tears streamed down her face.

"I thought your sister was ready for the truth and look how that turned out. We've been going to counselling ever since the abortion. The writers group was an outlet for her inner voice. She's come a long way, she's on the mend."

"But that doesn't give her an excuse to try and kill Jack."

"I am sorry Mrs. V but Valerie needs to be locked up," Jack interjected.

"So you're an expert now are you?" Mrs. Valentino said to Jack.

"No, but she's attempted to murder me a few times now so I guess that makes me pretty close."

"She's innocent," Mrs. Valentino said.

"But you just said she wrote the book?" Susan said.

"Yes she did, but I wrote the poems. With the help of yours, of course," Mrs. Valentino said.

"You what? I didn't know you could write let alone create poetry?" Susan said in shock.

"Where do you think you got your poetic interest from? Do you know how many hours I read nursery rhymes to you when you were a baby? Countless."

"But Mum, what the hell! Why did you write such harsh poetry, these are no nursery rhymes?"

"I wrote the poems and gave them to your sister to spice up her work. She thought they complemented her piece. Mr. Friar loved them too."

"What about all the stuff about the bus crash and the bus driver in the book? It was more than just the poems?" Jack said.

"What can I say? I helped with her editing as well," Mrs. Valentino said. "And I guess you thought she was talking to you about her resolve? Jack, she was talking to the guy that got her pregnant, it was her way of dealing with her state of mind!"

Jack thought about what he had read, to him it did seem very emotional and he was beginning to understand why Valerie had written the novel. One thing kept coming back to the front of his mind, and he needed more answers.

"If you wrote the poetry then you wanted to kill me! Why do you want to kill me? I thought you loved me?" Jack said.

"Every time you look at me it's a constant reminder of him," Mrs. Valentino said.

"Of who?" Jack demanded.

"Tony, my husband and your father," Mrs. Valentino said.

"Oh. My. God!" Jack was in shock.

"What Mum, how?" Susan said in disbelief.

Mrs. Valentino felt a release of pressure, she could finally let go and felt free to divulge all her grievances. "Your father fell out of love with me when we couldn't conceive. He had gotten someone pregnant while we were signing up the adoption papers for Valerie and Susan."

"But if Jack is Dad's child then why is he living next door? Did Dad have an affair with Mrs. Armstrong?" Susan asked.

"No."

"Then who is his mother and why is he next door?"

"Aunt Gillian," Frances Valentino said with conviction. She felt euphoric, like years of pent up angst had released from her body, she felt free – the family's dirty little secret was finally out on display.

"What? Your sister?"

"Yes, she's Jack's biological mother."

"What the fuck," Jack said.

"Jack and Gill!" Susan said in disbelief.

"Yes I thought that was trite too," she said, too ashamed to look at her daughter. She stared at her cradled hands like she was holding a newborn baby. "You see, your father slept with my sister and got her pregnant. She was too young to know better. I sent her away and I sent your father packing. The only reason I still talk to your sister is because I told her that she couldn't keep the baby. And I told your father that I wasn't going to raise three young children all by myself, so he could never see Jack again. Mrs. Armstrong agreed to look after Jack as though he was her own."

"I don't understand? Jack and I were born in the same year?"

"When the adoption agency called and said Valerie's biological mother had another child she couldn't keep, your father and I couldn't separate you from her - we took you in without thought," Mrs. Valentino said, she flexed her fingers and gripped them into a tight ball. "Little did I know that he had my sister pregnant at the same time! There was no way we could take Jack, and there was no way I wanted Gill and your father to play happy families around me."

"But why so much anger towards Jack?"

"I thought I would be okay with it. You two played lovely together as children but I could see that was getting more and more serious as you were getting older, and I didn't want anything like that going on."

"But you tried to kill him."

"It looks like that, but it was more to scare him away."

"But Jack isn't related to me by blood," Susan said, trying to make sense of the situation.

"Do you know how hard it is to look at Jack and not see your father? Imagine that when I see you two canoodling about. Do you think I sleep at night with the image of you two being intimate?"

"It doesn't have to be this way."

"It's the only way."

"Come on madam, I've heard enough. Let's go down to the station for further questioning, we need to sort this mess out, I'll need your statement regarding the alleged acts of violence towards this young man," said Constable Watson.

"I am not going anywhere!" Mrs. Valentino yelled, flailing her arms to lose the constable's grip.

"Either we walk out of here with your dignity intact or I can parade you in front of everybody with cuffs on," warned the constable.

"Just try me," Mrs. Valentino hissed and she picked up the pair of scissors on the ground, swinging her arm with force she connected with the constable's face.

Blood spewed out from his nose like a burst pipe. It flicked up across the wall beside them. He grabbed his face to stop the flow and in doing so tripped over his own feet, falling backwards his head cracked against the wall sending him to the floor in an unconscious state.

"Mum! What have you done?" Susan shouted.

Before there was a response Mrs. Valentino jumped behind Jack and took him off guard. She slipped her hand into her handbag and produced the large kitchen knife that Susan had used in her bedroom. Before he could defend himself Jack was frozen still with the blade firmly pressed against his throat.

"Mum! Jack!" Susan screamed. "What are you doing Mum!"

Ms. Smith ran into the auditorium, she was on her way back when she heard all the commotion. "What! Mrs. Valentino put the knife down!" she instructed.

"No, I won't!"

"Mum please!" Susan screeched through tears. "Why are you doing this?"

"I should have done this a long time ago," Mrs. Valentino said flatly. "This boy is a constant reminder of your bastard father!"

"But it's not his fault!"

"Mrs. Valentino, these children are innocent, let Jack go!" Mrs. Smith instructed in her best authoritative voice.

"Really, it's bits of fluff like you, that dress up all nice and innocent, that steal husbands," Mrs. Valentino said irrationally.

"You can't put the fault of your husband onto these poor kids," Ms. Smith said as she eyed Mrs. Valentino. She was frustrated as she couldn't see any way to diffuse the situation. There was no attack method that she had been taught by her father to overpower Mrs. Valentino without a potential fatal outcome.

Jack struggled to remain composed. The sharp blade was cutting deeper with each movement from each argument that Mrs. Valentino was putting forward. Jack saw no way out. This was where his life was going to end - Susan as his witness. His eyes welled as he looked across at her. He hated seeing her distraught, so with his final breaths of life he mouthed the words, "I love you," before he closed his eyes and accepted the inevitable.

"It's time to end this chapter," Mrs. Valentino whispered, "it's time to set you free, 'Stormbird Child'."

He felt the knife sear across his neck like he was being burnt, like a nylon noose was slipping across his skin. His mind flashed to memories in the backyard with his parents. To the fun they had running around playing tag, kicking balls and mucking about. He looked up into the sun and he was blinded, the heat coming back to him in the reality of his situation.

Outside the wind howled and grumbled across rooftops of the surrounding buildings, like the spirits of the earth were being unwillingly drawn out; clinging onto anything for dear life. Was it the life being drawn out of Jack? Was it the sound of screaming women around him or the sound of Death drawing him in with its gaping mouth?

Jack felt a shift of movement and a release of grip from Mrs. Valentino. He couldn't believe that all along, she was the assailant; the smiling assassin who bore baked goods. But now she had won, she had written the final chapter to Jack's short life.

A succession of bumps and tumbles bounced off of Jack. He figured there was a feeble attempt to catch his limp body. He dropped to his knees under the pressure that his own weight caused, his legs buckled under gravity. He lost the will to open his eyes; he didn't want to see Susan in a hysterical state - her hysterical screams were enough to endure. He could only imagine the way he looked to her in death.

"Stand up!" shouted a familiar voice, which was crisp and silenced the room.

Jack opened his eyes in surprise, he touched his neck and looked at his hand. There was blood but only a small trace. Turning his head he saw the formidable form of Daris standing over him. Jack looked to the side and saw Mrs. Valentino laying on her side; the knife was kicked a distance from her.

"Stand up Mrs. Valentino, you have got some explaining to do!" boomed Daris.

"Okay, okay, let me take over from here," Sargent McCloud said.

To Jack it looked like Daris had managed to knock her over in time to stop her. Susan rushed to Jack's side and held him tight.

"It's all his fault, he's the one you should be charging," Mrs. Valentino screeched.

"You were the one with the knife to the boy's throat," Sargent McCloud said.

"Yes, but Daris taught me all about explosives, he planted the seed."

"Bullshit!" Daris shouted. "You said you wanted to know about that stuff for research for your novel. Were you even writing a novel?"

"I was just trying to protect my daughter!"

"More bullshit," Daris said with clenched fists. "Jonas told me all about how you paid him to hurt your daughter. Was that trying to protect her or did you want to teach her a lesson? Is that what this is all about?"

"What?" Susan said with tears in her eyes, she couldn't believe it.

"He was never supposed to hurt her, he was only to teach her a lesson, to toughen her up, to teach her what men are really like!' she shouted as Sargent McCloud placed handcuffs on her and dragged her towards the door. "You've got the wrong person, it's that bastard's fault, now he's wrecked my relationship with my daughter!"

Daris folded his arms. His glare and steely demeanor made Mrs. Valentino look away, she unsuccessfully tried to seek remorse from her daughter's eyes.

"I think you've done a fine job of that yourself," Constable Watson said as he held a bloody towel against his face. "And you'll have plenty of time to think about it in the watch house."

This time Susan collapsed to the floor, sobbing uncontrollably as Jack put his arms around her for comfort. With tears streaming down her face, she looked into his eyes and sobbed, "sorry."

"Susan, this isn't your fault."

It was too late, she broke free from Jack and took off out the auditorium main doors and into the darkness.

"Wait! Susan!" Jack got up and sprinted after her, he wasn't letting her get away this time. "Susan, stop, please!"

"Let me go," she said, as he grabbed her arm and dragged her in close with his other arm. "Just let me be, can't you see you'd be better off without me? I am damaged goods, I'll always let you down."

They were standing under the awning of the office block, yet the wind was driving the rain underneath in sideways blasts. Wet hair stuck to Susan's face as she looked up mournfully into Jack's eyes. She wanted him to realise that the truth was more than anyone could rightfully endure, she wanted him to be free and for his life to be uncomplicated.

"Susan, we are in this together, you are my one and only love, I couldn't live without you."

"But..." Susan was cut off by Jack's sudden movement as he leant in and kissed her; stealing the words from her mouth. Her body relaxed and she slid a hand behind his wet head and pulled him in.

They were invisible in the darkness, in the wild weather, but the storm had exposed their naked souls to one another.

Two bodies moved slowly in one spot, turning gently and swaying to the music. They held each other at the waist and they looked into each other's eyes. To them there was nobody else in the parade hall. Their night was not going to be ruined by anyone - friend or family.

"I'm glad Ms. Smith encouraged us to stay until the end," Susan said as she let the music guide her movements. 'Another Night' by Real McCoy was playing, Susan didn't like dance music, but this song was growing on her.

"Yeah, this finally feels right," Jack agreed.

"It feels surreal though, all the family secrets."

"Yeah I know, my brain hurts thinking about it, our whole lives are a lie!"

"We're in this together," Susan said. "Let's make that promise."

"Okay."

"Jack, about Sissy, I am so sorry. I went off the deep end about her."

"It's okay."

"I guess we were both naive, we both put ourselves in stupid situations, me with Sissy and you with Jonas."

"How were we to know? I mean Sissy is crazy and Jonas was paid by my mother." Susan stared vacantly into Jack's chest.

"Sues, what *did* Jonas do to you?"

There was a long pause as that moment with Jonas flashed across her mind. She shook her head quickly, erasing the vision from her memory.

"Nothing," she spat quickly. "He made me realise that I wanted you all along."

Jack suspected there was more to the story but felt it best to let it go. They had both been through a lot emotionally.

"Yeah, and Sissy made me feel the same way about you. I guess she never really got over losing her mother, she saw my friendship as a way out of her torment. Problem is she didn't know when to let go."

"Yes, she certainly attached herself to you," Susan said. "I don't have anything to worry about, do I? It's concerning, all that talk about you two in her bedroom."

"No way!" Jack said. "Sissy looked too hard at every moment I spent with her, I had no interest and I didn't see her infatuation."

"Do you think they were capable of hurting us both, in their own ways?" Susan asked. "Mum and Sissy?"

"Probably, I think they were caught up in their own agendas."

"What about us? Do you want to reboot, start over again?"

"No Jack, I don't," Susan said with a curt look of frustration. "I want to pick up where we left off."

Susan leant forward and kissed him fully on the lips. Jack was taken by surprise at first but slowly melted into her. He felt dizzy, giddy with emotion. Her warmth pressed against him and he felt tingles all over his body. Her soft lips rolled over his as he wrapped his arms around her firmly. They continued kissing, everyone disappeared from their vision, from their thoughts.

They moved slowly around in small circles, in each other's arms on the dance floor. The mirror ball darting light across their faces as 'Time of Your Life' by Green Day started playing over the sound system.

The night was getting old, and they needed more time to process what had happened and where they were going. But Jack knew that from tonight his life would no longer be the same and he was ready to embrace the change - they were both emotionally scarred but together they would support each other through the darkness.

EPILOGUE

Waves rolled and crashed over the compacted sands on the beach. The roar was deafening. The cyclone had built to an imposing tempest but now meteorological influences changed its course and Tropical Cyclone Rona headed much further north to an unpopulated coastline. It hadn't intensified and was certain to turn into a tropical depression once it ploughed into the mainland - this meant more rain for Cairns and the surrounding coastal communities, and the threat of wind damage was over.

In the turbulent flow of the waves, sands tumbled and tickled about a piece of heavy driftwood which was stuck hard in the shoreline. Receding with the tide, and the diminishing waves, the water caressed and kissed the smooth surface of the driftwood. It played gingerly with some seaweed attached to its flank, rocking it gently to and fro in rhythmic surges. A rogue wave, one last pulse from the storm, rolled its hips, flexing and driving deep into the gutter of the beach, crashing against the driftwood and sending a spray of seafoam into the air. In the last throes of its existence it receded back into the ocean, gently dragging its fingers tenderly around the portions of driftwood that penetrated the sand. When calm returned they would once again be homogeneous - as one: the sand, the water and the driftwood.

The night grew tired of carrying the heavy clouds, it yawned, the heavens opened and the rains cascaded down in monsoonal fashion. It was loud, but the constant heavy fall was soothing. It blanketed the city, cleaning cuts and washing away the pain of old wounds. And not before too long the wind with the rain had also eased, casting a slumber across its reach.

With morning the rain had stopped, the wind was just a gentle breeze. The temperature had fallen which made it comfortable and cosy.

Clothes were strewn across her usually spotless bedroom floor. Tuxedo, slacks, ballroom dress, socks and bra lay clustered like fallen soldiers on a battlefield. His undies were twisted in a loop from being taken off in a hurry, hers were somewhere fallen in the space between her bed and the wall. Two bodies lay still, covered by a Doona which formed ridgelines on the bed. The sun was just starting to reach through the cracks in the window blind with its golden fingers.

Jack stirred and slowly opened his eyes. Her beauty came into focus and he smiled. She looked cute, her mouth slightly open and air drawing in and out making a gentle whistling sound. Her right arm had hooked under his pillow and he dared not move because he didn't want to wake her. He lay there, stealing the minutes drinking in her beauty. Her light pink lips, dry and puckered, reminded him of dusted Turkish Delights - and just as sweet.

He grinned thinking about the night and how they ended up falling asleep together. Susan's eyes slowly opened to see his cheeky grin being replaced with a look of concern.

Shit, did I wake her?

"Why do you look so cheery?" she croaked tiredly.

"You were snoring."

"Jack, stop teasing, I don't snore," she said. Not being a morning person was another thing Jack would have to learn about Susan.

"Oh, I was just admiring the view, it is beautiful you know?"

"Gee thanks." She rolled over and pushed her back towards him. She needed more sleep. She wasn't in the mood for cutesy.

"Oh come on grumble butt, you look cute with your mouth open, whistling away."

"Cute? I'll show you cute!" She threw the Doona off the bed and straddled his body. She pinned his arms down beside his head and clamped his torso between her strong thighs. He wasn't going anywhere. A wry smile formed across her face.

"What are you doing?"

"Wouldn't you like to know?"

Still holding him down she thrust her head forward quickly and she aggressively stuck her thick tongue into his ear.

"Ah, yuck!" He twisted his head to escape her wet proboscis.

"Guess that makes us even!" She said. "One wet willy for another."

"Yeah but at least you enjoyed my *wet-willy!*"

"That's what you think!" she said with a big smile, as she let go of his hands and started to tickle him.

They both wrestled on the bed, rolling around swapping positions of dominance trying to tickle one another.

Both were in fits, laughing in hysterics.

When they were finished they flopped back onto the bed, Susan slid off the bed and slinked away to the bathroom down the hall. Her naked form was slender and sleek, she moved like a cat ash she slipped through the doorway.

Now that's cute, Jack thought to himself. He couldn't help but stare at her beauty.

When she returned she detoured the bed for her dresser and pressed play on her personal stereo. She waited for the CD to load and skipped to her favourite song. The funky beat from 'Ava Adore' by Smashing Pumpkins started and Susan paused at the player like the song was lifting her spirits, like the lyrics mirrored her soul. She made her way back to the bed, picking up the Doona along the way, climbing back over Jack and giving him more than an eyeful of female anatomy as she flopped down beside him and covered them both with the Doona.

Susan had never been so naked in front of anyone before, not even her mother and especially not a boy. She felt invigorated and free from her emotional bounds that would have normally controlled her to cover herself up on her way back to the bed, but her nakedness was evidence to how much she trusted Jack, how much she loved him, and how much comfort she found in him.

After lying there in silence, listening to the tracks on the CD change, and reflecting on their situation she turned to him. "Jack, what do we do now?"

"I don't know."

"What do you think your parents will say?"

"I don't know, I'll have to face the music soon, but I guess they have some explaining to do as well."

"I wonder why they never told us earlier."

"I guess they thought it would mess us up, it was all about finishing school with good grades."

"How do you feel about it all, knowing that your parents aren't your parents?"

"I don't know, it still all feels surreal. I don't think I am angry if that's what you're asking. I think there was a pretty good reason for what happened, but I still can't come to terms with your aunt giving me up like that. If you were a parent wouldn't you try your hardest to keep your child?"

"Yeah but look at me, my parents couldn't keep me. There are things that are beyond our control I guess."

"And how do you feel about being adopted?"

"I was mad at first, but I don't know. I sort of feel hollow."

Jack prodded her from under the Doona and she laughed. "You don't feel hollow to me."

"You know what I mean."

"Do you want to meet her? Aunty Gillian?"

"I don't know. My parents now are my parents. Mum will always be my mum."

"Yeah, but don't you want to hear your real mother's side of the story?"

"I suppose, but I am kind of..."

"Scared?" Susan said, reading his mind. She also felt scared about approaching Aunty Gillian, without her mother, to get her side of the story.

"Yeah I suppose."

"You've heard too many farm house bawling stories that's all, she is quite lovely. At least *you* know who your real mother is."

"But what about my real father, where is he?

"Maybe he'll come back, to see you?"

"He's probably moved on by now, it's been quite a few years," Jack said.

"Yeah but I bet he's hanging around here somewhere. You're his only child and I am sure he's been keeping an eye out for you over the years."

"I am not too sure about that either."

"Come on Jack, things will get better." She leaned over and gave him a kiss full on the lips. He reciprocated and they kissed passionately with open mouths for a few moments. She pulled away before things went too far.

"Yes, things certainly are getting better," he said with a cheeky smile.

There was another long pause of thought between the two of them.

"What about you, you've got nobody to look after you?" Jack said.

"Yes, I guess by the time Mum goes to trial I'll be eighteen, but I have my sister take care of things, besides, school's over and I look forward to having a break from everything."

"I guess we crossed the line last night, from friend to..."

"We sure did, but I love that we did."

She traced a finger over his chest. It tickled him, but he resisted the urge to move as he watched her concentration. She followed the tufts of hair that grew down the centre of his chest, her fingers changed tack and floated from mole to mole like she was drawing a picture of join-the-dots. He watched her slender finger, with beautifully shaped pink nails swirl and dance across his torso.

"Can you guess what I am writing?" she asked, not taking her eyes off her trailing finger.

"No, what is it?" he breathed softly.

"I love you," she said. She rotated her finger on its tip and used her nail to run down just below his belly button. She loved how he squirmed when she got close to the 'danger zone'.

Finally not being able to take it any longer he took her hand gently and moved it to the top of his chest. He stared into her eyes. He loved how blue they were looking this morning, like they had an extra twinkle about them, like they belonged in a porcelain doll.

"I love you too Susan," he whispered and he lent over, closing his eyes he met her soft lips. They kissed tenderly. He didn't want it to end.

Finally she pulled away, a string of spittle bridged their mouths, they slowly opened their eyes in heavy, longing blinks and they laughed when they realised it was there.

After a moment Jack turned, lying on his back he studied her bedroom ceiling vacantly. Deep in thought and with a frown across his face he asked, "do you think what we are doing is wrong?"

"What do you mean?"

"We are technically brother and sister aren't we?"

"Not really, we're not related, even by blood, what we've done isn't illegal."

"I think what we did last night could be illegal in many countries."

"Ha ha, you're so naughty!"

"No, we aren't brother and sister, but you've been my best mate, like forever. I wouldn't want this any other way."

They kissed again, but this time Jack pulled away quickly. "Hey, I've been thinking, it's been playing on my mind..."

"Oh? Sounds serious," Susan laughed.

"...yeah, it sort of is. When you said that the poems in that novel were yours, but they were changed, how did you know?"

"Oh, it was kind of easy for me to tell. But I did have to read them over a couple of times, I couldn't believe it when I realised it," Susan explained.

"What do you mean?"

"Well she ended up making them quite dark, whereas my poem was a love poem."

"Really, I wouldn't have worked that out, which parts were yours?"

"I'll show you later but she broke one of my poems up and used each line as the first line in each of her poems."

"Wow, tricky. I'd love to read the proper poem. Who was it for?"

"*You* of course silly billy!"

She gave him a quick peck on the cheek for which he returned some cheeky affection by nibbling on her earlobe. She wrestled with him some more, deciding against wetting his ear again she grabbed her pillow and whacked him across the head. Before he could retaliate she sprang off of him and fled back to the main bathroom. Jack groaned on the bed and yelled out something about her unfair play.

She stood there looking at her tired reflection in the mirror. She smirked at the thought of the last few weeks. It wasn't long ago when both sets of parents had imposed strict rules about them spending time together. Perhaps it was all about their grades and ensuring they set themselves up for the best chances of entry into university - but she knew their parents couldn't afford to send them away. She realised that it was all about keeping Jack away from her, from becoming serious and inevitably ending up together. Heaven forbid they had sex - too late for that - she smirked again.

She felt giddy with freedom. Her restrictions had been quashed the instant her mother confessed the whole family secret - and what a secret it was. The table had been turned and now anything she knew or had been told was a lie. An element of her celebration was lying naked on her bed. But Jack was more than a triumph or a trophy. Apart from her damaged sister he was her everything and she knew he only really had her. She knew this new freedom had to be used wisely. She couldn't get caught up in the moment, but she did want to enjoy it. She didn't want to end up in a position her sister had two years ago. She loved her sister and wanted to hold onto her. She was the only blood relative she had.

Susan had to administer control, it couldn't be an open season on their feelings. One thing she thought her mother got right was the sound advice to keep things manageable. She felt safe with Jack and knew he was right. Her mixed emotions of fear and excitement sent a hot flush down her spine and her small translucent hairs on her arms stood on end. Their relationship couldn't be a firework that rockets out of control burning brightly at the start and petering out as quickly as it began. They had been friends for years, she hoped they would be lovers forever.

Susan had considered her mother's position but still couldn't get over the fact that she had tried to kill Jack. Maiming him wasn't in her sights; the bus crash, the food poisoning. She got the references to the birds. She thought she was a stormbird by having a child raised in another's nest. The instructions to Jonas were beyond belief. These were all lessons her mother wanted to teach that could not only kill youth but scar them for life. Jack and Susan were kindred spirits and their life journey was mirrored. She didn't know why her mother was like that, what she was capable of. She wished she had talked to her, told her everything, maybe the outcome would be different.

One thing stayed in her mind, if she did kill Jack how was she going to get away with murder?

Whether they liked it or not, Susan was Jack's step sister. Denial was their greatest friend. Susan wondered why her mother made her father leave after a couple of years when she was only two. Why not straight away? She probably needed the support bringing up two young children and knowing her mother probably stewed away with emotion until she finally erupted and told him to leave. And that was another lie which hurt, he didn't abandon them, he was ordered to leave. He was still out there somewhere and she had a small feeling to one day find him and ask what happened. Jack and Susan could do it together, she was sure he wouldn't mind. Up until this point she hadn't realised how similar their lives were. It was like fate that they were to be together; they were meant to be one.

With Jack she felt secure, she was happy and she hadn't felt that way for a long time.

She felt free from the angst of her childhood but all these new thoughts were overwhelming and she was feeling a bit restricted; hemmed in with cabin fever, she needed fresh air, so when she returned to Jack she suggested they go for a swim. And it was probably best to cool things down between them before it got too hot and steamy again. The creeks were flooded from the monsoonal rain, however as Tim was away on holiday, they could jump his fence and slip into his family's pool. Jack suggested she wear her fluorescent orange bikini and Susan agreed, but she suggested that wearing it for too long in the pool might be a little too restrictive.

The morning air was thick with the smell of disinfectant. A sobbing woman was heard down the passageway. The slow squeaking sound of the warden's rubber soled boots was heard as they kissed the linoleum floor. The hum of the fluorescent tubes overhead gave each cell an illuminated clinical feel.

"Frances Susan Valentino, your hearing is at eleven o'clock today. Your solicitor will collect you at ten," instructed the warden in a gruff, non-emotive manner. Frances didn't move, but gave a hand gesture to wave her away. The warden didn't mind, she could have disciplined the prisoner but she couldn't care less as she was finishing her long shift soon and didn't want the extra reporting. Besides she wasn't the one who was going to escort this alleged offender to the hearing room.

A frail woman in her seventies shared Frances' holding cell. She was incarcerated for the manslaughter of a child, she didn't see the boy run across the road chasing the ball. In her hands she was toying with a well-worn slip of paper. The words were carefully written in beautiful handwriting.

Frances looked across at the old woman and scowled. The woman stunk of body odor and her incessant desire to talk Frances' ear off annoyed Frances no end.

"Oh, it sounds lovely darling."

"What does?" Frances asked, not knowing what she was going on about. She was probably mad, her mind had probably gone years ago. *She shouldn't be allowed outside let alone behind the wheel of a vehicle.*

"Why his garden, Love," she said with a smile beaming across her cracked lips. "Adam and Eve's Garden of Eden I bet."

"Go away," Frances groaned. *She is definitely mad, probably gone all religious to pave her way to heaven - seeking her salvation for killing a child.*

"Sounds like you'll find out if you go to trial today," the old woman stated, changing the subject.

"Yes, but it's a given."

"At least you'll get to see your loved ones then," the old woman said trying to lift her spirits.

"I doubt it, I suspect I'll only see them at trial. They'll want to see me put away for a long time."

"Oh that's sad," the old woman said. "Perhaps you can meditate in this lovely garden, once you get bail that is."

"What? I won't be able to afford bail, nobody will pay it, and what's with all this nonsense about a garden?"

"Here Love, it's here, Tony sounds like he's got a green thumb," the old woman said with a big smile holding out the aged piece of paper, fold lines showing its age.

Frances turned pale, she recognised it straight away. Snatching the paper she quickly folded it up and returned it to the back page of her novel from where it had fallen out.

Tony's Garden

Flower spikes from heliconias rise like fireworks,
stabbing at the sky.
Their hollow heads dance and tap each other to a gentle breeze.

Frangipani flowers drop like summer snow,
littering the lawn.
And here you are weeding, dirt upon your knees.

No need to fight, don't struggle, it's calming here,
let the vines entwine.
Escape your breath with slow progressive ease.

My impatiens wilt for attention,
yearn for fertile ground.
Sprinkle your blood and bone to please.

Palm trees reach, fronds touching our neighbour's house,
an olive branch it seems.
This oasis harbours chicks, spiders and stingless bees.

Watch them grow from your luscious garden,
guide them from above.
You'll stand here in time, in one spot, under the cycad trees.

FV.

For my Jack

Conflicting is the day,
And vivid is the picture,
So take my hand in marriage,
Because we're a beautiful mixture.

Your strength is surely fragile,
I'll cup my wounded dove,
Bind our souls together,
And surrender to my love.

Susan.

Jack's Mixed Tape

1. Rush - Big Audio Dynamite II (1991)
2. Pretty Fly (For a White Guy) - The Offspring (1998)
3. Push th' Little Daisies – Ween (1993)
4. Master of Puppets – Metallica (1986)
5. It's Only the Beginning - Deborah Conway (1991)
6. Sweetest Thing – U2 (1998)
7. Boom Boom Boom Boom!! - Vengaboys (1998)
8. Dub Be Good To Me - Beats International (1990)
9. Pure Massacre - Silverchair (1995)
10. Glycerine - Bush (1995)
11. The day I tried to live- Soundgarden (1994)
12. You Don't Treat Me No Good - Sonia Dada (1992)
13. All Apologies (Unplugged) - Nirvana (1993)
14. This Is Your Night - Amber (1996)
15. Another Night - Real McCoy (1995)
16. Good Riddance (Time of Your Life) - Green Day (1997)
17. Ava Adore - Smashing Pumpkins (1998)

Search for 'Stormbird Playlist' on YouTube

Fact

The eastern koel, commonly known as a stormbird, migrates from southern Asia to the eastern coast of Australia during the Australian wet season. It comes to breed before the wet season and the male has a distinctive call. Because of this they are used by locals as an indicator to the onset of the wet season.

The eastern koel is also a parasitic breeder, meaning the female lays its eggs in a host bird's nest for that different species to raise its young. At the end of the season eastern koel parents and their biological young return to southern Asia.

The image on the front cover is an artistic impression of the distinctive male eastern koel, the stormbird.

Acknowledgments

First and foremost, I give my wholehearted thanks to my wife – my greatest critic – for without her unbiased review and unconditional support I would have never completed this work. I am grateful for her valuable insight and am glad this work was cut and trimmed while my imagination was guided in the right direction.

I would also like to thank you, the reader, for letting me share my fiction with you – and I hope you enjoyed the journey.

About the author

Leon Jane has always liked reading stories with a twist or with hidden messages, perhaps it stems from being a Gemini or that he loves being creative. He likes to delve into his imagination by creating stories and poetry which cover various genres. When he's not busy reading or writing he loves spending time in his tropical garden with his beautiful family in Far North Queensland, Australia.